Death of a King and other stories

SEAMUS DE FAOITE (1915–80), a native of Killarney, was a friend and contemporary of both Bryan MacMahon and Brendan Behan. He attended St Brendan's College, Kilkenny, and founded the Killarney Players, who performed his first play *The Night of the Moon*. After working as a postman, he moved to Dublin, where he worked in advertising to support his theatrical career and acted in The Gaiety's production of his play *The Cardinal and the Crows*. He was editor of the *Waterford Star* in 1950 and in 1955 became sub-editor and film critic of *The Irish Press* until the year of his death.

Death of a King
and other stories

Seamus de Faoite

THE LILLIPUT PRESS
DUBLIN

First published 2005 by
THE LILLIPUT PRESS
62–63 Sitric Road, Arbour Hill,
Dublin 7, Ireland
www.lilliputpress.ie

Copyright © Maurice White, 2005

A CIP record for this title is
available from The British
Library.

10 9 8 7 6 5 4 3 2 1

ISBN 1 84351 064 2

Set in 11.5 on 13.5 Granjon with
Zapfino titling
Printed by MPG Books, Cornwall

The publisher gratefully acknowledges the
following for permission to reproduce:

'Dry Train', *New Irish Writing*, 1980
'Like Father, Like Son', *The More We Are
Together*, Poolbeg Press, 1980
'No Day to Die', *New Irish Writing*, 1980
'A Hat My Father Wore', *New Irish Writing*, 1979
'My Uncle Was Santa', *Sunday World*, 1979
'Death of a King', *New Irish Writing*, 1970
'Timeen', *Our Games Annual*, 1958
'Pictures in a Pawnshop', *The Bell*, 1954
'Sky Is Plentiful', *The Bell*, 1951
'Law Abiding', *Irish Writing*, 1951
'The American Apples', *The Bell*, 1949
'The More We Are Together', *Irish Writing*, 1949
'New World's Eve', *The Bell*, 1948
'Kate's Grandchild', *Irish Writing*, 1948
'The Day Mary Clare Met the Bishop',
     The Standard Literary Supplement, 1948
'The Old Stock', *The Bell*, 1947
'Tailor's Rest', *Irish Bookman*, 1947
'Brownie', *Irish Bookman*, 1946
'Blindness', *The Irish Press*, 1946
'The Big Garden', *Capuchin Annual*, 1945
'The Poacher', *The Bell*, 1941

Dedication and acknowledgments
by Maurice White
For Eileen Fogarty de Faoite
I would like to particularly mention the
invaluable assistance of Frank O'Carroll in the
publication of this collection.

Contents

Foreword

Every wave of young people loves to see itself as a lost generation. My band of brothers and sisters in Cork University revelled in the role. Rousseau's 'Man was born free and is everywhere in chains,' was for us almost a mantra in reverse. I amended it to, 'Man was born free and is everywhere in digs—' and flattered myself that Rousseau would have approved. He had an acute sense of man's battle against petty humiliation. In this context his *Confessions* is very much a modern book. It tells of a world where the anti-heroic must be endured.

Samuel Beckett admired Seamus de Faoite's short stories. I can see why: they both tried to express a world where drama is seldom overt.

Joyce in *Ulysses* was on a similar quest. 'Two Gallants' in *Dubliners* is like a trailer for the alleged great Irish novel. We meet Lenehan sitting in a working-class café and thinking about how life is slipping away from him. He is an infinitely more tragic figure than Hamlet or Macbeth. Joyce ventured into territory that hadn't previously been deemed the stuff of literature. Beckett went even further.

Seamus de Faoite's short stories are anti-heroic to a heroic degree. He is the least literary of Irish writers. Sean O'Faolain and Frank O'Connor might dwell on another planet. Whence came his core of certainty? I cannot help feeling it owes something to his heartland.

Killarney is a town almost as famous for its lanes as for its lakes. It fosters intimacy; its people do not look outward for their values. A provincial is someone who believes that the capital of the world is elsewhere. For de Faoite, the capital was located somewhere between the cathedral and the friary.

I have long envied the citizens of that lake-blessed town: when they come to Castleisland to a game of Gaelic football or perhaps rugby, they speak as if they are on an expedition to a foreign country. I think of Samuel Johnson: 'Beyond Hyde Park all is wilderness.' It is a marvellous innocence. And if asked to apply one word to Seamus de Faoite's stories I wouldn't go beyond 'innocence'. It is, however, an innocence that goes hand in hand with wisdom—like that of Charles Kickham's in Knocknagow.

De Faoite's language varies from the candidly simple to the boldly metaphorical. And here John Millington Synge enters the picture. We all know the story about his meeting with W.B. Yeats in Paris and being advised to go to Aran, where the spirit of the people might enter his soul. The story is true but the message is not. Synge found nothing in Aran to inspire him. He admired the people for their hardihood and courage. He admired too their behaviour when a man who had killed someone on the mainland took refuge amongst them: although there was a price on his head they hid him until he could get away to America.

However, he also found them a people with a distrust of life. I am not being prejudiced in saying this. Synge found himself in Kerry and especially on the Great Blasket. He makes this abundantly clear in his journals and those critics who described Christy Mahon's language as Synge-song were profoundly mistaken. We tend to forget that Christy was a native of Kerry. His language was of a kind that Synge heard all around him in West Kerry. Even now, despite the cinema and television and the radio, that language is alive and vibrant. And it is not only colourful, it is precise.

I remember my father saying one evening after a few of us had returned from a day in the bog: 'I discerned ye as ye came over the brow of the mountain.'

'I saw' would have sufficed but 'I discerned' was more precise. Seamus de Faoite grew up in a world where that language was the common coin. It is hardly a coincidence that Joe Higgins, a native of West Kerry, is the most colourful speaker in Dáil Éireann.

Ernest Hemingway loved to talk about style and claimed to have learned much from the paintings of Paul Cézanne—perhaps he did. But a question pops up its head. Is there such a thing as style? There is a difference between describing a storm and cutting turf. I believe that the essence of style is to have no style. Seamus de Faoite had no style: his language is about as akin to that of conversation as writing can be.

Sherwood Anderson, sometimes called the father of American writing, would approve. He believed that writing should be rooted in speech. That, of course, is only partly true. John Milton couldn't have written *Paradise Lost* in common language. He had to go to the organ rather than the flute.

I doubt if Seamus de Faoite had any theory about language. He might occasionally have worried about the nature of his material. Almost every writer sympathizes with Robert Frost: 'How can I write a great novel when life goes on so unterribly in New England?' Thomas Wolfe, the great, half-forgotten American author of *Look Homeward, Angel*, harboured similar doubts. He used to lie awake in his lodgings in Chelsea and wonder how he could compete with Shakespeare and Wordsworth and the rest.

You can be sure that Patrick Kavanagh had his doubts too, but he could see the undying difference in a corner of a field. When we look at an old photograph, no matter how simple the theme, it touches something in us—time has made it significant in a strange way. This is especially true of us in Ireland.

I think of what Arnold Bennett said about his neighbours in the Potteries—'A people full of crushed tenderness.' We too hide our deeper selves. Some of Seamus de Faoite's stories are like the photograph—simple things expressed because he saw their significance.

My favourite of his stories is 'Pictures in a Pawnshop'—a tale of two men who set out from Killarney to the county final in Tralee. It embodies two of his passions—his belief that ordinary life is fraught with possibilities and his love of Gaelic football.

His work evokes Thomas Hardy's dictum: 'At the graveside of even the humblest man you see his life as dramatic.'

CON HOULIHAN
DUBLIN, MARCH 2005

Dry Train

A cool breeze from the window made candlelight lap against the walls of the room as Miah opened his eyes. Minnie stooped over him with a candlestick in one old hand and an alarm clock in the other. Her ancient red dressing gown was roped round her small body with a girdle like a monk's, her short grey pigtails stuck out behind her ears and with her eyes squinting into his face she had an oriental look about her.

'Time to stir, a quarter past five, you'll have a grand day for your trip, I can see by the stars in the window,' she said. 'Thanks be to God,' she put in like an afterthought as she moved out of the room in slippers as old as the dressing gown.

Starlight took over from candlelight at the window and the stillness made old Miah lie on for a while, trying to make sense of the train journey to Dublin ahead of him. No matter what way he looked at it he ended with the uncomfortable thought that a dry train, a rolling roaring pub with no beer, would be no place for a drinker of long standing and falling and always rising again.

'Tea is made,' Minnie called up from the foot of the stairs and he reached for his trousers. The smell of frying bacon met him on the top step to remind him of whiskey; most things in the morning reminded him of whiskey, especially frying bacon. 'Dry train how are you,' he told himself ruefully, but the smile that was never far away from his face came back as he stepped into the kitchen. 'I'll wash before I eat,' he told Minnie and she switched on the light in the pantry. Minnie was nervous of electricity but she allowed it downstairs for light. He washed, combed his white hair and beard, and finished dressing to collar and tie and the last button in the waistcoat.

'Tea is poured,' Minnie called and he went to join her at the table. Beside his plate of bacon and eggs and a few curls of kidney were a mug of steaming tea and a glass of whiskey. 'God spare you, girl,' he said, raising the glass.

'That'll be your last before Dublin so I gave it extra,' Minnie said.

'How do you mean last, girl?' he asked between sipping the whiskey and licking of lips.

'You don't mean to tell me you're bringing drink on a Pioneer train?' she said.

'Who else would bring it, in God's name?' he answered, draining the glass.

'Don't bring God into this,' Minnie said with shock in her voice.

'Who made water into wine at the wedding feast?' Miah was quick to ask.

'He never made whiskey and you're going to no wedding,' Minnie was even quicker to answer.

Miah palmed a smile off his face to say: 'I filled the hip-flask to the brim at Jack C's last night. For the train like, in case of emergency like.'

After a long pause Minnie said: 'In case of emergency. I suppose 'tis all right. Like.'

'The journey is a kind of emergency in itself,' he reminded her. 'With priests and nuns in the company I fancy I'll be darted with questions like "What's an old toper like you doing on a Pioneer pilgrimage?" Half in fun whole in earnest like.'

'Be serious,' Minnie said.

'Some of the other long-faces might think I was a spy in the camp.'

''Tis no pilgrimage. The Pioneer Total Abstinence Association is holding an All-Ireland rally in Dublin's Croke Park today.'

'How dare they,' Miah interjected. 'How dare they walk on sod made sacred by the footballers of this county for a century of All-Ireland finals.'

''Tis only for a day; we'll give it back to ye this evening,' Minnie said.

'Oh, thanks,' came from Miah in a way that made Minnie chuckle into her tea.

'Oh, I know you're having me on. 'Tis an old game of yours. I used to tell myself that laughing at me was better than being ignored,' she said, still chuckling.

'Who's laughing now? And who is she laughing at?'

'Herself maybe,' said Minnie, wiping tears of one kind or another out of her eyes with the sleeve of her dressing gown. 'But anyhow, you walk on that train as if you own it. Don't wear the cloak of a martyr with your tongue in your cheek. As a mason by trade, you can tame stone but sometimes you pretend you couldn't crack eggshells.'

'Oh here,' Miah protested but Minnie charged on. 'I'm the Pioneer and 'tis I bought the tickets. We weren't going to the rally, we were going to spend the day with our son Shay and his wife Kitty and their small sons, our grandsons, Mark and Danny. My sister Ellie was taken to hospital last night gasping for breath with bronchitis. So I have to stand by Ellie and you have to brave the dry train on your own. And if anyone, anyone, I say, if anyone says you have to be teetotal to travel on that train I'll deal with them personally, you tell them that.'

After a pause to draw breath she added: 'Now put on your hat, 'tis a quarter to six and 'tis Sunday, so you have to go to Mass in the friary on your way to the station.'

Miah finished his tea and got ready for the road while Minnie fussed about preparing for the send-off. 'Now,' she said, facing him on the porch, 'let me look at you.' She took his hat off and put it back on again to her liking. She tucked a well-pressed white handkerchief into the breast pocket of his jacket and put another into a side pocket.

'Have you your ticket?' she asked.

'Yes,' said Miah.

'Have you your pipe and tobacco?'

'Yes.'

'Have you your specs and the book you're reading?'

'Yes.'

'Is the paper money safe in your waistcoat pocket?'

'Yes.'

'And have you the flask for emergency?'

'On my hip,' said Miah as he opened the door.

The rag-doll shape with the stick-out pigtails was waving to him from the lighted porch as he closed the garden gate behind him. He raised his hand in answer before he stepped out of her sight.

The footsteps echoed across the street in the still starry dark until the silence was shattered by the tolling of the friary bell. When the silence settled back after the last toll a blackbird was singing in the friary orchard. Light in colours shone through the stained-glass windows of the chapel but by now there was just enough daylight to see the steps. They were littered with bagpipes and side-drums and kettle drums.

A big drum was where a banner hung from a crested pole in the porch; the town's pipe band was travelling with the teetotallers. As he treaded carefully past the instruments he couldn't help but think that as much whiskey and beer as spittle had dribbled though the pipes down the years. He would have laughed if he wasn't sidling past the big drum and the banner in to Mass.

He left the chapel a few minutes before Mass was over to find that daylight had won the battle with the stars. When he had negotiated the many steps down from the chapel hill he was only the width of a road and the length of an avenue away from the railway station. He was stepping into an empty carriage in the long train when he heard the pipes playing the remainder of the congregation up the avenue. By the time pipers and pilgrims were boarding the train Miah had his own pipe going and his cowboy book ready to hide in if his carriage was invaded by Pioneers.

He felt lucky when no one came near him until the train was on the move, and then it was a six-foot youngster who tugged the carriage door open, leaped aboard with a soft leather grip in his fist and said, 'Morning, sir,' with an American accent. A sunburst hit the tanned face and fair hair of the Yank as the train left the station. He put the grip on the seat opposite Miah and sat beside it.

'Morning, boy,' said Miah.

'I'm a soldier on short leave from Sam's Army in Berlin,' the Yank said.

'You have the cut of an officer,' Miah told him.

'Rookie second lootenant pilot on his last chance to toe the line,' said the Yank. 'As it is, I'm overdue at the base so I took advantage of the Sunday train to make time and grab a sleep.'

'You're in the right place for that,' Miah encouraged with the smile that people who didn't know him called saintly. 'I'm a stonemason and I'm the quietest man on earth when I haven't a hammer and chisel in my hands.'

'With that white beard and hair you look patriarchal,' the Yank told him.

'Moses without the stones,' said Miah and the Yank grinned and said, 'Yeah!' in approval.

'Look, sir,' said the Yank, 'last night I had one hell of a time at a goodbye party, so I'll grab a nap now if you'll excuse me.'

'I'll be the lookout,' said Miah, leaning forward in mock seriousness.

'Yeah,' said the Yank with a conspiratorial finger to his lips. He stretched full length on the long seat with the soft grip for a pillow. 'Yeah,' he said again before sleep came with the closing of his eyes.

Miah admired the way the mountains were taking the sun before the train swept him into lower ground where fields and trees and streams seemed nearer in the finger-flick glimpses that speed allowed. On the roads around wayside villages people were walking or cycling or driving to Mass; mostly driving.

He read through the rest of the way to Mallow where the train took on three more bands and hundreds of Pioneers. Any of the newcomers who approached the carriage went elsewhere on seeing that the long Yank occupied half of the seating space. That suited Miah down to the ground.

He read and smoked all the way to the stop at Limerick Junction, where again it was a case of more bands, more Pioneers and still more sleep for the Yank. Bareheaded women with white aprons sold fruit out of baskets from carriage to carriage along the platform. Miah bought six oranges in a brown paper bag for his grandchildren and the dealer told him he looked like Saint Francis as she gave him his change. 'Here's my blessing,' he told her, raising his hand as the train moved away, and she was waving and laughing in the last that he saw of her.

'Where am I?' The Yank was speaking with one eye open as the train beat out a top speed tattoo on the rails.

'You're not a long way from Tipperary now, soldier. You're in it,' Miah told him.

The Yank swung upright, combing his hair with his fingers. 'Cow country,' he said, looking through the window. 'Hey, you're a Wild West fan like myself,' he added, pointing to the bucking bronco on the cover of Miah's paperback.

'Heading into Arizona in this chapter,' Miah told him and the Yank said, 'Thirst country.' He added: 'Hey, which way is the bar on this train?' Miah said, 'No way,' and the Yank shot to his feet. 'Jesus,' he said, and it was no prayer.

Miah broke the news about the dry train but he cushioned the shock by taking the flask off his hip. 'My wife said to keep this for an emergency and this is an emergency surely,' he said. 'Take it and you'll feel better.' The Yank unscrewed the top of the flask and with a toss of his head drank half of what was in it. 'Fit for the gods, pardner,' he said. 'Now you drink the rest to seal the pardnership.' Miah drained the flask and said, 'Holy Water.'

'Now we'll break camp, pardner,' the Yank told him. 'You grab that cowboy book and your parcel and we'll hit the trail down these corridors.' He snatched his grip off the seat as he headed out of the carriage. 'Give your horse his head and stay on my tail. Yippee!'

The train was rocking and roaring with speed as they passed carriage after carriage with landscapes flicking by in the windows. 'Bumpy ride, pardner, like a stage coach. Stay in the saddle,' the Yank said as they swayed through a dining carriage that smelled of fried bacon where Pioneers were attacking rashers and eggs with knives and forks.

'End of trail will be in the guard's van,' said the Yank, and they passed five carriages more before he said: 'Here it is.'

He paused at the van door to take a crisp five-dollar bill out of a leather wallet. 'We'd better hope that the guard is a nice guy,' he told Miah.

'I'm praying,' said Miah with a face to match.

'Here goes,' said the Yank. Then he stepped ahead drawling: 'Hope we're not disturbing you, sir, but would you have the change of this?' He dropped the grip on the bare boards of the van floor and had the note between the guard's palms before he knew it.

'I'm afraid not,' the guard answered. He was sitting on one of four empty crates on the van floor.

'Keep it, I don't want it,' the Yank said.

The guard shot to his feet to get his bearings, but the way he made the note disappear into his waistcoat pocket would have done credit to a conjurer. He looked as young as the Yank as he sized up his visitors, but before he could get a word out the Yank was saying: 'Stand easy, guard, we come in peace for a powwow.'

'And for a powwow we need firewater,' he added as he sat on a vacant crate, put his grip on another between him and the guard, opened the grip with a flourish, and there on top of crumpled pyjamas and shirts were two bottles of whiskey.

The guard's dark eyes showed their whites in delight, a grin spread slowly across his face as he subsided onto his crate: "'Twas God that sent ye,' he said in the singsong accent of a Corkman. Miah smiled, preened his moustache with his fingers and pulled the fourth crate under him without a word.

As the Yank broke the seal on one of the bottles he explained: 'I was sick-sober when I got on this train without knowing it was dry. When he thought I was going to jump out the window this kind stranger snatched a flask off his hip in the fastest draw since Billy the Kid, and I murdered it. Now the stranger and I are pardners and I want to share a bottle with him to make up for the sudden death of his flask.' He raised the bottle to the light in the barred window of the carriage and added: 'And we want you to join us in the sealing of the pardnership.'

The guard reached into the corner behind him and put three cups one after the other on the makeshift table. He tossed the spoon that was in one of them over his shoulder and said: 'One thing I hate about cups for whiskey is that you can't see the colour of the liquor, and that's a shame.'

'Cups that leaked would be worse,' said the Yank as he poured for the three of them. 'Here's to temperance,' he added, raising his cup. 'To temperance,' echoed the other two, lifting their cups above their noses. The three heads leaned backward to drink and bowed forward between swallows like a ritual. The ritual kept going as the Yank kept pouring and no one said a word.

Then the guard took time out to admire the seasoned way Miah was relishing the liquor. He tilted his peaked cap back to let a lick of black hair spring loose on his forehead. 'How in God's name did a man like you stray onto a dry train?' he asked Miah, his round face wearing the ghost of a grin that is the seal of contentment.

'My son, only son, only child,' said Miah. 'He's a teacher in Dublin with a lovely girl for a wife and two small sons, my grandsons. Mark and Danny. Put in my wife Minnie and that's all there is of us. I know the kids because they come down to us for holidays, but I'm coming to see them for a day and this is the only train travelling. The return half of my ticket is in my pocket.'

'They'll say you're a spy in the camp. They'll say the three of us are spies,' said the guard, nodding his head in agreement with himself.

By this time a spotlight of sunshine slanted through the window on the three men, making the buttons on the guard's black uniform look like real silver. Miah had taken off his hat and his hair looked like platinum. The Yank was in a red pullover and blue slacks, and the tartan check in his shirt looked as loud as a fairground barker. Though still at top speed the train seemed more settled in itself. There was calypso rhythm in the sounds it made. It lulled the three into a silence of thinking and drinking not caring a damn as they sped through the miles.

All of a sudden the Yank said: 'Let's drink to Mark and Danny, the two very young colts in my pardner's far paddock. May they ride easy on all their trails.' And the three touched cups, looked upward, swallowed and bowed together again for a refill.

'What do you mean paddock?' asked the guard.

'Surely you must have read cowboy books, like me and my pardner. My old man at home had shelves of them. Books by Zane Grey,' said the Yank.

'*Lone Star Ranger*,' said Miah.

'Clarence E. Mulford,' said the Yank.

'*Bar-Twenty Days*,' said Miah.

'Buck Peters,' prompted the Yank.

'Johnny Nelson and Hopalong Cassidy,' said Miah.

And Miah kept on cue until the Yank had to laugh with delight at the way the guard was gaping at the verbal give and take.

'Old cowboys, old trails,' said the Yank.

'Men like Hoppy,' said Miah.

'They got saddle soreness so often they ended up with leather asses,' the Yank said.

'Leather asses,' echoed the guard, choking with chuckles.

'That's one of two reasons why you never heard of their being shot in the ass; the arrows and bullets hopped off. The other is that they never ran away,' the Yank told him.

'Good men,' said Miah, downing a drink.

'Good guns,' said the Yank, pouring another.

'The Winchester. The old Colt 45s worn on the hip by ordinary mortals, but slung low on the thigh by the gods of the lightning draw. Yippee!'

Miah smiled for the second time that day at something like the war cry of a Comanche being converted into the yelp of a cowhand on a spree. But the guard said: 'That was a bit on the loud side, partner. We mustn't forget that we're travelling with Pioneers.'

'Pioneers,' said the Yank. 'The men and women of the old West were the real pioneers. This is a diesel, theirs was a wagon train. And the Irish were up front in that kind of pioneering; opening up God's country between raid after raid by the Crow and the Cree and the Sioux and the Iroquois.'

'Here's to pioneers who drank firewater before breakfast,' said Miah.

'To pioneers,' said the others, and all three drank as one man.

Suddenly the Yank said: 'Hey, we're beginning to get into our cups.'

'We'll have to get out of them again in a hurry,' said the guard. 'We're not in the Wild West now. We're heading out of Kildare at a fair clip and 'tis Dublin City not Dodge City that's round the next few loops in the line.'

He got to his feet and put the empty cups back in the corner with the spoon. 'Tidy up, lads, leave no clues,' he said. The Yank closed his grip and gave what was left of the second bottle to the guard. 'You'll know what to do with that later.' The guard winked agreement and slid the bottle into the lining pocket in an overcoat that hung from a nail over the cups. 'I'll back-trail to check on the dry train Pioneers,' he said, putting a finger to his lips to signal caution as he left the van.

The Yank joined Miah at the window. 'We've passed the last wayside station,' Miah told him.

'I'll have to dash for a taxi to the airport the moment the train stops,' said the Yank. 'I'll have no time to say anything except so long. As a last favour I want you to give these to young Mark and Danny.' He handed two crisp dollar bills to Miah. 'I'd make it more but for the fact that if they've taken after their grandad they might go out and get drunk on a Pioneer train.'

'Ye're dead lucky,' said the guard from the doorway. 'The nearest car-

riage to us is empty, so grab yer gear and get into it now. From there ye
can leave with the rest of the passengers and no one will notice that ye've
been here in the van. Now good luck, ye were the best of company.'

Miah persuaded himself that it was the train and not the whiskey that
made him a bit unsteady on the way to the empty carriage with the
oranges, but he was glad to be on a soft seat again. It seemed only a few
minutes until the slowing train shuddered to a halt. 'I'm away,' said the
Yank. 'No yippees,' said Miah. 'No reason,' said the Yank as he leaped
onto the platform and raced away with the grip held high over his head.

For Miah it seemed a very deep step from carriage to platform. He
stumbled without falling but the bag with the oranges dropped and burst
on the ground. Four of the oranges rolled under the train; the other two
rolled together away from him. He hurried after them, picked them up
when they stopped, polished them with a cuff of his jacket and put one in
each of his side pockets. He was so vexed at the thought of how foolish he
must have looked that it was a relief to see that the hundreds who hurried
by hadn't the time to take notice.

He steered a wavering course through the Pioneers to the Liffey wall
at the far side of the platform. By that time the crowd was leaving by the
station gates or crossing the bridge over the river. And it was then that his
grandsons came bounding towards him with shouts of, 'Grandad,
Grandad!' His son Shay was on their heels. Miah had barely time to touch
his son's outstretched hand before the children grabbed him. One was as
dark as the other was fair and both were pulling at him as if they wanted
to make sure he was real. When he took the oranges out of his pockets
they stopped.

'Oranges all the way from Grandma,' he told them.

'Why didn't she come?' asked Shay.

'Your Aunt Ellie isn't well and your Mam stayed to keep an eye on
her,' Miah explained. 'Now, ye two young critters stand there before me
and close yer eyes so tight yer noses will crinkle.'

Knowing that the words always came before a gift of some kind, Mark
and Danny did as they were told. Shay grinned as Miah took the folded
dollars out of his waistcoat pocket, rubbed them flat between his palms
and with one in each hand raised them above the two young faces.

'Now open your eyes,' said Miah. Their big eyes got bigger at sight of the new notes. 'A real tall cowboy from Texas that I met on the train gave me these dollars for ye,' he told them. 'He said ye were to ride into town and paint it red and say "Yippee!"'

'Now say "Yippee",' he told them as he put the notes into their hands with a flourish. 'Yippee,' they yelled and they went on yelling 'Yippee' as they ran side by side towards the gates and the bridge with the notes held high over their heads.

Shay was grinning as he fell into step with his father to follow them. But Miah's smile looked fit for a halo.

Like Father, Like Son

Danny Coyle was a cross that teacher and pupils had to carry in our class at the monastery school. Except for him we were a lot of honourable hard-chaws. He was a slyboots. We rough and tumbled between us for survival; he stepped down from his nine years of age after school to bully innocents of eight and seven and so on down the line. And when lads of his age or older came between him and his victims with a boot on the rear or a punch on the kisser he wailed out—'I'll tell my Da!'

And most of the trouble about him was that same Da. Jack Coyle was easily the strongest man in our town or the country round it. He was so broad you hardly noticed how tall he was: six feet and an inch or two. His huge hands at the end of long arms were hung by his thumbs to his belt when he wasn't working. He earned a living at the sawmill where he tossed chunks of tree around like kindling. A show-off.

He'd as soon lift a barrel of porter onto a pub counter as drink it. But now, at forty-five or so, he opted for the ease of drinking and left the lift-ing to youngsters who tried to match feats of his they had heard about. The old grey suit he wore on Sundays he covered with an overall for work in the weekdays. His cap sloped to his right ear and his moustache bristled no matter what humour he was in. Give him his due, he was a quiet enough man till he was roused. And Danny was the rouser.

Outside of the classroom Danny meant 'I'll tell my Da' when he said it. He knew the way Jack doted on him as the son who came by special delivery from the Almighty after six daughters in a row. So he went to him with the names of the lads who stopped his bullying of others with a kick or a cuff in the right place. And Jack called on their fathers after work, flexing his muscles, opening and closing his fists at their doorsteps, warning them to control their sons if they didn't want their very own heads knocked off.

And believe me, no one's father wanted his son to be the cause of a visit from Jack Coyle. Even granted that it was holy and wholesome to save kids from being pushed about by a bully, they felt it would be wiser for their sons to win and wear haloes well clear of the Coyles. That meant that Danny went on strutting between whinges in Jack's shadow. So it would be true to say that the trouble with Danny was his father, the trouble with the father was his son. Like father like son in a way, with the father the better.

Inside the classroom when Danny talked of telling his Da, it was our teacher Tom Coffey who was at the receiving end of his barbs. Tom was a rawboned frame of a man with a mop of the kind of fair hair that brought freckles with it into his late twenties. It left him looking boyish when he was barely on the right side of thirty, especially when his lopsided smile made one of its rare appearances inside monastery walls. He was stroke oarsman for the Valley crew in regattas on the lakes that made our town world famous. He played good football and cycled eight miles every morning to the monastery from Beaufort, a scattered village with houses and shops hidden in trees on the banks of the Laune.

The long-drawn six feet of him had no chance to be anything but fit. His hands made pens and pencils and pieces of chalk look smaller than they were and when he was driven to use the cane you felt it all the way to the marrow in your palms. 'Do your homework. In class keep your eyes and ears open and your mouth shut,' was his code and the cane came your way when you stepped out of line. Fair enough.

In his favour too was the fact that he was the only layman on the school staff. All the rest were monks and anyone who was taught by monks will tell you it was always at the back of his mind that monks were neither priests nor people. Priests in personal sacrifice went up Calvary all the way. Monks stopped halfway and could go home any time they felt like it. Laymen like Tom Coffey had to put up with the world like the rest of us. They were some of our own and their faults, like our own, were as public as washing.

All told, Coffey was a fair man who gave you a square deal and got an honest hand back from everyone.

Except Danny. And it was the third part of Coffey's code that brought matters to a head between the pair of them. The third rule told you that if you were late for school you had to bring a note from your mother or father to explain why you weren't in the yard when the bell rang.

Danny was a half-hour late when he brazened into the room on a Monday morning that sent sunlight pouring through the tall peaked monastery windows. The sun gave the only brightness that morning. Coffey had the hang-dog look of a man who did too much celebration of a win on the lake for the Valley the day before. He was licking his lips and not liking the taste. Any smiles he owned he left at home.

And it was then that Danny walked in, letting the heavy door shut with a clatter behind him. Coffey never took his eyes off him as he strutted to his seat, dropped the bag at his feet and looked at his well-chewed fingernails. Bravado.

Coffey was still holding chalk at the blackboard when he said quietly: 'Where were you till this hour of the day, Coyle?'

'I was drawing water to shave my father,' said Danny, cool as always before the pay-off.

'You make it sound as if you should make a contract job of it. He must have a lot of face,' said Coffey.

'The pump is a long way up the lane from our house,' Danny explained.

'And that makes it a long way back of course. Did you wait to see him shave all that face?' Coffey asked, deadpan as you please.

'Only the half of it,' said Danny. 'When he cut himself with the oul' open razor he told me to get the hell out of there.'

'And only half the show kept you a half-hour late for school?' said Coffey, still nice and quietly.

'That and the walk here after,' Danny told him.

'With the note?' said Coffey.

'What note?' said Danny.

'The note you asked him to write for you to account for your being late.'

'Oh, that!' said Danny. 'He said he'd send that along later by carrier pigeon.'

'And get the pigeon to write it for him as well, I'm sure, but he wouldn't like us to know that, would he?' said Coffey.

'He wouldn't give a damn,' Danny rapped back. 'My Da don't give a damn about anything.' Then he added: 'Or anybody,' looking Coffey straight in the eye.

'Unfortunately I have to give a damn about you,' said Coffey. He reached for the cane at the back of the blackboard. 'Come up here,' he added.

Danny lost some of his cockiness with every step. By the time he was within cane's reach of the teacher he was beginning to cringe. Then he slipped into his familiar routine of putting on the boy martyr's face to look up at the torture stick. Then he whinged. 'Hold out your right hand,' said Coffey.

Danny's way of doing that was to put out his palm under cover of his elbow, where he kept darting it in and out like a stoat in a burrow while Coffey tried to get a shot at it. He struck air three times before he scored a direct hit on the wrong part of the hand: Danny's wrist.

Danny's howl hit the black oak rafters. He danced on one leg with the wrist wrapped in his armpit. 'I'll tell my Da,' he screamed. He had turned his back on Coffey and was facing us when he stole a look at the wrist. When he saw the red weal across the white skin the war cry about his Da had the true ring of outrage. 'I'll tell my Da,' he screamed up into the long man's face and Coffey, who hadn't seen the livid cane mark, said in his country drawl: 'You're always promising to do that, Danny.'

'But this time I'll bloody well do it!' Danny shouted over his shoulder as he scampered for the door, tugged it open and slammed it after him in a way that echoed in the monastery.

There was a silence before Coffey asked us: 'What was the new dimension in aid of?' and top of the class Con Nolan told him: 'You drew red on his wrist, sir.'

Coffey paused before he said, 'I wouldn't have hit his wrist if he hadn't played hide-and-seek with his palm.'

For the next two hours he took us through Mathematics and English with a few new twists off the boring routine. He was that kind of teacher: good. Then the bell rang at noon for the lunchtime break and we filed out through a porch as stone cool and empty as a mortuary.

The wide expanse of concrete yard was white with sun and hot as an oven. It had a shed, a handball alley and a lavatory that reeked with the piss of generations. Crows and gulls perched on eaves gawking at the crusts and crumbs the lads shed around them as they wolfed through milk and sandwiches. Finches and sparrows were spry enough to pick about the boys' feet where they stood around or sat on the warm concrete with their backs against walls.

It was a noon for siesta, but four of the senior lads were playing handball. Their shouts were finding echo in the hollow of the alley. Two monks were on the lunchtime watch. Tiny old Brother Eolan with snuff powder brown on the breast of his black habit was reading near the gate; a white handkerchief on his head to keep his bald skull from scorching. Brother Mark, the choirmaster, barrel-shaped as befitted a singer whose voice could make windows rattle, was in the peaked porch doorway; yawning. Tom Coffey had his bicycle upside down under our classroom window fixing a puncture.

The scene was so peaceful that the roar of 'Where's Coffey!' from the gate was a shock to us all. Sound and movement seemed to stop on the instant, except for the rubber ball bouncing loose from the alley and Coffey poking with a spanner at the bicycle. By that time Jack Coyle was walking on his own shadow towards Coffey: thumbs stuck in his belt, steely heels all but knocking sparks off the yard, Danny dancing in attendance like a pup on a lead.

'Are you Coffey?' he said to the back of the man bending over the bicycle.

'Mister Coffey inside the school walls,' Tom said without turning.

'I mister no man,' said Jack. 'Turn around till I talk to you.'

'So far I haven't seen you,' Tom told him in his country drawl. 'I'd like if it stayed that way.'

'I want to talk to you about my son,' said Jack.

'That's different,' said Tom, turning slowly.

When they stood face to face Jack snarled: 'Who the hell gave you the right to cut my son to pieces with a cane?'

'The pieces came together soon enough I see,' said Tom, glancing at Danny, who was hugging himself with satisfaction.

'I could take you to law,' said Jack. 'But I'll deal out my own justice by knocking your bloody head off.'

'I'm afraid I can't let you do that,' said Tom. 'Teachers are useless without heads in the way that you'd be useless without hands.' And the lopsided smile was there for the first time that morning.

He was raising his right hand to lift a lick of hair out of his eye when Jack hit him on the temple. It was a vicious blow that all but knocked him back over the bicycle.

'You shouldn't have done that,' he said, righting himself.

'You shouldn't have done the other,' said Jack, hitting out again.

But this time Coffey took the blow on his left forearm and let Jack have his right fist on his stained teeth. Jack looked as much surprised as offended. 'Now you did it,' he hissed as he drove forward with fists flailing. Youth and the fitness of an athlete were on Coffey's side. He took most of the blows on his arms, sidestepped others and swung his head side to side for safety in a way that would do credit to a trained scrapper. Needless to say, all of the 200 pupils in the yard had formed a ring around the two men, a ring that moved with them as each man in turn drove the other back towards the alley.

Blow after blow the two exchanged, all of them heavy, some of them sickeningly so. A left jab from Jack raised a bump on Coffey's forehead. A right from Coffey split Jack's moustache dead centre of the bristles and the taste of his own blood made Jack wilder than ever. By now we knew that youth was locked with prime in an epic. Danny was dancing and shouting and the rest of us were giving tongue in the raw excitement. It went on and on, with sweat running into their eyes, down their noses, dripping off their chins onto their chests. Their shirts were stained with it, Coffey's flaming hair was wet with it. Jack's cap was stuck to his temples with it. You could smell it.

And it was when a blow of Jack's drew blood from Coffey's nose that Brother Mark barrelled his bulk between them, shouting: 'This is gone far enough.' He gripped Coffey by the wrists and said: 'Have sense, Tom, you could lose your job on this.' Coffey said: 'Better lose my job than my manhood.' Mark said, 'Oh, heavens,' in vexation and Coffey said, 'Oh, hell,' in frustration. Jack said: 'Let him loose, in God's name, before my fire goes out.'

'He's right, Mark, let go of my wrists,' said Coffey, and when Mark hung on he said: 'Look, do you want it on my slate that I hit a religious?' As Mark hesitated he added: 'Can't you see that if I back down no teacher will ever again be respected in this school, monk or layman?' That clinched the issue for Mark. He stepped back to let the two men tear into each other again with a venom made fresh by the break.

With blow after blow they belted each other into the alley where knuckle knocked louder on bone. Coffey's fists were beating on the drum of Jack's chest and getting sound out of it. Jack's round-the-house swings were finding Coffey's ears. In a kind of last-stand slog, the fitness of the younger man was giving him the edge when Brother Eolan swept the handkerchief off his head and darted between them like a little old cur between mastiffs. 'In God's name, stop!' he cried in his reedy voice.

'You'll get hurt, Eolan,' said Coffey kindly. 'You'll get killed,' said Jack with no kindness at all. 'Would you waste a blow on me?' said Eolan to Jack whose fists hung limp by his sides. '*You* could kill me with a finger,' he told Coffey. '*You* could kill me with a fingernail,' he told Jack. 'Go on, go ahead, I won't stop you.' And with Eolan looking up at him like a willing martyr, Jack said: 'I won't start, small man.'

Eolan jerked like a clockwork toy as he faced each man in turn with the handkerchief raised as if it were a flag of surrender. 'I know you wanted to prove yourself to your son,' he told Jack. 'I know you wanted to make teaching safe in this place for another generation,' he told Coffey.

Then he stepped back to look at them both and said: 'Each of ye has proved his point to the hilt. Ye don't have to go to last breaths or death's doors or drive nails into coffins to make testimony. What do ye say to my calling it a draw, a draw with honour after a fair fight, what do ye say?'

Then the little tich made his master move. Without waiting for their answer he raised his palms to the yardful of silent faces and said: 'We'll call it a draw, lads, won't we?' At the top of our voices we all answered, 'Yes!'

The two battered men stood looking at each other without a word. We held breath. Then Jack broke the silence.

'No man ever stayed with me for so long,' he said.

'I had a notion I could overstay,' Coffey told him.

'I couldn't throw you out,' Jack said.

'I'll go now of my own accord,' Coffey said. 'I have a bike to fix.' His smile on a sore face was more lopsided than ever.

'Wait,' said Jack. He shuffled in his nailed boots, looked at his fist as if he never saw it before, closed a bruised eye and looked at Tom Coffey with the other. 'Any man who went so far to prove a point must be honest,' he said. 'Any time Danny won't do what you think is good for him, you tell me.'

'I'll do that,' said Coffey.

'Good luck to you now,' Jack told him.

'God speed,' said Coffey.

Jack walked away out of the yard with Danny in tow. Tom Coffey went back to his bicycle. Mark returned to the porch with all the yawns knocked out of him. Small Eolan put the handkerchief back on his head, opened his book and soon was reading as if nothing had happened.

It only remains to say that the next time Danny was called to the cane Coffey told him: 'And don't say you'll tell your Da, or I'll tell him for you. He told me so himself.' Then, taking a leaf out of Eolan's book, he turned to the class and said: 'Didn't he, lads?' And we answered, 'He did!' in a chorus. But the lopsider was back on his face when he turned back to Danny. 'I owe you a let-off for that bruise on your wrist, Danny. Go back to your seat.'

Danny put on a brave show of no surrender as he walked back to the empty seat. He stood at the desk and looked defiantly at all of us before he sat down at last. But he never said, 'I'll tell my Da,' in that room ever after.

No Day to Die

The trouble with Grandy, my grandfather, was that you didn't know what he would be doing next. I don't think he knew himself: he just found himself doing it, I think, and carried on regardless, whatever it was. Like the day he took us by surprise on the morning I was eight years old.

When you put seven behind you, you don't feel a child anymore, and piecing my new fishing rod together in the gun corner of our kitchen I felt as manly as ever I'll be. With the case of gamekeeping guns at my back and the split-cane rod bowing before me at the slightest twist of my wrist I felt as grown-up as Da, the tall man out there on the mountain as a gamekeeper.

The rod was my birthday present from Grandy, all the way from the ring at the tip to the reel that rattled like a crake when I twisted the handle: a lady's rod to be sure, but ladies are grown-ups anyway even when they're small like Ma, who was sweeping the floor.

It was so quiet in the kitchen you'd think it was as much silence as dust she was sweeping into the ashes. The kettle was boiling where it hung off an iron in the hearth. Coolness came over the half-door to keep the turf fire from heating more than the kettle and the chimney that drew the smoke away. Besides, the chimney was wide enough to let you see daylight or stars or let raindrops spit into the embers.

'Grandy is late in stirring,' Ma said.

'I know,' I said. 'I want to try this rod on the lake and I can't do that without Grandy.'

That was true. He wouldn't let me near the lake unless he was standing guard beside me on the bank or teaching me to drop a fly in the water the soft way a moth lands on a windowpane.

'He's stirring now,' said Ma, putting the brush away.

'Will I tell him to hurry?' I said, but she shook her head.

She took the greatest care not to hurry him since a stiff hip and a slowing of the heart put an end to any chance he had of going up or down the mountain ever again. From then on he had to content himself with the rough ledge the mountain allowed him for his white thatched house, with the small lake thrown in for good measure. With no call to put on his blue serge suit for Mass of a Sunday he put it folded away in a drawer in his room. The rumpled old tweed clobber he wore as a gardener in his good days went fishing on him now, with me running ahead of him or coming to heel like a pup when he called.

'The kettle is getting ready for your breakfast, Da, will I put the egg in the boil?' Ma said, raising her voice.

'I'll tell you when I'm ready,' he called back.

After a minute more the handle of his door rattled. The door opened inch by inch until there was space for an eye to show between a bushy eyebrow and a beard as thick as thatch. Then it was jerked open fully and there was Grandy framed with his stick in the doorway in a fashion that was one of his biggest ever surprises. From top to toe he was the Sunday man of old: from black felt hat with a brim wide enough for cowboys to the light black boots, with in between the suit that was getting away from mothballs for the first time in years. His stick had made four taps at least on the floor before Ma got a word out.

'You look real grand, Da,' she said, her voice cheerful but her face halfway between worry and wonder. He put his stick against the wall as he took his place at the table. She wiped the egg with her apron before she put it in the saucepan and swung the kettle to spill into the teapot.

'Where's the wedding?' she said.

'No wedding.'

'What then?'

'A wake,' he said.

'Whose wake?'

'Mine,' he said and the word dropped like a stone into a pool.

'You're joking surely.'

'Can't you hear me laughing,' he gave back, and silence said the rest for him. I had to hand it to Ma the way she hid alarm with a smile and a tone of chat in her voice.

'That cake went a bit hard in the crust on me, but I'll heat the butter so you can soften it,' she told him.

'There's nothing wrong with my teeth or my taste,' he said. 'Not yet anyhow.'

She put the egg in front of him and poured the tea before she tried again.

'Kevin here is charmed out with the rod,' she said. 'He can hardly wait for you to take him to the lake with it.'

'He'll have a long wait,' he said.

He looked sad, sounded sad, but his strong teeth were making mush out of the cake at the same time.

Ma took a stool from the hearth to sit at his feet, looking up into his weathered face the way she must often have done as a child when death was the last thing he'd talk about.

'Tell me what the matter is, Da,' she said in the coaxing way she had with him for all his surprises.

'They were in touch with me during the night. In touch, I tell you.'

'Who?'

'My people, our people, my mother and father and brother, your mother, Mollie. They're gone now a long time, all of them, but they came to me large as life to tell I'll be going to join them shortly,' he reeled off like a litany.

'How shortly?' said Ma as matter-of-fact as she could manage.

'Before another nightfall: that'll be tonight, so I must get ready. I must be ready, you see. Or do you see at all?' he said.

'I see a strong man sitting at his breakfast,' she told him.

'With a heart that could stop between mouthfuls,' he gave back.

'And a mind full of old wives' tales that mislead him,' she said.

'This is no tale,' he told her, calmer now. 'This is no tale, this is the truth. When the people of our blood left this world for the next, they kept in touch with the ones they left behind. They kept in touch. I did in my thoughts and whatever prayers I say. His father came to warn my father, now my father came to warn me. My father died on the hour his father told him. I'll die before nightfall the way my father told me.'

Ma put the stool back at the fire. Slowly. She pushed away the wisp of hair that always kept dipping over her eyes. Then she put a brave face on whatever thought she had.

'Yerrah, what will I do with you at all?' she scolded. ''Tis worse you're getting on me. You have Kevin frightened out of his wits on his birthday instead of helping him to catch a trout for his dinner.'

His words met hers on the volley. 'No, you're not going to talk me out of this with coaxing or scolding or downright temper of the kind you rise to when you're really vexed.'

He calmly put his pipe, tobacco and matches on the table. 'Call your Daddy, Kevin, if he's within shouting distance,' he told me.

'He is,' said Ma. 'He said he was only going above the lake a bit.'

'His bits make a lot of mountain, God spare him the legs. Tell him I have something to say to him,' he said.

'Go, son,' said Ma, and even with the rubber soles of my shoes I could hear myself walking out of the silence behind me.

No more than Ma did I believe a word of what the old man was saying. All I was worried about was the trout I might be missing by having my rod against the guncase. Da was easy to see above the lake with his gun and the telescope. I waved to him and he waved back. I beckoned and he came down to me.

'Grandy wants you,' I said.

'What is it now?' he said.

'He'll tell you himself,' I told him.

I was in no mood for telling him a ghost story with that sky full of fishing breeze mocking me and a heathery old mountain making me feel as small as a mouse. A minute later I was sorry I hadn't put him wise; for the first thing he said when he laid an eye on the old man was: 'Patch Leahy, you have the cut of a man who is going places.'

Grandy took a long draw on the pipe and said: 'I am.'

'A long journey?'

'Longer than long.'

'Well, wherever it takes you they'll say sir to you in that outfit,' said Da. 'But where? Or is it a mystery tour you're taking?'

'The next world. Heaven they call it,' said the old man.

'Where did you get a notion like that?' said Da, putting his gun and telescope on the clear end of the table.

The living and the dead of my family were always in touch with each other,' said the old man. 'Always. And in the night behind me they came to tell me I'd be with them on the other side before the night that's ahead.'

'It must be the drop of whiskey I put in your tea last night that set fire to your thoughts. You were dreaming,' Da told him.

'We're in touch, I tell you. It was no dream. It is no dream I tell you, Tom Lyne.'

'So you're going aloft. Just like that.'

'Before nightfall,' said the old man.

He went on to say: 'I'd like to bypass Purgatory if I can and you'll help me on that score.'

'How in the hell can I help?' said Da.

'We'll leave hell out of it too, if you don't mind,' said the old man. 'You can help me by shouldering your bicycle down the mountain till you get the wheels under you on the road below. Then you'll cycle the four miles to Killarney and bring me back any priest you can find in the presbytery. All priests have cars these days and he'll drive you here in style with your bike in the boot.'

'You're serious, Patch?'

'I have to be, Tom.'

'Then 'tis me for the road on my bike,' said Da.

I went beyond the door to watch him with the bicycle hanging off his shoulder, go down the mile of stone track between heather clumps and brakes of furze with here and there an ash in berry or a silver birch to remind you that some trees would grow anywhere. Behind me I could hear Ma chattering like a sparrow to Grandy, the way a mother says nonsensical things to a child to keep it from thinking it time for another blast of tears or temper. I kept drifting in and out of the kitchen, taking up the rod and putting it down again to remind him of his solemn promise of yesterday that we'd be luring trout to suicide, as he put it, at this very hour.

Ma got the message and put a spoke in nicely. 'That's a painted day for fishing,' she said, and followed up with hints as plain as the nose on your face, like: 'Would you believe it, 'tis two days now since we had fish on a plate.' But he just kept on puffing smoke to the ceiling through the black and white beard that would remind you of a badger.

It was only when vexation made me let off a rattle with the reel that he came to his senses. Then he pocketed the pipe, grabbed the stick and all but took the half-door with him on his way out onto the mountain. 'I thought you were taking me fishing today,' he snapped over his shoulder and I was at the tail of his coat with rod and net before a tinker could say tin.

The lake sent sound and smell to meet us. That lake smelled of trout the way trout that came out of it smelled of lake till you fried it away on a pan. The sound came from clear sheet water spreading itself out on the shore. A drowse day it was in the sun. A heron looked asleep on one leg in the shallows: he didn't give us a reck. A cock nodding a scarlet comb near the reeds didn't give a hang about us either. Grandy headed straight for the big grey rock with a dip in the middle that he called his chair. He shaded his eyes with his hat to look up at the sky that hadn't a speck on it except a hawk hanging on the prowl. He hadn't said a word since we left the house. Thinking he was, I thought, and if his thinking was anything like mine he was telling himself that this was no day to die.

Soon I was standing on the green bank in front of him with deep water below me and the rod ready in my hand.

'Right now, boy, let the fish know you're here,' he said.

The new rod had a tricky spring in it that took time to get used to, but after that it flicked the flies onto the ripples like a wand. The old man didn't say half as much as he used to. At the beginning, when myself and the rod were getting to know each other, he said things like: 'Don't whip the water, you're not riding on a horse.' Later, when I got better, he said: 'That's it. Lay the flies on the wind and 'twill lay them on the water. Nicely, nicely, any trout worth salt will admire that.'

And that's the way it was until a trout lepped clear of the water and struck like lighting at my tail fly on its way back. Quick as it was it was hardly quicker than the old man getting up off the rock. He was at my side, dropping his stick, spitting out the pipe, flinging away the hat and hopping on his good leg around me before the fish took a second good tug at the line. And tug it it did, game to the tail, an out-and-out battler that must be a pound if it was an ounce: a game fish.

Grandy called to whisper tactics as if the fish could hear. 'Give him the reel,'—'Halt him now,'—'Keep the tip of the rod up or he'll leave you,'— 'Nicely, nicely,'—'Lovely, lovely, beautiful, grand, lean on him now,'— 'Up with the tip, you whore you, I say,'—'You have him, you boy you, you're great.' The rod, line and cast felt like a whiplash in my two desperate fists. But in the end that trout was flashing gold and silver, spinning on his tail on top of the water all the way into the net in the old man's fist.

The old man gave a shout that must have been heard by our nearest neighbour a mountainy mile away. He swung the net clear, his black eyes with the whites widened were glaring at the fish threshing in the wet mesh as if it was the first he ever saw. His stiff hip was forgotten as he hobbled across the grass, walking on his hat on the way until the hoop of the net was prodding into a priest.

Young Father Slattery from town was standing on the bank, grinning bareheaded like a schoolboy with Da chuckling behind him. You could see how the old man had to remind himself that he was on his last legs.

'Forgive me, Father, I was carried away,' he said.

'I'll take this out of your way, old stock,' Da told him, relieving him of the net with the trout in it.

'I believe you want to talk to me, Patch,' said the priest.

'Isn't Kev here a great lad to land a trout that size on his eight years' birthday, Father?'

'He had a good teacher, hadn't you, boy?' the priest said, putting the flat of his hand on my head like a blessing.

'But what about that old chat we are to have?'

You could see the old man had again to remind himself about the last legs. Then he said: 'Come over here to my chair.'

I got his stick and pipe and his hat together and gave them to him on his way to the rock.

'Good boy,' he said. 'What would I do without you?'

'What would he do without you?' said Father Slattery.

It was a telling thing to say for a priest not all that much older than myself: it got me right below the belt I tell you.

'We'll leave them to it,' Da said. Before we were out of sight the priest was dropping a blue stole over his shoulders. As we rounded the elm that put us in line with the house I took another look. Under the high sky you never saw two people look more on their own at that rock, with only wild fowl in the rushes to hear what they were saying. 'He should be at peace now, whether he goes or not,' Da said, as much to himself as to me.

Da went on into the house but I leaned the rod against the wall near the door and went back to meet Grandy and the priest. To my surprise they parted company at the head of the track that led down to the road. 'He has more confessions than mine to hear this evening,' Grandy explained as we walked together to the house. 'But I got the Eucharist as well.'

He didn't say much at dinner: not even to say the new potatoes were the best ever the way he never failed to do day after day as if our potatoes stayed new into Christmas. Then he gathered himself with pipe and stick into his room, put his good suit with the hat back in the drawer with the mothballs, wound the clock on the window, heaved his old bones into the bed and told Ma: 'All I have to do now is wait.'

Before he went out on the mountain again Da told me to stand in the clearing near the elm on the hour every hour where he could see me with the telescope. 'If he takes a turn wave me down and I'll come to ye,' he said.

From then on Ma went about everything she did on tiptoe, whispering, as if a child was sleeping; or an old man dying, for that matter. I stayed near the door with a book, waiting on the clock on the hob to time my visits to the elm. Ma took a peek into the room now and then. I took a peek myself: he was lying on his back with his head raised on a pillow, his hands joined on a rosary beads. Like a corpse if he didn't look so healthy. And the big horny hands with the beads looked strong enough to punch holes on the wall under the picture of the Sacred Heart that leaned over him.

When the sky changed colour for dusk Da came down to us for supper. Ma took tea and a scone into Grandy but he waved her away without speaking.

'Let him be now,' said Da, lighting a fag.

''Tisn't easy,' said Ma.

'Going to him now you wouldn't know whether you were doing harm or good,' Da told her.

'I suppose,' said Ma.

'We'll wait with him,' said Da.

'Where?'

'Here.'

So we waited.

'When night comes nearer we'll know for sure,' Ma said after a while, her hands twisting in her apron.

'So will he,' said Da.

'Nightfall he said.'

'Nightfall.'

There was coolness now but I knew she was leaving the door open so she could see the sky. Da was looking at the sky too. So was I. Watching for nightfall, all of us. And it was then I began to feel that maybe the old man was going to leave us after all. Only coolness was in the air but I shivered. The ghost call of curlews homing to the lake made me feel like letting a gun go at them. That nightfall was the longest in coming I'll ever know. But come it did in the finish. With one star.

'Night is here, come in with me, Tom,' Ma said, and I followed the pair of them.

We tiptoed into the small room that was darker than the kitchen because the window was small. The clock was louder than ever I heard it. Ma leaned over the old face on the bed. 'He's alive and asleep,' she said. 'Thanks be to God.' Then she blessed herself, put a finger to her lips, and we stole out of the room the way we stole into it. We were just past the door when a string of snores came after us.

'So he missed the bus,' said Da, lighting a fag with his back to the fire.

'That's no way to put it,' Ma said.

'I feel like laughing, woman,' he told her. 'With relief.'

'Me too,' I found myself saying as I walked out for a ramble.

I felt older. I was finding that strain like that puts months on a man. There was quietness on the mountain. The curlews were gone to cover. The first star had plenty for company in a sky that had room for them. A time for bats to fly in tangles round the elm and the lake. Shadows had quenched the purples and yellows of heather and furze and the air was cooling their smell away. Things I took for granted, things not thought about before, things I found no time for were nudging me; like thinking that if it had been no day to die it was no night to die either. Like being glad that the old man in the dark room would see tomorrow with me. One way or another I'd get him to come fishing, I decided, as I walked back to the house.

Ma was taking a candle into his room. 'So he'll know he's not dead when he wakes,' she explained.

'He's snoring peaceful,' she told us when she came back. Then she lit the lamp and shut the night out with the tall door. The lamp put a ring of brightness on the hob for Da to see better the gun he was cleaning. I sat at one end of the table with the tin of barbed flies sorting them out for the fishing tomorrow. At the other end Ma was making more bread; that stray twig of hair bowing to every move she made.

It seemed no time at all until it was bedtime and Ma making the last tea of the day. And it was then that the old man came among us without a word or a nod in his worn clothes and the laces hanging loose from his old nailed boots. Da waited until he was well settled into his place at the table before he said: 'Welcome back.'

Grandy put his stick against the wall, put the pipe with the matches on the table and said: 'I'm hungry.'

'I'll soon cure that,' said Ma.

He lit the pipe for a few puffs while he waited.

'So you didn't die after all, old stock,' said Da, dipping with a spoon in his tea to cool it.

'I'm glad you noticed,' said the old man. Da was trying to get a grin out of him, help him back to himself. It was no use.

'Now, Dad, get that into you,' Ma said, putting a mug of steaming tea in front of him, with a chop on his plate and butter melting on the fried trout.

'You'll stay with us,' Da tried again.

'I might,' said the old man, breaking pieces off the cake with his fingers.

''Tis past the hour, the train is gone, you're safe,' said Da. 'Safe.'

'Yes.'

'And sound?'

'As a bell.'

'Thanks to God and Mary,' said Ma.

'And rearing to hop over the half-door again,' Da prompted.

'Hops like that are far behind me.'

'But you're strong as a horse.'

'A nag.'

'You're fine.'

'I'm lost.'

'You'll live to a hundred.'

'And that's what's bothering me,' said the old man, letting the knife fall with a clatter on the floor in vexation. I picked the knife up, gave it a rub on my jersey and put it back on the plate.

'Bothering you?' said Da.

'You wouldn't understand,' said the old man.

'Try me,' said Da.

'Damn it, man, can't you see? I'm out of touch. Out of touch, I say,' said the old man.

'Nonsense, Dad,' Ma soothed. 'Sure God Himself is only a prayer away.'

'I'm not talking about God, leave Him out of it,' he gave back. ''Tis them I'm angered with.'

'Who?' said Ma.

'Them. Them. Them,' he let out, like three blows of a fist.

'What did I ever do that they'd leave me alone like this?'

'Nonsense,' said Ma.

'I'm alone,' said the old man.

'I never saw a man so sorry he wasn't dead,' said Da with a smile as he put his empty cup on the table. But he was real serious when he looked the old man straight in the face and said: 'Only one thing you said was a nonsense, old stock, that last thing. Out of touch or into touch or over the bar you'll never be alone.'

Then he gripped a fist of my hair and led me to bed the way he would lead a colt from a fair with a hand on the mane. Ma stayed on with the old man by the fire.

A Hat My Father Wore

It was the suit that caused the hat and the hat that caused the bother, if bother you'd call it: a laugh really. The grey tweed suit with the heather fleck in it was lying in a drawer in the parents' room since Da brought it home from the tailor three months ago.

You could see how well he celebrated the suit by the limewash daubs on the right shoulder of the old dark jacket he was wearing: blue for Brady's, pink for Gleeson's, white for Leary's, the three houses on the lane he leaned against each time on the way to his own front door. The smell of whiskey followed him through the hall to the kitchen: I know because I was on his heels. When you're nine you feel you're old enough to see that your Da doesn't brain himself when he's jarred. My eight-year-old brother Donnie was a second Samaritan behind me when Da met one afflicted mother at the kitchen door.

'I have the suit, Kate,' he told her, as if that excused everything.

'But have you yourself?' said Ma as he waded like a tightrope walker to his chair by the fire. 'Give me that suit before it falls into the coals.'

'I'm easy about it,' he said. ''Twas you that said I needed it for Mass of a Sunday.'

'And 'twas I who put the money by that bought it,' she reminded him as she took the suit in the brown paper wrapping for safe keeping in their room.

'She's right of course,' Da told us, waving a hand to the ceiling before he sank back to sleep in the chair. Da was always admitting things like that when Ma wasn't there to hear.

But I must say he was right about the suit being Ma's idea. If he had his way the one suit would do him for a lifetime. He felt at home in the jacket he wore at his carpentry and carving, with the pockets wide open for his hands to drop into for pipe and pouch as he planned his next move on the bench. There was dandruff on his collar from his starve-the-barber periods but who'd see that if he let his greying locks grow longer. He liked nothing better than the nut smell of wood as he planed or chiselled or carved it into things that were as good to look at as to use. That was why Ma went easy on his binges. His craft and himself wore each other down so much that they needed a rest from each other to stay friends.

But how could a man rest in a new suit was his comeback when Ma mentioned it. 'By wearing it,' was Ma's answer, until finally he gave in and went to see Patsy Nagle the tailor. And so the suit came to rest in a drawer in their room.

All that was three months ago. But three days ago it was the hat. Da had stalled about wearing the suit on a plea that no sensible man would wear a new suit without a new hat to go with it.

So Ma started saving again. For Christmas she said. Christmas Eve for Midnight Mass the suit and a hat together on him, she said, as God was her judge.

That Christmas Eve began with a silver sun that saw Donnie and me on our bicycle all the way to the nearest mountain for a bart of holly. We hadn't to climb far to find a holly tree. When we had cut and corded a bart that was red with berries I sat on a tangle of bare heather to look at the lake below us. Maybe it was Christmas and cribs and the lake that did it, but I was thinking of Peter the fisherman and loaves and fishes when Donnie told me to get off my backside before the rain came down on us.

Donnie was the practical half of us. When he gnawed at the knuckles of his right hand you knew he was sizing up the situation; any situation. Just then he was telling me that a mountain was no place to be when a silver sky turned into lead as quick as that. He was right of course. After a mad dash on the bicycle, with Donnie on the back holding the holly in front of him, we were safe in our hallway when rain swept the lane with a squall.

Ma was busy cooking the dinner but she took snatches of time off to see that we put holly on the pictures, a few pads of moss round the crib and a ring of coloured paper round the tin of sand that held the candle.

She told us that the crib was great, the pictures looked grand and the candle was perfect, before she asked us to set the coal in the grate in the sitting room. Ma was a dab hand at showering you with praise for small chores before she saddled you with the big one.

We had the coal set and ready for a match when Da came in. He hung his work hat on a nail on the hob before he sat in his chair and he was hardly sitting before Donnie grabbed the old hat to play cowboys. Donnie's shock of hair made his head big enough to fit a hat of Da's perfect.

'Where's the hat you were to bring home for the fist of money I gave you?' Ma said.

'Ellie has it,' said Da. Ellie is Ma's youngest sister. She's a nurse in the local hospital.

'She was going on duty when I met her outside the shop,' said Da. 'I gave her that hat to hold in case I met whiskey company in Jack C's and lost it.'

'So?' said Ma.

'So she's coming here when she gets off duty at half-eleven. She's to stay with us for Christmas, you know that.'

'There's nothing wrong with her having the hat for safe keeping, but it will be a quarter to midnight by the time she gets here unless she flies.'

'And it only takes ten minutes to get from here to the friary.'

'We'll see,' said Ma. Then she spotted that Da had a bottle of whiskey he thought was hidden by a leg of his chair.

'What is that?' she said, as if she didn't know.

'A gift in the bar from the owner, Jack C,' he said.

'If fair was fair he'd have to give you the bar,' Ma told him.

'He only gives it to me a drop at a time,' said Da.

'When you pay for it,' she said.

'Oh now, Kate, you wouldn't expect him to give it to me for nothing,' said Da.

'I would,' she said, just like that. I often thought that if Ma meant all she said sometimes she'd be well on her way to being bonkers.

'Don't take the seal off that bottle until tonight,' she told him.

'As you say,' said Da, winking at Donnie, who was about to shoot Ma in the back with a shotgun. No doubt in his mind she was Calamity Jane and he was Sheriff of Dodge City.

'If you fire another shot with that toy thing I'll give you a swipe of the dishcloth,' she told him over her shoulder and Donnie said, 'Ah Ma,' in disgust at her insistence on being herself.

'Grab a chair for dinner, Sheriff,' she told him and he said, 'How did you know?'

'Your star is showing,' said Ma.

The only star we were likely to see that night was on the small tree in the sitting room. The coal fire was a great help in not caring about the rain that lashed at the window.

Before he joined us Da had put the finishing touches to a four-foot Saint Patrick he had carved to order for a small church near the mountain. The new suit made him look a perfect gentleman.

'He smiled nicely for me,' he said.

'Who?' said Donnie.

'Saint Patrick,' said Da. 'He was all for having a grin for the mood we were in but he smiled like a pal in the end.'

'I saw,' said Donnie.

'Did you smile back?'

'Sort of,' said Donnie.

'He told me to have a drink when I was leaving him,' Da said, putting the bottle beside a glass of water on the table. 'Very understanding is Saint Pat,' he added, pouring the honey-hued liquor into the empty glass in his hand.

He drank it neat. The water was for partly replacing in the bottle the amount of liquid he was pouring out of it to drink. So when Ma took short breaks from stuffing the turkey and making the pudding she thought he was going easy on the bottle by the look of it.

Poor Ma. When she expected him to be in the yearning stage in the whiskey he was in the singing stage. That was when she came to join us at eleven. She sipped lemonade with Donnie and me while Da made advances in the hard tack. She was in her best blue dress with her hair held together on a comb she wore on special occasions since her wedding.

Singing sessions with Da were interrupted to the point of annoyance

by his calls for 'one man, one voice' when anyone dared to join in the cho-
ruses. After many gnawings on the wisdom knuckles Donnie sometimes
said that was Da's way of making sure that his was a real solo when he
sang. 'As if he was a Jimmy Tormey,' said Donnie, shaking his head.
Jimmy Tormey was the best singer in a friary choir that never wore a
habit. All of them were lay people like ourselves, except the organist who
was a lay brother who had everything a friar had except a tonsure, and he
made up for that with a bald patch as round as a penny. Jimmy was a
butcher who looked like a boxer and could sing like a lark whether the air
was clear or not. Some people went to two Masses of a Sunday to hear him.
Da never went as far as that but he doted on that tenor voice as if it was
his own.

And his own just then on that Christmas Eve was hopping and trot-
ting with:

> *Goodbye, Johnny dear, and when you're far away*
> *Don't forget your poor ould mother far across the say …*

A catchy ditty that you'd love to join in if he didn't bring 'one man,
one voice' trumpeting in your ears.

I had to sing 'Killarney and Solo Angels' into folding their wings to
rest in that Eden of the West. Donnie's 'Rose of Tralee' had to be lovely
and fair on her own by the pure crystal fountain for his off-key wooing.
Ma's 'Last Rose of Summer' had to be blooming alone in real earnest.
When Donnie tried to help her in the low notes, he got the 'one man, one
voice' treatment in a way that sent him gnawing his knuckles like a squirrel with a bad nut.

And it was then that Auntie Ellie walked in with the new hat. Da had
hardly time to look at it before putting it on, the way Ma hustled us out
the hall and into a night that did everything bar be a show-off with thun-
der and lightning. The west wind had us clinging to each other out of the
lane into College Street and later up the hill of steps to where the chapel
window showed its colours like a banner in the dark.

Beyond white railings on our left as we climbed the steps were three
tiers of lawn sloping upward to a statue of Saint Francis if you could see
them. But the gale was blowing us towards the railings on our right.
Beyond the railings on that side was a field of tangled grass that had lime

and chestnut trees for shelter on two sides of the square—it was for open-air Benediction, but there was no seeing that either. And honestly I don't think Da could walk a straight line even if the gale stopped blowing.

He'd have fallen at the porch steps if I hadn't been holding him. As it was, the new hat was whipped off his head away towards the field and the trees.

'The wind took my hat,' he told Ma in the porch.

'It left you your head I hope,' said Ma.

The brightness in the chapel alone would make you feel good as you came in out of the cold. The smell of incense was escaping from the sacristy beside the High Altar where candles burned all the way to the roof almost.

A novice like an altar boy found us four seats, with Da on the outside nearest the aisle. Donnie was next to him and I was between Donnie and Ma. The organ loft was behind us. The organ was humming to itself tunes like 'Holy Night' and 'While Shepherds Watch Their Sheep by Night', drowsily, so that Da would have nodded off to sleep if Donnie didn't keep nudging him with his elbow. But Da was brought to order with the rest of us when the organ was joined by the choir in an 'Alleluia' to greet the three friars in gold cloth vestments who filed out of the sacristy to bow before the altar for the opening of High Mass. From then on to the Gospel the choir together and the organ on its own made lovely sound.

And it was when priests and people sat back after the Gospel for the 'Adeste' that it happened. The organ drifted into the hymn and Jimmy Tormey's voice floated with it off the loft onto the hush singing:

> *Adeste fideles,*
> *Laete triumphantes*
> *Venite, Venite,*
> *In Bethlehem.*

And once again I agreed with myself that if I had a voice like that I'd never be a butcher. Da was sitting with his eyes closed in a way you weren't sure if he was awake or asleep or halfway between.

He was that way until the full choir with a trumpeting organ joined the solo voice in the 'Natum videtes' but then he shot to his feet, stepped onto the aisle, swung round with his right hand pointing up at the choir and shouted loud and clear: 'One man, one voice.'

Ma stiffened in shock, looking straight at the altar. Da got as far as 'one man' second time round before Donnie tugged him by the new coat tail back into the pew, where he sat upright in a kind of shock himself before he came to his senses. That wasn't a situation where Donnie had time to gnaw a knuckle but he had done the right thing at the right time in a way I was proud to see.

In fact I was so lost in admiration for what Donnie did that I wasn't half as shocked as Ma and the rest of the congregation. From there on to the end of Mass and music Ma knelt facing the altar and Da at least kept one eye open.

He came fully awake for sure when he had to give himself up to the gale without a hat, with Donnie holding on to him all the way home. There wasn't a word out of him when he went straight for the bottle by the fire. By the look of him you'd swear he had committed sacrilege.

Ma put her coat and hat away and went to help Auntie Ellie with the tea. And it wasn't until Ellie's laughter came lilting from the kitchen that a grin tickled its way across Donnie's face.

Ellie was still laughing when she rushed into the room straight for Da with her hand out.

'Congratulations, Michael,' she said. 'I hear you were conducting the choir.'

'A farewell performance, I fear,' said Da, rising to the cue with a glass raised.

'I hope,' said Ma in a way that made all of us laugh together.

Then Ma told Donnie and me, 'Up at seven to the friary field for that hat. There ought to be enough light by that time to find it. A brand new brown hat from the glimpse I got of it before we were at the mercy of the storm.'

We were on our way to the field at seven in a bright morning that hadn't a breeze or a raindrop. When the trees came in sight Donnie said: 'What chance have we to find a hat in a place the size of that?' So we were all the more astonished when there was a hat in almost every part of it we searched. Thirteen we found, all of them brown except a grey like a nest in a lime tree that turned out to be a woman's hat with a blonde wig skewered to it on a hatpin.

We hid with our collection near the gate to the chapel as the people went down the steps away from seven o'clock Mass. We waited till they were good and gone before we considered the problem that five of the brown hats were new. 'How can we know which is Da's?' said Donnie.

And it was then I had what Da calls the inspiration of a lifetime when they happen to him. 'You fit them on,' I told Donnie. 'If one of them fits you for cowboys it will fit Da for wear.' He kept trying until the fourth fitted him and lucky we were: it looked the best of the lot. 'Now what'll we do with the twelve that's left over?' I said, as much to myself as to Donnie. And Donnie had his knuckles to help him before he said: 'Leave them at the Crib.'

The friary crib was second only to Santa Claus for the kids in our town at Christmas. The floor of it was covered with straw to soften the bumps of the apples and oranges and pennies that kids threw into it as offerings as long as Santa money lasted, and after. Old Brother Paul rolled each day's takings away in a wheelbarrow after the chapel doors were closed for the night.

We had the chapel to ourselves when we crept in on tiptoes to lay the leftover hats in a row on the pew before the crib, the grey with the blonde wig looking shameless in the middle. We felt as guilty as if we were raiding an orchard, which was ridiculous.

Mary and Joseph looked too taken with the Child to bother about us. Obviously the ox and the ass couldn't care less. The shepherds had no time for us either, except the fella with the beard who was raising his eyes the way teachers do when they feel there's no hope for you. Anyway, I felt that Joseph would understand about carpenters.

We didn't even say a prayer before we ran out of the chapel with a hat for Da, leaving it to Paul to sort out the hat trick with the rest.

Ma gave us an extra egg for breakfast and Ellie brought us our presents from the Christmas tree. They had to wait till noon to give Da the hat because on idle days he slept until it was time for the pubs to open. It was a perfect fit. We all went to the door to see him off and watch him in his new rig, strolling up a lane alive with children shouting about their new toys.

'He looks a new man,' said Ellie.

'Quite respectable, mind you,' said Ma. 'But I'd love to know who owns the hat he's wearing.'

My Uncle Was Santa

Yes, you heard me.

Santa was my Uncle Joe from Cabra West.

No white beard, no rosy cheeks, no merry eyes, no bellyful of laughs.

Just my scrawny Uncle Joe with a face pale from toil in Corporation drains: a drawn face with a look of long suffering (not without cause, fair dues to him), martyr's eyes that would remind you of saints in chapel windows if they weren't always bloodshot with booze, and a stomach that hung off his backbone as if it never knew anything but chips once a day and fish on a Friday.

True.

His bald skull was smothered in a red hat with white fur trimmings and a tassel that dangled under one of his ears.

His red coat had fur like snow on collar and cuffs.

A shiny black belt likes a belly and made a mock of his middle and I'd swear the gumboots that reached to his hasp were Corporation issue to drain men last August.

But you never saw such a sorry-looking Santa in your born days, and add to that the shock of knowing that Daddy Christmas was your Uncle Joe.

It all began when Ma lugged me along with her shopping bag to the heart of Dublin's own city this Christmas Eve.

Today that is.

She had me tethered to her side so hard with her right hand that the rings on it hurt when she got into her stride. Her pony-skin coat was worn thin but the plastic flowers in her hat were like April cocking a snook at December.

A great little battler, my Ma, when the chips are down and there's someone in the way. She scattered a lot of people at counters that morning, all elbows and old chat to cover for the digs she was giving besides hanging onto me and me hanging onto the bag.

The bag got so heavy in the finish that I simply had to have a rest.

I downed tools as Da says when himself and his mates on the buses go on their annual strike.

He's a driver.

We were in a shop that sold ice cream on the side, so Ma bought me a cone big as a clown's hat and one for herself to keep me company.

I could see she relished the ice cream as much as I did.

She kept wiping small moustaches of it off her lip with a hankie as she tidied that thing in the bag where I dropped it.

I was sitting on the floor where I could see myself in a huge mirror; with reflections behind my image of women launching themselves down the lines as if the counter was the last barrier to loot and liberation as Ma said. They cackled and crowed and called the Holy Name in vain in a way that made you think your ears were gone mad. But it was a fiery red toy in one of their bags that brought a thought in the back of my mind to the front of it …

'What about my visit to Santa?' I said.

'As if I'd forget,' said Ma. 'We're off to him now when you finish your ice cream.'

What was left in my cone was gone in one swallow and we were away.

Ma dragged me through traffic lights across the widest street in Europe, O'Connell's; causing cars and buses to grind to halts and drivers to call her everything they could think of with bitch for a start.

It was the mercy of God and Ma's luck of the Dubs that saw us safe into a shop bigger than four blocks of the flats we live in, with as many old ones and young ones and darting and squalling small ones as our flats ever knew.

Hands were grabbing at gaudy gifts as far as the eye could see.

Paper bells swung dumb from the ceiling. Tinfoil stars looked lost in a mile of mirrors.

I tell you I didn't mind Ma holding my hand there: I felt that if she let go I was a goner.

Ma was chasing her tail and me making circles after her until we saw a sign saying that Santa was upstairs. For real. I believed that the way kids hold on to a bit of brightness in their lives against all the hardchaws who tell them the old guy never lived, that he was never there, end of story, if you listened to them.

He was upstairs the sign said and I believed it.

And the way Ma climbed that stairs you'd say she was a believer too. But even at that she had to hold me back like a pup on a string; I wanted to run.

'Take your time. He won't run away while we're climbin' this Calvary,' she told me. 'He'll be there at the summit.'

She was right of course. He was sitting on a throne at the far end of a long room that had a varnished floor like a dance hall. Ahead of us was a queue of kids and mothers with tickets they bought for a pound from a lass in what looked like a phone box.

Hidden heat put sweat on you without a flame in sight. Ma put a pound down, got a ticket from the blonde and handed it to me as we took our place in the queue.

The walls and floor were covered with big toys and small so you could see there was no danger that Santa would run short if he stayed on for a week.

An old lad in a suit and bow tie that could have been for a wake or a wedding was pacing and sniffing between the kids and the wonderland of guns and bikes and trikes for boys and dolls and teddies and prams for girls.

As if we would nick something on the sly on our way to the throne. As if any kid in his right mind would have the gall to knock off as much as a whistle under the old lad's nose.

I mean you'd never get away with it. Not a chance. So maybe it was just as well; indeed maybe Ma was thinking it was just as well that her grip on my hand was even tighter than ever.

At long last we got to arm's reach of Santa without sin or omission. His throne was set into a half-lit igloo so it was more a case of being aware of his presence than seeing him.

Mysterious.

White beard and locks of long hair lay on his chest and shoulders and there was a smell of chewed cloves off his breath.

'Hello, hello, hello,' he said to me in a put-on voice as he poked in his bag and brought out a net stocking of geegaws you wouldn't give to a crow.

But when he looked closer at me his hand dived into the bag again and came up with a six-shooter in the fastest draw since Billy the Kid. Magic. I gave the stocking to Ma to stick in the bag and kept the gun in my grip all the way down to the cafe for tea and biscuits and a fag for Ma.

The snag was that after tea with crackers there wasn't a fag in the place. It was twelve by the clock when a loud speaker on the wall told us Santa was taking an hour's break for a meal and a smoke, in the roof garden if you don't mind. 'I should have asked him for a smoke in the igloo,' said Ma, and I remembered there was a small pub down the narrow lane beside the building. 'I'll get you fags in the pub outside,' I told her. 'Ten Woodbines,' she said like a light, handing me a pound. 'And don't keep the change,' she called after me.

I scraped past a glass door just in time to see Santa give a hop, skip and jump across the lane into the very pub I was going to. 'Roof garden how are you,' I said to myself, hardly believing my eyes.

With my heart in my mouth in awe I crept into the snug inside the door of that pub. I knocked on the partition under a small square hatch that was much too high for me.

Next minute a young man's face was in the hatch looking down at me. 'Ten Woodbines for my Ma,' I said, reaching up with the pound.

'Ten Woodbines coming down,' the man said, reaching me with fags and change while you'd say bingo. His freckled face was gone as quick as it came and there I was with the snug to myself. It had a round table, a long seat with its back to the window and a picture of the Dubs team before they were beaten by Kerry in the football All-Ireland at Croke Park.

There was only the partition between me and Santa. The only way I could see him without being seen was through the hatch that was too high for me.

So I climbed onto the table, knelt before the hatch and had a fine peephole into the bar. The barman with sleeves rolled to his elbows was washing glasses. There was holly between the coloured bottles on the shelves.

But no Santa. I thought he might have done one of his disappearance tricks again. But suddenly there was the sound of a doorknob twisting; and there was Santa, buttoning himself up as he backed out of the gents. Before he turned towards me I had visions of all the laughing Santas I ever saw in pictures.

But when he turned I was staring into the sad-sack deadpan face of my Uncle Joe. I hadn't time to be shocked before he was saying to the barman, 'Billy, pour me a large Jemmy while I thank God that I'm here. If I had to stay another minute in the sweat-box I'd have leaked into my boots.'

'Jemmy Ten chinning up, Daddy,' said Billy. 'Where's your reindeer?'

'Tethered to the lamp post outside your window,' said Joe. 'They're tired out. That red-nosed laddo sets them a hell of a pace. We cut Parnell Corner on one skate and shook the ass off every bus and car driver in sight. Oh there's no holding Rudolph when he wants to get that nose in front.'

Billy was chuckling at everything he said but Joe seemed not to notice. His mouth was saying funny things the rest of his face didn't seem to know about; as odd as an old crow making song like a lark. When he was clearing his pants pocket to pay for the drink he put a tin box on the counter.

'What's in the tin?' asked Billy with the usual curiosity of the barman.

'Cloves for chewing to keep the malt smell from the kids,' Joe told him.

A few old chiners he knew came in and called him Joe Christmas, asking what he had for them in the bag. They were settling with their drinks for a laugh at Joe when a high-heeled little woman sent her voice through the doorway ahead of her saying: 'Where is he? Where is he?' And the next thing I knew there was Ma in the middle of them. Her eyes nearly popped out of her head at her brother in his Santa suit.

'Oh Mother of God, will you look at the cut of the ghost from Cabra West?' she said. 'Slyboots Joe dressed up for the panto.'

'Cut it out, Mollie,' Joe pleaded.

'For a man who should be down the drain you're a disgrace to the costume you're wearing,' she told him, her voice climbing, the boyos in the bar in knots with the laughing and me mortified up in the hatch.

'I'm on holidays from the drain and this job is a nixer,' said Joe.

''Tis no nixer for kids to lose belief in Santa as a saint,' said Ma. 'One look at you would have them thinking Santa is a gurrier.'

'There's no kids here,' said Joe. Little did he know.

'None of yours anyway, for you've neither wife nor child,' she told him, throwing the shopping bag on the upturned toes of his wellies.

'What ill wind blew you my way,' said Joe, looking for the ceiling to have pity on him.

'I'm looking for my son, your nephew Mark I had with me when we called on your lordship in the igloo,' said Ma, stamping her toe at him.

'I gave him a gun, didn't I?' Joe whinged, all but toppling over in the big boots. 'That was extra, wasn't it? I'll have to pay for that on the side when I go back, won't I?'

'Ask Eskimo Nell in the igloo to help you,' Ma gave back, saying anything now that came into her head.

'There's no Eskimo Nell,' said Joe, as if there was a ghost of a chance that there might be.

'Then ask Charming Kate instead,' said Ma.

'And who's Charming Kate when she's at home?' said Joe.

'That's what they call the auld wan you chat up in Darcy's snug of a Saturday.'

'She's what you're not, a lady.'

'Lady Cabra West, no less. How's the poodle she haven't in the parlour she haven't ayther?'

'Oh, shut up, Mollie, till I get you a sup of something to be yourself,' said Joe at the end of his tether.

'I have to go looking for my lost son,' said Ma, grabbing the bag off the floor.

And in my haste to head her off at the doorway I fell ass over kettle from the table. I hit the floor with a thump and a yelp and a clatter. I was sitting on the floor in a dazed state when Bill's face filled the hatch again.

'I think I've found your young lad, ma'am,' he drawled out to Ma. 'He's here in the snug with your Woodbines.'

'And change,' I said up to him.

'And change,' Billy echoed for Ma's sake.

In seconds Ma was in the snug helping me to my feet. I could see she was between two minds whether to give me a hug or a clip on the ear, so I held out the fags in a hurry saying: 'Your Woodbines, Ma, and the change as well.' She grabbed for the fags like a druggie for a fix and after the first few puffs she was herself again. 'So now you seen all, heard all and know all, you little monkey,' she told me, leading me out to meet Joe and his friends.

'Sorry to wreck your notions about Santa, me ould flower,' Joe told me. 'But here.' His hand poked into his waistcoat pocket inside the white fur lining of the borrowed finery and came out with a twist of pound notes. 'Here,' he said, unwinding a note off the twist. 'Here, me ould flower, from your Uncle Joe,' he said, taking my hand and putting the pound on my palm with a flourish.

'And don't tell me you got the like of that from any sort of Santa since your cradle days,' he added with a wink.

His kindness was as good as a nudge in the ribs on his mates. They dipped into their pockets too but 'tis silver pieces they came up with. Still, I was never so rich in all my days.

Joe helped Ma onto a tall stool in a courtly way and she waved down to me with the gin he bought her. Billy poured me a fizzy red drink into a glass like a bubble.

'A drink on the house for the only gentleman in it,' he said. 'Come over to the fire, pal,' he added, leading me to a low seat under the holly on the hob. With a gun in one hand and a drink in the other all I was short of was high heels and a Stetson.

I drew the gun on the fire a few times just for practice. Then I settled down to some serious drinking.

After a few more sprinkles of gin the flowers on Ma's hat looked more brazen than ever. I knew she'd hit the roof if I told her, but the way her hair had sprung loose over her ears made it look like a wig. And the more Joe made them laugh the more he seemed to sink in sadness into his gumboots.

I felt as happy as a prince. Firelight winking through the bubble made my drink like wine. I had all the time in the world to set my thoughts straight about what the hardchaws said about *Ma*s and *Da*s and Daddy Christmas. There was room for suspicion that the Santas of this world might be *Ma*s and *Da*s and Uncle Joes, I granted them that.

But the Santa I had in mind was out of this world: on his way on a sleigh to our flats come hell or high water.

Anyway, I'll know for sure in the morning.

Death of a King

'The King is dead.' Liz Leary got the message by phone in her sweet-shop post office near the school gate and she gave it to the kids to scatter through the village on their way home.

'The King is dead,' they shouted to right and left, into houses and shops, and to the men in the fields. One line of girls linked together at the elbows sang it as they skipped down the Pike Hill: 'The King is dead, the King is dead, the King is dead.' In twenty minutes it was told to old Matt Harris at his cottage door by the kid who went farthest, one of the river Bradys named Mary.

'Did you hear that?' Matt called over his shoulder to Kate in the half-glow of firelight and whatever daylight got through the small window into the kitchen.

'God rest him,' said Kate, her hands wrist-deep in mash for the hens.

'Where did he die, did Liz say, child?' asked Matt.

'In Kilmurry Workhouse,' said Mary.

'And did she say where the King left his ass and cart?' asked Matt.

'No,' said Mary, 'Liz said he was taken bad by the heart near the town and they carried him to the workhouse to die.'

'His late majesty didn't like that,' said Matt. 'Didn't they know, child, that the King would rather die in a ditch than a workhouse?'

The child just shrugged and went on down the boreen.

'Don't mock the dead,' said Kate. 'Mocking is catching.'

'I'm not mocking him. I never did.'

'You never had reason. He was a civil little man.'

'Civil!' said Matt, scratching in his beard. 'The only time he thought of civility was when he was demanding it from someone else.'

'He was always civil to me.'

'When he came for the eggs and the butter and the spuds.'

'That he always paid for.'

'I gave him rest place in my boreen when Rossman and the council drove him off the main road with the by-law against tinkers.'

'He paid for that too. A pound every New Year's Day of the forty he lived there.'

'He forced it on me. It meant something for him to give that it never meant for me to take.'

'He was the only man in this place to ever lift his hat to a woman.'

'You would be the only woman in this place to ever notice that.'

'He was a cut above workhouses,' said Kate quietly.

'Then why the hell did he have to go rambling the roads yesterday as if he was a young fellah with a heart like a strong clock?'

'He went once a year to the mountains in Kilmurry when the heather was in bloom. Purple was the royal colour, he said, and the mountains looked a kingdom in it.'

'The mad little bastard,' said Matt.

'To get excited will do your own heart no good,' said Kate. 'You gave him more than the others.'

'And he paid for it all, didn't you say?'

'You gave him your company night after night by his fire until bedtime.'

'Ah, to hell with that for a story,' said Matt, lifting the pad of patches off the sun-hot stone beside the door and jabbing hard with his stick down the boreen.

On his right was a ditch topped with a fuschia hedge that had an ear-ring on every twig. Between it and the river was his strip of fields. On his left was the graveyard wall. The row of lime trees and one oak spreading over the wall gave the narrow road a green roof raftered with branches three centuries old. Matt tapped in and out of the gaps of sunshine between the trees until he came to the oak. At the foot of the graveyard wall under the oak were the ashes of the King's fires in a ring of cobbles. The smoke and flame marks of forty years were on the wall above the ashes. Beside the circle of ashes was a flat boulder to sit on.

'The King's Throne,' said Matt to himself, easing the pad of patches onto it and poking for his pipe.

He was amazed at the quiver in the hands that filled the pipe and lighted it. His eyes followed the smoke into the rafters of the oak. 'When my time comes I'll have only to go over the wall,' the King had said many a time. He could almost hear the quiet voice again in the stillness.

Was the man nearer to him dead than alive? In life he never gave him a thought until he saw him or passed him by. It amazed him that he was so upset by the death of someone who was a mystery to the whole world, never mind himself. A man with half a name who had bits of tinker, tramp and gypsy about him and yet was none of them, with piercing black eyes in skin tanned like glove leather, while pride could add inches to him when it was roused and make his old loose clothes look like the rig of a sheik.

'I'm King,' he said when he came over the hill with an upside-down section of a currach on the cart to sleep in and a sprig of bell heather under an ear of the ass.

'What goes with King?' he was asked, and he answered: 'Just King.' And the King they called him in mockery of his conceit.

Matt was cooling down from the smart of Kate's words when the sounds of the river began to remind him of worse. The King could hook or tickle trout onto the bank in daylight or gaff salmon by torchlight in a way no other man could do it. He knew fish the way Kate knew fowl, as if he reared them. What he didn't eat or sell he gave to Kate for Matt's table. With the pheasants and rabbits he bagged at will it was the same. He brought them a bart of berried holly from the hills at Christmas and was content with a sprig of the rib of the currach for himself.

Suddenly Matt was shocked into standing at the thought that the very stick in his hand was one of the blackthorns the King cut to sell to tourists in the summer. He held the stick out and looked at it as if he had never seen it before. It was a perfect stick, thorns spiralling to the twist, the gnarled head fitting snugly in the palm. And he had been tricked into taking it for nothing by the dark man's gift of making the thing he gave look nothing and the shoelace he took look good enough to pay for. Matt glared across the ashes and growled: 'It was trickery all the same.'

On impulse he hurried down the boreen, turning left at the green-stone bridge for the village, his burr of beard jutting under the clamped jaw. He passed the graveyard keeper's lodge and Rossman's big hotel and bar.

It was Rossman who refused to serve the King a drink at his counter. 'No road folk served here,' he said. 'Get out.' The King grew that two inches taller to ask: 'Is there a man here who would put a hand on me?' They told down the years how he gave Rossman time to stomach that one before he walked out the door with his head in the air.

Rossman was chairman of the council that had the by-law on the small man's heels when Matt gave him shelter in the boreen. Rossman was still chairman of the council that was sitting at that moment in an upstairs room in the parish hall. Across the road from the hall was Bill Murphy's snug little pub where the King drank with welcome any time he had thirst to quench.

Matt wheeled in the door of the concrete box of a hall as if a brass band were playing in his head. He stamped up the stairs and pushed the door to the council room open with a flourish.

'I suppose ye know that the King is dead,' he said, before the ten men in the room could draw breath.

'What King?' said Rossman, an ox of a man with clipped silver hair and moustache.

'We had only the one King ever,' said Matt, standing straight up between the door and the green-topped table.

'The gypsy in Matt's boreen,' said young Evans, with the wing of hair and bullfinch beak of his father before him.

'There isn't that many Kings left in the world these days that we couldn't look after our own,' said Matt. 'He's lying dead in Kilmurry Workhouse.'

'He was none of ours,' said Rossman.

'He was his very own man, I'll grant you,' said Matt. 'But forty years with us made him some of ours too.'

'What have you in mind that we should do, Matt?' asked young Evans.

'Buy him a coffin not lined with shavings. Give it a breastplate and handles of brass. Get him sent back to us by train and bury him here,' said Matt.

'Nonsense,' said Rossman.

'It wouldn't be the way of our people to leave him for strangers to put in a pauper's grave,' said Matt. 'I'll buy the grave for him myself, and if I had more in the waistcoat pocket I'd do the rest for him too.'

'What was he to us?' asked bald-headed Reilly, the grocer.

'Ask the kids. Ask the old ones. Ask anyone you like. The King, they called him,' said Matt.

'The chancer,' said Rossman.

'Big as you are you wouldn't say it to his face,' said Matt.

'Be careful,' said Rossman.

'I'm still here to answer for anything that I say, or you say,' said Matt.

'Easy, men,' said young Evans.

'He did harm to no one, owed no one a copper and went to Mass of a Sunday. God wouldn't ask much more of any man,' said Matt.

'This is all out of order,' said Rossman.

'His donkey's hooves were shod and polished. She wore silver in her harness,' said Matt. 'And she didn't bray about it.'

'Have sense,' said Reilly, fingers drumming on his head of bone.

'All ye're asked to do is get a coffin for one dead man and bring him by train to the grave I'll buy for him.'

'We have no power to spend ratepayers' money in that way, even if we wanted to,' said Ferris, the draper, butting over his specs.

'If a ratepayer objects he don't belong in this place,' said Matt.

'Facts are facts,' said Ferris.

'If you refuse the dead will rise this night and walk out of the grave-yard.'

'Ridiculous.'

'Our dead will disown us and most of our living will too.'

'He lived on us for years,' said Ferris.

'He lived on game without firing a shot, and that's more than can be said for the rest of the monarchs,' said Matt.

'You're a wrong-headed man,' said Ferris.

'All I want to know is will the council bring him back,' said Matt.

'As a council we can't,' said Ferris.

'Is that yer last word on it?' asked Matt.

'Yes, yes, yes,' said Rossman.

'Well, it isn't mine,' said Matt.

He walked three steps towards the door and turned.

'I'll do more than buy him a grave,' he said. 'I'll go as far as Killmurry by train in the morning. I'll load him there in his pauper's coffin onto his own cart and lead him here at the head of the ass. And I'll paint "The King" on the tin breastplate with my own hand.'

'Hold on a minute, Matt,' said Evans.

'He'll lie easy under the ribs of the currach for the last time. And if I die on the way the ass in the silver harness will know her way home.'

'Matt,' said young Evans.

'Then, Rossman, you'll have a chance to let Kate take the ass back for me,' said Matt.

'This is gone out of hand,' said Ferris.

'You wanted him out of the way when he was living, Rossman,' said Matt. 'And you were bested.'

'Matt,' said young Evans, quietly.

'You want him out of the way when he's dead, Rossman, and I'll best you there too,' said Matt.

'Put him out,' said Rossman, rising out of his chair.

'Is there a man here would lay a hand on me?' said Matt. 'They are words you should remember.'

'Steady on, chairman,' said Evans and Rossman eased back into the chair.

'Oh, go away,' said Rossman.

'I'll go because I want to go,' said Matt. 'I'll walk across the road, into a pub that was fit for a King.' Then he walked out of the room.

He was drinking whiskey in the snug across the road when young Evans poked his head in half an hour later.

'They're bringing the King here tomorrow, Matt,' he said. 'You scared them into it.'

'Scared!' said Matt.

'They realized that your ass-and-cart funeral would shame them forever through the whole country. So what they couldn't do as a council, some of them decided to do of themselves. Myself included.'

'I'll pay ye back.'

'Not if I have a say.'

'The grave I'll buy myself. 'Tis a personal thing between myself and the King.'

'Right,' said Evans. 'Now you'll drive with me to Kilmurry in the morning. We'll have the King coffined and on the train after dinner and we'll be back here by car to meet him at the station tomorrow evening.'

'We'll put him in the chapel overnight.'

'The chapel overnight.'

'Then away to the grave.'

'As you say, Matt.'

'Rossman isn't in this?'

'No,' said Evans.

'The King is glad,' said Matt.

A young moon was up when he went to the graveyard keeper's lodge and pushed in the half-door. Old Murt, the keeper, had a grandchild on his knee near the hearth. He flung a few kippins out of a basket into the fire for more light.

'What can I do for you, Matt?' he asked.

'You can give me a grave,' said Matt.

'You don't look like a man that will want it in a hurry.'

'I'll want it the day after tomorrow for the King.'

'You're late.'

'What do you mean, late?'

'Thirty-nine years late.'

'What, under God, do you mean?'

'The King bought it from me himself that long ago,' said Murt.

'Well, blast him,' said Matt, stabbing the fire with his stick. 'Blast him.'

'He wanted it in a special place I was glad to be able to give him,' said Murt.

'What special place?'

'Under the oak inside the wall. The same oak that was rooftree to the camp you gave him in your boreen,' said Murt.

'Over the wall,' said Matt.

'I'll have welcome for him. He was a gentleman,' said Murt. 'You could use the grave money as down payment on a headstone.'

'I'll put a bunch of headstones on his chest to keep him down,' said Matt, putting a half-pint of whiskey on the table for Murt.

The steam was suddenly gone out of him. He had the air of a man whose mind was miles away.

'Goodnight, Murt,' he said.

'He thought well of you,' said Murt.

'Goodnight,' said Matt.

'And good luck,' said Murt.

Matt looked more the old man he was as he went down his boreen, tapping with the blackthorn in and out of the gaps of moonlight between the trees. He gave a hard look at the cold ashes in the ring of stones. But he had to admit that the oak looked as royal against the moon as if the King were back in residence already.

Timeen

Although all of us in the gang were a head over Timeen no one ever questioned his leadership. We never made a wonder of this. Neither did he.

Boy or man short of stature who happens to have dark hair and eyes and skin looks smaller than he is. Breadth of shoulder and depth of chest seem to go unnoticed. Timeen was so dark he looked varnished. Only the long man who is on his back from a short-arm jab in the ring, or at football gropes in high air where he thought a ball should be, can bear real witness to the surprise in small packets. Timeen was full of surprises.

When we first came face to face I was from a different lane to his in our town. The ragball and bladder stages of football were well known to me. I was ripe for a ball with a better coat that would meet me halfway like a gentleman. Timeen had that kind of ball under his arm as he walked towards me. He was short a player for his team in a needle match on a green patch among houses so near that windows on all sides were in danger (we called it Glasshouse Square). Timeen palmed the ball to a redheaded referee whose whistle was the gap in his teeth.

'Where are you off to?' he asked.

'That's my own business,' I said.

'It can stay your own for all I care,' he said.

'I'm going to visit my grandmother, Mrs Riordan, in Tiller's Lane.'

'That's my lane,' he said. 'Is she in a hurry to see you?'

'Hardly,' I said.

'Maybe you'd have time to play right full forward for me. It won't matter if you're not too good so long as you keep the ball in play until someone gets a shot at it.'

'Fair enough,' I said.

'Add your jacket to the goalposts. Grab it first thing if there's a hunt from a Guard or an ould one.'

In the second of two goals scored the ball made smithereens of a pane in grey-haired Miss Mulberry's window. Timeen's black head missed collision with the mop of her duster by inches as he grabbed the ball off a bed of carnations. She was brandishing the mop at her gate and shouting for the Guards as we made our getaway from Glasshouse Square. When we got our breath back Timeen said he would let me hold my place in his team. Having my grandmother in custody gave Tiller's Lane a claim on me, he said. So that was that.

We played the next three or four matches on a narrow strip of commonage between the Shamrock Club's boathouse and Markie Shea's orchard. There were only two things wrong with Markie's orchard. It was hard to get into (especially when the apples were ripe) and it had a glasshouse. Once again a hard drive from a back under pressure sent the ball to crash like a homesick satellite through the glass into peppery Mark's tomatoes. Peering through tangles of thorny wire on the orchard wall we saw Markie jig and reel with rage on his hat, try to pull the wire-brush beard off his chin and ask Heaven with spread palms to look down on his torment. Then he locked the ball into his tool shed.

'We're back in the rag business again,' said Timeen.

And we were. Twine-tied scraps of mother coats and father jackets and great-grandfather shirt tails were touched into new life by young big-toes. Ground work had to be made as precise as step-dancing. A pick-up within the rules was an impossibility made possible by a mixture of mind and magic. In goal rushes shin bones sharpened on each other as they criss-crossed like blades in a cloak-and-dagger film.

'We'll get a bladder for a change,' said Timeen.

The slaughterhouse caretaker, Pa Carroll, looked the part with his head of grey bull curls and a moustache shaped like the horns of a ram. He blew and tied the bladder for us and we were away to the cobbles of

Tiller's Lane. The snub noses and bald pates of the cobbles were kind to bladder tissue and the bladder was kind to the windows. When it soared it taught the timing of the leap to a catch between fingertips. The way it was nosed this way and that by the cobbles made the swerve and sway of body a necessity that became Timeen's constant virtue later with the leather ball.

Our next leather ball came when Timeen led a door-to-door collection in the street that owned the lanes we lived in: High Street.

'We're known as the High Street boys,' he would tell the shopkeeper, a school copy and a stub of pencil in his hand, his berryblack eyes not much over the edge of the counter. 'That is the team,' he would say, thumbing over his shoulder at our tongue-tied collection of bashfuls.

The copy was the best part of a good act. When Timeen handed it to them, to mark in their offering, they often went back to the till to make themselves as good as their neighbour on the list.

All except Matt Carter, who put more store in a new penny than on the rarest bauble in the dusty half-light of his antique shop. Matt kept the cold off his tonsure of baldness with a round black skull-cap and kept a hand on the sharp point of his beard as if he were afraid it might stick into something. A moon and star-stoned snuff box had an edge over the left pocket of his waistcoat and snuff dust puffed off his paunch when he sneezed. People said all his pennies were prisoners but Timeen never failed to rescue a few during our collections. He would keep Matt for last on the list and say:

'Only thrupence more for the price of a ball, Mr Carter, so any ould odd thrupenny bit you have will be the winner.'

Matt would reply with the same bit of play-acting every time.

'Do you think thrupenny bits grow on trees like hazelnuts?' he would ask. Then he would start lifting and shaking antique jugs and mugs and vases, all as mute as tongue-tied bells till he came to a jug shaped like a fat man with a three-corner hat. That little grinning man always had a belly-ful of coins that spilled into Matt's palm through a hole in the hat when the old dealer stood him on his head. They were rare coins, gold and silver and bronze, each having the laurelled head of a man or woman who lived and died long ages ago. But the nail of Matt's finger would probe among them and up to the top would leap the hare on an Irish bit.

'I keep it here because the way business is going that little bit might soon be the rarest coin of the lot,' he would say, flicking it to Timeen. But he never put his name on the list. 'I'm a modest man, you see,' he would explain, grinning in his beard as daylight all but dazzled us at his door.

Glasshouse Square and the commonage got too small for the longer kicks that growing muscles ached for. The town's sports field had a wide deep river right beside it. The grown lads had first call on the pitch, so they used to evict us onto the broad strip of sideline on the riverbank. Too often it happened that a miskick sent the ball into the river to be swept by frothing water through one of the bridge's ten arches and we had to walk a mile and swim a pool to get it back.

So Timeen led us to Mikie Cronin's hilltop field, flat as a lawn, quilted with daisies and so kind to its twelve cows that they were too content to even moo when we drove them under the lime trees out of our way. In that high place to loft a ball was really to sky it. A long drive looked as if it might send the ball spinning over the toy people of the town below us into one of the three lakes with their more than three mountains just on the near side of where the sky curved down. A prayer sent from there hadn't far to travel, but the only prayer we ever sent was one to keep bowler-hatted Mikie and his tweeded wife a mile from us until the match was over. Anyhow Mikie's belled pony and the yapping of his ten pom-dogs always signalled his coming, with the missis, in the tub trap with the silver fittings and wheels shod with rubber.

Even the cows seemed to grin between chews as we grabbed our jackets and ran under the limes for the ivied wall and the drop onto the road-way. But before we dropped we would lay a row of sweaty smiles along the ivy as we watched the pom-dogs with pompom tails trying to look like police dogs among the daisies.

There came a time, of course, when Mikie and the missis and the poms and the cows must have wondered where we had been sent to. That was the time when Timeen and the rest of us were grown enough to take the pitch at the river field and evict smaller mortals on to the bank strip. Shortly after that the whole town began to know about Timeen. Too small, too small for the county minors, the half of them said. Too good, too good to be robbed by inches, said the other half. Timeen won two All-Ireland minor medals before age disqualified him in his early teens. Two years later it was a case of much, much too small for a senior jersey by half of the county, and counter-case of much, much too good to be baulked on stature by the other half. Timeen got his senior jersey and an All-Ireland medal.

Last year, that was. We were up there in Croke Park of course, the lads from Tiller's Lane, so long in the leg now that Timeen seems to have stopped growing in the days of the hill field. But the only chance we got of looking down at him was from the top row of the Cusack Stand. And we travelled in the train with him home to bonfires that looked like crashed stars on the mountains. More bonfires in the streets of the town. Blazes of brass-band music led the team in triumph where even dead stones sparked flint at a kick.

Ah, but Tiller's Lane. Timeen was claimed for his own at the archway. Only God's help and calm women's care kept the very granite in the two long rows of little man-high houses from bursting with the heat of yet more bonfires. What is left of Tiller's Lane fife and drum band, all ten of them, stood in a row in front of Timeen's place, and sure who cared that there was more drum than fife and that some of the fifes were getting lip service only? There were jars of liquor and yards of ballad song, and tea and sweet cake for the women and kids. The aged enjoyed the young and the young enjoyed each other.

Miss Mulberry came all the way down from Glasshouse Square to tell how near she came many a time to laying our hero low with a belt of her mop. Pa Carroll stopped blowing froth from time to time to show how he used to blow bladders. Markie Shea arrived with the ball under his arm from that tool shed, to be autographed by Timeen, if you don't mind. Matt Carter flicked a threepenny bit to Timeen in the firelight and chuckled out: 'Don't tell anyone, boy, I'm a modest man, you see.'

And in the end it was left to the careful woman to put things away for another year; the bits of good furniture and good crockery and the like, and to see that the empties found their way home to the snugs. When they looked at the sky it came as no surprise that someone had put the stars away too. But not for another year, of course.

Pictures in a Pawnshop

Jack is with us still, thank God, but Joe Jack has taken the only knock that ever put him down to stay down. God rest him. Jack was a man when Joe Jack was a boy. Joe Jack caught up with him later. They were butties together in that part of the town known as Below. The Bridge without a bridge that was ever known there to be below, and a few of the boys below the bridge were playing on the town's football team for the county championship in Tralee that war-time Sunday. The pair wanted to be at that match, twenty-one miles away.

Labouring life and fight broke Joe Jack's face into pieces and time in a hurry took a rough-and-ready gamble in putting it together again. The gamble came off in a half-and-half of knuckle-buster and rogue kid. Far at the end of a great-muscled arm his clenched fist looked fit to crush stones before it opened to spill coin—when it had coin—on froth among tall glasses with workmates, and the same from them, and the same again, and one for the singer, and one for the song, and one for yourself, Mick, and one for the road, until the light went out in the mirrors and it was mind the step after that. His feet were tortured by a more than six-foot spread of eighteen stone.

Jack does not drink, but he would back a horse at a ploughing match; and because horses have no part in this story they must give way to the schoolkids who gathered at his shop door and called down the steps:

'Count us, Jack.' Light had been ebbing in Jack's eyes, and now dimness was at arm's length from him.

'How many are ye?' he would say, coming up to the blur of colours in the door frame (it was mostly girls who went to school through the street).

'We're three, Jack.'

'A one, and a two, and a two and a three, counts out a tune that you'd dance with glee,' Jack would say, sparking with his nailed boots on the flagstones.

'We're five now, Jack,' a voice might come, with fresh colours to the blur.

'A one, and a two, plus a three, makes five; if ye're late for school, ye'll be flayed alive,' Jack would make up, and the soap-shiny faces would light in mock alarm and scream away schoolwards.

When Joe Jack came to him, the Saturday evening before that match in Tralee, with a tale of woe and a scowl, Jack said: 'Get yourself a few schoolkids, Joe Jack, and I'll count you.'

''Tis nuthin' to laugh at,' Joe Jack growled.

'Sit down, man, and tell us,' said Jack.

So the pair sat on the shutterless greengrocer's window as an August dusk came up the street to them.

'There's a world war on, so there's no trains to Tralee,' said Joe Jack, in disgust. 'There's no cars to hire, because there's no petrol to buy, and there's a law to say a car journey must have a life to save. For love or money there's no seat idle in the few cars that are taking the chance, and my feet are red-raw from walking.'

'I must see that match,' said Jack.

'If I have to walk it,' said Joe Jack.

'I seen desperate men with wheels in search of bicycles and men with bicycles in search of wheels,' Joe Jack said. 'A wagonette that didn't get a day out since Parnell is going to get a day out tomorra. I seen hens cooshed out of ould sidecars and six men wanting right-go-wrong to hire a hearse.'

'A splendid idea,' said Jack.

'Only the owner roared back that he might have to go there himself in it.'

''Twas true for the man,' said Jack.

'I seen stray donkeys lifted off ditches,' said Joe Jack. 'Big dogs got in dread they might be saddled, so they dropped tails and ran all roads.'

'You tell it well,' said Jack.

'Men are prodding the dump pit with crowbars for car parts and Guards are doing duty by all petrol pumps,' said Joe Jack, in a kind of relished melancholy. 'Ould women, in terror, are shawling paraffin oil cans into holes in ould walls for safekeeping, and chemists have a shotgun on all barrels of olive oil and linseed oil.'

'Only natural,' Jack got in.

'The only thing safe is tap, well or lake water,' said Joe Jack, 'and that's only because no wan have a steam engine to make it worth his while going in search of a man with an ould pair of tracks. The town, in wan word, is mad this minute.'

A silence settled between the pair. The cider smell of apples from Jack's fruit counter brought Joe Jack's thirst to the boil in spittle.

Then: 'I must see that match,' said Jack.

'If I have to walk it,' said Joe Jack.

Then suddenly Jack said: 'That's a bargain.'

'What is?'

'That we'll walk it.'

'Done,' said Joe Jack, easing his weight to his feet.

When they had made arrangements for Mass and meeting, Joe Jack went a few doors down to Mother's snug and Jack got his shutters to toe the line by touch, his little ebbing of light full out now in the dark of the shop. And where there was light again there was Sunday.

During that Sunday there were times when the tar road to Tralee looked like a scrap heap on the crawl to new quarters. A man with a three-speed gear on his bicycle could look down on the neighbours, and the odd man with a car felt he might be lynched by the rabble. One of the few wheeled rigs not used was the hearse, and only because an old footballer who should have known better mistimed his last kick. But from early morning Jack and Joe Jack were going the mountain road by Firies.

Jack was fearful for Joe Jack's feet and Joe Jack had fears for Jack's old heart. They fell into the habit of inviting each other to stand-easy on hilltops or sit on the brow of the road when Joe Jack had made sure there was no one looking. Jack called the first halt on Madam's Height and faced about towards the valley, with the town and the lakes in it.

'There's a view,' he said, waving his ashplant in the general direction.

'The view!' said Joe Jack, startled.

Jack tilted his head back until he was blinking skywards.

'No wind, blue air, white light,' he told himself. Then he blinked straight down into the valley. 'The Reeks, Tomies, Tore, Mangerton: they're puce under blue with the white of cloud in it, and the lakes are as smooth as well water.'

'Hey!' cried Joe Jack.

'So there's two of it all,' said Jack. 'Only wan is upside down, so you don't know if 'tis on your head or your legs you're standing.'

'I don't know,' said Joe Jack.

'There's a boat off Innisfallen like a fly on a mirror,' Jack said.

'There is,' cried Joe Jack.

'That'll be Son Leary, bound for the mouth of the Laune,' said Jack. 'That fellah would go fishing if all belonging to him was at a Kerry All-Ireland in Croke Park.'

'I'm off,' said Joe Jack.

'Where?'

'I wouldn't travel another peg of the road with a fraud. You can see as good as I can,' Joe Jack growled.

'When I could I couldn't see as clear,' said Jack. 'All my pictures now are framed, hanging in my head like in a pawnshop.'

'But look here,' said Joe Jack.

'I'm done with looking now for another year,' Jack told him, adding: 'How's the feet?'

'I'm no fraud,' growled Joe Jack. 'If I could hang 'em without hanging myself, they'd be hanging somewhere. I bet if there was a shilling on the road you'd see that, too.'

And arguing the toss about Jack's sight livened the road past the Two-Mile School: but from Ardagh to Ballyharr chapel the will to words was sapped slowly by the ripening heat of the day. The chapel itself looked the only cool thing under a sun that sent heat down in waves. Joe Jack floundered in the noontide of it so plainly that anyone but Jack would have seen how he stuck his head up for air every ten yards. Sweat from his bruised feet had seeped through his boots and dust had crusted white as lime on them. He called a halt for a smoke at the chapel gate, put his back to a pillar and all but scraped the coat off his back subsiding down the cool rough stone. Then he lit a fag and snorted smoke down the trumpet nostrils of his broken nose and said: 'Jackeen ... '

'Well?' asked Jack, the ashplant across his knees, stoking his pipe.

'How's the heart?' asked Joe Jack.

'I'd be shy about asking it,' Jack said.

'Do it sort of flutter when you draw breath?'

'So that's what it was,' said Jack. 'And I thinking 'twas a butterfly I swallyed.'

'Are you serious?' Joe Jack asked, after a pause.

'Oh, the butterfly is gone now.'

'That's something I'm glad to hear,' Joe Jack said, weightily.

'There's a man with a sledge in my temples instead,' said Jack, and Joe Jack rolled over onto his knees.

'Put away that pipe, Jack,' he pleaded. ''Twill suffocate you.'

''Twill suffocate the man with the sledge, you mean.'

'Godelmighty, can't you see that when he stops sledging you stop living, you bloody fool,' cried Joe Jack.

'I'll show him who's gaffer of this job, anyhow.'

'For God's sake have a thought for what I'll do with the dead gaffer.'

'Roll him under a hedge, say a prayer for his soul in the chapel here; then get your own dead feet a lift into Tralee.'

'They're not dead.'

'Then what are you doing on all fours like a donkey?' said Jack, blinking hard. 'Correct yourself before somewan hangs a cart on you.'

'There's a lift on the way here now, but not for me,' said Joe Jack, in real earnest. 'You don't look good, Jackeen; you look like I could fry a rasher on your face.'

'If you had the rasher, you'd be welcome,' said Jack.

A mahogany-coloured cob shone with condition down the road towards them. An oak-grained tub trap swayed cradle easy on good springs after him, with two men and a hefty youth in it. Joe Jack got to a sitting position, and when the cob slung alongside he raised a palm with a shell crust of welts on it.

'Whoa, men,' he said. What place are ye bound for?'

'Tralee, at our aise,' said the grey man with the reins.

'I don't like the look of my comrade, so would ye give him the spare seat to Tralee?'

'Take no notice of him, Pats Carty, if you're the sensible man I buy spuds from,' said Jack, without even bothering to blink towards the fresh voice. ''Tis the heat is at him.'

'Yeh, is it you that's there, Jack,' said Carty. 'Devil a bit I see the matter with you.'

Jack stirred: 'There's a man here, Pats, with two dead or dying feet. If your cob can take the weight, you might give him the spare seat he says you have.'

'Either wan or another of ye is welcome, Jack.'

'Not me,' said Jack.

'Nor me,' said Joe Jack. 'But I'd rather you'd take it.'

'Passed unanimous,' said Jack. 'Goodbye, Pats, and thanks for the offer.'

From the chapel up the Firies Cross there was more walk than talk. The heat was too much for all but the bees along the hedges and the butterflies that rose now and again off a hot stone under their feet. Joe Jack doped the pain in a daze of watching the coloured wings flap and skim ahead and flip shut on stones further on. Jack gave his mind to naming birds by their songs. His strong legs, in breeches and stockings, punished the stones with the nails of his boots. The peak of his cap was on his nose to shade his eyes from the hurt of light. Beads of sweat kept falling from Joe Jack's jowls to burst on a khaki shirt as tight as a drumskin on his big-drummer's chest. His step had collapsed into a shuffle that eased the brunt of his great weight to his bruised feet. With a fisted cap he kept mopping a balding skull and a face gritty with dust and stubble. At Firies he broke silence to say he would have to keep an eye out for spring water any time now, and Jack took the hint.

'Sullivan here in the village have it tapped in barrels,' Jack said. ''Tis a bit off colour from confinement, they say, but 'tis game ball when you blow the froth off.'

'Never heard of it,' said Joe Jack, heading for the village.

'That's why I mentioned it.'

'How much a barrel is it, tell me?'

'If you drink it off your head in wan go, you can have a barrel for nothing.'

'I'll have a barrel for nothing,' said Joe Jack, mopping the mat of hair at the open neck of his shirt with his cap.

The tiled snug was as cool as a cave. The water wimple in the mirror had ash leaves in it from the tree outside the window. The oak table was lime white from scrubbing and had a blue earthenware jug with bell heather in it. Froth slobbered over the barman's hand as he put the brimming pint on the table. Joe Jack's tongue licked parched lips loose enough to grin. The barman went to wrench a crown cork off a mineral for Jack. Joe Jack raised the pint to arm's stretch, reverently, above his grin; then drew it down in a slavering relish until it was at lip reach; then he bit out at the brim, like a dog snapping, and drew back his head. The pint sank in gulp after gulp that creamed the glass in gauzes of froth as a hissing, unheeded overflow cascaded down the stubbled jowls into the tangle of chest hair. Then suddenly he jerked the empty glass away and yelled loud and snapping as a dog's bark. Still grinning, but in kid-delight now, Joe Jack told the barman: 'Fill it again, my lovely son,' like to a child, as if the savage yell was never his, the rogue black eyes kind enough to own a lolling tongue.

'Let your feet out on the tiles, Joe Jack,' said Jack, still standing, the amber drink in the old hand looking as out of place as would a toy.

'I'd never get 'em back again,' Joe Jack said, looking at them as if he were talking about a litter of pups.

'Ah, the craythurs won't go far,' encouraged Jack.

'They're headstrong,' said Joe Jack, smiling up at the leaves in the mirror. 'Sometimes they do get too big for their boots.'

''Tis a big world,' Jack reminded.

'But rough underfoot,' said Joe Jack. If that road out there was a tar road, I'd let 'em out long ago, but that road out there wasn't made: it was quarried.' Suddenly he saw that Jack had stretched full length on the settle seat under the mirror. 'Oh, for the love of God, Jackeen, rise up out of that,' he implored.

'Why so?'

'All you're short to be a corpse is candles.'

Jack laid his cap reverently on his face.

'I can't stand it, I tell you,' Joe Jack appealed.

Jack crossed his hands solemnly on his chest.

'Oh, for the love of God, don't do that,' said Joe Jack.

'S-s-sh,' said Jack. That's no way to be carrying on at a wake.'

'Will you sit up, Jack!'

'No.'

'Even that I told you it gives me the creeps!'

'No.'

Joe Jack sulked. Even when Jack took two half-crowns out of a waist-coat pocket and told the barman to keep drawing pints for Joe Jack, the big man sulked. Because Jack went back to the dead man's pose. After three pints in ten minutes, and with a fourth in hand, Joe Jack began to look round the place to avoid looking at the old man. A picture of the 1903 Kerry team caught his eye.

'I suppose you can see this, too,' he said.

'What?'

'The 1903 team.'

'Oh, clear I see them,' said Jack from under the cap. 'Oh, God be good to you, Dickeen Fitz, you king in a kingdom of kings.'

'Are you sure you're not dead in earnest?'

'Certain, because Dickeen isn't looking a day older, God rest him, and I am.'

'Maybe you're not dead long enough,' said Joe Jack.

'There they all are now taking the pitch in their prime. Dickeen, Paddy Dillon, Austin Stack, Champion Sullivan, Dinny Kissane, Big Jack Myers. Fine, I can see them now skying balls to the sun and rising halfway to meet them coming back.'

Still in his dead-man's stretch, Jack's voice gloried out from under the cap, and Joe was stung into shouting: 'There was good men since.'

'Good men, Joe Jack, but never as good as the men I'm with now. Rocks in play for gallant men to break on, and men to laugh with and drink with when the waves were spent. Oh, God be with ye, the men I'm with now.'

'Was Paul Russell as good as any of them?' said Joe Jack.

'Was any son as good as his father?'

'Was any wan of them as good as Joe Barrett, or Con Brosnan, or John Joe Sheehy, or Miko Boyle, or Purty Landers, or Timmie Leary, or Jackie Lyne?'

'Good men all, but never as good as the men I'm with now. Fit to carry the game you shaped for them, Dickeen boy, but no more than that, Dickeen, you king in a kingdom of kings.'

'Time stopped for their last whistle, I suppose.'

'Don't mind him, Dickeen.'

'Did you see Russell in '32 at Croke Park driving a goal from fifty yards?'

'Don't mind him, Dickeen, carry on with your game.'

Joe Jack lunged past the table and towered up into a rage over Jack's dead-man's stretch.

'Will you listen, Jackeen!'

'We won't listen, Dickeen,' Jack gloated under the cap.

'Then you can go the rest of the way with Dickeen,' said Joe Jack, lunging for the snug door.

'I knew him well,' Jack called to a Joe Jack blundering about in the open bar.

'Give up the ghost and ye'll be shaking hands!'

'Go, if you're going.'

'Give up the ghost, Jackeen!'

'Go to the boneyard, Joe Jack!'

And the whole house shook as Joe Jack banged the front door after him. Rage carried him a quarter-mile at a jog-trot before his feet brought him to his senses. He fell on his rump onto the road with pain. Before him the road leaned up against the sky like a ladder against a blue-washed dome. It felt the easiest thing to roll back half a dozen miles into unconsciousness or sleep, but sweat came on tap to scar sleep off his lids. The hurt to his eyes put him thinking of Jack, and, when he looked back, Jack was striding after him, touching the road with the ashplant. When Jack was near enough to hear the boy's teeth-whistle from his old man's mouth, Joe Jack rose and lunged ahead in a shuffle of desperation that was the only way he knew how of getting the better of his bruised feet. Then he flopped back on the road again, mopped head, face and chest with the cap until the teeth-whistle slit the hush of heat and he had to heave ahead again, his power robbed of dignity in that lunatic shuffle. On top of the mountain he fell face down under the blue dome into the coolness of long grass by the roadside. When Jack laboured up the last rise Joe Jack found he was without the will to stir more than an eye his way. Jack stood mid-road on the mountain top, with the plant in his hand, like a blind shepherd under a Bible sky. He cocked an ear to right and left; then, after a pause, said:

'Joe Jack.'

Joe Jack neither moved nor spoke. The hush hummed with heat. Larksong ran out of the sky like grain through a rent in an apron. 'Joe Jack, are you all right?' Joe Jack began to relish the situation. 'Joe Jack, are you all right? Are you all right, I said? ... You must be near, because I could hear you ahead up to now ... Joe Jack, show a sign anyhow ... Joe Jack!'

'Stand in off the road before the larks do more than sing on top of you,' said Joe Jack, drowsily.

'You had me worried,' said Jack, at his ease now.

'I could see that,' said Joe Jack.

'Worried I might have to run all the way back for a gun to take you out of pain.'

'I got to the top of the mountain before you, all the same.'

'There's a view for you,' said Jack. 'The vale of Tralee. Do you want me to see it for you, you boneyard stray?'

'A postcard,' said Joe Jack, feeling with his face for cooler grass. 'I think I'll post it to John Joe Sheehey to hold the match until we hit Tralee this day week.'

'Here, I'll sit with you until the end comes,' said Jack.

He walked in the direction of Joe Jack's voice until he could see where he was. Then he lay in the dead-man's stretch on the grass beside him and retired under the cap. Neither was able to say afterward who went to sleep first, but Jack was first to awaken. To bring Joe Jack back he had to fist his ribs till he sounded like a barrel being tapped. 'I was dreaming I was in bed,' said Joe Jack.

''Tis time to get up now,' said Jack. 'What time do it look like?' Joe Jack said: 'Two by the sky.' Jack said: 'An hour to the match and the hill down with us. Come on.'

But it was Joe Jack who was first on his feet, to make ground in a kind of second wind he was afraid to mention lest it leave him. The downhill going changed the pressure on his feet but he wore sweat like a caul.

When the more sprightly shuffle sprawled again into new fatigue the firm step of Jack got on his nerves and he began to hulk ahead once more. Then he rounded another bend and cried out with the full of his lungs and shambling, stumbling, falling, rising, always shouting, he bulked downhill. Jack pulled up between strides and yelled at the top of his voice: 'Joe Jack!' Then, well ahead and below him, Joe Jack began to laugh great gusts of laughter that tossed a gibberish of words about like corks on a wave. Jack thought he had gone out of his mind. With the ashplant held straight out he began to run blindly down into booming chesty phlegmy laughter until the ash was whipped out of his hand and he hit the hulk of Joe Jack's bone and muscle the way he would a moss-plushed wall. Shaken and winded he blinked up into the porter-smelling laughter from the mouth of Joe Jack.

'What's the matter, Joe Jack?'

For answer Joe Jack lashed the road with the ash. 'Can't you see as far as the ground, Jackeen? Look!' Jack stooped and was blinking at a pair of broad, flat feet, boning red through holes in smelling socks.

'They're like something a flood would lave on a mud-bank, Joe Jack.'

'Only they're nayther dead nor drowned,' raved Joe Jack.

'They're on the tar road, man, no more stones, smooth as a dance floor, man, whistle a tune and I'll dance.'

'Wind's gone,' said Jack.

Then Joe Jack's high glee went out like a light. 'Hey, hold on there, old-timer,' he said. Jack's face had gone from red to a murky puce. His breathing came in jerks. 'Give us the ash, Joe Jack,' he said. Joe Jack put the plant in his fist and took him by the arm. 'Aisy now, sit on the ditch. Jack.' Jack shook the hand off. 'That run winded me, that's all,' he said, but he staggered as he spoke. When he tapped with the ash towards the ditch his legs trembled. He leaned against the ditch. 'Sledge gone. Butterfly back,' he said. Joe Jack slung his boots to hang fore and aft by the laces from his shoulders. That's what you get from drinking minerals,' he told Jack. 'Puts wind around the ticker. A few belches and you'll be game ball.' Jack blinked at the sky, as if listening to count heartbeats. Joe Jack's battered face had a deathbed concern that matched his feelings perfectly. Jack licked blue lips with a dry tongue, gasping. He slid down the ditch into a sitting position. Joe Jack began to massage his face as gently as huge hands and hard palms would let him, and Jack felt a benefit or was too weak to protest.

'Come on, Jackeen, we have a match to ketch. Two downhill miles and a pint that you'll buy for Joe Jack. Tay for Jack this time, no minerals, no arguments until after the match; then more pints for Joe Jack ... Ah, sure we're game ball again ...'

The gentle man-handling brought colour back to Jack's face. He raised a hand to push Joe Jack's palms away.

'Dickeen was asking for you, Joe,' he said.

Joe Jack stood over him with his hands hanging like a bear waiting for trainer's orders. He lit a fag and sucked it limp with one long drag. Not sure of how to bring Jack further towards the land of the living, he decided on singing.

'Good heart, Joe Jack,' said Jack. ''Tis strange, but you never sounded better than worse till now.' He began to help himself up along the ditch with his arms. 'If I can stand I'll walk,' he said. He got as far as standing, rested for a moment; then heaved himself onto the roadway, swayed, steadied up and began to walk and tap with the ash, but slowly. 'Come on, do you want to keep me all day on the road?' he asked Joe Jack and Joe Jack came up and fell into step. And anyone but Jack would have seen the blood stains Joe Jack left on the crust of the road until the sun baked the wounds on his feet.

Joe Jack was going better without the boots, but he pretended distress in hundred-yard intervals to give Jack a breather without having to admit that he needed it. Within the hour Tralee opened its eyes to the shuffling bear of a man on bruised feet in holed socks and boots dangling by the laces from his shoulder, mopping a balding head with a fisted cap: and beside him a man whose face sagged grey in near-exhaustion, touching the road with an ashplant, trying to persuade breeched and stockinged legs to keep his nailed boots moving. Joe Jack's trumpet nostrils smelled porter through pub doors, saw coolness and quietness through pub windows, but he was bent on knocking up the first chemist to get a doctor's draught for Jack.

The claret inside cut glass on the chemist's counter boiled Joe Jack's thirst into spittle again, but Jack got his draught, belched, broke wind, and said: 'Will you fix that fellah's feet so they'll fit his boots again and not be making a show of me.'

While the chemist patched his feet with lint, plaster and bandage, Joe Jack cut the uppers of his boots into sandal strips with a scalpel he took off a shelf. Then the chemist saw what he was at and howled at the indignity to the gleaming instrument, but the damage was done, and Joe Jack was able to ease his feet into the gartered brogues. Jack led off the main beat for a bite and a sup before they faced the Austin Stack Park.

'Better get some sort of Christian look about you before we face anywan we know,' he explained.

'You have the advantage on me, Jack; you can't see yourself,' Joe Jack growled.

Jack went upstairs in Con Clifford's for tea and a plate of ham, while Joe Jack stayed downstairs for porter and sandwiches. When Jack tapped his way down with the ash, he found Joe Jack well gone in liquor and reluctant to leave without a few more pints, but the clock was against him. They bought tickets at the gate to the ground and tickets on the ground to the stand. They found there was no room on the stand, and hundreds of the faces that tiered all the way to the roof at the back came alive in cheers and shouting the minute the pair came in sight.

'Sound man, Joe Jack! ... My life on you, Jack, with your twenty-wan miles when you should be at home with your rosary beads!'

'Ould Carty blew the gaff,' said Jack, in disgust, but Joe Jack revelled in the reception, the broken face fixed in a grin. Jack turned towards a white-lined pitch that gleamed green between lime-washed goalposts, but Joe Jack turned his back on it as home-town faces in the stand began to call: 'Speech, Joe Jack, speech!' Joe Jack took the cap off, tore at the tufts of hair with a huge hand, and every face known and unknown above him hissed, 'S-s-s-sh,' and called, 'Order! Order!' Joe Jack cleared his throat.

'We done it anyhow!' he said, and was cheered to the echo. 'The road was as hot as the hobs of hell!' he said, and they cheered again, and from there on they cheered every statement.

'My butty, Jack here, walked his sight back ... He seen Son Leary at Innisfallen off the top of Madam's Height.'

Jack's quick wheel caught the cheerleaders off guard: 'In hundreds wan, two, three and four, come away, Joe Jack, and say no more,' he said, for the loudest cheer of the lot. But Joe Jack was on cue.

'From Sullivan's snug in Firies he saw all the way back to 1903,' he said, and the cheers and laughter were his again. 'He wanted me to go back with him, but the ould feet wouldn't let me.'

Every face on the stand was laughing at him and with him now, and he gloried in his moment. Jack was straining to be away.

'Jack left me to go back there himself, and, God's truth, he nearly forgot to come back to me again.'

The tiers of faces were straining down to hear and Joe Jack obliged by bellowing up at them:

'I got corns in hindquarters from sitting on the road!'

The faces laughed louder, swayed and leaned nearer, and Joe Jack gloried on.

'There was the man called Carty with the trap—he—'

But the teams had burst into colour onto the pitch behind him and the faces forsook him on the instant.

'There was the man called Carty—' he tried again, but his bull-powerful bellow was drowned in cheers that broke over him in a wave onto the pitch.

'There was the man—' he insisted, but not a face turned his way.

'There was—'

The waves of sound quenched the words at his lips. His fighter's face looked punch drunk. Jack felt for his arm and gripped it.

'Come on, Joe Jack!' he shouted in the big man's ear, but he had to tug several times before he could get him headed toward the wall that bounded the pitch.

'I must see that match!' Jack shouted.

'If I have to walk it,' said Joe Jack. And no one, not even himself, was aware of what he had said.

Sky Is Plentiful

I never rightly understood the old man when he was there in the lane living, working, fighting an odd time with a man bigger than himself, or playing his tin whistle on a chair tilted over the back legs and braced by his shoulders against the hearth wall.

When I say the old man lived I don't mean that he had not yet died. There are people who have died long before they sigh themselves away on a last breath: the old man—my father—lived all the time. With his last breath he gave the word 'right' up to my mother's hovering face. 'Right' was his word for acceptance or for challenge. 'Right,' he said to the big man who wanted to stop words honed on the edge of his tongue on what the big lad called a daft idea and the old man called a principle. The other man was always bigger; men of the old man's small size were more cautious for being nearer to shoulders that would all but calm the drop in a spirit level at dead centre. The old man was a stone worker and big men are softer at the core than green stone or granite, but when stone had brought age to know his forties the big lads had their day.

It was said by my mother's view—I had not the wit then to see that she exaggerated to speed the moral—that his fighting arguments were sins against sense and dignity. Several times a week he was meeting Protestant Captain Martin in Carty's snug.

The Captain's skin and clipped beard, with their look of hoar frost and berries, gave him the cut of a superior Santa Claus in baggy tweeds. His eyes looked as if they never got over seeing sails vanish in steamer smoke like gulls in cloud, but because the sea at least was the same sea he remained a sailor, until the Navy decided that he was no longer seaworthy. He came home then to three dependent spinster daughters and had his own back, for their robbing him of even grandsons for the sea, by referring at all times to their Protestant household as 'The Nunnery'. But to eke out his pension for their genteel needs he forsook hot toddies for mulled porter, cigars for a big bay pipe on a galloping hoof, hotel lounges for pubs and parrots for pigeons.

In Carty's he and the old man would war with words until the very number of their disagreements stirred a common thought that sent hands in search of drinks and put minds to rest at a depth beyond depths sounded by too many too often. Then the Captain would stuff the big pipe-head with shag and ask for a tune on the whistle. The old man would take the whistle out of the coloured handkerchief in his inside pocket and play opera pieces, sea shanties, folk tunes with a hollow wind-sob of feeling, or the 'Blackbird', with the beat of the bramble under the sleek bird and the whirl of the song in the amber gorge.

After that they would have one for the road and part the best of friends, the old man to come home to the lane and the Captain to go to his orchard to scatter maize seed for his pigeons and pour water in the stone trough that he had had the old man chisel for them.

'In the sky they remind me of sails on the sea, Mac,' he told the old man one time. 'Gulls are better for that,' said the old man. 'Gulls won't be tamed and pigeons will be too tamed and overbred,' the Captain grumbled. 'My spoilt pigeons won't rise higher than my eave shoots. My toy sails are always in port and never at sea, like myself, always in port and never bloody anywhere. Don't you like pigeons, Mac?'

The old man did. The Captain told him that the brood pair mated for life. He liked that. Off his own bat he maintained that the pigeon was the one bird that lost nothing in grace or looks for being perched on a dung heap: and it was my own first pigeon that helped me on the way to my day-after-the-fair understanding of him.

*

I got that pigeon in the shell of an old granary, inside the lane archway, where pigeons came and went through the gold-dust of old grain by a hole in the slates. Street pigeons all, the low-spread cloaks of flight they made were grey: sea grey, slate grey, old head grey in dim light, or blue smoke or mist or washwater blue, until Captain Martin's thorougbreds after his death (to his last day he had liquor on his breath, a lash-lick to his tongue, rope welts in his palms and brine in his beard) missing his care in the shelter of the orchard, went for pot luck and royster in the granary.

Then the greys and blues of the flights began to have streaks of copper, bronze, amber, honey and white. In time the bright streaks narrowed in the flights, but began to show as a sheen or a graining, or both, in the colour of one in three of the separate birds. The one I got, with the aid of a ladder, out of a joist hole in the granary had the bare promise of copper among the grey first feathers.

It was a mid-June Saturday afternoon, the old man's pay day and half-day combined. Heat shimmered out of the round sun like sound from a bronze gong. It beaded the trout-speck freckles on my face so that I wore them like a mesh. Bread could have been browned on the cobblestones under my feet. I was lost in admiration of the pigeon and did not see the old man coming towards me at first, but I heard him.

For a small man he took a long step and hit the ground hard with it. Even as he was then, with the nailed boots off and the light Sunday boots on, you would hear his step before another man's. He had the good soft hat back-tilted so you could see his black hair giving ground to grey, curled hard in a close crop that would have been easy to work in stone. Clean shaven, except for his full moustache, his face had the furrows and colour of worn brown shoe leather and his eyes were as black as heelball.

His only offer to show was his great-grandfather's silver watch chain, securing his grandfather's keywinder watch to his waistcoat. He looked what he was: a craftsman on his day off with new coin in his pocket. Over his shoulder I could see my mother in our second-storey window looking on the old man and at me with my pigeon. But not for anything would I have let her know I had seen her and not for all the world would the old man have let her discover that he knew she was there. And he did know, because one time it was he with the bare feet and his father with the watch and watch chain, and his own mother in the window on pay day between two minds whether to rest easy with the good moment or worry right away about time to come.

'See my pigeon, Dad?' I asked. At rest he was a shy man. Even I made him shy out-of-doors and had always to speak first. 'So you robbed a nest?' he gave back. 'I left one and took one,' I said. 'The lad I left is all grey. This lad has copper in his feathers.' 'A pennyworth,' he said. 'Oh, more,' I argued. 'A penny-ha'penny so,' he said, 'but show him here to me.'

His hands, file rough in the palms, with a vein and sinew webbing on the backs that might have been plaited out of winter ivy by a creel maker, were always crouched at the stone man's bred halfway between grip and caress: controlled power worth stating in stone that moulded it. The hands closed over my young pigeon in a way that would not have spoilt the wing-dust of a moth.

'He's a good one, Dan,' he said. 'He's game.' He let the wings fall out to full point. 'Them toy sails will go to sea, Dan. He's not afraid of anything.'

'You'd know it in his eye,' I said. 'You'd know it from his heart, Dan,' he corrected, 'beating sure and steady in the hollow of my palm as if it rested in the mother's breast mould you took it out of. He'll fly, Dan, surely.'

'Where, Dad?' I asked. 'High, Dan, because the sky is always plentiful, and always home, Dan, because even birds must come to earth. Here, show him to your mother now.'

I gathered my pigeon back onto the hot wool of my gansey and said 'So long.' He did not answer, nor did he move and I knew what was coming. It came too. 'Dan,' he called.

When I turned his back was to me. His right hand was hooked by his thumb to his trouser pocket. 'Well, Dad?' 'Here,' he said. Still looking away, he turned the hand palm up under his best coat-tail. In the hollow was a shilling.

'Buy maize seed for that bird,' he said. 'It will strengthen the pinions and smoothen the feathers for clean flight. So long.' And that was the last coherent word I ever heard from him. I was too taken up with the young pigeon and the shilling to watch him go. But my mother in the window watched him out of sight. I went on into the two-storey, white-washed house through the stone-flagged hall and up the nine steps of shaky stairs to the landing of the two rooms we had on rent from the Irishean who lived on the ground floor by herself.

*

Fifteen years previous, the Irishean had come inland from Dingle when she had lost her two sons to the sea and her daughter in marriage to a fisherman. She knew as many words of English as helped her to buy her food and snuff and to ask for her pension at the post office on Fridays. But to herself, in the house, she spoke Irish that matched every mood of the sea she crooned over or cursed, moaned to or bemoaned, but could never forget. It was as if there was a hollow in her where words broke and healed like sea sounds in a cave.

From the landing I went past the parents' bedroom into the living room that had a nook for my own narrow bed. My mother tried hard to make a fuss over my pigeon. 'But the mother bird will be looking for it in the nest, Dan, 'tis a shame for you,' she complained.

'When he's big he'll meet her in the sky,' I defended. ''Tis not the same,' she said, 'but 'tis a good thing too.'

She took the thrush cage down off the glass case for me and I spent the hours till bedtime foraging among the tipped-up carts in the marketplace, stealing hay and straw from under the dreaming heads of donkeys tethered to the cartwheels, and buying tuppence-worth of maize seed at each of the town's six seed shops.

Day went out like a bank of new pennies, the light going as if door after door of the vaults were closed. But my mother was more interested in the closing of the pub doors at half-past ten, because the old man had not come home. By eleven he had still not come home, so she made me take off my clothes and go to bed. Having looked at the pigeon and eased my mind about his comfort on the clean straw I went between the blankets. I pretended sleep because my mother liked that she alone would have the strain of waiting.

The small window framed the bit of June night that I could see about her head. The blue-black sky had stars in it like candles being breathed on. The air was still enough to let the musk smell of geranium leaves into me from the outer sill. On her knees, elbows on the inner sill, motionless, the mother might have been kneeling at a shrine. On or about every hour she rose and put a sod on the hearth and the fire turned over on its doze, shrugged and dozed away again. Each time she came and stood over me. I felt her hands raising the bedclothes off my shoulders and putting them back again the same as they were before. I could feel her look on my face as if her eyes had breathed it down. Then she went back and put her greying head into the icon of stars.

Below the rickety flooring the Irishean's flow of Gaelic breathed like a litany. Beyond the window the barking of a dog echoed more as the night emptied. I was in the shallows of sleep when I heard his step. My mother was leaning further out at the window to see him better as he passed under the gas lamps. Then I heard a moan from her that she tried to clench with her fists at her open mouth. But her movements were quick and sure when she struck and lighted the wick of the hanging oil lamp on the hob and shaped the light with a round-bellied globe. She took the lamp off the nail and went with it over the landing, down the stairs and along the hall to within a pace of the closed hall door. With my pants held by a fist on my middle I followed with my bare feet on her shadow. The old man came nearer with step and stumble. The Irishean's litany of Gaelic sounded like she was answering herself, as if she had to hear herself above wave upon wave.

Statue-still my mother stood inside the door and in her shadow I hardly dared to breathe while the step and stumble on the stones drew nearer through the flow and ebb of strong-throated Gaelic. Then the steps stopped outside the door. The lamp in the mother's hand was motionless through a pause that seemed a deal longer than it was because I held breath and heard heartbeats against taut eardrums. I cried out as the door crashed open to show the old man. His good hat was gone and a gash on his crown showed in his thick hair like a crevice. There was blood on either side of his face and on the shoulders of his jacket. He must have lain unconscious where it happened for a time because the blood had crusted to the purple-black of sloes. The watch hung loose on the silver chain and where he swayed in the light it swung like a pendulum of time vacant in eternity.

He was not conscious yet or he would not be there in the lamplight with his face misshapen from kick or blows or both, because never before had he come home without getting skilled help to hide the worst. From his eyes I would have known that he was not fully there anyhow. They were empty. Then he moved forward under the raised lamp. My mother followed close. I was on her heels.

At the foot of the stairs he stopped, looked up and almost crumpled. My mother's hand went out but his right hand reached out to push it away, as if it was a thought he had thought himself before. Then he seemed to suddenly find his feet because his body grew up from them to straightness. His head took on the game cock of his best days.

'Right,' he said. Then he went on up the stairs and into the bedroom, to fall face first into full unconsciousness on the bed. ·

During twelve hours there was the doctor's head-shake, my mother's waiting for the old man to pass behind the glazed opes of his eyes, his pause as he passed to look at her and say, 'Right,' the stone man having a sea dirge ullagoaning in the voice of the Irishean, and the pigeon gone as cold in my mind as a sculpted dove on a tomb.

During twelve weeks there was the dovecote wrought for my pigeon by a craftsman in wood, the stone trough brought from Captain Martin's three daughters by their gardener, and the arrival of the daughters themselves to give my mother her first jobs at the dressmaking she took up to keep home and rear me.

I know now why I had that grudge against the pigeon but on the way to knowing there were a few confusions. Kids are quick enough to hop-step into stride with life away from the full stop of a grave. Any grave. But I brought with me hate for the man or men who had killed the old man.

The mother sensed a change in me since the old man went. She would complain that it was she and the Irishean who had to feed and water the pigeon. Part of a plan, no doubt, to stop the youth in one from curdling. I think if she could have played a tune on the dusty whistle on the hob she would. Whatever else had colour in our drab place was hers and of woman—the geranium blossoms, the small red lamp under the big picture of the Sacred Heart, even the wild flowers in the vases that flanked the light, because I brought them home under my gansey when I was told.

There again I would say that the daily call for fresh flowers was to send me away to places she knew I liked because I had talked so often about them: places of river and hill, lake and mountain, heron or lark in sun or in rain. They were out and about that town in renowned riches and they cost nothing to see and only thought to feel. But when I came back she was troubled again that when I spoke of what I saw it was to answer her questions and what I felt I never told her at all. The pigeon she took to be her main hope for cure of what ailed me and she used him for all he was worth.

One day she heeled up on the treadle of the sewing machine and told me to go and have a look at the bird. 'There is nothing the matter with him,' I said.

I had had the bit to eat after school and was waiting for Eddie McConnell to whistle me away to a game of handball in the alley of the airing court of the Mental Hospital. The school alleys were forbidden to us after school hours. The Mental Hospital alley was forbidden to us too but it was good, and anywhere was better than school.

'The dump pits at the back are alive with cats, Dan, and your bird is one to fly low,' the mother argued. 'That's what's wrong with him,' I said. 'What do you mean?' she asked. 'Only that's what's wrong with him,' I said.

She thought that out. She was nearer to a core now and she knew it. She was nearer still with the next thing she said and nearer the centre than I. 'The bird is young, son,' she said, 'and our world is so low. There is nothing higher than a two-storey house and no wall higher than a dump pit dyke.'

Her fourteen years in America before she married solved for her the Irish riddle between ditch and dyke. She called a tap a faucet and a Z a Zee.

'Our world is not far from the ground, Dan,' she added. 'Sky is plentiful,' I said, half to myself. That brought a pause. 'Dad used to say that,' she reminded. 'I know,' I said.

There was a pause longer that time. She ran a bobbin to fullness before she spoke again. 'I was only thirteen years when I went to Boston with the emigrants,' she said, 'working in the woollen mill and living near it in a kind of cellar of the city and not nice. I felt like an ant under a stone and lonely. Then, one Sunday I went with a lot of others for a trolley ride out of the city. It was a big adventure, Dan.'

I used to revel in stories of this kind and she knew that too. She paused to see how I was taking this one. I felt mean because I couldn't warm to her telling the way I used to. 'The last trolley stop put us where the city ended and the land began. There were orchards, I remember. Every tree drooped with weight of ripe red apples and yellow apples. But what I saw was the sky. I looked up at it, and into it, and cooled in it as if the blue was sea and the clouds were foam and the birds were flying upside down. It was nice, Dan.'

I felt that whatever she was hunting in me was hiding in me and I couldn't find it even for myself. I looked at my bare toes, felt the pause curl about them and look up at me with her eyes, and I tried to rise out of the chair. 'Listen a little more, Dan,' she said. 'It won't be long. When I came back to the mill and the boarding house and the cellar again I remembered every day to look up at the sky and it was the same sky. Sky is plentiful but we must see it. So, maybe, if you took the pigeon with you into the country he'd see the sky and remember ever after that the same sky was here too.'

'Cod,' I said. That really hurt her. It was a short word and easily out, but it was out and there it was. I didn't feel her eyes through the pause that time.

'Your Dad said "cod" about many things,' she said, 'but never about that. When I told him what I told you now was the first time I heard him say, "Sky is plentiful." '

She waited for a word of answer or comment but I had none to make. Then the machine whirred like angry crickets and I left the room. I went over the landing and down the stairs into the hallway. I opened the yard door by chinks to take the pigeon unawares.

He wasn't a bad bird to look at. He had the cheek that would age into pride with a burgeoned breast, spread tail and the full bass of the croon that would deepen down from mouse-squeak immaturity. The copper was still a penn'orth in the feathers but the grey was deepening to blue, the throat sheen rippled in the light, the legs were clawed crimson and the eye amber and fit for setting by a goldsmith. The cote was hanging on the back wall of the house from a brad that had held one end of a clothes line. I stepped into the yard.

On the ledge of the cote he squatted, preening the wing pinions. Feathers floated in the trough water where he had washed a time ago. When he saw me he rose up to full reach and cheeked me with one eye and the other. Then he lay on the air under spread wings and cut the loops of an eight of flight out over the dump pits and back to the ledge. But never for an instant was he higher than an eave.

I had tried to make him rise. I had gone the length of hurtling stones under his flights to drive him high but he mocked me with capering scoops of flight and fall, out of line but never out of range. And there he was back on the ledge again, shaping, trying to sell his ha'p'orth of coppers to the sun as pure gold, trying to win my interest with slitting of a silence full of sunlight (that smelled faintly of dump pits) with the slender zither pinging of his wings.

Eddie McConnell whistled in the hallway just then and I brought the pigeon with me. 'What are you doing with that?' he asked. 'Taking him with me,' I said. 'Is it a homer?' he asked. 'That's what I want to know,' I said and we left it at that.

The Mental Hospital is on a hill beyond the town and big enough to fool people into thinking it the town itself. The stone of it looked as if it needed a deluge to wash it down. The windows of it had very many small panes of glass and there was never a time when a window had all the panes or a minute without a patient's face mope-eyed in the light or a hand throwing pellets of paper through the space where a pane should have been. The ball alley was in the men's airing court west of the hospital. There was nothing between the patients and escape during airing time except a six-foot iron railing and attendants pacing each his own short stretch of railing like policemen on the beat.

The court was a field but what grass had the courage to grow near that ugly mass of masonry was scabbed with patches walked bare by patients' nailed boots and pocked with small and big enough holes where patients had scooped or kicked little graves for dead memories or for the want of anything at all to do. The big, plain alley, midway and inside the railing on the western end of the court, had no back wall, so that patients could watch attendants play during airing time. It looked like a bomb-damaged stone house that someone had healed up with old plaster. The whole court looked like a bombed area.

We got there about four on the late August afternoon. We climbed the railings by gripping the loop head to every first and third bar (the loop arched over the spike on each centre bar, on the principle that an escaped patient caused less uproar in a Board Room than a dead one) and walked with our bare feet up the centre bar.

I put the pigeon on the railings and he perched there as unconcerned as a hen on a roost feeling night wean light away out of the coop. I snatched him off the perch and walked with him to the centre of the court. 'What are you up to?' Eddie asked me. He was long and thin, with limp hair, and all his thoughts ended in a question and stayed there. 'I want him to see the sky,' I said. 'Is he blind?' asked Eddie. 'We'll see,' I said. 'Is this a good place for notions like that?' Eddie asked. 'Go to hell,' I said. 'I'll go out into the alley and loosen up,' he said. Not until he was away and I was alone with the pigeon did I feel that the old man was with me. When I looked at the sky I thought of the mother. It was high and clear of cloud in the dome, a deep blue womb, warm with light lambent on gull wings. Lark specks quivered high over the farm fields like soot motes blown up out of the fire of the westering sun. I showed the pigeon the sky. I willed him hard to see it and feel its vastness wooing for his wings. Then I flung him skywards. His wings beat wildly at house-eave's reach, fluttered for balance and skimmed down the air to the scabbed turf. Eddie's laughter echoed hollow in the valley. I turned my back on the bird and walked head down towards the laughter.

I worked off part of my venom against the pigeon in knocking the ball hard and fast, low and high against the drab concrete. Eddie had height and reach and a kind of dogged endurance that made a game with him close but always a winning one. That evening I played with an intensity that made for a nervy pallor instead of heat and sweat and Eddie broke the silence several times with—'Anything the matter with you?' and I shook my head and buried another ace on the bottom stone or knocked it well over his head. 'Where's that pigeon?' he asked me once. 'I don't care a damn,' I told him.

I remember it began when he tossed a long ball down the centre. I hit it hard and low to a butt that left him no chance even to get his toe to it because there was no hop. I was moving in to deal and he was coming out to play at the end of the alley when I saw his face stretch in terror that lit his eyes. 'Holy God!' he cried.

When I turned about there was a knock in my chest like a hammer-top. Half the court was full of patients, walking towards us with myopic eyes, their hands hanging below short coat cuffs and feet striding in nailed boots. One or two in straitjackets looked like part-clad divers without a helmet and all strode towards us like men stalking a life on lynch law. That was how it seemed to me. One man with the peak of his cap over his left ear and eyes grey-cold ran at us. 'Run,' I shouted to Eddie. 'Jesus,' he cried and ran out of the alley and back to the railings.

His being ahead of me heightened my terror of the pounding boots behind me. Eddie was up and over the railing before I started to climb. 'He's coming, hurry!' he cried.

I missed my foothold a few times but in the end I fell face forward onto the avenue as the railings rattled from the force of the patient's run against it. I heard the too-loud lunatic laughter of the patients before I could pick myself up. I heard the more measured laughter join it and when I turned around I saw the patient and the attendant in his white coat, both as breathless as I was.

'That will teach ye lads to leave us our alley to ourselves,' the attendant said. 'Little snipes, they were,' the patient said, 'little frightened snipes skittering out of cover above a gun. Little ladeens, 'twas a shame.'

'Well, blast you anyway,' Eddie said on his first even breath. The patient laughed again and the attendant put a calming hand on his shoulder. 'You did your work, Pats. That's enough, boy. Enough,' he said.

But just then the whole court full of patients started a gale of crazy laughter on their own. The cause was my pigeon. The patients were chasing it from perch to perch along the north railing, their arms looking extra long in the shank from the shortness of the sleeves of their thick suits. The nearest hand to each new perch grabbed at the blue bird that rose on the full spread of white-lined wings out of reach to sway away to another perch further down the railing. In the brown shapeless suits that somehow smelt collectively of smoke-damp they hunted the bird, grabbing at it with great hands on long red shanks of wrist.

The white coats rushed here and there among the brown, pushing, holding, knocking as the laughter rose and the great hands reached out of the mass and grabbed at the bird that rose in white-lined flights always out of reach away to perch again, to rise and sway again along the railings.

Somehow the old man was in that laughter-mad pursuit and I was watching, waiting for the kill.

'That's my pigeon,' I said to the white coat near me. 'He'll be all right,' he said. 'I'm going for him,' I said.

I made to climb back over the railings but he put a hand on my shoulder that weighed heavier than lead. I fell away under it and ran down the railing to climb again. The white coat followed along, place after place I tried. I began to cry with rage and frustration. The white coat got into a kind of a frenzy. On my sixth or seventh attempt to get over he hit me with the knuckles of a big fist over the ear. I fell stunned to the ground and Eddie asked was I all right.

I had to fight through tears and daze to get the place in focus. Through the swirl several times I found even keel and each time I began to notice something. It was this. Each time the pigeon rode a reaching hand he rose higher above the railings. Sitting on the ground I watched the brown mass of humanity laugh and grab and saw the pigeon rise higher than the eaves he knew. Then suddenly when he was beyond tree height he began to soar. I watched him rise, and watching, the fears fell away and the white coat was forgotten as I saw him soar into the womb of sky.

The flight fountained up and up through crow flap and gull scroll until the white of the wing linings turned silver in the light. Higher and higher he rowed the air with the silver wings till there was nothing above him but larks. You could imagine the wings feeling the fall of larksong to hush on fields to dew on grass, to breast of mate and warmth of scalding. And high between the highest gull and lowest lark my pigeon was a silver flash that suddenly ceased to circle and sped arrow-straight towards the town.

*

As I picked myself up I felt the silence. The brown mass and the white coats stood with their faces raised silent to the sky. I looked back for the

wings of my pigeon and they weren't there. I began to run. Eddie followed with his long legs, shouting: 'Where are you going? What are you
doing?' But I didn't answer. He ran with me until he could run no longer.
I shouldn't have been running that long without stopping but I was. My
body seemed to have made a rhythmic habit of running, my lungs a rhythmic pain of breathing.

Running into the town from the asylum was downhill work. When
the heat and sweat swelled the blood in my head I felt the bump big and
painful over my right ear where the attendant had hit me. I ran on down
Rock Road, down Meara's Hill, down High Street, through Main Street,
up Henn Street, across the Square and down New Lane where I lived.
The mother was watering the geraniums on the window sill. When she
saw me she showed fright in her face that for a moment was a shadow of
the way she looked the night the old man dragged death all the way home
in spite of itself.

She went in from the window and was standing inside the door when
I turned in at the hall.

'The pigeon,' I said.

'What about him, son?'

'I took him up Asylum Hill. He flew right up into the sky. Then he
flew right down towards town. I think he's home.'

'We'll see,' she said.

We ran down the hall, threw open the door into the yard. But there
was no pigeon.

'He's not home yet,' she said.

'He should be,' I said.

''Tis a long flight, Dan,' she said.

'I ran as far,' I said.

'You knew the way,' she reminded me. 'We'll wait here in the doorway till he comes.'

Beyond the dumps—the width of a livery stable beyond—was a store-
house roof and over the roof was the crown of a beech tree. The sun bed-
ded down red into the west beyond the tree and the crown of leaves was
like a brazier. We stood motionless in the doorway, silent for minute upon
minute of waiting, looking ahead. Then of a sudden the pigeon sped out
of the brazier tree of skyfire like a flame, to swoop low over the dump

walls and glide up to claw to a perch on the ledge of the cote.

'Right,' said the mother and the word was in my mind to say.

I felt her smile before I looked up into it. When I smiled back I felt the bruise over my ear where I was hit but I kept on smiling anyway. She was still smiling when she turned her face from me. But for a long while after I only saw her back.

Law Abiding

The two policemen were big, with the fat of their sixties added to the bone and body of their prime, but as they approached the smallest pub in the village they looked enormous. The heat of the day had put a dew of sweat from brows to double-chins. When they butted under the white horse figure in the fanlight it seemed as if they would rob the flagged and shadowed place of a coolness that bottles gave the deep green of a trout pool.

The owner of the pub was asleep on his palms, braced by an elbow on either side of an open ledger. A fly winging about the ripe tip of his nose was upset in each act of alighting by a whistle of breath like mild surprise. His specs, halfway up the furrows of his forehead, were secured to his bald head by a piece of twine. The policeman with the round parcel in brown paper hit the counter with it, but the wizened sleeper slept on.

The two big men stood over him for a moment without comment. Then, drilled by long custom, without knowing, they followed a slow ritual in perfect accord. Brows and cap-bands were wiped with handkerchiefs out of pants pockets, caps were placed at the sleeper's elbows, bar stools were drawn up to the old face as if the pouted lips were about to utter something extremely confidential. One of the policemen stooped to look into the wry expression.

'If 'tis dreaming he is, Dowd, the dreams are not nice,' he told the other.

'Ah, with a man of his years even sleep without dreams do turn sour, Mac,' said Dowd.

'Give us two, Darcy,' said Mac, but old Darcy went on whistling at the persistent fly.

'If you don't make a move, Darcy,' said Dowd into the ear near him, 'we'll fill 'em ourselves.'

'Darcy, we'll make away with your money,' Mac confided to the other ear, and Darcy collapsed out of sleep onto the counter.

'What is it, what is it, what is it?' he gasped. 'What, what, what?' he exclaimed with petulance, and 'What now!' until the specs fell into place on his nose. Then, 'Good day, men,' he greeted, as if nothing unusual had happened at all.

'Two, Darcy,' said Mac, but Darcy was already reaching for two pint glasses off the zinc draining board.

He raised the glasses between him and the window to make sure they were clear enough to catch the lime leaves in the yard without misting their freshness. While he filled the pints the two policemen made themselves comfortable. Dowd undid the belt and collar of his tunic and the neckband of the striped woollen shirt. His ruddy good-natured face was frosted on the loose jowls with stubble. Mac was satisfied with loosening the laces on boots that had a little half-moon of upper missing over each small toe. His mop of hair had aged from red to rust and his freckles were like the blotches on a blackbird's eggs. But his grey collie's eyes were lively and roving constantly. They lighted now on a calendar that showed a sheening cob bearing a foxy barefoot boy over a pad of date tags.

'Ah, Darcy,' he complained.

'Yes, yes, yes,' grunted Darcy.

''Tis easy known I was away four days.'

'How, now?'

'The calendar is four days behind time,' Mac said.

As he walked to the calendar with his loose boots and his mop on end he might be just up out of bed. A yawn added to the likeness.

'One, two, three, four,' he counted, tearing the dead numbers off the pad. 'Now, Darcy, that brings us up to date.'

Darcy put the two pints on the counter into two pools of their own froth.

'If so small a thing brings us up to date, a smaller should put us ahead of time,' he said. 'Take off one more.'

'An up-to-date village is one thing, Darcy,' Dowd put in. 'A village ahead of time would be a place of pilgrimage, however, and we want your good porter, Darcy, for ourselves.'

'Maybe that explains why ye're so strict on my after-hours trade,' Darcy countered.

'Now, Darcy, fair is fair. We didn't raid you so often that there was ever an endorsement on your licence. Would you, as a mere matter of interest, care to be told how many men you let in after Mass on Sunday?'

'I wouldn't, I wouldn't, I wouldn't,' growled Darcy. 'But would you care to hear how much I have paid out in fines on the head of yer summonses?'

'The sum didn't stop you from paying the way of two sons to be priests, a son for a vet and a son with a bar business in Dublin that wouldn't own this hole in the wall as a cellar for bottles,' Mac butted in.

He raised his drink, scraped the tip off the base of the glass on the edge of the counter, blew a shape for his lips in the high cap of froth, fitted his lip with care into the shape and allowed his shock head to tilt gradually back in the first long draught.

'Here's luck,' he said, out of a wet mouth over the rim of the glass.

'The best,' wished Dowd, raising his pint with an odd kind of crude grace to the toast.

'God bless the pair of ye,' prayed Darcy.

Then for a matter of minutes the two policemen loitered with their liquor, content out of the hot day as plough horses at a stone trough.

'Two more, Darcy,' said Dowd, at length. 'That was a master pint. Like new milk. May God never give me more mind for it than I have now.'

'Amen, amen, amen,' prayed Darcy, distaste for the thought hanging in every loop line of his sour old face.

'To hell with you, Darcy, you ould hypocrite,' laughed Dowd.

'Amen to that too,' said Darcy. 'Your business in Dublin went off all right, Guard Mac?' he added, from a milker's squat at the barrels. 'Our poor neighbour was taken where the weight of his cross will be lightened for him?'

'He was in Grangegorman asylum a half-hour after we sighted the Liffey,' Mac answered.

'Mac was at Green Street courthouse for the murder trial of the tramp tinsmith, Darcy,' Dowd put in.

Darcy put Dowd's drink on the counter and looked at Mac over the specs.

'What did the young man on trial look like?' he asked.

'A good figure of a man and well-featured,' Mac admitted. 'A man too young to die, who must die.'

'He wouldn't have to die, if there ever was such a thing as an intelligent jury,' said Dowd.

'Are you serious?' Mac asked him, his very voice suggesting the curve of the question mark.

'Why not?' Dowd gave back, his new pint snuggled in the crotch of his elbow.

'Only that it don't sound like you,' said Mac. 'A man of your years, and your experience and your understanding to make so unthinking a statement as that.'

'It wasn't unthinking,' Dowd said, snuggling the pint still, caressing it with his big paw as if it were a pup. 'Sure I'm always thinking. With nothing but your ould boots for company in years of solitary watch as a keeper of the law, sure you'd go as mad as the creature you took to Grangegorman if you didn't keep the mind occupied with thought. It was long thinking brought me to the opinion that the jury system is no use because juries, without exception, have less legal intelligence than the old brogues that I talk to on my beat.'

'I'll have another free trip to Dublin shortly,' said Mac.

'Your pint, Guard Mac,' Darcy got in, putting the glass into the imprint of the last.

'Explain yourself, Dowd, about the jury system,' Mac challenged, sparks of temper in his lively eyes.

'Take the case of the journeyman tinsmith,' Dowd said. 'There was no witness to say what happened between that lad and the ould fellah that's dead now from a belt of a mallet on the forehead.'

'There's plenty to say they saw him with a mallet in his fist over the prostrate body of the victim.'

'With one rap of a mallet the prostrate body wouldn't be prostrate at all if the victim was forty-eight instead of eighty.'

'Even at a hundred-and-eighty we have the same right to life as a lad of eighteen.'

'But if he travels the woods under the first star, grabbing money out of people's hands, he have to suffer the strength of their objection.'

'The victim stated in deathbed evidence that it was he who was counting the shillings by the holly bush when the lad attacked him,' Mac cried, venting his venom in a savage attack on his drink.

Dowd raised his glass with due respect.

'The lad who travelled the roads of Ireland was a journeyman tinsmith, don't forget. The mallet was a necessary tool of his trade. The shillings he said were hard earned putting bottoms on old pans and making new ponnies for the neighbourhood. He wouldn't have hit so hard, he said, but that 'tis a man's bulk and not his age you notice as a first impression when dusk is in a wood and last light in a sky beyond treetops. As a man who had to act quick in dusk and dark I agree with him. And so should you, Mac.'

'A man of years who knows he has only minutes before he goes before his God is not likely to tell lies,' Mac cried.

'A man of years who gets a belt of a mallet on the head could say a questionable thing to God Himself,' Dowd almost whispered to the top of his pint. His voice strengthened when he added: 'And the ignorant members of the jury are unlikely to take that into account. That one tap of the mallet too many will probably lead to a condemned cell and the long drop in Mountjoy for that young lad.'

Darcy was so interested in the argument that he forgot to have an eye for the Sergeant on behalf of the two dishevelled policemen. He moved now along the counter to look through the open doorway. It seemed as if the parched stone road was drinking from the light-flecked pools of shadow under the lime trees and the hot air thirsted for the sound of the river. Downhill towards the bridge a caravan rocked after the light-shod hooves of a cob. Midway between the bright red wheels a piebald terrier bobbed along on three legs. At a window in the round green gable of the hood a young woman with jet black hair was talking to a young man with a crop in his armpit who walked after. The ivory of the woman's teeth and the gold of her earrings had a perfect setting in the chestnut darkness of her skin. Apart from these there was no one on the road down to the bridge, and no one at all showed where the road beyond rose in a leap to a bluebelled hilltop.

'Did you ever summon a jury?' Mac shot at Dowd as Darcy shuffled back.

'I did. I did four years in Store Street Station in Dublin before I was sent to the foreign missions of the force, where a man's wife is his chief superintendent and the barmen are all like Darcy.'

'Your wife is a fine woman, a fine woman,' said Darcy, raising his palms to the ceiling and nodding a wry thanks to God for the nature of Dowd's wife.

'What did you think of the jurymen you summoned?' Mac pursued.

'Cute enough, clever enough, cagey enough in their own business, but ignorant men inside the door of a courthouse, especially in the ins and outs of human frailty that are brought into play to make a capital charge.'

On the last word Dowd's tunic belt was buckled far out on his paunch, the collar was fastened, and his glass was ready for the rite of the three last swallows.

'Law is more than law,' he added. ''Tis justice too, and justice would be better administered by trained lawmen who had to bear the full brunt of their own findings in any case that carried their name. As it is they can blame any miscarriage of justice on the stupidity of the jury that use the lawman's brains in place of using a bit of their own.'

Mac was retying his laces while Dowd spoke. He was made so angry by what he heard that he broke a lace. That made him even more angry. On Dowd's final word he rounded on him with a tirade.

'Mother of God, man, do you not see that the jury system is a legal institution framed by trial and error over years upon years to down the criminal while giving the criminal every chance?'

'Criminal is a broad term that has a lot of room for the lights and shades that no juryman has the wit to fathom,' Dowd said amiably.

'Ninety-nine criminal cases out of a hundred carry a guilty man in the box. For one innocent man that would benefit by doing away with the jury system ninety-nine criminals would roam the world at large to prey upon innocent people. If we argued a thousand cases from our own side of the fence, the two of us, you'd probably be right in one, and I'd be right in the rest.'

Mac coughed down the last of his drink, and before Dowd could answer, he had his brown paper parcel like a baton under his arm and was making for the doorway. Dowd emptied his glass in three slow swallows and savoured the dregs on pleased lips. Mac turned at the doorway.

'On that level of law you're dealing with criminals, remember,' he said. 'Criminals! And you speak of them as if they were plaster saints that an ill-wind only shook on the pedestals. Criminals, they are, the most of them, and the most of the most were criminals in undetected cases many times before the once they were caught. Criminals!' he cried and struck the door with his huge fist. He narrowed his eyes to look for the set of the relentless sun in the bluebell blue of the sky. 'And on top of it all 'tis all hours of the day and the wife will kill me,' he added.

'Ah well, you would appear to have your excuse under your oxter,' Dowd said, tapping the baton-shaped parcel.

Mac smiled. 'I might have at that,' he said. 'Dammit I might at that,' he said as if he were easing in to awareness of possibilities.

He chuckled. The weight of previous thought was shed for the pleasure of the new. He came back two steps to meet Dowd inside the door. He tore a portion of the paper off the contents.

'Do you see what it is, Dowd? A roll of flyscreen. Zinc with very small holes in it. You'd see it in old pub snugs and confession boxes in old churches—and where else? Come now, Dowd, where else would you see it?'

'In a stone-breaker's goggles,' said Dowd. 'If there's a stone-breaker left in the world.'

'Good,' Mac replied. 'But you'd see it too in a kitchen safe you'd have standing on stilts in the yard. We have a little girl from the next village for skivvy below at the house. She's a nice little one and a good worker but she have one fault. She's light-fingered. Hardly anything not nailed down or under lock and key but will walk. All in the house is sealed down by the missus from her. But in one side of the safe in the yard there's a hole, and the eggs and things are goin' through that hole at a rate would set up a small business. So I'm putting a sound piece of wire on that side after dinner, and the missus have a key for the door, and the eggs and such will be out of the way of the creature's temptation.'

'That's a prime idea,' said Dowd.

'Good luck, Darcy,' Mac called.

'Good luck,' said Dowd.

'Safe home, men,' said Darcy.

As the two big men left the cave and pool cut and coolness of the flagged and shadowed pub, and strode down the parched stone road towards the bridge, Darcy's old face twitched and trembled all the way to what passed for a smile among those who knew he meant it for a smile.

'Well, well, well,' he whispered. 'Well, well, well.'

He straddled the ledger with his elbows. In fitting his wrinkled wedge of face into his palms his finger-tips pushed his specs far up on his forehead. The sleep came back, and the fly came back as if in answer to the very first whistle.

The American Apples

The only plants she had grown before were geraniums. They blossomed for her the way cats purr for spinsters. I can't recall the names of the varieties but I remember the blossoms: the one that was a crimson stray— away from elegance and somehow a stranger to all but herself in the place, the pinks with a blush that set with the sun on the youth of our grandmothers, the purples, the red that was a rose without smell and the white that smelled like a veil away for years in lavender. I know with what prim docility they grew for her in greying earth in sweet tins brought from shops to the sills of the rooms in New Lane where we lived.

As an altar boy I went often onto the High Altar of the cathedral when the priest away below in the pulpit droned the last prayers of Holy Hour. I would fit the long lighted taper into the brass tube on the cone cowl of the extinguisher and light the hundreds of candles, from the Tabernacle all the way down red-carpeted steps to the patterned tiles of the Sanctuary. Every cluster of candles I lit raised a richness of flowers out of stained-glassed dusk. Flowers from the hothouses of the earl and the agent and the manager and the doctor; in root and on stem they were there in their thousands, smelling like cool incense, but never was there a geranium in the lot that was better than my mother's.

Even that the sweet tins had discreet burial there in urns of beaten brass and bronze I used to recognize her few flowers when my butterfly flame hovered over them, holding their own with the best.

So when the old man laughed on the day of the apples, I let laughter alone while she prised the pips from the hearts with her nail: no hard task because the brother and I had gnawed our way to the core. They were sleek, cider-wry yellow apples, freckled where they had out-bowed leaf shade on the branch.

She was sitting on the edge of the chair near the hearth. The hat she had brought, after fourteen years in Boston to her wedding, flaunted the wear and tear in fur felt with one defiant feather. The black nap of the coat that travelled with it wore a silver clip in the right lapel for the same reason. The ten years since she was twenty-five showed in her heart-shaped face only in a slight slackness of flesh below her chin.

The brother sat cross-legged on the floor looking up at her. I too sat on the floor between a basket of groceries and two heads of cabbage. The old man stood over us, hat at angle, thumb hooked to the watch pocket of his waistcoat.

While she had shopped he was detailed to have an eye on the brother and me in that one of two rooms near the slates of a two-storey tenement, and his ear had been at full cock for her step on the cobbles. Tap-a-tap-tap she came, eighteen to the dozen down the lane, in the hall and up the stairs. He drew on his hat, poked for pipe and plug, and felt for coin in pants pockets, but by then she was in at the door. One in each hand she held the apples, the basket on her arm and the cabbage cuddled by her elbows.

'Look what I got for the boys,' she said, a bit breathless, her eyes making more of the gift than was usual.

'Apples.'

'More, boys!'

'What, woman?' asked the father.

'American apples!' she said.

'Only that you told us, they could be out of Pat Carty's sour half-acre in Ballydribeen,' the old man joked.

'Here Michael, here Kevin,' she said, and then put her load on the floor.

'Eat them,' she urged, before we had a tooth in them.

'God, I thought we were to have them under a glass globe with a lamp burning in worship of their highnesses,' the old man said.

'I'm not rushing ye, boys,' she told us, 'but I'm going to keep the seeds and save them till 'tis spring again. I'll save the seeds.'

'And save your soul,' mocked the old man.

'If saving seeds would save a soul I'd have to rob an orchard for yours.'

'A Boston orchard.'

'One tree out of a Boston orchard would do.'

'No, woman, mine is one Irish soul that's not for sale in American dollars.'

'I brought my soul home with me, and some dollars too,' she snapped.

When she held the seeds in her palm the old man laughed. Moving to the door, he ballad-sang:

> *The Yanks are coming.*
> *You can hear them humming*
> *Over there ...*

She pretended not to hear as she put the seeds in an envelope and put the envelope between the Sacred Heart picture and the warmth of the hob.

'Over there. Neither here nor there,' mocked the old man in doorway.

'When spring comes we'll see,' she called after him as he went to slake a summer thirst.

The lane gave spring no easy coming amongst us. Flowering weeds had laboured birth in old mortar along old walls. Grass stems overreached in lankness so that bright green tips might show between and above the slug-backed cobbles. House-bound old people had to wait for their cage-bound birds to sing again before they could be sure that they had weathered another winter. But ahead of weed and grass and finch song, she took the seeds from hob-warmth. Next morning she took a distemper tin with her to her usual first Mass at the friary. Coming home, she reached through the friary railings for fists of earth from a flower bed. Then on she came with another tin full of monastery garden for her sills.

She waited until the hour between the father's going to work and ours to school before she brought tin and seeds together on the sill. School bags on hip, the brother and I watched her prod four holes in the earth with one of the old man's chisels and drop a seed into each hole.

A murmur of mist soothered on the lane. Rain beads roped and broke along the rusty chute above the open window.

'A wonderful day to plant seeds, but bad for the pay-packet if it gets any more rainy, so you don't know where you are,' she told us. 'A stone set in damp sweats for years after, whereas a seed set in mist is set in growth, they say. Ye remember ye said the apples were nice tasted?' We said we did.

'Were they real sweet?'

'Sweet with a tang.'

'And juicy?'

'Oh, yes.'

'Remember how they looked myself. Yellowy-goldy and marked like blackbirds' eggs. Maybe from these four seeds four trees of them will grow. The ways of God are wonderful.' She looked from the tins to us and back to the tins again. 'I wonder are they that wonderful?' Then, wide-eyed, she looked at me and said, 'Oh, God forgive me.'

'We can say a prayer,' Kevin encouraged in all earnestness and her laughter raced up and down and up its scale. Then, suddenly serious herself, she said: 'School now; off to school; school is important.'

'I wonder do I know about that looney Cromwell's killings all over the country?' Kevin asked, scratching behind an ear.

'We can say a prayer,' she mimicked, laughing again. 'But you do, Kevin,' she added, all concern.

But Kevin's sleepy-headed solemnity was too much for her. Her laughter followed us down the stairs. When we reached the lane her serious face was waiting over the sill of flowers for us.

'Kevin, Cromwell happened in sixteen-something. He was a bad man, but the strange thing was that when he had slaughtered hundreds of peo ple he—'

'I know,' Kevin interrupted. He gave her one of his slow-fashion grins. 'He said a prayer.'

The three of us laughed that time. Then Kevin butted his thick thatch into the mist with the two steps he always held ahead of me. I listened to her laughter gentling over the planted seeds and wondered idly whether a thing would grow from them.

I don't think she wondered though. So far as I know she never wondered where her gift for growing things came from. She was bred of a lane like our lane, daughter of a stonemason, married to a stonemason bred of a lane that like ours was wrought of stone, paved with stone that let nothing of root thrive on it but lichen and moss and nothing between but the weed and the striplet of grass. In fact our lane's very bareness may have been a reason why she wanted us out of it, but certain it is that she wanted Kevin and me to stay longer in school than our kind, to have Boston at home, no less, and she had an idea that a lane was a bad start for that.

Two years from the morning of the seeds she had us a walk distant from town in a stone house that had two cat-swings of flower plot in front, a crusty quarter-acre of one-time commonage to pass for garden at the back. How that came about is another story. But in the way the peacock-feather and the silver clip had more to be defiant about everyday.

But a bank manager had been persuaded that a meagre-enough warren of dollars would bed and breed issue with docile rows of shillings kidnapped on the roll from a four-pound pay-packet to butcher, baker, grocer, tailor and the old man's pocket on Saturday pay day, when there was pay. Urban councillors were persuaded that the manager was persuaded that the old man was convinced that the age of miracles was not dead.

The old man argued, angered, mocked and then laughed the way he did about the seeds. But it was on the night that we left the lane for the house in the country that he had reason to remember the seeds again.

Daylight for the flitting would be merciless on the few sticks of furniture, she thought, and her hopes were answered by an October night without moon or stars. In a rumble of iron-shod wheels Mick Breen's dray lantern rocked down the lane like a buoy-light in an inshore harbour. The shoes of his Clydesdale chipped flint sparks big as match-spurts off the cobbles. The old man's face loomed bronze-like in the museum half-glow of the lantern before Mick knew who he had and where he was.

She helped the lantern with her hob-lamp in the doorway while the old man gave Mick a hand. The old man held the lamp while she fetched the geraniums tin by tin for careful placing in a packing case at the back of the dray. When the last geranium was in place and she faced for the house he asked her: 'What now?'

'You'll see,' she told him.

Mick put me sitting on a folded sack under a sleek slope of the horse's rump and put the lantern in my grip. 'The heat of it will keep you warm,' he told me. He himself sat opposite, with Kevin in the old man's timber armchair, in line with the horse's tail, between us. With her footsteps in the hall came the old man's question: 'And what the hell might they be, woman?'

'Two Boston apple trees to save your soul.'

'Well, I'll be damned.'

'Not if you don't decide to leave us before these two little plants that grew are trees.'

'Put them in the ould box with the flowers.'

'Indeed I will not.'

'Then what'll you do, woman?'

'Why, carry them myself, of course.'

'Not with me, you won't.'

'Then I'll have to walk alone.'

'You damn well will.'

She was standing in the doorway with the tins held against her body. He was facing her with the hob lamp still lighting in his hand.

'It will be a poor journey to the new house if I have to walk alone to it,' she said.

'Then dump the ould weeds out of my sight,' he said.

'They're not weeds. They're only stems with a few leaves now but they'll be trees one day.'

'All right, put 'em in the box.'

'No,' she insisted, and as if to ease over the firm finality of the word she added: 'They had the courage to grow in the old house so 'twould be a shame if anything happened them before they saw the new house.'

'Their ould lad saw the new world, isn't that enough?' he jibed, but you could tell that he was near the end of patience. Her answer did not help either.

'They're going to a new world now. I'm taking them there myself.'

'What!' he cried, and on the word she tried a pleasantry.

'A wonder the lamp wouldn't help you to see light.'

She could hardly have said a more unsuitable thing. Suddenly made aware of the lamp he saw how ridiculous he looked.

'To hell with the light,' he cried, swinging the lamp arm violently. The lamp arced over the dray and quenched in a globe-burst against the blank wall opposite. The horse heaved forward. The dray rattled my teeth together. I had a glimpse of the mother following on with the tins before

I had to look ahead for balance on the jigging perch. Sound of the wheels must have been listened for by the neighbours. Door after door to lane's end opened.

Families called out of kitchen glow of light and warmth, 'God go with ye, good luck, safe home!'

When I could venture to look back I saw her and the old man walking together through doorway light. She was bowing and smiling like a celebrity on parade. He was carrying the seedlings in their tins.

On more and roomier sills of windows more generous with light she tended her tin-can garden throughout the winter, but I think that from Christmas onward she watched through the windows for the spring. Back of the house she saw fields swell in a green wave to foam along the skyline into firs. The air was full of free birds' wings. The air itself felt free, it seemed to have hinted to her about spring even before the trees or the fields or the birds showed awareness of it. Anyhow she was out one morning in the back plot with a digging fork where there was a skim of frost tinselled in sun that had only lit to boast about.

Again it was in that hour between the old man's departure for work and ours for school. Small-spare in the quarter-acre she picked at the hard earth like a robin at a crust in the schoolyard. Her palms let down her willpower in that first day but she had done enough for the old man to notice the bird scratch on the alligator hide of our domain. He was always suspicious of her motives in these displays of industry, especially in departments where he felt she must have known how futile her own attempts must be. He never could decide how much honest effort went into the work and how much was stage-setting for intimidation to stalk on and leer up at his place in the gods.

To be on the safe side he staged a show of his own: champing, tossing his head at the roof, roaring murder to the rafters, then blaspheming his way to a door-bang exit for the fork to the tool shed to dig between dinner and dark of that evening—and every evening after he pickaxed and forked in that plot till the crows flapped home to their rookeryring of beeches. So when spring came down the hill of fields she was there in the torn earth, intimidating with a young tree in each hand, the empty distemper tins beside the cast-off work boots of the old man.

I can't recall how many springs went by before the men of the house realized that the way of God with trees was wonderful after all. She had known before us that her forlorn-looking hopes had bole and branch and leaf. Her worry had been that never in any spring had the trees held blossoms and never in autumn were there apples to pick. Every spring she had watched, but for every summer there were only leaf for every autumn to wither.

Her garden otherwise was all that a garden should be. Cabbages, carrots, parsnips, radishes, rhubarb, thyme; currants like drops of claret and sherry and currants black as pitch blobs; gooseberries green and bitter, gooseberries red and amber and kind; raspberries, strawberries, melons and parsley thronged from the earth to her. All of them travelled with her in baskets to market to keep the shillings rolling dollarwards in the bank for the house. The shilling that came home with her travelled back on other days to pay for each term of mine as a day-boy in the town's seminary and out of town once a week to Kevin, who had got a scholarship to a college a train-day journey up country.

Hardly a root stirred in the earth without her knowing. Cat-like she watched for weeds and pounced on them, bearing them away by the apron-ful to dump under the privet hedge where cats slumbered with one eye awake for other quarry. With the slumbering cats' quietness of pleasure she saw the colour of the crops richen between soil and stalk and stem and leaf. But always, I think, there was one dreaming eye on the apple trees, and year by year the dream was chilling in it.

Then one Saturday afternoon, when the garden was prostrate in autumnal dying and the trees humped in a tattered shroud of withering, the old man stood at the kitchen back window looking out at them, kindling his pipe, smoke oozing about the hat he had on for the road to a pub with pay-day substance. Without moving his gaze from the garden he said: 'I see the Yanks are yet to come?'

The flat-iron slowed to a stop on his shirt for Mass in the morning. Still looking at the kitchen tabletop she said with careful carelessness: 'I know that well.'

'I wonder is it how the haggart isn't grand enough for 'em?'

'The trees weren't too grand to grow in it.'

'Like hens without eggs, only we could eat the hens.'

'And use the trees for firing,' she countered.

'Green burning,' he gave back, going to the front door. 'Is there any-thing you want from town?'

'You home early and sober,' she told him.

He laughed and closed the door. She finished her ironing without a word, cleared the table and then went to look out the window. I was greasing the leather of a football boot out of washboard curl and stiffness.

'I wonder why the trees don't bear fruit, Michael?' she asked me with-out turning.

'I don't know,' I said.

With that the old man returned to the doorway.

'Do you know where Tommy Cronin lives, Mick? I couldn't know his pub because he never takes a wet, but you knock around with his son?'

He went when I told him where Tommy lived. I wondered at his clos-ing the door as if there was a child to wake with the sound of the lock. But in the feel of the silence he left after him I knew why. She was at the core of it, and my gaze was drawn by it to her. Her stillness might have had no breathing in it, so still she stood, yet the silence it summoned to her had unease. Hers was the blank back of a woman in a moment when she relin-quishes yet another illusion to leak away from her in tears. When she turned there were no tears but I caught her unawares by the look I had not time to take away from her. She winced at it, recovered instantly, but what she meant for a smile of not-caring ended in one of never-mind.

Without a word she went through the pantry into the yard. I heard her poking in the tool shed. I took a turn at the window myself, in time to see her walk up the centre path of the garden toward the apple trees, standing together in an oval green patch halfway up. Her hands were held in front of her. Her back had lost anonymity now, as when the belief relinquished makes room for a belief less easy to give home to. She looked who she was, but not quite what she had been, somehow.

When she was some paces from the oval she paused for an instant, then she walked on purposefully and went sidewise on her knees beside the right-hand tree. With a sweep she rasped the teeth of a saw through tender bark to blossom-white pith of the young tree and sawed till the shock head bowed inch by inch, to collapse in a sigh of near spent leaves onto the ground. When she stepped over the stump toward the comrade tree I felt I should persuade her to stop, without quite knowing why. I was in the act of moving when she paused in the act of kneeling. She straightened slowly and looked intently from the lowest to the highest branch of that remaining tree. Then she let the saw fall from her hand, stood on for another moment and walked back quickly towards the house.

I schooled my impulse to look up from the boots when she arrived in the kitchen. Between the laying of a saucer and a cup she paused.

'I cut one of the trees, Michael,' she said. Before I could comment she ran on with: 'I was going to cut the other but I felt that the patch would be bare without something in it.' She paused again, the pause of an instant, then she added: 'Wouldn't that be the thing?'

'Just so,' I said, without any inflection whatever.

There was a longer pause then, as if my saying of my say left the situation wholly hers again.

'What would you like for tea, Michael?' she asked me suddenly, and I felt as if she were home from a journey.

That evening, on plea of a football club meeting, I got away to fourpenny hop in the Old Town Hall. The evening felt as if winter was near enough to have chilled it with the breath of cold that I could feel at the open neck of my shirt. I had gone several hundred yards when I heard her calling my name. When I turned she was running towards me with my mackintosh. The manner of her running made me see how worn-out-of-time she was going. The heart shape of her face was that of an old heart now and in the folds of loose flesh under her chin I could see the pulse beats of an old heart floundering in her breathlessness.

'Those meeting rooms are draughty, Michael, and there is quite a cold out this evening. Better wear your coat.'

I was about to refuse it when I remembered I had in mind to lure a harpie from the dance and that the coat would be handy. I took the coat. 'Goodbye now, Michael,' she said as if we had not met for a year and would not meet again for another.

On her way back to the house she paused to wave to me but after the second occasion I looked back no more.

The harpie delayed me longer than I bargained for, and I walked home under a mooned midnight, bright as a wan-gone noon. The key was in the front-door lock and I let myself into the hall without a sound. My hand was on the kitchen light switch when I saw her shape between me and the smouldering fire. I switched on the light. Wearing what had been a rich blue dressing gown, gold roped on the edges—the last remaining item of her American trousseau—now gone to fadedness, she sat slippered in the old man's armchair in front of the fire. She turned to look at me intently, her hair hanging loose about her face from a shoestring on her nape.

'Michael, this is no hour for a seminary boy to come home. What would the priests say if they knew of it?'

'The meeting was heated and lasted longer than anyone thought,' I lied.

'Besides, 'tis after twelve and you can't have supper, going to Communion in the morning.'

'I'm not hungry,' I said.

'And your father has not come home yet. Drinking money that we could do with to hold house and home where he is the only wage-earner, while I run myself to rags to keep up appearances in ye. 'Tis at the point now that one week of idleness for him and disaster faces all my hopes.'

The banging of the front gate and a lurched step signalled the old man's coming in his cups. Slurring of footsoles on concrete told of effort to find balance before facing the four steps and the pathway to the door.

'Come quickly. Leave the light on or he'll brain himself. If he finds you here there'll be questions about where you were.'

She pulled me by the arm after her up the stairs. We were hardly on the landing before he fell in at the door. She held me until he had picked himself up, telling himself to steady up, let there be no panic, woman and children first and God for us all. Without question of the light in the kitchen he sidestepped into it in a half keel-over that ended in the slap of his palm against the hob to keep from falling again. When the chair-joints screeched under his sudden weight she relaxed her grip on my wrist. She firmed it again in reassurance, put a finger to her lips and tiptoed to her room. I followed suit to mine.

Moonlight through the open window had transformed it into a place of grace like a mendicant's cell. A moth fluttering upstream towards the moon's face was ivory white as a prayer of grace underway might be. When I thought of the harpie, the thought felt like a stain but I brought it with me to the ivory moth in the moonlight and looked out the window. I felt I was fighting that pure fierce light with my life for repossession of a room that had been mine, and that the harpie was merely a spectator at the struggle, leering-luring with her eyes for my eyes under a loop of her oil-heavy hair. Moonlight was focused direct upon the earth, with such intensity that the butt of the cut tree showed like a bleached wound in the withered garden.

A chair crashed in the kitchen and the old man's unsteady steps sounded through the pantry. The back door banged open. The steps stumbled across the yard and presently I could see him hatless at the garden gate. Up the centre path he went, his head huddled in his left shoulder-blade, his left hand straight out, like a punch-drunk has-been of the ring reliving in perpetuity the moment before the final crash to canvas. When he was four paces from the trees he stopped in his tracks. After a long pause the outstretched hand counted one-two, one-two where the comrade trees should have been: then one, and one again it counted, then it wove a nought over the fallen tree. He was talking aloud but I could not hear what he was saying.

He blundered up to the rooted tree and gripped a branch. Holding on with one hand he groped in his pocket with the other. What he removed from the pocket was recognizable when the two hands came to play on it and a blade flashed for an instant in the moonlight. His pocket-knife. Head down he butted through the lower branches of the tree to the bole. Then round the bole slowly, carefully he groped, his right hand obviously working on it all the time.

When he had come full circle he shadow-boxed down the garden to the house again, face swollen, eyes glazed, to make the punch-drunk likeness nearer true than ever. Through the house he barged without closing a door; up the stairs and into their room.

'What the hell happened up there?' he shouted in the room doorway.

'Up where?' she asked, coolly and firm.

'Woman, I said!'

'What now?'

'That tree!'

'Oh, I cut it down with the saw.'

'What did you do that for?'

'Why shouldn't I?'

'Why should you?'

'Up to now 'twas you supplied all the reasons for that. The Yanks are coming. Dump the old weeds. A hen without eggs.'

That last gave him pause. Sufficient for her to run in explanation: 'Trees without fruit have no place in that garden. Fruit would sell and we need all we can sell with our purse the way it is and our commitments the way they are.'

'Was that what you were thinking when you saved the seeds and planted 'em?'

'Times have changed.'

'And who the hell changed 'em?'

'I did. And 'tis up to me to see to it, as far as I can, that the change is for the better.'

'By God, 'tis mighty practical you got of a sudden.'

'I'm practical now, yes.'

'Full-blown practical.'

'Yes, I have to be.'

'Then why didn't you cut down the second tree?'

After a pause she said: 'Come to bed and don't disgrace us with that shouting.'

'I'll shout all I like, when I like, how I like and where I like.'

'Come to bed.'

'Listen, woman,' he shouted, 'leave that second tree.'

I lay on the bed for a while, hearing his voice drone on in querulousness, then drowsiness, then it was lost into silence and snoring. I went down to close the doors. At the back door, curiosity got the better of me and I went up the garden to the apple tree. A band of bark was cut with surprising neatness from the bole at the point where he had used the knife. I wondered why. Then I remembered that the Tommy Cronin he had enquired about last evening was by way of being a gardener.

From that I guessed correctly that, by what seemed to me like rule of thumb, he had performed a grafting operation on the barren tree. I never told him I knew about it. She neither knew nor noticed that it had been done.

She had other things to occupy her mind. Christmas ended the best of winter in beginning a period of idleness for the old man. She dreaded idleness for many reasons, he for one special reason, his inability to live without working. Signing at the Labour Exchange hurt his dignity in craft and taking the palm-ful of silver every Friday seemed to him like cadging, doing Judas on his principles.

He would return from signing with a paper in his pocket and read slowly through patched-up spectacles, rising to pace the kitchen, window to window, when his eyes got tired of a combination of bad glasses and unlovely print.

Noticeable in particular was the restlessness of his squat strong hands. Again and again he would anchor them with his thumbs to his leather belt but always they broke free to poke for a pipe he could not light that often on short tobacco, to grope in trousers pocket for coin that was not there, to punish each other's leathern palms with prominent knuckles or plunder a matchbox for stems to chew to ease his craving for tobacco. His hands seemed to live a life of their own in a period like that. They were of him but not quite with him, like gun dogs fidgeting about the master's heels on a day when hills held promise for the hunt.

She made much to-do with little and less to do with. She whipped lean meals to lively mealtimes with rush and bustle in the making. Her bustle irritated him because he was missing the customary pint off the neck of the bottle before drawing his chair to table. His careful pacing between the windows irritated her because it seemed to knell the futility of her make-believe when the meals were met by hunger. They snapped at each other when their minds met, then they stood on opposite sides of a palpable silence. Buff bank envelopes cut with elegant edge to the heart of the matter at intervals. Then the wedding-present silver and the mantel clock and her American gold watch travelled with her to the pawnshop. In the lane she would have had her dollars to draw on. In crop time she would have had baskets for market. Now there was an arid garden and in the centre a barren tree.

Until spring. Spring's first flowering showed on her geraniums. Tending them eased odd hours for her between house chores and questing visits to chapel. Spring brought the fork to the old man's hands and they drove it into the earth, with a will for the job that in time of craft they had done with contumely. Spring brought sun to the sills, song to the silence, growth to the soil and leaves to the apple tree.

Spring brought her into the garden to plant while he prepared the ground ahead of her. In the first days she looked at the leafing tree when she entered the garden. She did that every day, until the third or fourth day after leafing was complete, and the tree looked as if it had given all it could to the year and was content. I can say that with certainty because, in guise of study at the window of my room, I brooded on how I was going to ease over to her the fact that I was not going on for the priesthood; my reason for going to the seminary in the first place and her strongest wish.

I was at the window on the morning that the tree had blossom for the sun, a white froth of blossom broken by the leaves so it looked like the lace on a surplice, a garland for a bride, a quilt for a marriage bed.

The old man had seen it first because he was in the garden before I came to the window. She came into the garden with an apron of seed potatoes, dragging the loose boots. Propped by the handle of the spade in his armpit the old man watched her as she moved along the drill spacing the seed, her cloth-bound head bowing towards the tree. Seeing me at the window the old man nodded at the tree and beckoned me down. When I arrived in the garden her unconsciously ceremonial, ritual-like bows in the spacing of the seed had brought her blue-clothed head under the white blossom. She put seed in the last place, put her hands on the small of her back to help her straighten. Her head touched a branch of blossom as it raised, then the branch flicked before her like a wand and she was looking at the transformed tree. Her body tensed. She stood staring at the tree without expression for several seconds. Then, 'Oh, oh, oh,' she whispered. Then hardly above a whisper, 'Oh, oh, oh God, isn't it lovely!'

Her face broke on all its lines into a smile. Her eyes brightened slowly from glow to real brightness. The leftover potato seed dropped on her boots and she was walking into the tree. She walked right on into the bole. She cupped her palms about the slim stem.

'Michael, Dad! Look at my tree, look at my tree!' she called.

'The Yanks are here at last,' said the old man.

'Oh, God, isn't it lovely?' she cried.

With a smile she emerged out of the tree looking straight at the old man.

'Now didn't I tell you I would have a fruiting tree,' she said.

He said: 'Wonders will never cease,' then he began to smooth the earth over the drill of new-set potato seed. Before she could turn her smile towards me I walked down the garden, away from both of them.

The More We Are Together

The brothers were the last two coopers left in that town.

Other crafts were going: theirs was gone. Now they got a few pocket-warm shillings from farmers for repairing things they had made years ago. Mick, with a head full of reading at his beck (Shakespeare, Service and the Bible were all the one as long as they came under candlelight without cost) was apt to dramatize their position. Charlie would tell him to have a bit of sense, if he would spare the words. The two lived together in the narrowest lane in that town, in a house so small that even under-sized Mick looked big in it and Charlie looked like a heron in a hencoop.

Charlie looked like a heron anywhere. Long and lean and droop-nosed, eye-weary with boredom even in a pub, when he stood he drew one leg up till the flat of a thin sole against wall, bar or lamp post braced the cushion of the calf for the right buttock: then his stubbled craw collapsed into a loop of neck band, hands dug into trouser pockets, elbows hugged the shelter of his withers, a Woodbine hung limp from his sad mouth like a sprat from the beak of the bird he resembled. He spoke when he had to speak, but mostly he used a high sweet whistle of a tune for ironic com-ment on things about him. Although he grudged life every step he gave to it he would walk any distance in the funeral of a man he liked. He was never known to walk in the funeral of a woman.

Mick was partial to women, but his square chunk of body on short legs and the music-hall humour of his face never prompted their love sense to sacrifice, and hard times to his trade estranged their sense of good business. In the wind-up he drew consolation from their nearness passing in the narrow lane. His small blue-bright eyes signalled his moods as far in daylight as a cat's eyes show at night. They told if he was liquored and ready for a spate on the passing away of the old stock, probing for doubtful beginnings to a new townsman or romancing about all the comely women who had loved and lost him up the laneway to Charlie.

The under half of the house was their workshop, its floor a good twelve inches above the cobbled lane level with whole generations of coopers' chips and shavings. In a deep poke of window in the back wall was a statue of Our Lady and a corkscrew. Over the workshop was the loft, where they slept on two beds in two whorls of old clothes. A ladder led to the loft and it was when Charlie was one night climbing the ladder that Mick first noticed he was having trouble with his left leg.

'What's up with you?' Mick asked.

'My leg,' Charlie gave back on two darts of a Woodbine.

'I know 'tis your leg, man,' said Mick.

'Then you know as much as I do,' said Charlie.

Lying on the doss that night Mick lighted a second pipeful of twist. The smoke plumed up out of murk to full whiteness in a splinter of moonlight from a chink in the slates. Charlie's head lay in the light, his face becalmed in sleep. The candle, stuck with its own grease to the bed above Mick's head, was not lighted that night for reading.

2

Down in the workshop in the morning, boiling a can of water in the oil stove, Mick talked up through the hole where the ladder reached the loft.

'Charleen! Charleen, I said!'

'I can't hear you,' said Charlie, half out of sleep.

'Why so, man?'

'I don't want to.'

'Why so, man?'

'Guess away.'

'Charleen! Charleen, I said!'

'Well?'

'What about the leg, Charleen?'

'What about the cup of tay?'

'Will you see a doctor?'

'In hell with the rest.'

'If I was you I would, man,' Mick ventured.

'You're not me,' said Charlie.

Mick jambed his hat down to an inch above his eyebrows. He allowed a pause, then tried again.

'Charleen!'

'Go to hell.'

'About the leg.'

'That's what I mean.'

'I was looking at you last night ... You were asleep. There was moon light through the hole above my left ear slantin' ... You were pinned by the light like Saint Paul near Damascus ... You made such a spittin' image of a corpse that I smoked half the night over it ... Maybe if you don't see a doctor we'll play the piece out in rale earnest—will you see a doctor?'

'No,' Charlie grunted at last.

'Then I'm as well layin' in the tobaccy and drink?'

'You're as well.'

'Then come down and wet your own bloody tay!' Mick shouted up through the hole.

But he thought of opening the door in time to see the women from Mass.

3

The leg got worse. Charlie's heron-perch against uprights became as much necessity as the habit of years. Climbing the ladder was as difficult sober as ever it had been in drink. Mick heckled him from all angles without success. In time the night came when Charlie could not climb the ladder at all. He tried drawing himself up the stilts of the ladder with his arms. He failed because the old strength had all but left him. He crouched to sit on the third rung, lit a Woodbine and looked up to find Mick's shadow between him and the doorway of starlight. With the slightly swaying shadow had come the smell of drink. There was derision in the croon of Mick's voice when he spoke.

'Home is the sailor, home from sea,' he quoted. 'Home for good an' all,' he added, circling a finger in the air towards Charlie.

'When the sailor can't climb the riggin' his sailin' days are done. He didn't make off the ould medicine chest in time. Or throw the bottle overboard in time. So now the stars will sail without him … and gulls will bring their cards to him a mile inshore.'

Charlie's strong tugs at the fag put little haloes of warm light about his head that found his face unmoved.

"Tis a grand night for a man with two legs,' he said.

Mick rocked, toppled and went out of sight to the shavings.

'If he could stand on 'em,' Charlie added.

From where Mick lay came a stirring of shavings, the jerk of a breath as he heaved himself to sitting, then the voice crooning: 'Joke away, Charleen, split the ould sides with choked laughin' at boozed Mick but remember … Remember, Charleen, remember, my man, that Mick will be game ball in the mornin' …'

In a high sweet whistle Charlie began 'After the Ball Was Over'. Mick shook himself for the rattle of his matches. He lighted a match to find the pocket with his pipe. The match dropped from his hand and lit an oak chip. The chip flared and passed the flame to chips near it, all seasoned with years of shelter. In a minute there was a small steady blaze and the sweet smell of mellow wood burning. Hat askew, Mick gaped at the firm growing blaze. Of a sudden his eyes widened and brightened in the rising light with a wild, unuttered laughter. The quick jog of a thought enlivened the body. He tensed inside his loose hand-me-down clothes and rose to his feet to teeter about the workshop, grabbing and groping for bits and pieces of solid timber, piling them on the strengthening blaze from the floor. He began to shout wide-mouthed, snapping at the words with his stained teeth.

'I know now what we'll do, Captain. We'll burn the ould ship in dry dock, Captain, and go from sight and sound in a blaze of glory. No creepin' to death and crawlin' to graves for the last of the coopers. O Merciful God, that thought of this for us! O Merciful God, to save our face!

We'll go out on our legs! Out on our legs we'll go, Charleen, and the strangers round us dazzled by the blaze! Charleen, Captain, stand up and give me a hand with the glory, lend me a hand for the blazin' way home! Charleen!'

Charlie never stirred. He lit a second smoke from the end of the first. By this time Mick's shadow was large on the wall, dancing with Mick who danced with the flames, his voice kindling with the rising heat into round after round of mad merriment, louder and stronger. In the middle of it all he thought of the oil stove. He unscrewed the cap of the oil container and flung paraffin to burst above the blaze into sickles of hissing flame.

'Climb!' he shouted. 'Climb to the roof, ye sweet bitches of flame. Climb! Burn! Burn and roast us out of here forever more! Charleen, come and stand with me, opposite them out we'll stand together and laugh! They thought they were great coming to take our town away from us and our living away from us and our women away from us! Charleen, come here and cock your game leg in their foolish bloody stranger faces—and we'll laugh! Laugh, Charleen!'

The flames were licking the boards of the loft when the first of the townspeople arrived with buckets of water from the lane pump. Mick raved and cursed and got in their way till they lifted him kicking out of the place. Out in the lane his ravings followed the bucket chain from pump to house and back again, over and over. They grew in abandon as the fire was gapped with water and thick shrouds of smoke wound about each dancing shape of flame. When the last flame fell under weight of water he stopped shouting. He went limp as if the fire had been a part of the demon in him. The small house hissed in its walls like a shower on sheet water and belched great clouds of smelling smoke through the doorway.

Suddenly Mick's body shuddered. It straightened itself quietly and slowly as with a long-drawn breath. Then suddenly his wide mouth opened full out and sharp as a dog's bark he cried—'Charleen!' He began to run towards the house thudding people right and left off his road and shouting—'Charleen!' But as he got to the house the heron-spare length of Charlie brought the game leg leisurely through the doorway. His clothes were sodden with flung water. His face and hands were as black as a sweep's. Mick blundered up, gripped his shoulders and shouted to his face as if it were up among the stars: 'Are you all right, Charleen? Are you all right, boy?'

'The least you might have done was to wet the cup of tay,' said Charlie.

4

They spent the night sitting by the hearth of the only old stock neighbour left to them: Mick drained of strength and sore for liquor, Charlie's sick bones craving heat through wet clothes from a fading fire. Charlie was still smoking when Mick nodded off in the small hours.

When Mick woke the first splink of cold dawn at the window showed him Charlie's long-drawn body limp in sleep over the chair. He had to fight an urge to listen for his brother's breathing. Sense arrived in time to remind him what Charlie would put into a few words if he opened an eye and found him fussing. Then memory had the firing antic ready for him: when he blasphemed a thick tongue disturbed the coat of wryness in his mouth. He went to grope for milk in the stale-smelling cupboard. He found enough to cool his mouth and leave a drop for the breakfast crust. Then he moved towards the door and tripped over a potato sack on the floor. He thought of a use for the sack: it would keep the dawn cold from Charlie's sick leg. He had the sack raised over the leg when a doubt about the depth of Charlie's sleep again unnerved him. Charlie could put a lot into a few words. A fire in the hearth would do, he thought. A timber cat-box of straw against the hob would kindle and spit sparks at a touch of a match. But Charlie would remember the last match he struck. Charlie might open an eye. Charlie could put a lot into a few words.

He stood over Charlie's face, grey and drawn in the white weak light, and glared down at it.

'If you die of the cold you can blame your own bloody self,' he hissed.

Then he went and raised the latch with care and let himself onto the narrow lane.

Going to the small house now was like easing his way back to a near one he had offended during a skite on whiskey: like nearing the mother's presence knowing he had broken the last of her marriage teacups in a drunken tantrum. There was the silence, the meeting side-face, the wait-ing of each for a sign from the other that it was all in a life and could go to the dead day that brought it. But unlike the old mother the small house gave no sign. He felt that maybe it was whatever of the mother was left in the house that gave no sign. He told himself to hell with that too. Still he stood there between the night and day in the narrow place, looking lost, until full daylight sent the dregs of night away and the presence lifted from inside the walls. Then he chucked at the hat for courage and hummed his way into what was left of the workshop.

The carpet of chips and shavings had a great black hole in it. The steel of the tools lay in the hole, where bench and boxes and handles had left them in the fire. Metal hoops lay where the old barrel or firkin had been, or the tubs that farmers' wives had used to wash for the family or stall-feed a beast. Against one wall a hole was burned in the loft and a leg of Mick's bed stuck through. The ladder and Charlie had been farthest from the flames: the ladder still was there, leading to the loft. As he surveyed the damage a thought about the loft came to Mick. It sent him searching till he located a handsaw. He gave a grunt of satisfaction that enough of the handle was there to grip it.

He took off his jacket and hung it on the door latch. First he cleared the litter from the floor onto the lane cobbles. Then he journeyed up and down the ladder until he had rid the loft of all on it, from the pair of beds to the ha'penny candle. That done he returned into the workshop with the saw.

Three spars of timber, embedded in the stone of the side walls, supported the loft. Because a board was missing on either side the spars were clear for sawing where they met the walls. Standing on the ladder he sawed the centre spar free. Next he sawed the spar-shanks in the opposite blind angles. The loft still held above his head. Then he tackled the shank in the angle opposite the open door. Here he had to be careful that the ladder braced the corner of the loft when the saw had cut through. He backed slowly towards the doorway, easing the ladder with its burden down the wall. The loft now listed above him. Only the corner near the door held a grip on the house. Bracing it in turn with the ladder he sawed it free. Then he stepped onto the lane and jerked the ladder through the doorway after him. The loft fell to the ground, and there and then was a floor of boards.

Straight away he reassembled the beds in the workshop and put the

litter from the lane into order inside. That done he sat on his bed to wait
for Charlie. But the day aged without Charlie's coming. Mick went and
dogged the sunlight through hour after hour, from street to street, gable
to gable: knowing Charlie's custom in an idle day. When the sun had set
he searched the pubs, without result. Night came down in a drizzle of
mist. Globules of the mist on the leaf of Mick's hat glistened in the lane
gaslight as he returned to the shelter of the house.

He was in an hour before Charlie limped up the narrow way, the long
body crow-black against the silver the gaslight made out of wet cobbles.
When he stooped in at the doorway the quiet light of the ha'penny dip was
all the welcome he got. Mick was stretched on his bed, the hat on his face,
his bald crown airing. Charlie abandoned his exhaustion to the bed opposite and lit another fag. There was a long silence before Mick raised the
hat off his mouth.

'Well?' he challenged.

'Well?' Charlie gave back.

'What the hell were you doin' all day?'

'Makin' up my mind to see a doctor,' said Charlie.

'And where were you all night?'

'Seein' wan.'

Mick lay quiet for a while. Then he tilted the hat off the near eye and
fixed Charlie with a glare.

'What the hell did he say, man, what did he say, tell us that much!'

Charlie took his time. Mick's barrel chest filled with a long breath.

'That I'll not do a long journey on two legs, but I might go a bit farther on one,' said Charlie.

Mick let the breath out easy. He let the hat fall back on his face. There
was another silence before he spoke from under it.

'Well, wan leg is better than no leg at all,' he said.

'I'd rather the short journey,' said Charlie.

'What do you mane?'

'When I lave I'll lave all in wan piece.'

'You must have it in your mind to lave early,' said Mick.

'All in wan piece,' Charlie repeated amicably.

Suddenly Mick jerked to a tailor squat on the heap of old clothes. The
hat fell in his lap. Tufts of hair stood out over his temples. The whites of

his eyes looked genuinely clean against dark stubble and the prickles of a black moustache. The eyes glared at Charlie.

'Why all in wan piece, tell me?'

''Tis what any wan of them would have done.'

'Who's them?'

'Your old stock.'

'Through bloody ignorance,' said Mick. 'I know the story backwards. Better die of what ails you than own it and admit it as a weakness in the blood. Ignorance, I say.'

'We're ignorant people,' said Charlie.

'Not all of us,' said Mick.

Charlie stretched his hand to make an arc of smoke with the Woodbine that for an instant linked the two beds.

'The half of what's left of us is,' he said.

'I won't argue with you,' said Mick. 'I'll spare my breath to blow froth, or whistle for a woman in a lonesome night.'

As another silence settled Charlie pierced it with a thin ironic whistle of a lovely air. The irony was in the beauty of his rendering. The tune was 'She Moved Through the Fair' and Mick was caught in the imagery of its words: the young girl went from him through the country fair and away along a lakeside homeward under one star—until the irony went home to him and he hit back like a goaded animal.

'You're as ignorant as all the obstinate ould codgers that went before us,' he said.

'What do their ignorance matter to them now?' asked Charlie.

'It don't matter to them,' said Mick, 'but it do matter to us. They left us a legacy in a way of life it would puzzle a hermit to follow. Nothin' would do 'em but principle. They must have slept it, ate it and used it for firin'. Honesty was the best policy. A good day's work for a beggar's pay an' the rest was in the hands of the Good God Above. What did principle give 'em?'

'They could meet themselves in the mornin' shavin',' Charlie answered.

'What did honesty give 'em?'

'Sleep of a night.'

'And from the hands of the Good God Above?'

'The five of trumps in the last card dealt.'

'Aye, but sometimes you'd wonder if there's damn all in the "kitty",' growled Mick.

He rose, hat in hand, to pace the boards between the two beds. Suddenly he wheeled on Charlie.

'What I can't understand is why you feel you owe it to them to die sooner than you can help,' he said.

'What do extra time mean in the wind-up?' asked Charlie.

Mick gave the answer in a breath.

'A few times more to blow froth. A few times more to covet a young girl well made under the gloss of her white pelt. A few times more to tell the stranger to his face that he's no good.'

'A few times more to hold forth in praise of the old stock,' Charlie reminded.

'Oh, may God forgive me,' Mick prayed.

'As two of 'em we lived,' Charlie reminded.

''Tis time for a change,' Mick argued.

'Change before death,' smiled Charlie.

Mick jambed the hat on his head and flung open the door. The rain was falling fast and heavy now. It pounded the cobbles so that their silver leaped like a meshful of moonlit fish.

'O God, is it any wonder that sooner and later the sky has a leak on all the bloody world!' he called aloud into the lane.

5

The burning of the house brought problems they had not bargained for. Neither house nor workshop was insured. Property not theirs was burned and the code of their kind took for granted that the owners should be compensated. More customers were needed with tubs and firkins to mend.

They prepared by whittling handles for the damaged tools and edging the steel on whetstones wetted with spittle. The beds with their tatters were rolled against the back wall and hidden from callers with a patchwork of old sacking on thick twine. In the new sleeping place the statue of Our Lady, coomed with untroubled dust as soft as moth wings, came into its own in time of candlelight.

No further clients came their way. For four days the two appeared and

disappeared through the parting in the canvas curtains, like two actors of
the fit-up stage impatient for the arrival of an audience: Mick, a blubber-
faced comic in trouble with remembering his lines; Charlie, the tragedian
rehearsing a limp and limbering a selection from his store of smiles. After
that much waiting the comic downed tools.

'Charleen.'

'Well?'

'For all we'd know, stayin' here, the world might be dead.'

'Or we might be dead to the world,' said Charlie.

'Well either we or the world must find out, an' I see no sign of the
world flockin' to the door,' Mick said. 'There's only three days to market
day an' then the rustics will be in to moan over their few relics like they
were gold. Be the holy, talkin' to their big fed bodies with their warm fat
purses I feel like a corpse with the pennies on my lids. What'll we do at all?'

Charlie's answer was a whistle. The tune had run its course before
Mick recognized it as a comment, and only then because in his mind the
air was wedded to its words:

> *The more we are together, together, together,*
> *The more we are together the merrier we will be:*
> *For your friends are my friends*
> *And my friends are your friends,*
> *So the more we are together the merrier we will be.*

Mick flung his hat on the floor and kicked it.

'Put a string on the whistle,' he said. 'What'll we do about the long
faces from the fields?'

'There's three days before us,' said Charlie.

'An' three centuries behind us that ended with the fire,' said Mick in
a breath. ''Tis no use. Ah, can't you see 'tis no use. When the smell of the
craft went out of the house the craft went with it and all the soul of the
craftsmen, damned or saved, sad or merry. All they thought and felt and
fought for, all they lived and hoped for, all the sport they ever had and all
the memories of all they did at work or in drink: 'tis all gone now with the
smell of the shavin's. An' the ghosts of their women rose in the smoke: all
but my mother—an' she only delayed long enough to give me the back of
her hand. By my soul, there in the middle of the new mornin' she gave me

the cold creeps for burnin' the house.'

Charlie merely smiled.

'What'll we do about the rustic demand-notes?' Mick challenged.

'Sell the house,' said Charlie without a pause.

'Oh, then, begod, the mother will be back,' Mick said.

'Maybe she left the thought here before goin',' Charlie told him.

'Who'd buy it?' asked Mick.

'Them with shops in the street below.'

'For what use?'

'You should know that,' said Charlie.

'I never bothered my neck with home matters,' Mick defended himself.

'Stripped of their insides, houses like this are handy for stores,' Charlie explained.

'An' we can perch like a thrush on a hawthorn bush, I suppose?'

'We'll sell it on condition that it shelters us while we need shelter.'

'Will they buy it that way?'

'Half the houses in the lane are bought that way,' said Charlie.

6

'Come away!' said Mick, making for the door.

They got twenty pounds for the house. Five pounds satisfied the owners of the burned articles. Drink took the rest inside ten days. On the morning of the tenth day Charlie raised himself out of a stupor, stood, swayed and fell face forward onto Mick's bed. Mick straightened him where he lay, listened at the sad mouth for breathing, felt for heartbeats in the big-boned vault of the chest. Satisfied that he was alive, Mick began to call in his ear and shake him at the shoulders, till Charlie stirred of his own accord. His eyes opened and humour gathered in them, taking time.

'I heard you over the way,' he told Mick.

'It must be wan hell of a distance,' Mick mumbled. 'How are you now?'

'Like I came back to know what time it was.'

'Time for a doctor.'

'Not till after nightfall,' said Charlie.

Mick stayed with him through the day, now and again brewing cups of tea for him in the battered tin on the recovered oil stove: not talking much and hardly being spoken to at all. He waited until night seeped in at the small window and settled in the crannies before he lit the candle. Then he went for the doctor.

The doctor, a young man in a hurry, had no reason to delay with his opinion. He took Mick aside and told him it was a matter of where he wished that his brother should die.

'How long will it be?' Mick asked.

'Longer than you can look after him here,' the doctor told him. 'Weeks, a month maybe.'

The doctor also knew his people.

'Look here,' he added, 'I can get him a bed. I can't get him into hospital on the ticket. His being an incurable will mean ...'

'I know, I know,' Mick cut in. He added: 'Do you mind goin' as far as the door, doctor, till I have a word with himself?'

The doctor went to the door as Mick returned inside the sacking. Mick walked up and down a few times, raking the boards with the look of offence in his small peevish eyes, as if the floor had swallowed his last threepenny bit. He sat on his bed and poked for the pipe inside the lining of his jacket. He frowned at the pipe as if he blamed it for hiding. He bit viciously on the chewed stem and lit a match. The match paused on the way to the pipe head. The match burned out in his fingers. He lit another match and lighted the tobacco with it in the leisurely way of the lead-up to a drink: the hurt had left his eyes.

'I suppose I'll have to poke out a supply of smokes for you first thing in the mornin',' he said. 'You'll want them in ... that place.'

'Oh ... that place,' echoed Charlie, with Mick's emphasis on the two words.

Mick spoke at length then, from a quick opening gradually taking time and sparing breath.

'We went there with my mother wan time, you remember. We were young lads, and she was young in her Sunday clothes. 'Twas a great thing to feel Sunday clothes in the middle of the week, or any ordinary day. She took us there that day: we were young and she was young herself in a Sunday bonnet and coat. She had a basket of things, with oranges on top. We wanted to do for so many of the oranges that she asked us was it we were sick or the neighbour in ... that place.'

'That place ...' said Charlie.

''Tis quare how you remember a thing,' said Mick. 'I remember she saying that day: it was a fine sunny day the way it is in my mind now—I remember she sayin' an' the sun shinin' on the world that it didn't matter; that it didn't matter at all that the old stock neighbour would go the rest of the way in that place. 'Tisn't where, but how, that matters, she told us. Then she put a smilin' eye on me an' said: "The thing is, not to finish in jail, of course." Thinkin' she saw me stealin' that other orange, I put it back. And she laughed out. And we laughed. We all laughed together. Then she gave us an orange each and said that was the last now, and no more: not to spoil the clane white collars now, and no more. 'Tis quare how you remember a thing.'

'The doctor is waitin' at the door,' Charlie reminded.

'Oh, be damned, yes,' said Mick.

He got to his feet, but he did not move away. After a pause he walked as far as the sacking.

'I suppose I'll tell him,' he said.

'I suppose,' said Charlie. 'Tell him that as a doctor he's a sound judge.'

Mick joined the doctor at the door.

'That'll be all right, doctor,' he said.

'I'll phone the ambulance and have him removed straight away,' the doctor decided. 'I can fill in the red tape in the morning.'

'Fill it in tonight, doctor,' Mick told him. 'An' while you're at it fill out a form for me. You know the names. He's Charlie, I'm Mick. I'll call for mine tonight.'

'For—' the doctor began.

'That place,' said Mick.

With the last threepenny bit snuggled in the right peak of his waistcoat he followed the doctor down the lane and bought Charlie a packet of smokes for the road.

7

When the ambulance came Mick held the door of the house open for the driver and his helper to pass out with the prostrate Charlie on the stretcher. When Charlie was laid in the ambulance he went and hovered about the door. He could not make up his mind whether it was better that Charlie had either no breath or no mind to whistle. He called into the gloom of the cab, below the glow of gaslight through the high, square cab windows.

'Charleen.'

'Well?'

'Are you there?'

'I think so.'

'I'll see you tomorra.'

'If I'm not there I'll be elsewhere.'

'I'll bring a drop,' said Mick.

'You can launch me with it,' said Charlie.

The driver brought the engine to life. The helper entered the cab and closed the doors. The ambulance felt its way down the narrow place, bumping gently on the cobbles. Before it was out of sight Mick went back into the house. The dead smell of the place repelled any memories the walls might have huddled between them. He went beyond the sacking into the candlelight. Apart from the candle flame the only bright thing in the small space was the statue; the too-bright blue of cloak and white of gown was toned by the dust, and in the soft light the gilt-gold of the rosary had the patina of the antique. The corkscrew put Mick in mind of a thirst he had no way of relieving. He snuffed the candle out, crushing the frail blossom of light with his fingers. Then he left the house to call on the doctor for his workhouse ticket.

New World's Eve

Old Mac lay quietly on the bed, smoking to while away the night till time to rise. It was his custom to rise when the old town clock struck midnight, but tonight the twelfth stroke must find him elsewhere. It was New Year's Eve.

Ever since the town as he knew it became a thing of the past he took to walking out by night when the streets were deserted. In daylight he could see the new names over the shops and the faces of the new people. Resting on his stick in the archway of the lane where he lived he muttered after women passing. Several times he raised the ferruled ash growth to the men. But when bitterness took him as far as resenting the child-play of the new children Mac began to spend the days in bed and use the night to walk abroad in; filling the empty streets with remembered people, seeing old daylight through the new nights.

The darkness in the small room smelled of tobacco. Each pull at the pipe put a berry-red glow on his face and beard that daylight would have drained. Between pulls the glow dwindled back into the bowl and the old head went back into darkness. Night beyond the poke of a window was thinned by moon and starlight and the silver of frost. Within and beyond was utter stillness, because Mac's was the only house left standing in the laneway. When the lane was condemned by the town council Mac refused to leave it. Before the council workers came to level it Mac gave word out that the gun of an old Fusilier had a shot left for the first man who put a crowbar against a stone of his place. They knocked the lane into rubble about him, but they left him his house. While Mac, with nothing more harmful to life than the sour pipe in his hands, peered through a hole in rotting curtains, tasting the words of bitter humour with his wry old mouth.

A dribble of cold spittle in the stem gave notice that the pipe was empty. His big hand fumbled for a crease in the grimy pillow and laid the pipe in it. Without the company of the live pipe he felt the silence more. Outside was night hanging in cold space, space touching on old stone, stone heaped upon dead earth: and earth covered a bulk of the men and women who once gave life to the emptiness. While they lived it would have been hard to persuade them that it mattered to Mac whether they went or stayed. He never gave more than a sharp answer to a question, or a look more than was needed to mark who spoke. When the two old people passed away no other member of the family would live with him. When he would have married no one would marry him. He carpentered and drank and went his way, alone. But in each New Year's Eve there was one moment when they found him perfect.

They would have had uses for this high night of stars on the roof and frost on the floor. The door of each house would be open wide so that every doorway laid a welcome of light on the cobbles for all. Fires of turf and timber heaped high on the hearth held the cold at a wholesome distance. There was help for the oil lamp on the hob from the Christmas candle burning in each unblinded kitchen window: enough to cast shadows of geranium and birdcage to crumple on the lumpy limewashed wall of the house opposite. Berried holly gleamed like new enamel on dresser and pictures, and where it was stuck in the gallon of sand supporting the tall white pole of wax.

The voices of the women would be crisp and eager, their faces living fiercely in the telling of trifles as intently heard as if they were the timely story of God on earth. They visited from neighbour to neighbour until each was in a house not her own. Here an old one would be fighting for breath enough to finish a comic ballad; there a clear young voice sang of sad love. Somewhere a battered concertina chuckled out a jig or a reel or a hornpipe: somewhere else a fiddle high on the E string cried over a lost cause. Children played day games in the window and door lights. Lovers would be together in the shadows.

Then the men came trooping up the lane from the pubs to drink on in each other's kitchens: hats at angles, words at will. Telling the worn stories as if they were fresh from yesterday: using the names of their dead to boast about their living blood, laughing with the living about the laughter of the dead until they brought the dead so near that each was struck with the thought that so near was so far, forever. There would be a silence then. Then someone would surely mumble:

> *Should auld acquaintance be forgot,*
> *And never brought to mind …*

But as surely one wife would wink towards another and the two together would call for help to clear the floor for dancing. And through it all Mac would be just as much on his own as he was now.

Eight music-box notes fell on the broken lane from the clock-tower of the Protestant church. It was half-past eleven, and at this time in the past Mac's moment would be only thirty minutes away. For just about now Jer Blaze would walk in at the archway and go from house to house, calling his brass band to order. Known as Blaze because he never tired of saying that the blaze of brass was a blaze of glory, the name suited the fiery look in his eyes and the brandy glow on skin that age had marked but little. His white moustache was schooled to two upturned points that matched the upturned peaks of his two white eyebrows. His way of walking, pushing his middle as if he was proud of his watch chain, he brought from the Munster Fusiliers to lead his band as befitted its music, and his players jumped to his heels like recruits for inspection. Mac would be first in the hurry because his moment was near, proud that he was the only man in the band with a silver cornet.

Front row, second from the right, was his place as they followed Blaze out through the archway to the town. On the street Blaze did a round of inspection as if they were a guard of honour giving him a civic reception. Then—'Ready? All ready! By the one, two, three!' And there would be Blaze bringing music after him through the town. 'The Minstrel Boy'. 'Who Fears to Speak'. 'A Nation Once Again'. The martial airs would beat like wings against the faces of the gathering townspeople. All who could walk followed the band. In their hundreds strong they followed the band, while the babes and infirm were together in windows. All had smiles, or smiles in their eyes. All were alive with a swing to their gait. Plate-glass windows shivered in their sockets. Window-frames rattled in their slots. Clod-horses waiting beside pubs for farmers arched their necks and reared like chargers. The very sky seemed to leap and shake its stars like a jewelled harness. But every now and again Blaze would lower his eyes from their high-headed stare to look at his nickel-plated timepiece: keeping a check on Mac's moment.

And Blaze had his band in the right place at the right time. At ten to twelve they were playing under the clock on the Old Town Hall in the centre of the town. Thought-stirring music now. 'The Kerry Dance'. 'The Maid with the Nut-Brown Hair'. 'Oft in the Stilly Night'. Built of red sandstone the hall had worn into an old, brown, crusted age. Blind in all its forty windows, its one gesture towards the new times reposed in the centre of its grooved old brow—the great, yellow, strong-featured face of the old town clock: living on to record the hammer-hard pulse beats of the clock's great, iron heart.

The flag pavement beneath was honoured with the tallest gas-lamp standard in the town. Under a wide arc of blue-white light the band played as the minute hand, with the girth and length of a Viking sword, lifted towards the comrade centring on the Roman twelve. When the minute hand touched the mark for a minute to twelve Blaze halted the music. Silence settled on the thousand faces, all upraised towards the face of the clock. As the great clock-spring gave in infinitesimal fractions of an inch of steel the silence tightened to the point of nerve-break. Because the minds of all were reaching for the past, the past was fastened to a thousand thoughts as taut as harp-strings and drawn as near as breathing with all who lived in it. A thousand living stood with thousands dead as the long hand lifted imperceptibly towards the Roman twelve.

Then quietly it was on it. A cough from hoarse metal. A succession of creaks and knocks as if a great chain laboured in a socket. The chain stopped. A finger-flick of silence—then—CLANG! That first anvil clang of the great clock was like a sledge blow on the chain link of that moment binding the future with the past, forging the mark that guided all succeeding eleven blows to unmoor the past to drift with time into time beyond memory. NINE, TEN, ELEVEN. On the instant of the eleventh stroke Blaze took three steps back as Mac took three steps forward. Mac raised the silver cornet to the light. With the care of a kiss he put his lips to the mouthpiece. TWELVE! And there was Mac's moment. He had inhaled so much breath that the lungs sighed in ecstatic release as he breathed through the silver cornet into the first breath of the fresh, young year.

The full round notes of ripe sound followed on to the air as smooth as swans launching white breasts on still lake water:

> *Should auld acquaintance be forgot,*
> *And never brought to mind?*
> *Should auld acquaintance be forgot,*
> *And days of auld lang syne?*

That was Mac's moment and they, the people he regarded with hidden feeling, felt towards him in their fluent way. For this they needed him and after it was over he would act again as though he had never needed them …

Mac felt for the watch under his pillow and struck a match. Twenty-five minutes to twelve. With the match he lighted the candle, stuck with its own grease to the seat of the old chair beside his bed. The taxed bedspring groaned as he heaved himself off it. The bed shook. The old wooden beads looped on the bedstead knocked against the metal. His few clothes went on in no time: trousers, waistcoat, jacket, a knotted scarf for his neck. The stiff, corrugated leather of his strong boots made the lacing with thongs a job of patience for old fingers. But they were put right, and then the hat—a black, felt affair with a wide, limp brim. The stick next, from where it lay beside his lair in the mattress, tokening his fear of intruders.

He was ready to go now, but tonight there was one other matter. With the stiffness of the first steps after rising he made his way to the orange-box in the corner that served as a shrine to the Virgin. The statue was cowled in dust and the top of the box was grey with bed fluff. The curtain that careful hands had fashioned to cover the crude timber was so far invaded by dust that its one-time colour could no longer be told. Mac lifted the cloth and groped beneath it. In a moment he was holding his silver cornet.

He brought it to the candlelight. It still shone. Gripping a sleeve against his wrist he rubbed the cornet with it. It shone brighter. Slowly, as if he were afraid, he raised it to his lips: not for sound, but to make sure that there was no stoppage in the coils. The breath he gave it, it gave back in a long sigh, like relief. He tried the keys with his big-knuckled fingers: they obeyed his pressure. He snuffed the candle with his fingers and groped down into the dark house by the old, complaining stairs. Through the kitchen then, its stillness staring like an old face. Bolts were drawn. The click of a latch, a step, and he was under the star- and moonlight, breathing the frosty air into his rheumy old lungs. Jabbing with his stick he made his way over the heaps of jagged stone and time-dozed mortar. Now and again the dark outline of his stoop was stabbed with a silver splinter when the moon- and starlight found the cornet. Out under the archway of the town he went, to where Blaze used to hold his brisk inspections. He stopped there and stood. By the one, two, three! he told himself in a whisper. Then with the stick tapping and the cornet in his grip he followed over every step of the familiar way.

Blinds yellow with light and taut as drumskins sealed the privacy of each separate celebration of the new townspeople. Dance halls, three of them, muted their bedlam with closed doors. Hardly anyone at all kept the night company, and all the beauty of the high, calm sky was going a-begging. But Mac barely noticed that it was so. Because he followed Blaze's band the ash growth may as well have been with him of itself. Because he was filling the streets with remembered people the few who followed, out of chance loitering, had a thousand added to them. And the old tunes were sounding in his mind. 'O'Donnell Abú'. 'Who Fears to Speak'. 'A Nation Once Again'. And all the thousand remembered people trod the ground hard and smiled as they marched.

At ten to twelve Mac was standing under the arc of light under the old town clock. For an instant he became aware that his behaviour had gathered a score of new townspeople about him. He was gripped by his hatred of their stranger faces, but then the remembered band was playing 'The Kerry Dance' and his mood changed. At the minute to twelve the music was gone from him. He was left with the thousand remembered faces, all looking through his face at the face of the old town clock. As the iron hand reached through the last minute Mac's heart knocked at his ribs with the strength of knuckle blows. Fear felt for a grip on him all through that minute: fear that when his moment came the old mastery over the cornet would have departed with all his years on lungs and hands, and thirty years of silence.

At last the hand was home. The metal coughed. The chain laboured: and stopped. The instant of silence and—CLANG! Then sledge blows, one after another until NINE, TEN, ELEVEN! Mac shuffled through the three steps forward: hooked the head of his stick on the loose mouth of his pocket. TWELVE! The old head went back. The black hat tilted. The old drawn face with the grey coarse beard was bared to the light like a death mask. The stiff-thewed hands raised the silver cornet till the crusted lips were pursed against the mouthpiece. The slack lungs outraged at the intake of so much breath, then gladly let the breath free into the shining coils. A key-head bowed under the cramped pressure of an old finger. A long, strong, quavering note tore free of the horn. '*Should ...*'

Then silence. But sound was heartening. The lungs complained again, but further notes, off-key and reeling, gapped out the first phrase:

> *Should auld ... acquaint ... ance ... be ... forgot,*

Beads of sweat, whole as the bubble in a spirit level, appeared on the grooves of the brow. More breath. More sound tearing free like strips from a ragged banner.

> *And nev ... er ... brought ... to ... mind?*
> *Should ... auld acquaint ... ance ... be ... forgot,*
> *And ... days ... of ... auld ... lang ... syne?*

The chest-blows from his heart beat in his breathing now. The next two phrases of the tune made a sound like sobbing:

> *For auld ... lang syne ... my lads,*
> *For auld ... la ... ang ... syne ...*

One more breath, a heave of the stooped shoulders, and the final phrases steadied into blaring, brazen notes like an old man's boast:

> *We'll tak' a cup o' kindness yet,*
> *For auld lang syne.*

Mac's big, bent frame lost height and breadth. His head bobbed down to crush his beard against his chest. The cornet fell to arm's length and swung a little. It was a while till he could raise his head again to look into the smiles of the thousand faces: before they dissolved in his worn eyes into a silver swirl of smiling light. A while more left him with the steady silver of the cornet, and the score of faces of the new townspeople, staring steadily.

Then the twitches on his old face made him feel the smile on it. He left it there. It was there as he gripped the stick with his right hand, gripped the cornet with his left hand, and went back to the house among the crumbled homes.

Kate's Grandchild

It was my mother who told me, long after, the way it was with old Kate Flahive when the last of her five children had left the laneway. Her husband had been a woodman in a local estate, until he met his death under a cross-grained tree. In my time all that remained of Pat Flahive were his nailed boots, worn thongless by Kate herself. Kate did well for the children, carrying each to the last school year by scrubbing floors the years round and making the most of ha'pence. Age found her bones and her eyes ahead of time, her eyes in particular. The children were a battle to control, it seems, especially the two girls with their handsome prancing bodies and hot blood. One after another they left the lane and the country and ever after gave Kate or the neighbours no reason to believe that they looked back.

The postman never stopped at Kate's door and yet it took many days to cure her of waiting in the doorway during post times.

'That's a grand morning, Mrs Flahive.'

'A grand morning, thank God, that will make a brave day,' Kate would agree with the postman.

Then she would pull the tails of her three-cornered shawl tighter into her armpits and lean farther over the half-door, her mouth wearing away a gumdrop for her asthma. Later in the day she would be there again.

'That's a great day now, Mrs Flahive.'

'A great day, thank God, that will bring a good night too.'

The postman's footsteps would have gone beyond her hearing and his shape would have faded in her failing sight before she turned in for the dim kitchen. The fire would guide her to the hearth seat, a cut from the bole of a long-gone tree where flame light would flow over her face like sunny water over an old porous stone. Then her ringed hand would reach towards the cradle of her illegitimate grandchild.

Because she was a next-door neighbour and trusted by Kate, my mother was asked to stand as godmother of the lad. The parish clerk was asked in the baptistry to be godfather, since he would know anyhow.

'What do you want the boy to be called, Mrs Flahive?' the priest asked.

'Making you no short answer, Father,' Kate answered, 'you can call him the day of the week for all I care.'

'Today is the feast of Saint Anthony,' the priest said. 'How about the name Anthony?'

So Anthony he was named during that hour stolen from public notice for the christening.

For his first seven months of life Anthony was no more to Kate than a presence with her in the quiet house. Twice a day she waited for the postman and after he had passed she would brood over the memory of her scattered children, only remembering Anthony through remembering them. It was easy to disremember the sort of child he was, with hardly more sound or stir from him than from the flat-faced china dogs on the dresser or the stopped three-cornered clock on its bracket on the hob in common with the dogs and the clock and the picture of Our Lady on the back wall and every piece and scrap of ornament or usefulness in the place, the child was visited by the soft white ash flakes that drifted from the fire when Kate used the bellows on it.

My mother was able to tell me all this because as often as not she was there in the kitchen, making a meal of milk for Anthony or changing his child-clothes. It was twenty years since Kate had done for her own in that way, and what with peering and poking in the half-light she was lost for the sure, quick-fingered touch it called for. My mother understood and for this Kate was grateful.

'You're very good, Lena child,' Kate would tell her.

'Good how-are-you, woman,' my mother would say, making light of it.

'You have your own care indeed,' Kate would insist.

'So my hands are in practice, Kate.'

'A whisper, Lena. What sort of a child is it to look at?'

'A lovely child, Kate, with a nice long set of limbs, blue eyes, and a sprinkle of fair, silky hair that haven't to ask the sun for the gloss on it. Far and away a nicer child than the black lad I have next door.'

I was the black lad. I am that today.

'Ah, now you're only saying, Lena. Sure I know what you are like yourself and what your boy's father is like. But my girl who left that child with me was no fair-haired.'

'I have left more milk in the saucepan, ready to your hand,' my mother would say, or something like it, to take Kate away from herself. 'The bottle will be beside him in the cradle after he is finished what I gave him now. Anyhow I'll run out again when I have my own lad settled.'

'A whisper, child. Isn't it queer for a baby to be as quiet as that for so long? Night or day time he do hardly give a stir or a sound. Now and again, when I remember, I do put my ear down to his mouth till I hear him breathing. For though I don't want him, I don't want without him through fault of mine.'

Now by this time every mother and grandmother in the lane was concerned about Anthony, and about Kate herself. Every hand's turn for their own reminded them of the child who was hidden in the half-light near Kate. No one of them was more put out than my mother, because she felt that her place in Kate's confidence put the brunt of the blame on her shoulders. No other woman in the lane could as much as talk to Kate about Anthony, until such time as Kate owned to his existence among them. They talked and plotted among themselves and gathered their ripest wisdom for my mother, who was expected to use it at the right times between Kate and the child. But Kate had a will and a way of her own. She even shortened the scope of my mother's helpfulness, as much as she could manage. In the matter of shopping for Anthony, for instance, my mother could have done the needful when she was buying for me: but Kate would not hear of it. The rule was, when my mother could spare the time to sit with Anthony, Kate would cowl herself in a street shawl that breathed of smoke and paraffin. Huddled under it, to save her worn eyes from daylight, she eased one loose boot before the other towards lane's end and the shops.

Having to buy the extra milk was an embarrassment for her, Johnny

Downey the huckster told me.

'A half-pint of milk,' she would say, stealing the old crock out from under her shawl.

She would wait until the milk was ladled into the crock. Then she would take it into her hands and peer into it, the bridge of her smudged nose against the earthenware.

'Is the milk going scarce?' she would ask.

'No, mam,' Johnny would tell her.

'Will it be scarce tomorrow, do you think?'

'No, mam.'

'But you never know all the same?' would come from her: near to pleading, peering anxiously in the direction of his face.

'Not a chance this time of year, ma'am.'

'Oh,' she would say, and go two steps, come two steps, go and come back again.

'If I got a pint more, would it be sour tomorrow for baking?' she would ask this time, the old face hanging loose as she bent her head to peer once more.

'It would indeed, mam,' Johnny would say, glad to agree with her in something.

'Then give me the pint, if you please,' she would tell him, holding the crock out in a quake of eagerness.

When Anthony was seven months old and still a stranger to daylight and sky the women of the lane were beside themselves. During their to and fro going past Kate's door their footsteps got slower on the cobblestones, as they plucked for the courage to walk in and breast whatever way Kate would take them. My mother was very upset but she hid her feeling with a show of cheerfulness and bided her time. Kate carried on taking each day as a day in itself. The child went on being untroublesome, as if his scrap of young life, when it stirred, touched Kate's old life in the quiet place and so had learned to stir but little. Now and then he gave a mild complaint because of wind pain or loneliness. What happened on those rare occasions when my mother was not there, no one knew; but when they happened in her presence she had to take and calm the child herself, because Kate made no move. During all that more than seven months Kate never touched the baby while my mother was in the kitchen, until one midday in the August of that year. My mother was holding Anthony in her arms after he had been fed and freshened with clean clothes. For Kate's benefit she began to cluck to Anthony in the proud mother-hen way that women use to make a child feel its importance to the world.

'Wouldn't your granny love to see you now, Anthony pet?' she began.

'Granny,' Kate grunted.

'Clean as a new pin and smiling,' my mother went on. 'Wouldn't your granny love to see you? Ask her, pet, ask her there in a huddle by the fire.'

'My eyes are as dim as dusk,' Kate grumbled.

'There's a big splash of sunlight over the half-door, Anthony,' my mother ran on, 'that is just as if the Lord sent it for your granny to see it shining on your bright head.'

When Kate held her ground my mother tried another approach.

'Feel the weight of him, Kate,' she said.

'My old hands are clumsy,' Kate protested.

Each big hand was on an opposite elbow in her crouch by the heart-light, their vein-roots high against the skin as if groping after the slow ebb of life through the blood. Kate drew them into her lap and leaned over them.

'Clumsy how-are-you, Kate,' my mother assured her. ''Tis only to feel the weight of him.'

Kate paid no heed.

'Here,' said my mother.

She reached forward with the child and put him against Kate's face. The old body straightened on the hearth seat.

'No,' she said.

'Yes, Kate,' said my mother. 'As a favour for me.'

Kate's heavy hands lifted slowly and gathered the child down against her big, slack bosom.

'Sure I know his weight, Lena,' she said. 'The weight of a cork.'

'Air and light will put weight and strength in him,' said my mother. 'Watch him, will you, looking at the sunlight over the half-door. Ah God love him, take him to the light, Kate, take him to the light.'

Kate lifted an ear towards the doorway. The sounds of child-play in the lane were distant. Near at hand there was nothing to hear. Then she reached up to offer the child to my mother.

'Here, Lena. Let you take it to the light.'

'In the sunlight a body could see him plain,' my mother remarked.

There was a long pause, but Kate raised herself off the hearth seat and moved slowly towards the sunlight. Except for the grey house shawl on her shoulders Kate was clad in black. In his white and blue wrappings the child lay like a big posy on her breast. The light met them as if the day's brightness was hungry for them. The child's white skin and fair hair met the light halfway and gave a glow back. Kate's crumpled face took it dully and gave no change. The boy's blue eyes beat their lids, like butterflies awakening to wings. Kate's head came between them and the light as she peered an inch above his face. The touch of the sun called his limbs to life. He began to kick and glaum. His legs encircled her neck. His hands caught in her tangled hair. Then in the shadow of her head he gave suddenly the first cry of pleasure in his life.

'Did you hear that, Kate?' my mother called out of the half-dark maw of the kitchen.

Kate moved enough to give a blank back to her eagerness.

'Did you hear that crow of delight?' my mother asked.

Kate gave no answer, but continued to stand there, the old heavy body in a stillness like stupor, half-crouched over the live child.

'Kate,' my mother called.

Kate turned slowly until her eyes found the guide of the hearth-light. The wide black bulk of her returned to the dusk with the child wriggling on her breast.

'Kate, did you hear him?' my mother said with a determined loudness.

'Hear what, child?' asked Kate.

'The cry of delight he gave when he met the sun?'

A moment went by before Kate answered.

'Sometimes my ears are as bad as my eyes,' she answered.

'But you surely saw him in that strong light,' my mother said. 'And what do you think of him?'

'The glare of the sun put a cloud of colour over the splink I have,' Kate told her. 'Here, Lena, put him back in the cradle.'

'You're a dogged old woman,' my mother told her outright.

But Kate's ears were not hearing again.

One good came out of the occurrence. It gave Kate the custom of holding Anthony in the doorway any hours her ears told her were free of footsteps. She stood far enough in from the half-door to be hidden from sight at right or left. Facing her across the considerable width of the lane was the whitewashed wall of an orchard, owned by a publican with a shopfront in the street beyond the lane archway. The cool green of the apple trees showed above the wall, as thick as thatch. The friary steeple rose in the background, near enough to show the bell-wheel and the bell. In the brightest days, Kate saw the view as a strip of misty white below a wide, blue mist of sky; and the steeple as a mast looming out of a blue fog. But the child could see it all and feel the sunlight fawning on him. He crowed and crooned, kicked and glaumed over the old heart. The moment Kate heard a footstep on the cobblestones she backed away into the kitchen. The neighbour women tried to catch her off her guard by treading lightly, but it seemed as if Kate could hear their very breathing, because she was always gone. As well as the women and the men, the children came to know about Anthony. But even their barefoot swiftness and its soft sound on the stones failed to get past Kate's sensitive ear range. Young and old were at an end of patience when the night came that brought the whole affair to a head.

My mother remembered the night well because she did a lot of looking at it. It was a Monday night in that September. That Sunday the County football team had won the All-Ireland Final in Dublin and the team were due to arrive in town by train at half-past ten. From the first dust of dusk the whole town was preparing a welcome. Bonfires were lit in the streets, on the outlying hills and in every lane. Our lane was fortunate in that Bill Horan, the blacksmith, had been shoeing wheels all day, because he left a ring of fire for the lane youths to build on when he was done with it. They built on Bill's ring of fire until it was a stack of burning turf, driving red heat and ripe cherry light against the hands and faces of the crowd that gathered to it.

When my mother had got me to sleep she poked her head through the window of the little room to watch the fun. Young and old of the lane made a ring around the fire. Seats had been made with builder's planks on stone heaps. Bare-necked men were filling jugs and mugs with porter, out of earthenware jars that youngsters brought between them from the pubs beyond the archway. There was singing and dancing and courting and laughter. Over it all, my mother said, were stars as big and near as rush-lights. The sky was a deeper than day blue from them and so glowing that patches of it showed through the bell tower of the friary. The whole length of the lane had mothers looking through bedroom windows, with the capering crowd before them and the quiet breathing of their babies behind. The only house-front that showed a blank was Kate's. My mother went next door to see how she was. It was firelight there too, but smaller and quieter. When Kate used a light at all she used a candle and only to keep her company.

'Ah, there you are!' my mother greeted. ''Tis a wonder you wouldn't give yourself a light, Kate.'

'To light what?' said Kate. 'For what to see?'

She was sitting with her back to the hob. Spittle from the gumdrop stuck her lips together. Each time they came asunder they made a noise like a tap dripping.

'Open that door there,' my mother coaxed.

'Wisha, no, child.'

'Ah, do, Kate. There's great life,' said my mother.

Kate chuckled a bit, then went still-quiet.

'My life is behind my eyes, Lena,' she said. 'I do go wandering in it. And I do get lost.'

'How is Anthony?' my mother asked, peering into the cradle to find the child's forehead for her hand.

'How is your son?' Kate countered.

'As quiet as your grandchild, Kate,' said my mother, edging the words with rebuke.

She left without a word more, hurrying to me, in fear that the lusty singing around the bonfire would wake me. As the train-time of the team drew nearer the crowd thinned gradually. The singing weakened the way a hymn would if the choir went one by one away out of the organ-loft; the quiet the merrymakers left about the fire was as deep as church quiet.

The station was beyond the church, and near the ten-thirty, the train came in a long roar of carriages through the quiet night. Fog-signals laid on the tracks burst in a volley like rifle fire. Cheering rose in gusts and each echo gave a notion of the sky swaying. With that the town's brass band blared in a marching tune. Tune and cheering drifted nearer as the players were driven down the street beyond the archway, towards a dinner reception in the centre of the town. The mothers left behind in the lane pulled shawls and coats over their shoulders and ran up the lane and under the archway, to see the procession passing by, my mother among them.

What happened to Kate after they left she told my mother later. Wandering in the life behind her eyes took her so much out of her way that she was lost to the lane since my mother's leaving of her. When she came back the lane was silent beyond the quiet house. The cheering and band playing was distant beyond the closed door and she hardly remarked about them at all.

Then it was that Anthony suddenly screamed. He cried bitterly and screamed again. Kate groped to him and found him with her hands. Rigid with pain, he was crying and screaming when she lifted him out of the cradle. The next thing she knew she was crooning to him and rocking him in her arms, but he gave no heed to her. Her fingers closed over his body. It was like a stick. In a moment she had flung the door and the half-door open and was rushing through our hallway with the screaming child, calling, 'Lena! Lena!'

When she got no answer she groped back into the lane and pounded with her fists on the door of the neighbour on the other side.

There was no answer again. All the time the child's screams were gathering in vehemence. Kate rushed towards the bonfire and fell forward over one of the plank seats.

'Oh merciful Christ!' she cried.

As she fell she rolled, out of instinct, onto her back. Her always weak breathing all but left her entirely. With a stare of terror in her half-dead eyes, she lay there in a lifeless heap with the screaming, writhing child on her body. Her breath came back again, bringing life with it and she groped back over the plank. She stood there with the child in her arms, her face to the houses.

'Neighbours! Neighbours!' she shouted.

'Neighbours!'

All the while the band was pounding with the rhythm of her heart so that it took her a while to think that it was a band, and then it took her a while to think of the band as a reason for the empty lane. But in the end she did. When she did she began to run towards the glow in the eye of the archway above the dark outline of the crowd standing in it. Breathing in gasps Kate came with the screaming child behind the crowd. But the band was just passing.

'Neighbours! Neighbours!' she cried, but the blare of the band tore through the archway like a wind and drowned her cries.

'Neighbours!'

She groped and caught at sleeves and coat-tails but they pulled away, thinking it was someone fighting for a view.

Then the band was beyond the archway, and suddenly they heard her. When they turned, my mother said, they saw a demented old woman that they hardly recognized as Kate at all. Her thin hair hung from her head in wet tails. Her eyes were raw-wet and the folds of her face were wet. One of the hands that held the screaming child was torn on the knuckles and dark blood made tracks to her elbow.

'Neighbours!' she said, with not enough breath to make it a cry.

'Neighbours, neighbours, neighbours,' she kept on saying after my mother had taken Anthony from her.

'Don't worry, Kate, 'tis nothing,' my mother told her.

'Oh, 'tis, 'tis, Lena,' said Kate.

'I'll take him to the chemist,' said my mother.

And she did. Kate dragged the old boots down the lighted street after her, followed by what looked like the entire lane of people, all of them telling her, 'Shah, Kate.'—'Now Kate'—'Don't worry Kate.'

'Where's Lena?' Kate kept saying, her hands feeling in front of her.

Bill Horan, the blacksmith, gave her his hand and led her towards the chemist. By the time they got there, the chemist had already dispensed gripe-water to Anthony and already his crying was quieter.

'Now, Kate,' said my mother, 'there is Anthony, as right as rain.'

As Kate took the child the chemist noticed the blood on her arm.

'Let me see that hand, Mrs Flahive,' he said.

'Tomorrow, child, tomorrow,' Kate told him.

'But Mrs Flahive,' he began.

'Tomorrow, child, tomorrow. Can't you see me. Can't you see me. I'm taking my grandchild home. I'm taking my grandchild home.'

Holding Anthony in her arms she pushed the old boots homeward through the lighted street, followed by all the lane of neighbours.

The Day Mary Clare Met the Bishop

Mary Clare is eight years old, and even her mother has despaired of making her look pretty. Because the heel click of her left shoe collapses after one week of hardship, the shoe has to be dragged along wherever she goes. This dog-and-drag gait of going makes her pigtail ribbon to bob on her spine, like a butterfly too full of flower milk to rise as high as hedges.

It is often taken where hedges are, because Mary Clare likes to bring flowers to the tall glass vase before the statue of Our Lady, in the bedroom she shares with her two sisters. Snowdrops come with the dots and the drags out of the frost-grey early dews of spring. Daffodils arrive from riverbanks, their crisp shanks still damp with weir-spray. Ivory-spindled bluebells shake blue belfries as the old boards sway under the white shrine when the sisters come into the room. Wood and field flowers, hill and bog flowers: every flower that grows up out of a wild root has been brought to that vase on the top floor of that tenement. But it was bluebells were in it the day Mary Clare met the bishop.

It was the white hour before noon of a sunny day. The world felt as sheltered as if God had closed the skylight of its blue roof. Mary Clare was alone with the two rooms and a pantry at the top of the tenement. Her father was hodding mortar up plank gangways. Her mother was washing the tiles of the church floor. The two sisters had stolen away from her to a street game.

The mood of rebellion began when she felt a hole in her sock. Examining the hole made her notice the shabbiness of her shoes. When her hands stretched her faded jumper, in vexation at both calamities, a weakness in its weave burst into a tear. At this she made the mistake of stamping her left foot, and the loose shoe fell off. As she hopped on the right foot in putting the left shoe on again, she saw the withered state of Our Lady's bluebells. The need to spill them out of the vase brought her to the window, and it was then she saw Bishop O'Donnell in front of his palace, less than a quarter-mile away, gathering a basketful of the richest blossoms in the country. As he stooped over the rounds and ovals of his flower beds in the palace lawn, his red biretta might have been an outsize rose bowing friendly greeting to flower neighbours. Mary Clare took one look from the withered bluebells in Our Lady's vase to the coloured riches in the bishop's basket and straight away the mood of rebellion was with her. On its heel came her decision to visit the bishop, once and for all.

*

Her next thought was to get out of the tenement without having to tell nosy neighbours down the way what her errand was and how long she intended to be about it. In her peaceful moods she understood that their curiosity was part of a duty to her mother, who asked that they have an eye to her goings and comings when she was not there to do it herself, but in her present state they were enemies to be thwarted. First she spilled the withered bluebells all the way down to the tenement yard. Next she returned the vase to Our Lady. Then she took off the loose shoe for going down the rickety stairs. Step below step she went quietly as far as the third-floor landing. Matty Dowd's grandchildren were playing a noisy game in his living room and Mary Clare was pleased by their screams of laughter because Matty had the kind of deafness that would hear a candle burning when he wanted to. Very satisfied with herself she was three steps down towards the second floor when Matty's voice came at her from behind.

'What have I done that went agin you, Mary Clare?' he asked her.

'What do you mean, Matty Dowd?' she asked.

'Well I thought I must have offended you some way when you didn't bid me the time of this grand day as you were passing by,' Matty told her.

In shirt sleeves and stockinged feet, and with the peaks of his waist-coat flapping, he was cutting a green sod with a rusty scissors to the shape of a lark-cage window.

'I was in a hurry, Matty Dowd,' said Mary Clare, going down a step.

'You'll forgive me now,' said Matty, 'when I say that, no matter how big the reason for the hurry, you will have time to watch me sodding the lark.'

He had a way of butting with his head when talking down to children, as if he were looking over a pair of spectacles and it crushed his curly grey beard against his muffler and partly hid the humour in his moist eyes with a bushy screen of eyebrows.

*

'I'm afraid I can't wait,' said Mary Clare, going down another step.

'He's giving song to the sun that's dripping on the street below,' said Matty, 'and when he saw me coming with a fresh sod he started a hymn.'

'I suppose he did,' Mary Clare said and went down two steps before he spoke again.

'I brought the children a blue balloon that cost me a penny,' Matty told her, 'an' 'tis bobbing in the kitchen as big as a ball. Do you hear 'em? Man, now I can't hear the music of my lark! Would you care to be playing with that blue balloon with 'em?'

'I said I was in a hurry, Matty Dowd,' Mary Clare reminded him.

'Oh the hurry, that's right,' said Matty. 'You have a big reason for that hurry, I'm sure. Look now, there's another thing I nearly forgot. The children's mother is making a griddle cake. 'Twill be cool for eatin' on the ledge of the window inside twenty minutes. Do you think now that your hurry could be over in twenty minutes?'

'It might, Matty Dowd,' said Mary Clare and was gone three steps before Matty's shout to Mrs Cassidy of the second floor echoed between the bare walls of the tenement.

'Are you there, Mrs Cassidy?'

'What ails you, Matty?' The answer came up on the instant.

'What time do you make it?'

'A minute to half-past by me,' Mrs Cassidy called.

'There now, Mary Clare,' said Matty. 'If you're back at ten to twelve you'll be right for a spoke off that wheel of a griddle cake.'

Then he raised his voice to a shout again:

'Mary Clare is goin' out in a hurry, ma'am, so I gave her time and a reason for hurrying back.'

'Come on, Mary Clare, until I see you this morning,' Mrs Cassidy called.

'So long, Mary Clare,' said Matty, going away with the sod to his lark, through a floor full of noisy children.

*

Mrs Cassidy's collection of brightly coloured aprons hid her tatters from the world the way her cheerful face hid her troubles. Only when she turned her back did she look poor and old and shabby. She was wearing her pink apron today and her smile, as always, was somehow to match.

'I was thinking about you, Mary Clare,' she greeted, at the closed door of her room.

'Were you, ma'am?' said Mary Clare.

'My man is practising new tunes on the fiddle and here you come just in time,' she said.

'I'm in a desperate hurry,' said Mary Clare.

But Mrs Cassidy opened the door as she passed and the notes of the fiddle flew out on the stairs with their gay, frolicsome flight a hornpipe. She closed the door again.

'There's a taste,' she said. 'Don't it sound good enough for sitting to hear?'

'I have the very urgentest place to go,' Mary Clare defended.

'One taste more and a look at himself,' smiled Mrs Cassidy.

This time she opened the door fully and the notes seem to curl in wilder arcs in the wider space. The doorway gave a view of the crooked room; the floor so uneven that the legs of the bits of furniture had to be of different lengths to have the tops of them level. The sunlight by the window had a pearl brightness, and out of it the hornpipe came because the player sat in it, on the bare boards of the floor. The grey stubble of his tanned cheeks was made white by the light and the hair of his bow was made ivory. But even for so bright a light, the weathered fiddle had no gloss. The head that was cramped onto the chin-piece of the fiddle wore a battered hat. Closed eyes put the last calm on the long, hollowed face. It seemed as if all of the man was peacefully away in the last sleep of all, except the arms and the hands and the fingers. They were young-alive, and the fiddle and the bow were alive in the May-day sunlight, in the white hour before noon, and the air was alive with gay music.

*

'There he is,' smiled Mrs Cassidy, 'practisin' fresh tunes, because street fiddlers must have new wares to sell or go without pennies. If you come in now, he'd tell you we're in the room without opening his eyes, because one time we had so many children of our own that the breath of a child we could feel near us, and the sturdy beat of a child's heart in our place. And we can still, after all the years, the both of us. Maybe you'll delay awhile in your hurry, Mary Clare?'

"Tis a terrible, terrible important hurry,' Mary Clare fought out.

'Will it take you far?'

'Not so far, ma'am.'

'Will it keep you long away?'

'Not so long, ma'am.'

'Is it a great secret?'

'It is, ma'am.'

'Are you there, Mr Coffey?' Mrs Cassidy called down to the ground floor.

'Yes, Mrs Cassidy,' came the answer up in the voice of a man who should be no stranger to long words.

'How do you like Pat's new hornpipe?' Mrs Cassidy called down.

'Delightful,' the ready answer arrived up.

'I tried to coax Mary Clare here to listen awhile, but she is in the world and all of a hurry.'

'Whatever the reason for the hurry, I shall be very offended if she doesn't call to see me on her way,' called Mr Coffey.

'Goodbye for awhile, Mary Clare,' said Mrs Cassidy.

'Goodbye, Mrs Cassidy,' said Mary Clare, none too pleased.

*

As Mrs Cassidy came back to the music, Mary Clare went down into the flagged hallway. She sat on the last step to put on her left shoe. At the other end of the hallway a heavy door weighed tired hinges down as far as the flags let it. The weather of three generations had worn, burned and washed both oil and shine out of paint that long ago had relinquished colour. Chalk-marks on the four panels showed where a child had tried to do a sum of subtraction and two others had put their names. At one time someone resented the snarl of the lion-faced knocker and broke its nose. In the doorway of sunlight a red cat dozed standing, because to lie on the cold flags would have wakened it again. The door inside the hall door belonged to Mr Coffey's room, and when she knocked there his rich voice told her to come in.

'Ah, if it isn't my very good friend, Mary Clare,' he greeted, rising painfully from the high back and deep seat of his otherwise battered armchair.

'Sit down, my dear,' he told her, indicating his petrol tin footstool with a courtly motion of his hand.

'I can't stay, Mr Coffey,' Mary Clare told him.

'I didn't expect that you should stay, my dear. I merely want you to delay a while.'

'I can't delay either, Mr Coffey.'

'Not even if I were to tell you a little incident from my books?' he questioned, the two waxed points of his moustache standing to attention for her answer.

'I'm in the most awful hurry,' said Mary Clare, fit to be tied at having to repeat it so often.

The moustache points twitched, and were calmed by a very elegant thumb and finger. The hand held a white handkerchief in the palm, and only Mary Clare knew that it was kept thus convenient to cover the ring on the middle finger at short notice. The gold of the ring burned like an ember, quietly, as if it knew that it was just a background for the emerald glowing in its oval shield. The emerald lived with an intense light, as if it in turn knew how fine was the craft of the goldsmith. So intensely did it live in all the day shades and shadows of the room that Mary Clare felt it must even glow in darkness. The occasions when the handkerchief was

called to cover it arose with the friendly visits of charitable societies, looking after those who live in tenements. His ring, his books, his speech and
manners, and the threadbare state of his clothes were all he owned of an
expensive past; but only his clothes (and his bones) had worn in the new
surroundings. Even his books had suffered no more than a careful dust-
ing once a month, because their duty was done in simply reminding him
of friends within them that he knew to a shoelace. He was looking at all
twenty of them now, where they leaned on each other against the slant of
the mantel.

'Well now, let us see,' he said. 'There are a few little odds and ends—
pipe cleaners, matches, a tin of sardines—which I want from the shops, so
are you, by any possible chance, hurrying up left through the streets?'

'No, Mr Coffey.'

'Then you must be turning right for the river and the woods,' he rea-
soned, 'so perhaps you would be good enough to bring me a few flowers,
some bluebells for preference?'

'I'm not going to the river or the woods, Mr Coffey.'

'Not to the town, not to the woods—then you are going to the cathedral to your Mother, and that will make it most convenient for you to
bring me a bottle of holy water. I declare, there wasn't enough in the font
to bless myself with before sleep last night.'

'I am not going to the cathedral, Mr Coffey.'

'Not to the town, not to the woods, not to the church. Then you must
be hurrying to the palace to see his Lordship the bishop.'

Mary Clare had no answer for this. His calm acceptance of the thought
that she might take it into her head to visit the bishop gave her courage to
face the problem on hand.

'I'm going now, Mr Coffey,' she told him.

'Just one last moment, Mary Clare,' Mr Coffey requested.

'Tell the bishop that I liked his sermon on Sunday very much and that
I hope the head cold which ruined his delivery is very much better by
now.'

'I didn't say I was meeting the bishop, Mr Coffey.'

'I didn't say you did, Mary Clare.'

She went as far as the door and then paused. 'Mr Coffey,' she said,
without turning.

'Yes, my dear?'

'Suppose I was visiting the bishop?'

'Suppose indeed?'

'What would you call the bishop when you were talking to him?'

'The rule is, whatever you says, put "my Lord" in at the end.'

'Thank you, Mr Coffey,' said Mary Clare, letting in the chill flag-breath of the hallway as she opened the door.

'One last request, Mary Clare,' Mr Coffey said to her. 'Please call again on your way back.'

Hardly was she clear of the hallway when Mr Coffey called to Mrs Cassidy that Mary Clare was visiting the bishop today, and Mrs Cassidy called the news up to Matty Dowd.

Meanwhile Mary Clare was hurrying around the scythe-sweep bend the street took towards the country, the left shoe dragging and the hair ribbon bobbing. Round the bend a river bridge made the road rise as if it leaped towards the sun-dappled silence of the woods beyond. Birds sang and flew away among the tall trees, and the river spread noisy water over the weir. Halfway to the river she reached the railed grey walls of the cathedral grounds, on her right. The first gate of gracefully curled iron did a double service, because as well as giving entry to the cathedral grounds it gave a straight run to the bishop's car up the bishop's path, to the palace at the far end. Each lawn between the paths of the cathedral grounds was as large as a field. The groundsman walked quickly after a motor mower on one of them, guiding it over a lawn as level as the bed of a billiard table. The mower droned as drowsily as the bees, for all its speed, and thrushes hopped with hair-spring ease after it, stabbing the shallow green with beaks that took pot luck for the worms beneath it.

*

Up the bishop's path Mary Clare hurried, looking as small and dishevelled as a year-old doll beside the high, grey harmony of the great cathedral. Pigeons on wheeling flight about the cross on the spire looked like coloured leaves on a spinning breeze, until the beat of their strong wings came down the still air for hearing. Past the lawns and the cathedral Mary Clare hurried, until the bishop's path spread its own gravel between the bishop's laurel hedges. From there on the very air seemed to hold its breath with awe at what Mary Clare was about to do. The white hour seemed to be stealing by with held breath, too, at the thought. Once, on the way, Mary Clare dragged her shoe less hurriedly, the ribbon bobbed more lazily. That was the moment when she nearly turned back, but the moment passed and Mary Clare moved on towards the peaceful world of the bishop.

*

The palace grounds grew out of the pathway the way that a pipe bowl grows out of the stem. The grounds were wide, deep, perfectly planned, and so still that the drag of her left shoe on the gravel sounded to Mary Clare as if it could be heard for miles. Here every living thing seemed to be posing for a photograph. The lawns were mown and rolled. Flower beds were cut to even edges. Flowered trees had rule-straight boles, and it seemed as if each branch over-reached the one above it by a measured inch. Hedged birds flew from place to place in direct lines. Mary Clare was made to feel as if only birds with the ripest, most reverent song, would dare to sing in so whole a silence. Every cubic inch of silence was filled with flower scent. Every flower had petals as thick and soft as velvet; their colours so rich and many that it would sound true to say that a few were not known to the rainbow. In the strong sunlight the palace stone was bleached white in its cool, dark, shelterbelt of firs. The roof of the orchard greenhouse blazed like a mirror and apple blossoms shone like broken snow.

*

Held awestruck on the edge of that sweet-scented world of colour and silence Mary Clare felt the hole in her sock grow as large as Matty Dowd's penny balloon. Frightened by her own foot sounds on the gravel she stepped onto the lawn. Robbed of her foot sounds she heard her heart beating in her narrow chest as if she was a caged lark, like Matty Dowd's beating with wings against the bars. To persuade her feet to move one beyond the other towards the bishop, she had to keep remembering the empty vase at home before the statue of Our Lady; and the hole in the sock did the rest.

As silent as her own shadow on the lawn she drew inch by inch towards the bishop. Fractions of an inch took over when she came within speaking distance, but in spite of the intensity of the stare from her wide eyes at his stooped, white head, the bishop remained unaware of her approach. Finally she was standing at the other side of the flower bed from him. Standing and staring there, she was astonished to hear the bishop's breath, edged by his meeting teeth, hissing a hornpipe. When she had stood so long that she could wait no longer, she drew a deep breath and blurted out:

'My Lord!'

The hornpipe halted, the ringed hand braced the small of the back, and slowly the bishop raised his face, till his grey pair of eyes saw the wide-eyed urchin over his rimless spectacles.

'Bless my soul,' he said.

*

'I'm Mary Clare Looney,' said the urchin.

'When I was your height, I was Timmy Joe Donnell,' said the bishop. 'And look at me now.'

He straightened to his full height and smiled down at her. If age had not leaned so hard on his shoulders, he would be a very tall man: but if the same age had not scored a heavy web of wrinkles on his long face, he would look a very stern man.

'Now where in the world do you fall from?' he asked her.

'I live over there,' Mary Clare told him. 'I can see my window from here.' Then she added, after a pause, 'My Lord.'

'Which window now?' he asked.

Mary Clare directed his eyes to the window by pointing out that it was in the last house in the street, and again there was a pause before a look at the bishop's ring reminded her of Mr Coffey, and that reminded her to add—'My Lord.' The bishop must have known that the house was a tenement, because he said: 'So you live on the top floor? High enough in the world to look into crows' nests.'

*

'I was looking out of the window, spilling withered bluebells out of Our Lady's vase, and I saw you here picking those gorgeous flowers.'

'Yes.'

'All I can get for Our Lady is wild flowers.'

'Yes.'

'So I made up my mind to ...'

'Yes, yes.'

'To come and ask you for some of your flowers ... my Lord.'

'And you're vexed with the world, aren't you?' the bishop asked.

'I am, my Lord.'

That made him chuckle.

'Come over here to the steps till we talk,' he said.

There were three sets of steps for the three levels of the lawns. The bishop led the way to the top step of all, outside the palace entrance. There he sat and motioned to Mary Clare to sit beside him. He waited till she was settled before he said:

'Now tell me all about the state of the world, as you see it, Mary Clare.'

Mary Clare was slow in starting, but once she got used to the sound of her own voice putting words into the great silence she talked freely. For a pause or a halt in her tale the bishop was ready with the right question or statement that gave her a fresh spate of words. One by one she unloaded her grudges of the morning: bringing in about Matty Dowd and his lark and his grandchildren, Mr and Mrs Cassidy and the fiddle, Mr Coffey with his ring and his books. But first and last, she mentioned the empty vase before the statue of Our Lady. The bishop smiled and chuckled and gave back the silence, all at the right time, and finally he said simply: 'Mary Clare, it was no chance that sent you to see the bishop today.' With that he rose up and went over the lawn to the flower beds and returned with two baskets of flowers.

*

'Now that is for you and that is for you,' he told her, putting a basket on either side of where she sat on the step.

'And now I want you to come with me because there is something I want you to see.'

Taking her hand he led her towards the palace. Beyond the three slender pillars of the porch, the oaken door showed eight clean panels and a polished brass knocker. It glided away before the bishop's push with a sound as soft as a sigh. The deep hallway was floored with white tiles, had a white ornamental ceiling and a door inside the oaken door that sighed as easily open for the bishop's hand. The room shone quietly with smooth furniture. Against the far wall was a great glass case of its height and breadth, full of leather-bound volumes. The deep straight mantel ledge of black marble was centred with the refined face of a slow-ticking clock. From the rich carpet to the ornamental ceiling, from wall to wall, and wall to tall clear windows, the room was full of stillness.

'Now, who is it is in this room in your place?' asked the bishop.

'Mr Coffey,' whispered Mary Clare.

'Mr Coffey indeed,' said the bishop. 'Now, Mary Clare, follow me!' said the bishop.

Slowly she followed the bishop to the second floor. The carpeted steps stifled the sound of their feet. A carpeted corridor led to the oaken doors of the rooms. It seemed to Mary Clare that if a moth were to fly there they would hear its wings.

'Now who is it is on this floor in your place?' asked the bishop.

'Mr and Mrs Cassidy.'

'Mr and Mrs Cassidy indeed?'

The third floor was as silent as the second. The bishop paused there too and let the stillness settle about them like a shaded pool.

'Now who is it is on this floor in your place?'

'The Matty Dowds.'

'The Matty Dowds indeed.'

Then he was leading her up the last flight of steps to the top floor. Here was a carpeted corridor again quiet as an aisle of a church locked for night-time.

*

'Now on this floor in your place you are living yourself, Mary Clare? Isn't that right?'

'Yes, my Lord.'

The bishop put his ringed hand on the handle of the first oaken door, but he did not open it immediately.

'At home I always liked the attic, Mary Clare. Through the skylight you can see the sky, by day full of clouds and by night full of stars. Through the skylight, you can see the drops of rain falling towards you but they break on the glass before they reach you, and run off the glass like long tears of light. And you are high enough in the world to look into crows' nests. That's the way it was when I was Timmy Joe Donnell and it is the same with me now that I am a bishop, no less. And now here is what I brought you to see!'

He opened the door on a room full of sunlight. Facing Mary Clare at the centre of the wall opposite was a white shrine. On it was a statue of Our Lady. In front of the statue was a tall glass vase. And the vase was empty.

'See the vase, Mary Clare?' said the bishop.

'Yes, my Lord,' said Mary Clare.

*

'Now in or about the time that you were emptying your vase for Our Lady, I was emptying mine and I left it empty for the moment, because I thought to myself there were few things in the world I wouldn't do for one bunch of bluebells to fill it with ... Now away we go down.'

And as he led the way down through the corridored stillness he spoke back to her.

'So now, Mary Clare, you can do me a favour. When you're bringing me back the baskets, have them full to the top with bluebells ... hundreds of bluebells.'

And as she followed, Mary Clare's mind widened and brightened to the size of a certain clearing in the sun-dappled woods beyond the river, where bluebells grow with the curves of the green ground into waves like the sea.

The Old Stock

It was the last thing we owned in that town: the well-field. In law and in daylight it belonged to the two Leary brothers but they were two of us. Two of the old stock in that town that used to be ours. Through them and with them in daylight we owned the well-field. By night it neither belonged to us nor to the two Leary brothers. By night it belonged to the ghosts of our people: the ghosts of the old stock. And even by night we were nearer to the well-field than were the new people who were the new owners of our town, because the old stock living this life were near to the old stock living that other life the length of a last breath away.

We were craftsmen, those of us who were born with that feeling for the grain in green stone, the vein in sweet timber, the glow in the heart of dark iron, the gloss in the hide of dull leather, the white lightness in grey troughs of dough. Those of us in whom the feeling for these things was dulled by the will of God or the blood of mothers not of our kind were skilled tenders of craftsmen.

We were quiet men, quiet-spoken in the weekdays. Our work-hour concentration relaxed at home into the comfort of unlaced boots, the ease of old wooden chairs with long arms and straight backs that braced the ache in tired spines until the specs fell from the bone of the nose and the newspaper was crushed between thighs and the weight of hands. Then our wives came from their mending for a moment to put the specs where our boots when we walked out of sleep would not crush them.

And while we slept it was that our wives took the looks that showed what Time and the grind were doing to us. And while we slept the house was quiet because our very young were put to bed and those of an age were out at play. And while we slept our ghosts slept in the well-field: because our ghosts worked our day with us and were tired when we were tired.

We drank two pints of stout each working day: a pint at home before midday meal and a pint before bed with our own, in a pub that our own made their own of. Our bodies felt the need of those workday pints. On the Saturday half-day we drank more than two because our minds it was that felt the need.

The need to talk long until we talked loud without knowing, to talk loud until we raised our voices further without knowing. Then we sang one by one until we sang together without knowing: and then we laughed without rightly knowing what all the laughter was about.

Our talk was about the past of our people when a craftsman was a man of substance with the past the present and the future of his children in his two craftsman's hands: it was then we talked long. We talked of our own day when a craftsman in his workshop spread the job of a day till it covered a week because the idle hand became a fist: it was then we talked loud. We talked of the new world of new people where the foot was forced to the shape of the boot, houses were poured with buckets into casings of board; where the house of prayer looked more a hall for song. It was then our voices climbed and travelled to the unheeding street.

Then someone would sing. Someone young would sing and the throat would be proud in the open neck of the Sunday shirt as the notes went from it loud and soft to rise and die, to ripple and leap, to laugh and sob and sigh and melt in quiet above our tilted faces. The singer was ours and the song was ours. The singer was theirs—the dead ones'. The song was theirs for the words had not changed. Nor had the singer changed. The face of his father and his father's father was under the tilt of the brown soft hat and the forelock heavy on the forehead. The power in the body, the blood in the veins, the heart crying in the voice were the power and the blood and the heart and the voice of his father's on through the listening years that were part of eternity now with the ghosts who walked when night put a careful corner of her shawl over the well-field, and pinned it there with four sharp, shining stars.

And it was in the pause between a song and a song that the two Leary brothers came the night we thought of giving them the well-field.

There was the usual space between the coming of one brother and the other—a half dozen of the long one's long strides. Two days previous an uncle had died leaving only a childless wife and the two Leary brothers for his land and his riches. We never liked the uncle or the shrewd, stranger wife he was punished with. But we liked the two Leary brothers. When the short one stepped from the street we would have jibed at him about his chance of good fortune in the will, but for something about the way he walked to the counter. He was always quick on his feet and bold in display of his prominent belly: like the new town clerk when God gave him bad news about the old stock for the ears of the new town council. This time he was even quicker on his feet but less the big-drummer with his middle.

'Double whiskies,' he ordered.

'How are we, lads?' said the long one coming in.

There was something about him too. What he had in height was matched with weight well moulded onto big bones. He was smiling, but there was nothing new in that. His face under the tweed cap always hung in the part-sad, part-mocking smile of the born fighter who has been hit with all the other has and still is standing, and yet is powerless to get home with his own sledge-hammer blow. This time it was that the smile had a new shape: as if the other had hit him in a mean way and the smile was salted with a bleeding lip.

'Here's to the old stock anyhow,' he said and the glass only parted the smile as he drank.

'May they rest,' said the short one.

Suddenly a chuckle put sound to the long one's smile.

'I'm thinking what a hell of a hard time they're giving the uncle now,' he said.

And we knew straight away that the uncle had left them out of his will.

'How bad is it?' Jim Lannigan asked.

Jim was a woodcarver and the oldest of the old stock living.

'Couldn't be worse,' the short one answered.

'It could,' the long one disagreed. 'We could be dead with him and known to relatives for all eternity.'

'Nothing at all then?' Old Lannigan asked.

'Not even a mention,' said the short one.

'Not even to ask us for prayers for his soul,' said the long one. 'Because he knew he'd have them after the reading of the will.'

We had been certain of good fortune for them in the will. We all wished for it. Our women prayed for it. Our children knew it as the happy story waiting for an end. Our dead watched for it to make their Heaven whole before they turned their faces smiling on eternity.

'Herself will have it all so,' Tom Breen, the oldest blacksmith, said, his big hand gentle on his grey moustache.

'And she'll bring a stranger brood to fill the place of children,' growled Lyne, the painter.

'More new owners for old goods,' MacGillicuddy the stonecutter agreed, his dead left eye indifferent to the anger in the right.

'Changes for the better don't happen any more,' said Casey the stone-mason. It was not the uncle's money that mattered. It was not the houses or the car—or his power because that came from selling the soul of our kind for the new kind of soul. All we wanted for the two Leary brothers were the sandpit, the quarry and the two workshops. For here then would be two of the old stock who were men of substance still among the new people. Here would be a part of our town belonging where it properly belonged. Here would be two of our own who had it in their power to will a portion of our town to some of our own coming after: a stake to hold till maybe the new people would wear old and the old stock would come new into their own again. And then it was that someone said:

'What about the well-field?'

There was a silence: in it the old and the young faces were as still as the pewter and bronze amid the gleam of the bottles. The sounds of the street grew big and drew near like a challenge. Sunlight through a high window lit up the nook where Old Lannigan sat, his grandson standing tall and young at his shoulder. The old man's hair and beard shone quiet like the pewter. The young one's red hair shone bold like the bronze. The dust in the sunlight softened the picture they made to tone like old masters. When Old Lannigan spoke the challenge of the street drew away again.

'The well-field,' he said. 'What about the well-field?'

'It belongs to the Learys,' said the son of the blacksmith.

'It belonged to them one time,' Old Lannigan corrected.

'It belongs to them still.'

'By right it do, but in law it don't.'

'Why so?' asked the son of the blacksmith.

'I'm no law man,' Old Lannigan said. 'But the way I heard of the law in this matter, the well-field belongs to no one man or no one family anymore.'

'The Learys never signed it over to any man,' the grandson of the stonemason argued.

'The law don't always look for a signature,' Old Lannigan explained. 'It seems that if a man laves a thing like a field open to public trespass for a number of years, that field becomes common property.'

'What is the number of years?' asked the grandson of a cooper.

Old Lannigan smiled.

'Far less than the years between us and the Learys who made that mistake,' he said.

'There's four generations of Learys between them and the two Leary brothers.'

'Time enough for a change in worlds,' said Tom Breen, the blacksmith.

'And for a change in Learys,' said the long Leary out of his new smile.

'Our kind don't change,' MacGillicuddy said quietly, his good eye as mild as the dead one.

'The world has changed,' the short Leary said. 'The only way we can have a place in life at all is to bring a bit of our own world back.'

'We'll begin with the well-field,' Young Lannigan said.

'What can we do about the well-field?' asked Old Lannigan, looking up at him.

'The town has a right to trespass on the well-field—right?' asked the grandson.

Old Lannigan nodded agreement.

'Supposing the town gave up the right of trespass, wouldn't the field come back to the two Leary brothers?' Young Lannigan went on.

Old Lannigan thought for a moment, then shook his head.

'You'll never get them all to agree,' he said. 'If there isn't one way there's another,' said Young Lannigan.

'Yes!' said the youngsters to a man.

'But is it fair to ask or to force?' Old Lannigan insisted.

'Aye,' the old ones gave agreement to the wisdom of the question.

But Young Lannigan would not be shaken.

'What's not fair?' he said.

'Every scar on the crust of that field was made by our people before the new people ever came. The football part, the circus part, the tinkers' part along the wall, the courting pathway under the trees, the grass worn on the bank of the stream, the stone steps worn to the flag kneeler of the well itself: every single sign of life going and coming to that field is a sign made by our lives and the lives of no one else.'

'True!' agreed the young ones in a body.

Old Lannigan cupped his hands over the head of his stick. There was silence for a moment. Then his old voice dreamed away to agreement.

'And the dew on the trampled grass, and the webs that we break in the arch to take water from the well in the morning: they are put there while the ghosts of our kind walk the old ways when night is on the world.'

'Aye,' said the old man and the young together like an Amen to a prayer.

'We can try anyhow,' Old Lannigan said.

'We can start straight away,' Young Lannigan said.

'We will start after last Mass tomorrow,' said Old Lannigan. 'When we have less of the drink in us and more of the grace of God.'

'After last Mass.'

Last Mass was our Mass on Sundays. At six o'clock, through the last of night and the first of day our women, cowled in shawls, went to Mass and Holy Communion. Mass and Holy Communion for our children at nine: but last Mass for our men always, except on Christmas mornings and Easter mornings when we went to Holy Communion too. To keep in the memory of our God, and ease the minds of our women and our priests.

Our God was a strong and a fair God. Our sins were made weak by the strength of their manner. Our church was worthy of our God.

The spire was so high that a twenty-foot cross at the top looked the size for a rosary. The dark oak ceilings were so far overhead that a lost bird lit by the eave windows looked as small and as bright as a moth near a candle. Candles on the altar looked remote from the porch as stars when they are nearest. The great organ broke like a storm of singing winds against the grey-blue granite of the walls. Yet even the high hidden inches that never would know the eye of man were a credit to the skill and care of our ghosts who built it.

Over the road from our church was our river. Over the river was our green-stone bridge, where the old stock met after last Mass for as long as our town was a town.

That Sunday in the shade of the alders by the bridge we began to talk again about the well-field. The upshot of the talk was the final decision to ask each person of the new people to forgo their right of trespass on it. For thoroughness we agreed on a door-to-door talk with them, beginning with the business class.

Old Lannigan led the way, withered the way a tree withers, bent but with strength to the minute of the fall. Tom Breen the blacksmith on his left, the smooth clear skin of all blacksmiths clear and smooth still in spite of his years. On his right MacGillicuddy the stonecutter, like all stonecutters hewn into age as if Time in its turn used a mallet and chisel: his good eye watching Old Lannigan's stick so that his feet would not come in the way of it. All together in that town of new people we did not add to one hundred men. Age and near-aged at the front, youth in the middle and rear: the halter of years on old bones was a check on young tempers. The check was needed before all was said. The check did not hold before all was done.

Give them their due, the new business people agreed almost to a man. But in some cases the way they agreed left room for improvement. The well-field meant nothing to them. Their lovers' walk led more imposing ways. Their children kicked football in a field that boasted regular goal-posts in place of the heap of little patched jackets. The circus of their day brought them richer and bigger wonders than cantering horses and tumbling clowns, so it called for more space than our field could give. Many of them hardly knew that our field was there at all. But some grew a new interest when we explained our errand. A new clutch tightened on the poor coin in the corner of the purse. Nevertheless, Old Lannigan's calm face or the blacksmith's great shoulders, or the quiet stare of the stonecutter's dead eye had their way. Where they had not, the flare of devil in younger eyes had. By nightfall we had accounted for the business portion of the new people.

Next evening after work we began on the new working class. Here we were taking our case to a harder court and we knew it. Many times on our rounds it took all the elders could do to hold young fists from flailing. We had never welcomed the new worker. It was not in our nature to say one thing and mean another, to hide a grudge with a show of smiles. Openly, honestly but none the less hurtfully we and our dead despised their jack-of-all-trades invasion of our world. One man one craft, was our motto; and the man for the craft must be bred to it. We shared the secrets of our craft with each other only. We refused to work with any but our own kind whose name in a craft was as old as the craft. As one man we walked away from an employer who took on any but men who were indentured to work with us. To get work the new worker had to cut wages and work a longer day. Their chances were poor enough, until the makeshift and the jerry-built became the order of the day. Then it was their turn to be up and our turn to be down. Their better fortune had not healed old wounds because day by day the handful that was left of us made the wounds to sting again. Nevertheless, we faced them, and they faced us.

For our direct question they had a direct answer: a quiet 'no' that for all its quietness bore a hint of challenge. Old Lannigan led us away to talk the matter over. Age at the front, youth in the middle and rear; and age was a good way gone before they discovered that youth had slipped back and away from the slow procession.

As Old Lannigan led the old ones towards the river bridge, Young Lannigan was leading the young ones into the new workers' district. The young ones of the new workers expected this and were advancing along the road to meet them. Not a voice was raised, no word was spoken as the two groups walked step for step towards a meeting on the quiet road. Only the trees could have seen, and beyond the trees the cross on the spire, beyond the cross the evening star: beyond the star the eyes of our dead looking back. From some faces colour drained, in others colour strength-ened as the quiet road gave full value to the unhurried steps. No face showed a trace of the fear which panics where the shout is not there to dull the thud of the heart on the eardrum and words are not shared to steel the stiffened arm for the violence of the blow. No word, no shout, no tremor on the mask-set face. There never are where hate is seasoned through many years and blows are struck in the secret dream before life itself brings the time and the place. No sound on the quiet road, only march of men towards march of men, till man to man they met and fought with only the thud of the blow and the hiss of the breath to hear in the quietness that trees dusked with their shadows. The blows are hard that seasoned hate can strike. The blows are hard that seasoned hate can stand. Blood was the wine to quicken the spirit, hurt was the spur to hurt more. Quick, strong, vicious but always silent, the young men fought in a moving, wheeling tangled mass as Old Lannigan led the old ones back in search of the young.

'Stop!' he shouted on the fringe of the fight, but no one heeded.

'In God's name, stop!' he shouted again.

The bent back almost straightened as he raised his face like an angry old saint. But the fight went on. It was then that the long Leary, with a touch of the old smile on the shape of the new, spread his long arms and forced a way for Old Lannigan into the thick of the fighting so that he suffered no more than the loss of his hat.

'In the name of God, stop!' he shouted again, the stick raised high over his bare head.

'Stop, stop, stop!'

This time they heeded him. Their fury was bright in their eyes as they looked his way, so that for the instant it seemed as if their hate was for him.

'I'm ashamed of ye,' he said.

'When you were young yourself you did the same,' Young Lannigan defended.

'And the old ones of my time did what I'm doing now,' said Old Lannigan. 'We were all of us in this from the start. It matters to all of us, whether young or old, and ye shouldn't have made a move that wasn't decided by all.'

'On our side the story is the same,' a voice as old as Lannigan's stated.

Even men of medium height hid the speaker from sight. When they stood aside a little bearded man with a skin as brown and wrinkled as an old leaf walked up to Old Lannigan and peered into his gundog face with a terrier's cheek. It was Timmie Hartigan, the oldest man among the new workers.

'It do seem,' said he, 'that the new and the old know the language of the fist.'

'The cunning of the craft don't rob the hand of force in a blow,' said Old Lannigan.

'It do seem,' said Old Hartigan, 'that ye were in earnest about the well-field. Is there gold in it?'

'What's in it for us is not in it for ye,' said Old Lannigan.

'There's an answer for that, if I knew it,' said Hartigan.

'If you were born again,' said Old Lannigan.

'I wouldn't be born again if they made me the son of a king,' said Hartigan. 'Because there was bound to be trouble in my reign. But tell me, the answer ye got to that question ye put was deserved.'

'I don't follow,' Old Lannigan told him.

'The way the question is put calls the tune of the answer,' Hartigan explained. 'The way ye put the question ignored the fact that we had rights in that field. Ye didn't ask us, ye told us.'

'No one but a Leary has a right in life to the well-field,' Old Lannigan stated.

'The world and its mother—may God forgive her—have a right in law,' said Hartigan.

'Do ye recognize that we have a share in that right? Do ye admit that it is right ye should ask us in a fair way for what it is our right to keep or to give? Do ye, now?'

'Are you talking in law or in life?' asked Old Lannigan.

'In law then,' said Hartigan.

'We're no law men,' Old Lannigan told him.

'We are when it suits us,' said Hartigan, jerking his quick little terrier head in impatience.

'So here then, do ye recognize our right in law to take the stand we took?'

'We have to,' said Old Lannigan. 'And here and now, we do.'

'Come home, lads, the battle is over,' said Hartigan, turning on his heel.

'One way or another it would end the same,' said Old Lannigan. 'Good evening to you.'

Then the two old men led their followers away, as dusk filled the lengthening space between them on the quiet road that the trees could see, and the cross on the spire, and beyond the cross the star. But beyond the star our dead no longer looked back. They had turned their faces smiling on eternity.

The high heads of the old ones were good to see. The pain of the bruise was good to feel. The smile on the face of the long one was the smile of the game fighter who has been hit for almost the once too often, but at last has himself been able to hit. Steps were firm. Tongues were tied. Feeling was tight in the throat and hot at the back of the eyes. With fists clenched hard and teeth hard pressed together for control we walked high-headed past the new owners of that town that used to be ours.

Perhaps we knew it was the last time we all would walk together in that town. That could be. Because we knew where we came from we knew where we were going. Because we had had our day we knew the night was near. As night drew down about us we remembered the brightness of the morning and how strong the sun was on our faces when it struck upon our noon. Maybe we felt that when we walked together on the earth again there would be one the less with us, and one the more the length of a last breath away. Maybe we felt it in our bones that each new time we ever after walked together on the earth there would be one the less on the earth with us, and one the more walking the old ways when night spread that special corner of her shawl over the well-field and pinned it there till dawn with four, sharp, shining stars. Lannigan. Breen. MacGillicuddy. Casey. One by one they left us. But leaving they left with us the well-field for our daylight, and we left it for them when the daylight was gone.

We did proudly by the well-field for them. Our blacksmiths gave it a gate. Our masons gave it a wall. Our carpenters gave it trellised fences to brace the young spines of the cypress trees, which our gardeners borrowed from the new rich tenders of old gardens while their dogs were away. Our stonecutters gave it new grey steps to the old stone kneeler by the well. Our woodcarvers gave it a story in seasoned oak for the niche above the arch of the well shelter.

And maybe we felt it was the last time we would have full freedom in our crafts in this new world of new methods. The iron gates were fit to stand between an eye and the moon: fine in the light as the art of the spider, all curl and scroll and flowering into shapes as graceful as blossom on drooped stem. And the story being forever told in mellow oak was about Joseph our patron saint, and Mary the nearest neighbour of our women, and Jesus whom our children knew well. Joseph stood at his carpenter's bench, Mary was in the doorway of the workshop holding an earthenware jar full to the brink with clear-cool water from the nearest well, Jesus with His child's hand was raising a cupful to the craftsman's hand of the carpenter.

As the years went by the cypresses grew into tall and dark green plumes. The field each year grew the shining golden mane of a meadow. With scythes we swept it gently from the root and let it lie, for the sun by day and the feet of our dead by night. When it was dry and the colour of pale light we drew it away and sold it to buy winter boots for our children. Shorn of the shining mane the crust of the field showed through the glinting stubble. And there they were again. The football pitch where we ran and rose and gripped and kicked, and argued after as we panned the stream water with a plate of palms against our fire-hot faces. The circus ring, where mild-eyed horses, bits strapped to the breastband on short leash to arch the columned necks, circled big and broad as if cast in bronze for bronze-cast horsemen, while little clowns with great noses and wide check trousers cartwheeled for the laughter of our children. The tinkers' camping ground along the wall, where big-bosomed women combed long copper-coloured hair by faggot fires at night while their young fought sleep away with giddy laughter under the tilted spring-carts, and their men sang in drink together on the road home with ashplants beating time while ready to defend defenceless heads. The lovers' walk under the lime trees, where love grew that was blessed in the church of our God to last forever without end.

But each year fewer scythes were needed for fewer reapers, as more of our aged went on to our dead and more of our primed went on into age. And fewer pairs of boots were needed as our very young moved on into youth and went to care for themselves in other countries. The men of our kind were the first to pass on nearly always: and always their women followed in the next spring, if worry about a child or a grandchild did not hold them from going a while more. Men and women, they went on to our dead ones: the aged ones. The younger and young went over the seas, in search of a town where crafts were not forgotten and craftsmen not wholly neglected.

Each year there were faces missing among the gathering on the green-stone bridge after last Mass. Until the year came when the shadow of the alders purpled the pipe-smoke of only the two Leary brothers. They held the field for our departed living and our dead departed and would not leave it. For five years there were only the two Leary brothers. Then in the spring of the sixth year the short Leary brother passed fussily away, and there was only the long one each Sunday on the bridge: elbows on the parapet, old smiling face between old gnarled craftsman's hands, smiling down on the amber river until the need to eat called him away. One Sunday he never left the bridge at all, or never stirred at all, but no one noticed because there was no one left to care whether he ate or not. No one noticed until a dog in the evening shivered on the leash and would not pass. The owner drew near the long one and looked into the old smiling face between old gnarled craftsman's hands, and knew that the eyes were not seeing the river. But he did not know, as we would have known, that the last had joined the rest to walk that night in the well-field.

It was the last thing we owned in that town: the well-field. But when we were all gone the new town clerk confided to the new town council that he knew all along that we never owned the well-field at all, that it would have taken an Act of Parliament to give back to Learys what the law of trespass had taken from their ancestors, that anyhow it did not matter because the long Leary had willed the field to the old stock, and there were none of the old stock left, so even if the will were valid the field would belong to the government of the country. But he did not know, as we would have known, that the old stock walked together after nightfall in the well-field. Further, the new town clerk suggested that the field, with its magnificent gate, shrined well and tall cypresses was ideal for what the new people had had need of for a long time: a new cemetery.

And so it came to pass that even our dead, to be together, must walk unfamiliar ways, or lie forever in unrest.

Tailor's Rest

Long Ned Friel's small devil of humour was a shy one. To the people of Tower Lane it seemed as if it lived among his big bones as a squirrel lives in a tree. Loop-swings up to a chatter to the brain, a spring to the eyes to see its inspiration happen, then a long drop to laugh deep where no one ever heard it. All they ever saw of it was the dart of its bright eye in Ned's quiet eyes and its touch on his lip as it dropped.

At one time Ned owned the first shop to the right in the world beyond the lane archway. It was a small shop with a big ledger. When hard times came to the lane the ledger was full from cover to cover with the names of lane people. In the long run Ned gave the empty boxes and coloured showcards to the lane children, put up the shutters for the last time, locked the door and accepted the only return the lane people could give him for favours received—a place among themselves.

He strode with his small devil down the cobbled lane between the two rows of coloured one-storey houses to number 13 on the right, the bachelor home of Mickey Rice.

Mickey was the tailor tail-end of a long line of seamen. One look at him was enough to know that the past of the blood was disappointed in the present. All he had in common with the seamen was the hint of a sea roll, a liking for come-all-ye sea shanties and a few phrases of south-west Gaelic. Shoulders straight, head on a back tilt, Mickey carried his paunch as if it braced the big drum of a brass band. His little black eyes in their pouches had a big-drummer's fanatical glare. Every three steps he gave a big-drummer's puff at his black moustache. He wore a big-drummer's mask of moisture in warm weather and owned the father and mother of a big-drummer's thirst.

His way of carrying the paunch had another reason in his fondness for fancy waistcoats. In a way he took himself seriously as a leader of fashions for the poor man. Waistcoats became his obsession because any stray piece of material made the front of a waistcoat and what the rest was like went under the jacket. His taste ran to large checks in three colours, red predominating. As long as red predominated and the checks were large enough the run of the rainbow held no fears for Mickey after that.

A nickel-plated watch chain hung on the waistcoats like the upside-down of a seagull's flight. He was very proud of that watch chain. The lane admired its silver wings. Children were reminded by it to ask him the time and smile in the knowledge that he had no watch. And in secret, all that suited Mickey down to the ground.

One more word about Mickey. He was not known at all until an idea is had of the pride he took in his seafaring ancestors.

'They came from Dingle. From Dingle, think of that, man. If it hurts you to think, sit down to it. From the nearest parish to America they came: from so far to the edge of that parish that they let the sea in to quench the fire. *Tá sé sin go ceart*, man.'

'A strange thing for them to breed a tailor, Mickey?'

'Sitting didn't do your thinking any good. Stand up again. Hadn't they to stitch sails and knit nets, hadn't they? *Tá tú ag rádh* damn nonsense now, man. Have another drink anyhow ...'

And sooner or later in a mood like that he would tell of how he brought his mother back to rest with the seamen. A frail little wisp of a woman, timid as a doe, the limitations of her mind and body fibre it surely was that robbed the sea of Mickey. When the sea gave back the body of her man she had it buried with his own, in the cliff-top grave in Inniscara, and fled with her three-year-old son to Tower Lane, forty miles inland.

Church cleaner was her job until she died. She left with the lane the memory of a gentle presence, and with Mickey a pride in strong forebears when all the time her concern was to make him hate the sea that claimed them. But living in her mind with that hatred she had for the sea was a great wish to rest with her man above it at the end.

'I'd like to go back to him, Michael, when my days are up. But we're too poor. Too poor to pay for the long way back …'

'We'll see now, we'll see,' Mickey would tell her, then go to sit with another stout while he thought the matter over.

When the mother died he still was poor, but the thinking was done for him by the people of Tower Lane.

That week the pawnshop in the world beyond the archway did a record business. Wearables that never surrendered their Sunday dignity before were marshalled with warrior garments of long pawn experience against the brass barrier that topped the counter.

Old Pat Nagle's bowler hat ranked with Foley the sweeper's corduroy breeches. Big Mane Leary's shawl of many colours was a cushion of brightness among its plainer sisters. Gentle Norrie Sugrue's cameo brooch was brave among strong watches, like a lavender lady in a worker's pub. The seven remaining pieces of old Moll Flanagan's china teaset appeared to have accepted her breathed apology in the spirit given, for they shone in that dim place when Moll had taken her shillings to Ned Friel.

Ned was collector, organizer and adviser to Mickey. When the offerings were four pounds short of the right height on his counter, Ned's till and his wallet were emptied on the pile. And for a finish he had to go with Mickey in the motor hearse on that long journey to Inniscara above the sea.

'Look, Ned, I'd be blind if I didn't know I was a quare hawk for appearance. *Tuigeann tú*, Ned, do you understand me? I don't want the lads in Dingle to know that a man of my blood is that big of a mistake. So I'm thinking that when we come to the end of our journey, and meet the people who knew my people: I'm thinking that I can be you then, Ned, and you can be me …'

And there by the grave in Inniscara it was as if Mickey's mother came to him and gave him the wish to rest with the seamen that had possessed her.

'I'm thinking, Ned, that I'd like to come here when I'm done myself. 'Tis far away from everything and everybody. Great peace and no distractions. This is the place to rest, Ned, and I'd like to come back.'

In the years that followed he went as far as having several tries at putting the bit by for the way back, but the publican in the world beyond the archway got every penny of it when tailoring failed to take care of his thirst. Finally it was left to Ned's small devil of humour to start the wheels in the right direction.

To liven the air during a time of despondency, and for want of a better inspiration to get Mickey talking, Ned's small devil prompted Ned to draw the tailor's attention to the number on his door. Number 13. Unlucky 13. Instead of a tirade Ned was greeted by a request for a screwdriver. With the screwdriver Mickey removed the brass numbers, but their imprint remained; so he scraped the timber with the point of the screwdriver till the imprint had gone in a flurry of splinters. When Ned thought to get under his skin by pointing out the fact that the raw mark looked unsightly, Mickey gave back that he would think of something to cover it.

What he thought of came as a surprise to everyone: nothing less than a metal disc, representing Saint Christopher walking the angry waters of a river with the Infant on his shoulder. The disc was meant for the dashboard of a motor car, but it covered the raw patch on the door to perfection. Through a perforation on either side Mickey had fitted a thumbtack to keep it in place.

'What's the idea?' Ned asked when he saw it on the door.

'Saint Christopher, man,' said Mickey, thumbs crooked in the pockets of his technicolour waistcoat. 'He's the patron saint of sure journeys.'

'But this ship is going nowhere,' argued Ned.

'But I am,' said Mickey. 'Any day now I might be called away, and maybe that man will take me all the way to Inniscara above the sea.'

Every day for five years more Mickey polished the Saint Christopher till it shone in the sun like the wings of his watch chain. Children turned to asking him why it was there on his door, because they knew he would tell them the legend of Saint Christopher all over again. It challenged waistcoats and watch chain for hold on his mind. It took full possession when Mickey had the accident in the world beyond the archway.

The driver of the car was on his right side, and travelling sober. It was the other way round with Mickey. A half-hour later, when Ned walked the long ward of the county hospital, he was prepared for the worst. He knew the worst had happened when he saw the tailor. All but the black eyes and the mouth, under its shelter of black moustache, was wound about with bandage. 'What I can see is sound anyhow,' Ned greeted.

'Did you bring it, Ned?' said the mouth, and the eyes had sparks like frost on two sloes.

'Trust me,' said Ned, taking four bottles of stout and a corkscrew out of various pockets.

'Not that,' complained the mouth.

'What so?' Ned asked.

'The Saint Christopher, Ned, the Saint Christopher,' said the mouth.

'I brought that, too, thumbtack and all,' said Ned, and the frost sparks melted on the two sloes.

'Show it here to me,' Mickey said. 'And drink the stout yourself, Ned, because the way it is, Ned, I'm a done duck where I lie.'

'Ah, no,' said Ned.

'Ah, yes,' said Mickey. 'The priest was here after the doctors put me together. I had a long chat with him, Ned, and the sacraments, Ned, and I'm ready to go now. But whisper. Where are you, Ned?'

'I'm here, Mike,' Ned told him.

'The eyes are dimming on me,' said Mickey. 'Any time now it will be lights out, and there's this I want to say. There's nothing for me but the pauper's plot, but no matter. I'm not insured. That car didn't shake a penny in my pocket. There was no penny there to shake. All the people of Tower Lane are the same these days. If an earthquake shook the lane the way the car shook me all that would be heard is falling stone on empty ware. What they have don't let them spend on me, Ned. *Bhfuil tú ag éisteacht liom?* Are you listening?'

'I'm listening, Mike,' Ned told him.

'Good,' said Mickey, 'because this is important. Fix the Saint Christopher on the lid of the ould box, Ned. He didn't see his way to lead me to the right spot in this world. He'll maybe make up for it by finding the right spot for me in the next. And one thing more, Ned.'

'What is it, Mike?' asked Ned.

'Rest here for the while till it happens.'

'I'm resting, Mike.'

'And drink the stout, Ned, because the way it is, Ned, I'd sooner it was in good hands than in bad.'

An hour later Mickey was dead.

Ned felt awkward about facing the lane people. When he turned in at the archway the half-door awnings of the little houses glowed with lamp-light. When his steps sounded on the cobbles each glowing square was broken by their coming to the doors. In the broken light their half-lit faces waited for news. But when Ned walked by them without a word, they understood.

Hands were raised for a sign of the cross. Lips moved in prayer. Latches sounded quietly as doors closed behind the half-doors to seal the glow of light away. Grown-ups in the kitchens talked of the heart behind the waistcoats. Children, in their beds, lit their minds for a moment with the silver wings of a watch chain, and went to sleep again.

They were asleep for a long time before the elders broke from thinking how Mickey was to be saved from a pauper's grave. And for hours after all the lane was at last asleep Ned sat on in Number 13, pondering how he could get Mickey all the way to Inniscara above the sea.

In the morning the lane birds had hardly stirred in their cages when window-blinds were up, and fires sending the first cold curl of smoke up the wide chimneys. Daylight was barely on the colours of the houses when the women were moving to the pump for pails of water. The taste of breakfast on their lips, the men and women together were early in to Ned in Number 13. Small silver from purses, pennies from pockets, ha'pennies from money boxes that still had Christmas newness on them were put among the scraps on the tailor's table.

But the money brought together was only just enough for the people's wish, the pounds short of what Ned's wish needed.

Ned's first concern was the securing, with the thumbtack, of the Saint Christopher to the lid of Mickey's coffin in the hospital mortuary. When he got back he set about preparing for the funeral.

Gentle Norrie Sugrue was given to buy the good habit, warm socks and underwear, and to see to it that Mickey was clad in them and laid in his coffin. Big Mane Leary bought the green plot in the new cemetery: not too near a wall for fear of dampness, well in the centre of a row for company's sake, near to an oak tree for easy finding with a visit and a prayer. In the matter of expensive fittings to hide the makeshift of the workhouse coffin, old Moll Flanagan stuck four purple tassels on the handles. Because they were stylish, she explained, and Mickey was a great man for his bit of style; and to have her wish she borrowed from the postmaster on the strength of Friday's pension. Everyone was satisfied except Ned.

As Ned brought Jack the carpenter to put the fittings on the coffin he still was troubled about Mickey's resting-place.

On the way they met gentle Norrie Sugrue, quietly pleased about the success of her errand, breathless with the tale of how lucky they were to have put the Saint Christopher on Mickey's coffin. Because not one, but two workhouse coffins were in the mortuary now, she said; both waiting for the fancy fittings, so that the Saint Christopher was the only way of telling which was which.

The mortuary was locked, the key in the keeping of the hospital matron, so Ned sent Jack the carpenter in search of her. A look into the mortuary through the window while he waited confirmed Norrie's story of the two coffins. The two were there on trestles inside, Mickey's Saint Christopher claiming him, centred at the foot of the lid.

Ned had just lighted his pipe when a strange motor hearse drew up at the mortuary door. With the driver was an old lady, weathered and worn of face, in a shawl as brave with colour as big Mane Leary's, and a young man in coarse tweeds who carried the breastplate, screws and side handles of a coffin.

'I sent for the key,' Ned told them when they got down from the hearse. 'I see we have the same job on our hands.'

'That we have,' said the young man, almost cheerfully for one on his errand.

'Ye came a journey,' Ned ventured.

'Dingle,' said the young man. Ned hid the quickening of his interest by taking his time.

'I know Inniscara well,' he said at last.

'The very place we're taking the ould wan that's dead,' said the young man.

'Is she a relation?' Ned asked.

'No then,' said the old woman. 'She just drifted among us from God knows where a year ago, and died with us. She had a bit of insurance and there's worse ways for spending it than taking her back to Inniscara, we thought.'

'Inniscara above the sea,' said Ned.

'Above the sea, then,' said the old lady. 'The cliff graveyard.'

'Here's my man with the key,' said Ned.

As he went towards Jack the carpenter for the key he hid an eagerness with a slow stride. Having the key made sure of being first into the mortuary. One stride had him at the foot of the coffins. His broad back shielded his hands as they changed the Saint Christopher from Mickey's coffin to the strange lady's.

'Which coffin is which, stranger?' the young man asked.

'Ours is the one with the Saint Christopher on the lid.' Ned lied, the small devil peeping in his eyes for an instant, and faintly touching his lip as it dropped.

'Inniscara above the sea,' he breathed to himself as he walked from the gloom into the bright day.

It took Tower Lane a whole month to get over a worry about Ned. For had they not seen him with their own eyes, walking five miles in the direction of the wrong funeral.

Brownie

Brownie the poacher was as lean as his black-and-white mongrel terrier, and as brown as the hazelnut ready for the hammer on the hearthstone of Halloween. And a tidy size for his job: small enough to have cover from the golden mop of a stunted furze or a tangle of briar barely big enough to fill a child's bright tin with blackberries. To see him climb a wall with the terrier on his shoulder and Glinnane the gamekeeper's hounds pounding a wood walk after him with the big chamois pads of their paws was a lesson in cool and collected hurry. The oldest of very old soft hats would be as near to the age of Brownie's as makes no matter. His heather tweed jacket was as shorn of wool from wear and weather as if he scraped it with the penknife he used for skinning rabbits or slitting the silver belly of a fish. Knee-breeches kneecapped with layers of patches, puttees that he wore in Mons, brown boots that a thoughtful butty had brought safely through the Dardanelles made the sum of what he wore: except, of course the grey army shirt, the navy waistcoat, and the red patterned handkerchief tied gypsy-way round his neck. One other item he wore constantly: the Woodbine in the corner of his mouth. Once lit he never touched it, except with the tip of his tongue to swing it to whatever side of his face he wished. When an eighth of an inch of tobacco held the smouldering top from his lips he spat it out.

The right-handed waistcoat pocket in a pub was a teller of Brownie's finances after the day, as was the tail of his jacket the giver-away on his day's luck when you met him homing over the road through the coloured dusk of evening. The tail of his jacket was his bag, the waistcoat pocket was his bank. Under cover of dusk he would walk the back ways of the town to the back doors of his customers. As he progressed in the general direction of Will Hegarty's pub the bulge of the bag subsided as the protuberance of the bank swelled gradually. He would hardly have passed the door of the pub when Will had the pint glass under the tap. While the tawny froth of liquor climbed the glass there would be no word between the two. Hoisting his great stomach against the ledge of the counter Will would put the part-full glass on the counter for a moment and wait, his lips making little puffs of breath under his moustache, while the froth blackened on the bottom and the black crept upward devouring the froth. Then he would give the glass back to the tap of the barrel again till all was black with a collar of cream.

'A good pint, Will.'

'Not bad, Brownie.'

'Not bad is good, Will.'

'That's fine, Brownie.'

'That's logic, Will.'

Perhaps another deep swig from which, with watching, Will drew full satisfaction at second hand.

'Had you a good day, Brownie?'

'Not bad, Will.'

'Not bad is good, Brownie, accordin' to logic.'

'Right, Will.'

And so it would go between them, Brownie sitting on a barrel with the pint at his elbow on the counter, Will leaning against shelves of Spanish and Portugese and French-sounding empties under the great yellow face of his great-grandfather's clock, while the terrier's stretch on the saw-dusted floor curved with the barrel-end as she dozed between delicately touching forepaws.

Brownie and his dog were inseparable. But one day the gamekeeper's two hounds surprised the pair of them when the poacher was in the act of emptying his snares.

With a fair start he beat them to the ivied wall. He was beyond reach of their jaws with the terrier on his shoulder when a stone broke from the wall. He swayed, recovered, but the terrier fell like a bright toy into the jaws of the Great Dane. If the terrier fawned she had a chance but she fought like a game rat in a corner. Brownie jumped clear off the wall and broke the spine of the setter with his nail-shod boots and swung for the Dane. There was sweep, sway and ripple of muscle from the Dane and Brownie's boots lunged and ripped at the gleaming body. There was growl, snarl, and terrier's yelp and Brownie's venom-hissed curses. There was a shrill whistle through a vent in strong teeth: Glinnane was on the scene. Silence fell like a dropped hat. The Great Dane let go of the terrier and slunk in a half-circle towards the keeper. The setter dragged maimed hindquarters towards him in a direct line. The terrier lay on red-stained grass at Brownie's feet. Brownie made no attempt to escape. Glinnane strode steadily up till the setter flung its weight on his feet. The two stood without words for a while.

'I'm sorry about your dog, Brownie,' Glinnane broke silence.

'Can't be helped now,' Brownie gave back. Then he added, 'I suppose the yoke is loaded.'

'The gun?'

'What else!'

'Yes, 'tis loaded.'

'Would you be good enough to—'

Brownie stopped and motioned towards the terrier. Glinnane stepped back to let his own dog lie on the grass. He strode to within a yard of the terrier.

'Step back, Brownie, like a good lad.'

Brownie's step and the shot were simultaneous. Glinnane held the gun out to Brownie.

'Give mine the other barrel,' he said.

Brownie raised, aimed and fired in the one movement, but the setter heaved and keeled over.

'You haven't lost your use of the gun, Brownie,' Glinnane said.

'If it had a third barrel I'd be tempted to try at a movin' target,' Brownie said with an eye on the shifting fretfulness of the Great Dane.

Glinnane took back the gun with one hand and struck the tail of Brownie's coat with the other.

'I hate to spoil the party, Brownie.'

'That's your trade, Glinnane.'

'How many is in it?'

'I lost count.'

'I'll have to make a charge, Brownie'

'I suppose 'tis time you had a chance, Glinnane,' said Brownie; then he stuck his hands in his pockets and walked away.

During the following week, there was no good to be got of him. He moped like an owl in daylight from corner to corner of the town for the first day or two. Then he took to standing with his back and the sole of his right boot against the coat-grimed bricks of the Town Hall, his hat tilted to hide his eyes, his lips jerking the Woodbine as they dropped a limp hello to every greeting, waiting for the clanging hammer of the Town Hall clock above him to unchain the hours. To make matters worse the weather was perfect: sunshine all the time. You would pity him, God's truth, you would miss that terrier yourself. If he had lost a limb he wouldn't have looked as incomplete. With the fall of dusk he would move up to Will's place, and Will would reach for the pint glass, as always.

'Get out the slate, Will.'

'Polished and ready, Brownie.'

'You can chalk up two at least, Will.'

'I'm a good man to make figures, Brownie.'

It was noticeable that Brownie no longer perched on the barrel. With unbecoming respectability he sat on one of the long wooden stools with his back to where he used to sit while Will studied him with sidelong concern. One evening, late in the week, he left the bar and returned inside the counter towards Brownie with his hands behind his back.

'I want to show you somethin', Brownie.'

'If 'tis the cut of the slate I'm blind, Will.'

'Devil take the slate.'

'Give him the somethin', too, Will, while you're at it.'

'You'd be a better judge of what it is.'

'If 'tis handy for the pocket I'll give the court judge a look at it Tuesday.'

'You're not curious, Brownie?'

'I'm curious, Will.'

'Well, that's somethin' to be thankful for.'

'I'm curious to know is it the heat or the customers that's drivin' you balmy, Will.'

'Here, to hell to it, have a look anyway.'

Will swept his hand from cover to conjure onto the counter a black-and-white pup, a mongrel terrier pup with a spot the size of an ink-blob over the right eye and a left ear that stood to attention for no reason at all. The pup floundered under the sudden weight of its distended belly, heaved it onto splayed legs, wobbled, righted itself, sniffed high, sideways and downward, then settled to licking a moist spot on the counter. For a moment Will thought he had won. Brownie's eyes lit. He started in his seat, but relaxed again into indifference.

''Tis makin' a good start, Will.'

''Tis a young lady, Brownie.'

'Worse still, I hate to see ladies drinkin', Will.'

'What else can you expect when she has no one to give her a proper upbringing?'

'A proper end, Will, in deep water.'

'She belongs to no one, Brownie.'

'I don't doubt it, Will.'

'She has a nice head, Brownie.'

'And curiously enough, Will, she is wearin' her tail at the other end.'

'You wouldn't fancy her for yourself, Brownie?'

'No, then, Will.'

''Twas strange all the same, the way she staggered in the door there an' not a word out of her.'

'You must be on the booze-up when you brought her so, Will.'

'When who brought her?'

'She never found her way to this place without somewan bringin' her. I had to be brought here myself the first time.'

'You wouldn't be for takin' the orphan under your wing so, Brownie?'

'She wouldn't have shelter, Will. My wings are clipped.'

'Ah, no!'

'Fill it again, Will.'

'Sure. But about—'

'Fill it again, Will.'

A week later Brownie was in court. The Justice was an ex-British-

army man himself and known to be partial towards the like of Brownie.
He heard the charge with his one good ear, then looked over his specs at
the defendant.

'Have you anything to say?'

'Not a word, y'r h'n'r.'

'Well, I have.'

'Is that so, y'r h'n'r?'

'You went through Mons?'

'I don't boast about it, y'r h'n'r.'

'Why, Sugrue?'

'Many a better man saw less of life because I thought I wanted to see
more of it.'

'You were decorated, I've been told.'

''Twas either a medal or a breast-plate, y'r h'n'r. I got a medal.'

'There is no need to be insolent, Sugrue.'

'Meant what I said, y'r h'n'r.'

'Look here, can you not get honest employment?'

'I never tried.'

'Why?'

'I was afraid I'd get it, y'r h'n'r.'

'Hmm, would you pay a fine of say—say ten shillings?'

'I would not, y'r h'n'r.'

'Then you will have to do a week in jail.'

'Right, y'r h'n'r.'

And be it recorded to his honour's credit that his honour had to draw
a smile from his long wedge of face with a grapple of fingers.

Will was at the door of the courthouse when Brownie's erect small figure stepped into the sunlight between two tall round pillars of the law.
Will spoke a word to the nearer guard. The guard passed the word over
Brownie's old hat to the comrade pillar. The two took one step forward
and looked towards the cross on the friary steeple opposite. Will, mum-
bling a jumble of words that his moustache sieved of all sense, put a brown
paper package of Woodbines and matches and a half-pint of whiskey into
Brownie's pocket.

'You have a note of these, Will?'

'On the cuff, Brownie.'

'Fine, Will.'

'I'm sending the shirt to the laundry tomorrow, Brownie.'

"'Tis a pity I can't send my memory to the laundry as well, Will.'

'I'll send it with the shirt this time, Brownie.'

'No use, Will, I'll have too much time to think where I'm goin'.'

'You might think of what a dog you could make out of that pup I have, Brownie.'

'She's a nice thing, Will, but you can keep her all the same.'

'We'll see.'

'See you in jail, Will.'

'A nice day for a motor drive, Brownie.'

'The best.'

'I'll be tappin' a barrel this day week.'

'I'll drink it, Will.'

Brownie stepped between the pillars of the law.

'Gentlemen! By the left, quick march!'

The pillars moved with him over the pavement, then broke to get into the car. As the car drew away from the kerbing Brownie poked his head through the window and raised a palm.

'Right, Will!'

'Right, Brownie!'

True to his word, Will tapped a barrel the evening of Brownie's return. The small poacher walked in without a greeting, again avoided his perch on the barrel. Nor was there a word from Will as he introduced the glass to the fresh liquor. Neither hinted by even the flicker of an eyelid that a week had passed since they met last. Will leant against the shelves of foreign-sounding empties under the clock, hands touching beyond his expansive middle, puffing little breaths at his walrus moustache as Brownie did a grand job on the first pint.

'A good pint, Will.'

'And well drunk, Brownie.'

'Encore, Will.'

'I bow from the waist, Brownie.'

'I have no way of tellin', Will, but I'll take your word for it.'

'But ... as we were sayin', Brownie.'

'Yes?'

'That pup is still an orphan.'

'You ought to write to the papers, Will.'

'She's thrivin'.'

'Lave it to a lady.'

'She's cute.'

'Which of 'em isn't?'

'She's in a bad way for a right ramble, Brownie, an' my ould feet can't carry me far enough for her to see what she should be seein'. An ould rabbit under a green ditch, an' so on.'

Brownie didn't answer. There was a silence. Will began to curl a tune in a high sweet whistle like a boy's.

> *And my soul soars enchanted,*
> *When I hear the sweet lark sing*
> *In the clear of the day.*

Brownie shifted in his seat.

'Have you all that, Will?'

'I know, Brownie, you have enough of it.'

'Right.'

'I could sing it, Brownie.'

'Whistle again, Will.'

'I'll tell you a story then.'

''Tis too early for bed.'

'Glinnane is boastin', Brownie. Says he performed the miracle feat of killing the spirit in Brownie Sugrue.'

Brownie cocked an angry eye at Will and as quickly collapsed into comfort again, chuckling.

'What's so funny, Brownie?' asked Will.

'There's only the two of us here, Will, an' I'm the wan that's laughin'.'

'What's so funny about me?—unless the way it was the will of God to make me, an' the wonder of that ought to be well worn on you by now?'

'Even Glinnane wouldn't be that big a gom,' Brownie explained.

Daylight darkened in the open door. It was Glinnane, his tall, broad body choking the light away.

'Who do I hear callin' my name in vain?' he greeted.

'You were never called anywhere you ever came, Glinnane,' Brownie gave back.

'My name was used by wan of the two of ye, an' I'd like to hear the nice thing was said,' Glinnane persisted.

Daylight splintered on his powerful shoulders as he stepped into the bar. The Great Dane was ambling at his heels.

'I see you have the horse with you,' said Brownie, tilting his hat back and looking at the dog.

'That's a good animal,' Glinnane defended amiably, as he leaned his big frame against the counter.

'You ought to win races with him,' said Brownie. 'That's if he don't stop on the way to ate the jockey.'

'Now all that is nayther here nor there,' Glinnane said. 'Fill us two pints, Will. What I want to know is what was said about me before I came in here.'

'Makin' no bones about it, I was tellin' Brownie that you boasted you had broken the spirit in him.'

'Well, now, I don't know if you'd call it a boast, Will, but I made the statement all right,' said Glinnane.

Brownie shot upright in his seat and edged round till he was facing the gamekeeper.

'You made the statement, Glinnane?' he asked, his tone barely soaring above a whisper. Glinnane took his time in the explanation.

'Since the day I caught you with the stuff, Brownie, the rabbits rise earlier than they used to, an' go to bed later. Day by day they're fattenin' on peace of mind. Pheasants have their chests out far enough to wear watch chains, an' no light shines on salmon pools at night except the light of stars. If this goes on my boss will have to hire an army to thin the game so there's room on the ground for flowers to grow, an' net the river to make room between the banks for trout to swish a tail. Now all this can only add up to wan thing, says I. That I killed the spirit in Brownie Sugrue.'

Brownie flung his hat away and jumped to his feet. Glinnane raised his full pint to pursed lips. Brownie's hand shot from the shoulder and hit the pint out of the keeper's hand. The glass smashed. Liquor slunk with the slant towards the counter. The Dane growled and Glinnane said, 'Down,' as matter of fact as if the dog had threatened a neighbour's cat.

'You're big, Glinnane,' said Brownie, 'but you were never as big as I feel this minute. Put up your fists, man, till I give you a hidin'.'

He began to half-circle on his toes on the floor, his small gnarled fists troubling the air under the keeper's nose.

'Come on, Glinnane, you mile of misery,' he called. 'Come on, you killer of poachers' terriers!'

Glinnane was as unconcerned as if Brownie was talking to someone else. Will was the same. Glinnane reached for the second pint.

'I'll come nowhere,' he told Brownie.

Brownie pulled into stock stillness, at a loss. He peered into the keeper's face.

'Surely to God you're not afraid,' he said.

'I'm afraid I'm right in that boast of mine,' said Glinnane.

'O, put up your hands, Glinnane,' Brownie implored. 'Because I want a belt at your long jowl and I can't hit you while your hands are down. For God's sake and the good of my soul will you raise your hands to defend yourself!'

'And what will a fist-fight prove between us, Brownie?' asked Glinnane.

'It will prove whether the spirit is broken in Brownie Sugrue!'

'Ah, have sense, man,' said Glinnane.

'What do you mane?' asked Brownie, more at a loss than ever.

'Jack Delaney,' said Glinnane, 'has a wife and three children that he never worked a day for in the past five years. He can wreck two men at a time on dole night, but do his power with the fists in a pub brawl prove that he's a man with spirit, Brownie?'

Brownie dropped his hands and looked at Will, but Will was looking at his great-grandfather's clock as if he was timing Brownie's answer.

'Go on, Glinnane,' said Brownie. 'My ears are feelin' as big as yours, God help 'em.'

'Now Brownie,' Glinnane began, 'as I see it, the day I caught you was the day you retired from poachin'. Would it be the way now that you hould the week in jail against me?'

'In the first place,' said Brownie, 'you didn't catch me. You never caught me in all our days without an accident was in your favour. An' in the second place, a week in jail was never more to me than a chance to see ould friends again.'

'How's Jack the Tailor?' said Glinnane.

'Lookin' forward to bein' out for Christman, an' sewin' buttons on the warder's pants.'

'Good,' said Glinnane. 'But seein' it isn't the week in jail you hould against me, what can it be at all?'

'Ask him was it the loss of the terrier,' said Will.

'You stay out of this, you heavy tail-end of a wasted life you,' Brownie growled.

'And I have a pup in the backyard that could near sell the rabbits after killin' 'em for him,' Will continued.

'Did you make him an offer of the pup, Will?' asked Glinnane.

'Did I what?' said Will. 'Did I near go down on my knees to him to take her!'

'Show me the pup,' said Glinnane.

Will waddled away to the yard and the two waited without a word. Will returned with the pup hanging from the scruff of her neck. He dropped the pup on the floor. The pup shook the bristle from her neck and went straight to Brownie's feet. Brownie pretended not to notice. Glinnane eyed the pup, then winked at Will.

'Well now, Will,' he said, 'I must agree with Brownie that this handful of bones isn't worth regardin'.'

Brownie grabbed the pup from between his feet and ran with it to the counter.

'Ah, for the Lord's sake man, don't be more of a fool than you can help,' he shouted.

The pup put a head to one side and looked askance at Brownie's pointing finger.

'Look at that eye, that cock of the head, that listenin' ear,' said Brownie. 'If that isn't a poacher's terrier I was never a poacher.'

'That week in jail did no good to your judgement, Brownie,' said Glinnane and Brownie jumped with temper.

'Them tall donkeys an' small horses you call dogs have you now where you don't know a dog when you see wan, Glinnane,' he countered.

'I still know enough to know that thing is an oil rag,' Glinnane gave back.

'You're wrong,' said Brownie.

'I'm dead right.'

'Are you doubtin' my judgement?'

'I am, Brownie.'

'What'll you bet, Glinnane?'

'A pound a head on the first five rabbits of mine that thing will have a hand in catchin'.'

'I'm your man, Glinnane,' said Brownie.

Then he paused. The light of battle dimmed in his eyes.

'Ah, what am I sayin'?' he asked himself. 'Here, Will, take the pup away out of my sight.'

The pup mistook his push for playfulness and took Brownie's finger between his teeth.

'Why should I take her away?' said Will.

'I'm done with dogs an' all that goes with 'em,' said Brownie, but he let his finger to the playful pup.

'That's the lamest excuse for gettin' out of a bet that I ever seen,' Glinnane said, with a great show of contempt.

'I'm not gettin' out of the bet,' Brownie argued.

'I'll hould my opinion till 'tis proved wrong,' Glinnane persisted. 'An' my opinion covers two things, Brownie, yourself an' the pup. If you do a man's part in stickin' to your guns the opinion will cover the pup only.'

'You're an ignorant man, Glinnane, but I'll change the two opinions if 'tis the last thing I do before God calls.'

'Your efforts will cost you many another week in jail, Brownie,' Glinnane warned.

'I'll lift game from under your nose so fast 'twill cost you your job, Glinnane, an' long before that you'll be after payin' a pound a head on this pup's first five rabbits. The money will be handy to clane the slate that Will have against me, an' after that Will can take a jump at himself.'

Brownie stopped to stuff the pup inside his coat.

'Come on, dog,' he said, 'an' don't blame me for the present company. I promise you that this is as near as ever you'll be to a gamekeeper.'

Head in the air he walked out the door. Glinnane and Will gave him a minute's start, then they followed into the street and to the archway of the lane where Brownie lived. Brownie was halfway to his house when they got there. When Brownie got to his own door he put the pup on the

cobbles of the lane while he searched for his key. He let himself in. The
pup stood for a moment outside, sniffing the trapped air of the little house.
Then she wagged her stump of tail and followed Brownie indoors.

'Thanks for the help, Glinnane,' said Will.

''Twas a pleasure, Will,' said Glinnane.

And chuckling the two heavy men went back to the bar.

Blindness

In a few minutes I would be leaving her. I had the uncle's leather case on the kitchen table and was putting my few belongings into it. The amber evening was as quiet in the valley as the firelight in the bruised metal of the urn she pulped the mash in for the hens. Big Jack Healy, her husband and my grandfather, had come on the urn in the bog ten years before, only a week ahead of the day the byre crumbled and crushed him to death: so she held on to it ever since. The opposite wither of the valley might have been of bruised bronze too, the way it looked under the amber light, with here and there in it the star-dazzle of a stone under falling water. A Leghorn pullet was picking at the dried scum of mash in the neck of the urn and the metal rang under the hard beak like an altar gong. The thick bulk of the uncle was in the open doorway. He was looking away downward into the valley's one winding road, uneasy, wishing to have it over and be away.

'The days don't be long after all,' he said.

'No day is long enough here for all there is to do in it,' she said.

Her words were slow, quiet-spoken. He sensed the sting behind their tonelessness and bridled.

'Now, Mother, we went over all that a hundred times. I know you will be short-handed without Michael, but he has his own life to live, and a perfect right to expect more from it than drudgery.'

'I didn't hear Michael say a word of that,' she gave back.

'I'm saying it for him. It is what his father, my own brother, and your son would be saying if he was here.'

She never moved a stir from where she was standing in front of the open hearth, her two dead eyes fixed forever upward with the same torture of entreaty that you see in the eyes of saints in chapel windows, strands of her coarse grey hair briaring out and downward from the few pins she used for holding it together.

'Words like them were in his father's mouth when he left for John Bull,' she said. 'If he stayed here he wouldn't be killed by a train and his wife wouldn't belong now to an Englishman in England, and Michael would have a mother's hand in his rearing in place of the hand of a blind grandmother.'

'If he stayed he could have been killed by the wall of a byre the way our Dad was,' the uncle hit back.

'The byre was Big Jack's own, and would have been a better byre when he was finished with it, if it wasn't for what happened. But Michael built it again from where it lay in rubble, with the gap still in the pile that I cleared with my own hands when I lifted the stones from him an' he half dead and groanin'. Michael finished the job for Jack and that's a credit to him. Many a thing here is a credit to him. But 'tis all for the stranger after me, because Michael is the last of the blood with a feelin' for the land in him.'

'Land!' said the uncle, spitting the word as if it were a pellet of the substance it stood for.

I knew what he meant. Hungry land. Hungry growing things, tree, plant and stalk clinging with claw-grip of root to starved stone. Drive a spade hard into the earth of this place, and nine times out of ten, the blade strikes stone. The stone of it wears the earth like an old coarse blanket, fibre by fibre fighting to keep its grey bones from the wind and the cold. Coarse, hungry earth it is that hungers for male children with the spare men that work it: sons to care for it after the bones and stringy muscle of the spare men are part of its moist marrow and strong bitter smell.

'Land, yes,' she said.

'Look, mother, we'll leave it at that,' the uncle implored.

'We went over the ground a hundred times, I know,' she agreed. 'But 'tis you that took it wan beyond the hundred. All I said was that the day was never as long with light as we have use for here, an' what I said was for myself only now, because how long or how short the days will be in this place won't trouble you or Michael in the town.'

'There you go again,' the uncle complained.

'I'm going no place,' she said, in the same low, unhurried way. ''Tis ye that's going back to the town where, when daylight lifts out of where ye work, ye can pull a button an' 'twill be day again. While I'll be here where the day and the night are as long or as short as the hand of God did make 'em, an' the two of 'em quenched forever in my two blind eyes.'

'Oh, for God's sake leave me alone,' the uncle begged.

'I'm lavin' myself alone by lavin' you take Michael from me. I'm alone now but for Shone here. Poor Shone.'

Shone was the son of a neighbour. He wasn't bright in the wits, but the brightness of a child's first wonder at the world was in his blue eyes. Dark to anybody's meaning but hers, he was never far from her. His eyes were hers while the sky coloured all the way from morning grey to blue-black and stars. When it went towards midnight, his fear of whatever his child's mind told him lay beyond would tell him it was time to go home, and he would take her hand. 'Home,' he would say, and the two of them would climb the goat track through the grey night mists that lay on the heather, up and over another ridge to where his father mumbled alone to the black rafters of his room. I used to come out under the night to watch for her return in needless concern for her safety, because she had travelled the way back so often that a pebble would not be on it without her knowing. Besides, out of instinct, Shone would have cleared the track on his way up of anything likely to stumble her coming down. And standing there I would hear her talk to him, and in his mumbled, eager answers have another proof of her power to make him understand. His eyes were hers: her thought about things of the day was for the two of them. He was sitting by the fire at her feet just then. At the sound of his name, he straightened out of his huddled, half-smiling interest in the pullet's picking at the urn. He craned his neck out of his ragged jacket, and the half-smile lit into fullness towards her face. As if sight guided her free hand, it gripped his cow's-lick of fair, fine-spun hair.

'Myself and poor Shone it will be from here on,' she said.

The uncle turned on me with anger and impatience.

'Look, aren't you ready yet?' he asked. 'Or what the devil are up to at all?'

'In a minute, there's something I forgot,' I said.

I went down into my room off the kitchen for the rosary beads that hung from a nail above my bed. I could hear them as I went.

'Ah sure, give him time,' she was saying. 'It will maybe be a while till he's back here to the house again.'

The uncle made an effort to bring his voice down to the calm of plain statement.

'Look, Mother,' he said. 'I want you to know that where Michael is going he will stay.'

'He'll be back,' she said.

'He won't be back, no more than his father would be back if he was alive. No more than Denis in America. No more than me.'

'He'll be back,' she repeated in that toneless way he could never stand.

'He won't be back, no more than any of the rest of us, so for all our sakes will you consider again what I am sick of saying—come on into town to my place with us. There's plenty of room in the big airy house, and Agnes will be every bit as pleased as me about it.'

'Ah sure, your good wife isn't over-strong, the craythur, and with you an' Michael an'—'

'I told you before there was nothing wrong with her health,' the uncle interrupted, his voice rising again.

'That's right, so you did,' she agreed. Then she added, 'Michael will give her an interest. It is grey for a young woman in a childless house.'

The uncle fumed back towards the door again.

'God, Mother, you'd try the soul of a saint,' he said.

'I would, I suppose,' she agreed.

He wheeled back, as if drawing his head away from the wisdom that prompted him to hold his tongue.

'How many times will I have to repeat that it is the will of God that we have no children?' he cried.

'If she worked on the land and lived on the land now—what do you think? And in the spring of the year ... I wonder?'

The uncle threw up his hands in despair. It was then that he saw me standing there, waiting. He came and snatched the bag out of my hand.

'Come on,' he said viciously and strode out the door.

I stood there looking at her while his footfalls died downward to the road where his car was waiting to take us to town. She would be nearly as tall as I am, but for the stoop her blindness brought with it. The black of her blouse was crumpled, coomed with dust and turf ash. Blindness had made shapeless the flesh of her face, but the strong bone undid a good deal of the damage. The gong-notes of the urn had ceased.

'Come here,' she said.

I walked through the silence to her. She let me come till I hit her ready hands with my breastbone. Her hands closed and tapped together against my body, then were guided upward to my long, lean face. Her heavy, gnarled hands followed the bone-structure of my face, beginning on my forehead, round and into the sockets of my eyes, along my nose, then outwards and down to the point of my chin. Her right hand closed at that and the knuckles rapped once against my jaw-bone.

'You'll be back,' she said.

And Shone was smiling as I turned and walked out of the house.

I got along well enough in town. Things were slack in the uncle's building trade, so he got me a job in the boot factory as apprentice to the lasting machine.

'Mind yourself,' he told me, 'and from here on the look of the sky won't trouble you anymore.'

But he reckoned without the glass roof over where I worked. The first six months of drilling my farmer's hands into doing what the head had learned by rote left small time for thought to go sky-rambling. It was after that I became properly aware of the glass roof, or more truly, the sky over it. My mates were town lads mostly, without watches all of them. In the beginning they made a wonder of how accurate I could be in telling time from a look upward: soon the wonder wore down to a taking for granted. But those looks told me more than the cut of the hands on a clock face. What I saw of the sky might be over the house in the valley so perfect the picture of what she would be doing there at the time was in my eyes.

'Ten o'clock,' I would say to the mate who asked.

Then my mind would go on to see her coming with Shone into the sunlight through the kitchen doorway with the urn of mash for the hens. I would hear the richness of the hen-call in her throat, and see the shiny rooster stiffen on the dry dung-heap beside the byre, then streak to her to be ahead of his women-folk. Speckled and black and brown and white they raced from all corners, from under the sally row that hid the haggard, from low on the ash that shaded the zinc roof of the piggery, from hole and corner crag and cranny with necks at full stretch, tongues needle-rigid in open amber gorges, a gloss on wings half raised to give the driving legs a power of spring; then heads together at her feet, jostling, hard beaks hammering the squashed handfuls of the steaming mash adhering to the cobbled yard. All day long that patch of sky through the glass roof would have its reminders, from feeding of hens in the bright morning to evening and the driving of cows home through soft light and cool shadow. I would see the colours of the three cows, white, red and white, and smoke blue live in the light of the gaps in the hawthorn and quench in shadows of the unbroken blossom. All the way up the boreen from the low field to the byre I would follow her and Shone while they followed after the cows. In the byre I would feel the satiny flank of the smoke blue against my face, smell and hear the warm milk drilling into the pail.

In the uncle's comfortable home after work it was the same. After the tasty evening meal we would sit in the comfort of soft chairs, the uncle in slippers reading a paper, lipping on the pipe-stem like drops falling from thatch to barrel in rain-time beside her door; his wife Agnes quiet-faced and kind darning socks or knitting new ones. Myself, soaking my mind in quietness after the clamour of the factory the way I used to soak the body in a pool of the river after a day on the quiet land. When I said goodnight it sounded under rough rafters instead of a ceiling. When I climbed the stairs she was there before me, up climbing through the night mists with Shone. As I knelt in my room for the few prayers the town door was the door into the country kitchen and she kneeling by the urn beyond, the torture of entreaty in the fixed upslant of her blind eyes out of keeping with the slow, unhurried, almost familiar talk with the Almighty. Now I am aware of all this. I wasn't rightly then. It wasn't till long after that I realized what all along was happening; I was measuring the days by her life, not by mine.

Another thing, the clamour, whine and rattle of lasters, trimmers, peggers and the rest at the factory sent me back to the land's quietness on the Saturday half-day, and more often than not the Sunday as well. I tried going to a different country but what I wanted wasn't in any of the places for me. Quietness is deep for a man according to his familiarity with the place where it lives. When familiar it holds memories of his, and whether his mind reaches in to gather them or not the quietness that holds them gives peace.

So once a week at least I took the bicycle out of the uncle's garage and cycled into the valley here. Back to the place but not to the house, back to the quietness but not to her I would promise myself, and for an hour or more wherever I hid myself in the valley I had no trouble with that promise. I would put the bicycle over a ditch and walk nowhere special because I had what I wanted if I sat beside the machine and put a hand on the grass. At an end of an aimless ramble maybe I would find myself on the high bank of the river, above the river's rush over stones, with shapeless, water-sounds to hear, and spray to feel cool on my face faintly as if a small bird shook it from a wet wing. But after that the stillness would stir with hints of her so sly that for a time they made no impression: as if she herself had shuffle-groped with her blindness into the place to stand there without greeting till I looked there and found her. Maybe it was that the sound of the river or a bird song would call to mind the liking for sound her blindness gave her; maybe it was the spray on my face would bring up the way she used to go all the way to the pew under the pulpit during a mission or retreat, to feel on her face the fall of holy water from the brush in the missioner's hand when he gave the Pope's blessing at the close. Whether or which, soon I would be climbing the boreen to the house and her in it.

Shone always would see me coming. Before I laid an eye on him I would hear his child-cry of surprise. Beyond whatever bend in the boreen was between us I would hear the stumbling headlong pounding of his nailed boots on the hard ground, see the uncontrolled rush of his tatter-clad gangling body round the bend ending in the grunt of the breath leaving him when he hit the ditch. Then gurgling with excitement he would half-circle over and back ahead of me to her door, the two arms held away from the body, the hands hanging limp from them: like a big dishevelled bird challenging my way to where a brood of scaldings huddled low for heat in a grounded nest, like that kind of bird but for the wide-open blue of the eyes, shining bright with welcome.

Hers was no welcome at all. Not by voice or saying or movement was there a hint that I had ever been away. And a curious thing, she was always standing in front of the hearth in the exact spot where she was the day I left her, the face calm, the mouth firm out of keeping with the eyes' lofted entreaty, the briaring hair astray from the pins and the grey dust on the black of the crumpled blouse.

'How do you think the spuds are doing?' she would say, matter of fact, or, 'What way do you think the turnips is doing?'

An ordinary thing like that she would say in an ordinary way and for the hour or hours I would be there I would be seeing her as I never did when I lived with her. I marked how accurate was her shuffle-grope about the business of the kitchen or the yard, how near to the tongs or the pot or the urn was her reaching when she needed them, and how, when she laid the table for a meal of strong tea, fresh eggs and home-made cake her weathered hands, heavy-ringed on the marriage finger, moved as if they had eyes to guide them. That meal was never put on the table until the proper every-day hour for it, no matter how long I came to the kitchen ahead of it. The long silences settled about us as naturally as when we lived the days together so close that each knew what the other was think-ing, or knew that if it was a new or strange thought it would out in its own good time for the other to hear or add to.

When I stood to go she would say, 'Suit yourself now,' or, 'All right, son,' as if I had told her I thought it time to take the horse to Tom the blacksmith to be shod, or that I felt like a game of twenty-five in the Mas-ter's bachelor house a half-mile of the hill away. But she would rise and stand, tall and gaunt and bony on that spot before the hearth again. And Shone would be smiling where the firelight made a golden wing out of his glib of fine-spun hair.

Then the day came when I climbed the hill and Shone wasn't stum-bling to welcome me on the boreen. Without hearing a sound or stir any-where I walked towards the house. I went in the door and there she was standing before the fire again, a thumb rubbing the green stone of her brooch, and the urn alone in the firelight without Shone to have an eye on. It was the first time she gave me the welcome of one who had been away.

'You're late today,' she said. 'You left it a long time.'

'I didn't notice the minutes,' I said.

"Tis nice to be away from clocks for a while,' she said.

She walked to where the chair I used to own was standing by the table and brushed it with her palm.

'Sit a while,' she said.

I sat, and she went to a nail on the hob for her black head-cloth. She was sure of where it was and her hands were sure in the tying of it under her long jaw.

'The kettle will be boiled by the time I'm back,' she said.

I looked over the fire flame and there was the kettle hanging.

'I'll come for the cows with you,' I said.

'Please yourself now,' she said.

I rose and followed after her slow but sure progress over the cobbled yard and down the hawthorn shelter of the boreen. I asked after a while what was in my mind all along to ask.

'Where's Shone from you?'

She took a while to answer.

'Away,' she said simply.

'Away, away in the Big Place?' I ventured.

"Tis a big place where he's gone,' she said. 'It must be. But thank the Good God it isn't the big place you mean.'

'You mean he's ...'

'He's gone on,' she said.

'The Lord have mercy on him,' I said.

'Ah don't ask the mercy of God for the soul of a child,' she said with heat. 'It doesn't need it. 'Tis for Shone now to ask favours for us.'

I lifted the baulks from the gap for her, and straight away the three cows took their slow wide turn towards us: heavy bellies swaying, drowsy heads swaying, full udders swaying above the cool grass, and their colours cool in the soft light. We were following them up the boreen when I questioned again.

'When did he die?'

'A week ago.'

'How?'

'It was towards midnight when I was takin' him over the hill home. His breathin' was short and quick in the climb but I gave it no heed. At the top of the hill he fell without a sound, his face to the sky. I listened for his breathin' an' it wasn't there. I put my hand on his chest. His heart in the hand of God fluttered like a moth ... Then the hand closed.'

We milked the cows and had a drop of tea. I sat longer with her than was my habit in my visits to her. Night had arrived stars and all and still I sat. Every time I rose to go I missed the smile of Shone from my going and I sat again. With my mind I saw myself gone out into the night while with my eyes I was seeing the way she would be after my going. Sitting by the fire, her hand on the neck of the urn. Alone. Blind eyes entreating the silence hanging in the cowl of darkness above the firelight. There in the minutes going heavy with silence by us I struggled against that nameless, timeless thing, constant and strong and tugging me back—she a part of it, it a part of her—searching for a grip on my resisting will: the claw-grip of root to starved stone. And suddenly I was angry with this thing. I rose with a jerk and stepped purposefully out into the centre of the kitchen.

'I'm going,' I said, the anger in my tones leaving her unmoved.

'I said I was going,' I repeated.

'Sit a while more,' she said quietly.

'No,' I said.

'Poor Michael,' she said, in the way she used the word of Shone.

'I'll be poor if I stay,' I said brutally.

'You won't be the poorer for the minute more you sit, Michael. So sit, Michael son,' she said.

She was a while without speaking. Then she said:

'Michael.'

'Yes,' I said.

'You're happy where you are?—in the town, in the factory, I mane?'

'Yes.'

'You're rale happy I mane.'

'I told you yes,' I fired back, angry.

She let the silence gather about us again before she said in a firm, quiet way: 'You're not.'

I said: 'What do you mean?' indignant.

'Me bein' here is a trial to you,' she said. 'Me bein' here with only Shone was a trial to you an' your uncle. Me bein' here without even Shone will be more of a trial. O, sure I know, I'm not a fool. I lasted it out because I thought you'd come back. I was sure you'd come back. Even now I can't believe you're not comin' back.'

I held my mouth tight shut. I was afraid of what I would say if I didn't. A minute more went by. Then:

'Tell your uncle I'll come into the town any time he's ready,' she said.

It was what I fought for a long time to hear her say. Now that it was said I felt empty of any satisfaction. And in my going out under the sky of stars again I missed the smile of Shone.

The uncle was away making plans on the wind of the word. In three days he had arranged with the valley neighbours that they had an eye to land and stock till the auctioneer was ready for auction. He shed years, foostered and smiled and rubbed his hands together: even the coolness of the neighbours made no matter to him.

'Bejay you'd think I was a grabber or a bailiff. But they gave their promise.'

He did gaffer over Agnes's careful preparation of one of the ground-floor bedrooms for the old lady.

'Wouldn't the bed be safer for her lying against the wall now, Agnes?'

'Wouldn't a solid chair now be better than the rockin' wan, and more likely to be there under her when she sits? That's right ...'

'Nice paper or no nice paper a nail must go in the wall above her head to hold her rosary beads ... That's right ...'

And Agnes smiled and nodded and indulged his childishness, as any woman will who never gave her husband child.

The old lady asked that I go with him to fetch her. It was middle evening as we drove out. The evening was more gold than amber and wrapped the valley in rich silence. He told me to walk up on my own for her. The song of the one lark in the sky as I climbed was like a running ravel in cloth of gold. That silence was oppressive: thickening the breaths I drew, slowing the strides I took, exaggerating the sound of the footfall on the stony way up as if the world was empty except for myself and the one bird. I was the best part of the climb before I noticed the figures moving to right and left of me and high on the brow of the hill against the sky. Young men and old, old women with cloth-bound heads and girls and women with free-hanging hair. And children, holding with young hands to older, harder hands. Moving slowly, or standing still as stone. All of them silent. Some stood on the boreen itself, close to the ditches, under the hawthorn beside the gaps to her small fields. Others were on ledges of the high rocks, on goat tracks, the rusted bed of a dried-up stream; others high on the brow of the hill against the golden sky. None of them smiled. None gave greeting. They were the neighbours, the virile dregs of dead genera-tions of valley men and women. The Learys, the Leahys, the Flemings and O'Donoghues; the Kennys, McCarthys and O'Sullivans. It was like walking through the twilit valley of the watching, waiting, not hoping dead. Fear was in me and the fear might be fright if I didn't hold my legs from heeding the heart thumping in my chest.

I tell you I thought the time was long till I was in the door of the house. She was standing, as ever, before the fireplace. The hearth was empty of ember flame. Her best shawl was about her shoulders, partly cowling her grey hair; her second-best shawl was wrapped round a bundle of keep-sakes, which lay on the floor beside her. Her two strong hands held the urn against her body. Her lips, as I entered, shaped a smile.

'I'm all ready, Michael,' she said.

'I'll take the bundle,' I said, avoiding the look of entreaty in the blind eyes.

'Do, Michael son, do, do,' she said.

I raised the bundle from the floor, but she made no move to follow. In the doorway I paused.

'You go ahead, Michael,' she told me. 'I'll not keep you long.'

I took a few paces over the cobbled yard, and stopped. I had to stop. The thing that was fighting in her was fighting in me. It was then that her words fell on the silence softly.

'Don't you be minding, Jack,' she was saying. 'Don't you be minding now at all. This house is a strong and a wise house yet, and young in spite of the years. 'Tis strong with the strength of the men who walked in it, and wise with the heads who thought in it, and young with the youth of them that crawled the floor. If I stay in it, a dried-up crust of a good woman in her day, I'll make it die with me … So I'm goin', Jack, while 'tis still a living house. Them that will come to it will not have our blood, I know. But I know that what's left of our way between the walls and in the walls of our house will mould their way. They will not have our blood, but they will have our way. I'm carrying with me the tokens of the things we lived between us. The things themselves are in my heart, Jack … They will be in my clay … So come with me now, Jack, come with me out the door …'

I heard the soles of her spring boots drag over the floor as if the floor itself was fighting not to leave her go. They were held to stopping again. Still they were. Her voice rose a little.

'Come, Jack … Come, I said … Jack! Ah, come will you … Jack! Jack, I said! Ah, God, will you come, will you come, will you come!'

Her voice had risen to a broken half-anger, half-pleading. I faced round for the door, but as I moved I heard the one cry, 'Jack!' Her feet scrope the floor. Again she cried, 'Jack!' The urn crashed to the floor with one angry boom, as from a hard throat. Then her feet were moving freely over the floor. In a moment she was running through the doorway. A groping, stumbling run it was, but nevertheless a run and well directed towards the mouth of the boreen. I stood rooted as she passed. Her face was thrust forward, her blind eyes imploring the sky, arms outstretched, the shawl clear of the grey tangle of her hair. She was crying aloud:

'He wouldn't come, he wouldn't come, he wouldn't come!'

The cry softened to a continuous sob as it drifted from me down the boreen. The neighbours from above by now had joined the ones who were gathered against the ditches on either side of the stony way, and calling she hurried down the lane of faces: faces grey where old, dark where young and wondering where little. I followed after, feeling that they were the faces of the valley dead of all time, and I the last and the lost one of all, being accused. I lengthened my stride to overtake her where the boreen met road in a maw of broken stone. The uncle was holding the door of the car open. I caught her arm and guided her flight towards him and she suffered my leading as if she was in a daze. Her words were coming brittle now out of a dry throat:

'Jack wouldn't come, lads, Jack wouldn't come. But sure he was always headstrong, headstrong. All the men of the house were headstrong always …'

As I closed the door a glance showed me the neighbours looking with hard eyes down out of faces hard as oak.

'All the men of the house were headstrong always …'

The uncle set the car to moving. It gathered speed, rode down the valley and still she gave no sign that travel in a car was new to her, or strange, she who never saw a car or rode in one. In a dazed way she wrung her empty hands and over and over said, 'He wouldn't come, he wouldn't come, he wouldn't come, Jack wouldn't come … ' Then suddenly she stopped. Her hands stilled and hardened in a grip. Her long body reached up into a rigid questioning that had voice in her one cry, 'Where am I?'

'You're bowlin' along in one of the best little cars in the country,' the uncle assured.

'Car?'

'A motor car, woman, you're off the land now and away from the iron wheel,' he went on in his kindly way.

'Lave me out of it,' she cried.

'Ah, 'tisn't worth your while now, Mother, for there's the town below us an' your friend Patey Keogh at the door of his grocery,' the uncle tried to soothe.

'Michael!' she called.

'Easy now,' I told her. 'Here's the house to our right.'

'Stop the thing, Michael, stop it!'

Her groping hand had caught my wrist. The strong nails bit into my flesh: she was frightened.

'Stop it, Michael, I said!'

'Now we're pulling up,' I told her.

And we were. The car curved in and straightened to a stop against the flagged path. The door of the house was open and Agnes was in the doorway, waiting, quietly smiling. The old lady was silent, her body as rigid as the hand that held my wrist, her pale, dry lips twitching like dying things, a curling vein swollen on either temple.

I opened the door, still giving her the guidance of my hand. But I wasn't prepared for what she did when her feet touched the fence. With a short, dry gasp of fright, she flung herself into what would have been headlong flight. The lunge of her strong body flung Agnes aside. The step of the door tripped her and she fell full length in the narrow hall. Her forehead hit a brass umbrella stand that toppled to clang on the tiles. Without a sound, but with quickened breathing, she heaved herself to her feet. We stood in the middle of our rush to help her. Her long body swayed for a moment, then straightened to a stillness that held the air itself to stillness. The blind eyes twitched. The nostrils gaped. The hair was loose from the scattered pins and the shawl loose from her shoulders. A thin thread of blood curled with the curling vein on her right temple. And then it was she gave the cry that broke the crust I had held about the soul in me.

'I'm blind, I'm blind, I'm blind!' was the cry. 'Michael, I'm blind, I'm blind, I'm blind!'

'Wheest, Mother, you'll be right as the rain from here on,' the uncle said, moving towards her.

'I'm blind this minute an' never before was I blind,' she complained.

With pain in her kindly eyes Agnes came quietly behind her with one of the hall chairs.

'Sit for a while, Mrs,' she said, and the old lady sat without trouble.

'Never before did I know that I was blind,' she went on.

Agnes took herself quietly into the kitchen. The uncle stood beside the old lady, hands on his knees, bracing the concerned lean of his body towards her.

'Wheest, woman, wheest,' he kept saying.

'In the house or in the valley I never was blind. The door of the sight was shut with me, but it closed on the world I knew along with me. Even without Shone, I could make my way around. Now I'm blind, I'm blind …'

As Agnes came out of the kitchen with the things to wash and cover the cut on her temple, I walked out of the house.

In five minutes I was talking to one of the uncle's carters. In the next five I was in his stable putting the harness on his cob. A minute more and the cob was tackled to the cart I had stripped of the guards. I drove to the uncle's door and pulled in behind his car. The uncle was drawn to the door by the sound of the wheels.

'What the hell are you up to?' was his greeting.

I didn't answer. I took her shawl-ful of tokens from car to cart.

'Mick, what do ye mane?' he kept saying, hopping about me.

I went into the hall to find Agnes sticking plaster over the lint she had put on the cleaned cut.

'That's you, Michael,' the old lady said.

'Are you all right?' I asked her.

'Yes,' she told me.

'Do you feel able for the journey back?' I said.

'Back!' she said. 'Back where?'

'Back to the house,' I said.

'The house,' she repeated.

'The house,' I said again.

'What's this?' the uncle cried.

'Do you feel able?' I asked again.

'But—' she hesitated.

'No buts,' I said. 'Do you feel able?'

'If it was the last breath was in me I would stretch it the length of the way,' she said.

She rose and I took her arm, and Agnes gave me a look that said she understood. The uncle was silent as I led her to the cart. Whatever his lips were saying as I gave the cob her head was crushed under the noise of the iron-shod wheels.

Evening had gone when we entered the valley: the velvet black of a starless night was in its place. The cob had shed a shoe on the way, but Tom the blacksmith was on a late job and I had the shoe handy. The cart-wheels brought him to the door of the forge, and the shape of her sitting in the car at the spent end of his forge light was enough for him.

'God an' glory, but herself is back!' he shouted.

'I'm back, Tom, and Michael is back,' she told him.

'Ah, God an' glory, ma'am, but you're powerful to see,' he said.

He shook her hand and shouted to the wife to come from her kitchen. With her four sturdy children she came, and her welcome was warm. The old lady wouldn't leave the cart so the cup of tea had to be brought to her. When Tom's wife brought the tea the children were not with her. While the tea was being taken I held a candle while Tom put the shoe back. He took longer than the job called for, stretching the time with talk of the old times. But it wasn't till we were on the road again that I knew why he delayed and why the children were gone after the one appearance.

For all the hills, by all the tracks that led to the house, were acrawl with lanterns. As we progressed on the road, the lanterns drifted down-ward to the house, like worn, wandering stars astray in the darkness. By the time we turned for the boreen, it was lined on either side with lanterns all the way to the door. In the friendly drowse of light the faces of all the

neighbours smiled welcome on our return. As we drove up the lighted
way the faces opened their mouths and gave welcome with words: voices
of men and women, young and old, voices high and low, rich and plain,
and all of them happy.

'Welcome!' they called.

'Welcome to ye!'

'Thanks be to God!'

'Ah, God is good!'

'God is very good.'

'Welcome to ye!'

'Welcome back!'

'Welcome!'

And to the babble of voices she gave her blind face smiling, and a
raised hand like the blessing of a priest.

At the door of the house she stopped, and I read her thought. I passed
in and lighted the oil lamp on the hob. The urn lay on its side on the floor.
I lifted it up and gave it into her hands.

'You're good, Michael,' she said.

She walked slowly to the hearth and laid the urn in its corner. With
sure hands she took the tongs, shook the seed of the fire from the smoor
of ashes, and laid a crib of bog-oak splinters on the coals. She put the snout
of the bellows where the second snort brought a bright flame.

Then she took off her shawl and hung it on the hob. And there with
the shine of the urn in the fire flame, I felt the smile of Shone.

'We could do with a bite to ate now, Michael,' she said.

The Big Garden

Never mind about now; it was a big garden. Think any way you like, but I *know*. I remember.

This wicket, this wicket was every inch of ten feet high, and leaf green to rest an eye in the sun. These three steps had a carpet of moss; a broken carpet that wasn't ravelled like rope or tattered like paper, but rounded in the breaks like snow melting. Up there on the top of the ten feet there was an arch of roses that were the hoarded secret of Pats, the gardener, who gave them to the big garden long before June arrived with the others. Weighed down with scent, they were; deep velvet red like thick blood, hanging in clumps. The arch shut away the sunlight and the sky, so there was always shadow on the steps. The sky was always blue. There was always sunlight. Always.

All through the night spiders swung their webs from the arch to the uprights of the wicket. I could never tell why, because they never caught more than a tail of mist or beads of the dew falling. It looked like the spiders arranged the patterns of the drops so fine they were, and spaced perfect. Sometimes the spiders forgot themselves and swung the webs from the arch to the whittled ribs of the wicket itself: then when you opened the wicket you tore away those tracings as fine as lines in young skin.

The wicket opened with a creak of hinges, blobs of dew toppled out of the roses on your head and shoulders; and there you were on the path of white gravel that led away between hedges of box palm, a mile, three miles, any distance. Other white paths went to right and left between the dark green of the box to the pale green of hawthorn rows, knee-deep in fern. The box, a foot high, was as bristled as a yard brush: The Bush. The fern was soft-wet as the tongue of a stream: Forest Shade. Miles and miles of them.

Suppose you followed the straight path. The gravel slewed to either side under your feet, swinging the body, a sway to the mind, sending up langour in waves of heat: Canyon Country, Sweat, Thirst, Gold in the Withers of Mountains. Miles on miles of them.

Then a veil of coolth fell over you, breaths of thin fragrance trailed apast your nostrils—you were under the twisted apple tree. The apple tree, the twisted one, hung a draggled head low over the path, from a bole halfway to being fallen. So low the blossoms dipped that the head of a child would be lost in them. Beyond the twisted tree were other apple trees. Four, one-hundred-and-four: orchards dipping with the sweep of hills from skies of white cloud, women with copper heads that glinted, white-dressed, eyes sloe-dark, green leaves lining gold baskets where the red fruit dropped from white hands: Spain!

Once there was a nest in the twisted tree. We found it by accident, the brother and me ... We were after tracking down a band of Sioux to their wigwams (the beehives over there). A struggle took place with the enemy (the brother) for the beautiful captive (Doctor Murphy's ringletted daughter in the village). The enemy won.

We came back into ourselves to squat on our hunkers for breath. The brother was worrying the gravel between his sandalled feet with a stick, a knot of hair stuck to the sweat on his forehead. Suddenly a thrush swung out of the hawthorn, braked in mid-air with a swish of wings, and chortling dived head first into the old tree. The chortling went out like a light to leave the air stiller than ever.

'A nest!' said the brother. He had a sudden way of saying things that were true, with nothing to go on.

'A nest!' he said again, looking a question. I didn't know. We had never seen a real nest, only pictures in a book with bars of music growing out of the maw of the mother bird.

'We'll try,' I said, moving away to the tree. He followed on my heels.

That was the way always. He would say the thing, and wait, watching me. I would act, and he'd follow.

We crept under the tree. So still it was you could hear a creaking in the white gravel of beetles foraging. Shade put cool fingers to our sun-broiled bodies as we peered up into the blossoms. There was nothing of a nest that we could see.

'Climb,' said the brother. 'Might be between the leaves.'

I scrambled up the leaning bole. A beetle tacking through the gravel underneath seemed a long way down. Up I went into the blossoms where bees moaned like a distant wind. Of a sudden a little spear of cold fright darted across my chest: I was looking into the eyes of the mother bird. Amber pinpoints of eyes, they were, full of anger or fright, I couldn't say for certain. I didn't dare to move a muscle. I don't know why: I didn't. I wanted to tell the brother, but words wouldn't come to me. We battled with our eyes, the bird and me. The point of her beak made me feel a point in the middle of my forehead. I stirred: she jerked taut. I breathed in, and suddenly screaming she shot away in a whirl of wings and feathers. A wisp of down arched backward from the whirr of her flight, settled on the air, and floated to rest on the rim of the nest.

''Tis a nest,' the brother shouted up.

'With eggs in it!' I gave back.

Then the whole tree shivered and shook as if it were at grips with a wind as he stampeded up to my side.

'You gom! You'll knock it!' I shouted, digging back with my elbow at his chest. His body jerked to the thulk, there was a hiss of breath from between his teeth: he never noticed. Eyes bright in his round face, he looked at me.

'Where?' he asked.

'Look at it,' I said, pointing a finger, all my spleen forgotten where I looked.

That nest of clay and moss was a lovely thing.

'Janie!' he said above a whisper, shoulders hugging his neck in a little jerk.

'There's four eggs. Four.'

The eggs were like four drops of the sky, with black specks.

'Isn't it funny?' I said.

'What?'

'I dunno,' I answered, for my mind hadn't closed on the thought as it passed.

The nest was built into a fork in the tree, where a handful of cool leaves stuck out all round it. The eggs glowed in their shadow like sky in a dark pool.

'Take one out in your hand,' said the brother.

'No. I read in a book once that if you touch them she'll know, and forsake them altogether.'

'What's forsake?'

'Fly away, you gom, and never come back. So the eggs would go cold.'

'Touch them. See if the book was right,' he tempted, all eagerness.

'No!'

'Let me take one in my hand. I'd like to. Let me!' he wheedled.

For answer I reached my hand just below the rim of the nest. It was warm, a soft heat swelled up from it, like from a coal. The brother did the same.

'Janie, the book was right,' he cried.

'We'll go away now, and let her come back to them,' I decided.

'We'll come tomorrow, won't we?' he said.

'Won't we?' he persisted, till I agreed. Then he smiled.

That night I lay awake in the warm dusk, thinking about the nest. I didn't take note of the stars framed in the murk of the open window. But out in the garden I saw a thrush, under a handful of leaves, squatting on four warm eggs that were blue with black specks.

'Rob!'

I heard my name above a whisper. The brother. I thought he was asleep, like always.

'Well?'

'Will it be there tomorrow?—the nest, I mean. Will it be there, do you think?'

'Well, it won't fly away, will it?' I gave back. Somehow I resented that he should be thinking of it too.

'That's good.'

Content, he hitched the clothes up about him, and burrowed deeper into the tick.

'Goodnight, Rob,' he called. I didn't answer. Long minutes went by, and repentance growing inside me for the short way I had taken him. I was filled with affection for the slob he was, but by that time he had slipped away into sleep. I nudged him with my elbow and he awakened with a start.

'Goodnight, Tim,' I said.

'Goodnight, Rob,' he answered without question. Then sleep came down on both of us. Poor Tim! I wonder if he tells them about the big garden, in some snug, somewhere; in between telling them true things he never heeds, with nothing to go on.

*

Now here! You walk past the old apple tree, and there is the first of the branch paths. You could go with it, if you had a mind to, away between the onions and the cabbages to the bed of scarlet wallflowers by the hawthorn. A cloak, the bed was; a cloak flung off the shoulders of The Prince when he drew steel to battle for The Lady. And the scent of the flowers was The Lady herself. Sun on the glass frame, to the left, was the silver of the sword leaping. Silver is in many things. Many men are in one man when you have eyes that see. Take Pats, the gardener.

Pats was king of the big garden, as old as the hills he came from: ageless. From his knotty frame thick tweeds hung in troughs, like in a curtain. His battered hat was any old way on his grey-black crop of hair. Bushy brows dipped over his black eyes: crow's feet wriggled under them in his frequent smiles. A wedge of black beard stuck out from his chin, curled up at the end like a duck's tail. He had broad shoulders, bow legs, and a mind like a brake of furze blossom—the edges swamped in the mellow waves of it.

Four miles he walked to us, at cock-crow, from his cottage on the jaw of a ravine; four miles he had to climb in the evening, to his rods and the streams he grew beside. There was hardly a day that he hadn't a portion of a catch to bring us, a trout each for Tim and me, and the rest for my mother.

One day he forgot them in the bag, where they lay, for freshness, on green reeds beside the whole-bread meal. When he went to fetch his lunch from the kitchen (he always shared it with us in the big garden) he thought of the fish. So here he comes up the white path, the bag slung over his shoulder, the gallon of tea swinging off the left hand, and in the right, on a tray of reeds, our two brown trout.

As usual, Tim and me were waiting under the twisted apple tree: Tim lying flat, his poll on cupped palms; and me with the tale of Ali Baba propped between my knees. So taken I was with the story that Pats was on top of me before I was aware of him; I looked up with a start. The silver of fish in sunlight caught my eye, the bearded brown crag of face above it: in that flash Pats was a dervish diving to fight with a dagger between his teeth. Only an instant, then Pats was Pats, squatting on a tussock of sod between us, settling to eat, and smoke his clay, and yarn at heart's content.

And Pats's yarns had colour all their own: grey of crags, purple of hills, green seas laced with white foam, angry brass of the corselet, steel of swords cold as sunlit ice, bronze goblets of amber wine. They had sound: the roar of waves among granite cliffs, the clash of sword on shield, the ring of sword on sword, swish of kirtle and cloak, the drip of notes from the strings of the harp. Sagas of kings, bards, fighting men, vikings from afar that cleaved the sea with ships. And listening, in my mind Pats would walk the ground he spoke of, doing the things he said they did. One minute he would be a viking, a sword brandished in a hairy paw, a leg reached out to grip the prow that cut the mane of sea. The next, he was standing, legs apart on the brown sand at the head of the Irish host, strung out on the white sand, waiting.

Mechanically we would take the brown bread from his hands, Tim and me, and mechanically we would wash it down in gulps of hot tea out of the gallon. The wine of the goblets had the tang of tea. The pine smoke of the banquet fires had the odour of plug tobacco. Our minds were in the old days that fell, young again, out of the rumbling tones of Pats. In books I found the other worlds beyond the hills. In the talk of Pats was Ireland. From under his gritty paws grew the colour and smell of the far worlds; all here in the big garden. But, for the sight and smell of Ireland you had to travel further. Right down the white path apast the apple trees, you went, on by the ridges of Kerr Pinks and Golden Wonders, up to the far hedge, right up to the gap in the hedge. And there you craned up out of yourself, to spy the blue sky, to smell the wind—that was Ireland. Straight into Ireland the fledglings flew one day, out of the nest in the apple tree.

Pats was showing us Cuchulainn racing over the heather that day, I remember. All the sunlight that ever was seemed to have dropped in waves out of the high sky, to lie in the big garden. Even in the shade of the tree the heat was thick as a print of butter. The smoke of Pats's pipe hung in bellied veils out of the lowest branches. His jacket was in a ball under him. Sweat beaded the knot of hair that peeped at the open neck of his shirt. Only Pats could have made Cuchulainn race after the ball in heat the like of that. All of a sudden Cuchulainn was called to a dead halt by the shiver and shake of feathers up amongst the blossoms.

'They're leaving!' Tim whispered, gripping Pats's arm at the elbow.

'It could be. It could so,' Pats said, taking the pipe from his mouth, with care, between a finger and his horn of thumb.

'Easy now. Easy,' he cautioned, dealing the decks for action by shifting the gallon from between his boots.

We lifted slowly to our feet, our eyes screwed up to peer up into the branches. Sure enough, Tim was dead to rights again. The four young things were perched on a loop of bough above the nest, shifting and shuffling their feathers, twitching their pinions like they didn't know for sure what they were for. Anxious, fussy as a crone, the mother bird hopped about them, with a nudge of her beak here and a pat of it there, throating encouragement out of her amber maw.

'Take a look around you, now,' she seemed to be saying. 'Don't be afraid. All this you can see is the big garden of the troublesome lads that used to visit ye, even before ye were born. But the garden, big as it is, is only a pebble on the beach of the world that is yours. Yours is the earth and the sky. And the earth is big enough for a race of lads like the two you know to be lost in. And the sky is vast enough for the winds to lose themselves in.'

About at that point, maybe, it was that Tim kicked the gallon in his eagerness. The mother bird let a scream of warning out of her and took to flight straight down the white path. Like veterans the four young shot away in her wake. Tripping over one another in our haste Tim and me ran onto the path, just in time to see mother and family safe and sound on that gap in the hedge.

We walked towards them.

'They're gone from us now,' Tim said.

'They'll be back,' I said.

'Will they? Did you read it in a book?'

'I did,' I lied, and Tim smiled, to show his white uneven teeth.

A chuckle behind made me look over my shoulder, to meet a broad grin on the face of Pats. He winked at me. He was pleased. As we drew nearer to the birds we stole forward inches at a time. A few strides from the gap we halted. Pats moved up to stand between us and his smile had the crow's feet still wriggling under his eyes.

The mother bird never took her eyes off us. Silence trembled in the heat between us. Then suddenly she shot away into the blue sky. One by one the youngsters took wing, on her tail, chirping to the feel of freedom as they rowed through sunlit space. Away into Ireland.

'I wish I had wings,' said Tim, words for himself that broke a long silence.

'But you have, my son,' Pats said, putting a hand on both our heads. And words for himself they sounded too.

Now I know what Pats meant when he said that. Pats was right. We had wings then, Tim and me: and then too, this was a big garden. This *is* a big garden. Ask your youngsters, or mine. We see a wicket five feet high, not ten feet: a quarter-acre of garden, four apple trees. But we are wrong. It's just that we have lost our wings. Our minds then were the fledglings winging out into the blue that was Ireland. Now—they're the big of the egg in a cold nest—forsaken.

The Poacher

I laughed with him today. Loud and long we laughed together, startling the quiet of the bridge and the sweep of the river between the dreaming alders. And suddenly in the middle of my mirth a scalpel of thought bit deep into my consciousness: that I had not had a laugh the like of it in years.

'Man alive, if it isn't the poacher's curate himself,' he had said when we met at the familiar spot on the bridge, 'and look at him now! Just look at him! A dressed-up tailor's dummy of a man, and respectability oozing from the sleek of his hair.'

And he spat over the parapet with all the high disdain that he can pack into that gesture. That started it.

'Pull over against the wall till I be talking to you,' I said.

'Hould on a minute till I prepare Ballydowney for Grafton Street,' and with that big, red handkerchief that reeks of baccy and the scales of ill-gotten fish he made great show of wiping the lip of the parapet.

'There. Now plank yourself against your own ould spot on the wall, an' I'll do me level best to forget your respectability. When the wall feels harder on the blades of yer back than it used ye'll learn that ould places aren't as forgiving as ould friends.'

Taking my cue from the vein of his welcome I measured my back against the spot he had wiped, and dug in my pocket for my pipe. That gave him cause for another one of the chuckles that makes the stubble of hair to jerk on his throat.

'So you're as saucy as ever I see,' he remarked, 'as damned saucy as the first evening I took you under my wing.'

I will go bail to the limit that the pipe in my hand looked every bit as abashed as I did. While he laughed at me through the gimlet-green eyes of him I could swear that his cutty-pipe laughed at my elegant briar. There is more 'giddum' in that cutty than there is in many a man.

'By all that's good an' holy,' he said, 'I'm getting my first good gander at what a poacher looks like when he goes all respectable, and damn glad I am in my heart that I didn't take your turn at the crossroads. That choker of a collar is an insult to any gullet that ever jerked to a pint of flat porter, an' me ould limbs would go back on me entirely if I put 'em behind creases the like of them there in your trousers. They would so.'

'Well, how is the world using you?' I asked as we palmed the baccy, and I doing my best to hide my hands from his sight. Beside his they had the pallor of a lily against the withered leaves of a beech. He chuckled again.

'The devil a wan cares a ha'p'orth whether I live or die. But Faith, I'm kickin' the ould heel in spite of them.'

While we crunched the baccy between heel and palm I took stock of him out of the corner of my eye. About the same as ever, I reckoned. A wee bit more stoop in the shoulder, maybe, and a trifle more crinkle on the crust; but otherwise the same, identical gnarled little knot of a man, in what looked like the very identical suit of thick tweeds. And the dog was there to be sure; but not the spiky-backed Bilbo of golden memory that used to give me welcome with the soft look in his amber eyes that I have seen nowhere else but in a woman, and the top of his tongue on my bare shins.

'Old Bilbo is gone to the happy hunting grounds, I suppose,' I ventured. Bob gave a slow shake of the head.

'He's gone, the craythur. Killed by wan of Glinnane's bloodthirsty baters of hounds when he went between him and the sate of my pants. But I'd bet a quare penny he didn't go to e'er a happier hunting ground than the two of us ranged together,' Bob said, and for the moment the twinkle was gone from his eyes.

Bowls packed and ready for the match, we dawdled, as men will with their supreme moments. So I stole another look at Bob's baggy coat. Like all of his calling the round of his coat is his pocket. If the coat bulges at the bottom Bob has had a good day in the hills. If it sags it can speak of either two things: that he has had a day among days, or no day at all. You see it is like this: when his catch is so big that it would act like a magnet on the eye of the law, he transfers his spoils to a certain black bag that once was a pillow-case, white as the sap of the sycamore. Then when he dallies on the bridge for his smoke the bag squats snug in a sconce behind the stile on the town side of the parapet. When I stole that peek at the coat today and found it innocent at the tail as the child from the cradle, I craned back for a look at the sconce. And there it was as in the old days, that bonny, black bag, and bulging like the belly of the fatted calf.

'Do you mind now,' said he, 'the first time I gave you a game of talk about my profession? The same evening I made you my poacher's curate,' and with the dint of his chuckle the Adam's apple rippled like a trout in the hair of his neck. 'Here on the bridge it was, an' you a gorsoon. The divil a boot ye had on yer feet an' …'

As the words sparked off the rasp of his voice that November evening of the far past built itself afresh before the eye of my mind. Things were worse than plain bad at home just then. The old man was going on his second year of idleness, and Mother's needle was stock-still on the breast of her blouse. Tea and bread was the fodder for every meal, and meat was the food of the gods. I was homing from the Mill Grove that evening. The highway meandered before me to where the town of Killarney huddles on the valley floor. On the extreme right of that sprawl of grey roofs the spire of the cathedral hoisted its cross to where the rooks wheeled like blown leaves about it. The chimneys of the community belched plumes of smoke to the leaden winter sky. A splay of white gaslight lay like a cloak upon the roofs, still feeble in the trail of fading day. Beyond, Tomies and Mangerton mountains laboured with a weight of grey cloud.

My way beckoned over the bridge, through the stile, and on by the river path home. I was almost on top of the bridge when a wee wing of orange light played about the faded brown of a hat, and I knew that the man on the bridge was Bob the Poacher.

'I give you good evening, Master Jimmy,' said Bob.

'Hello, Bob,' I answered.

A white wraith glided out from behind his heels, the soft padding of paws on the asphalt, and Bilbo (of golden memory) was giving me greeting of wet warmth with the top of his tongue on my shins.

'And where are you off for in the cold of the evening? Ye'll be famished an' you with no boot to your feet,' said Bob.

'I'm going home, Bob,' I answered, 'I was up at the Mill Grove for a bit.'

'Well, so you were up at the Grove ye tell me. I notice that the Grove is a great haunt of yours entirely,' he said.

That his words were baited with question I gathered from the lift of his scraggy brows, and the perch of his head to one side like a robin.

'True enough,' I said, 'I do go there often. I got the habit of skelping there when Mother gives me a spell off from my lessons.'

Bob wagged a head in assent.

'Aye, 'tis a nice place an' no mistake. But whisper. A word of advice. Don't ye let ould Mother Nature make a hare of ye entirely. If ever that lady gets under your skin ye'll be only fit for one of two things: the life of the gentleman with the money to pay court to her ladyship, or the life of a man like me that promotes his courtship to take care of his own four bones.'

By now, Bob's words were stuffed out between puffs on the cutty. Then, as now, the bowl of that pipe slanted on a bare two inches and a half of stem. A thin silk scarf tucked its knot under his Adam's apple. As always, the pair of gimlet-green eyes made game of the world in its passing.

'Is there a lot out of the game?' I asked as I sidled up to ape his lurch against the parapet.

With another shuffle for more comfort Bob launched out on his favourite subject.

'Well now, if yer out for the luxuries of the belly kind 'tis a failure. Ah, but there's more to life than just that. There's the sky over you, an' the earth under you, an' the air as clean as a whistle between.'

'It must be great sport,' I agreed, and meant it with all my heart.

'An' why wouldn't it? With you matching your wits with the wild places.'

'You must know their ways like a book,' I said.

'Aye, but they know mine. The rabbit an' the hare an' the pheasant get to know yer movements like you get to know theirs. Sometimes they're laughing at you an' sometimes you're laughing at them; an' always either you or them has the last laugh of all.'

'Do they fetch much at the market?' I asked.

'There's a sixpence for the carcass of the rabbit an' a thruppenny bit for his hide; five bobs for a pheasant, an' a quid, maybe, for a salmon off the long gaff or the biteen of net.'

'It must be fair exciting,' I blurted.

'Enough to put life in the heart that is dead. There's the excitement of the hunt to put fire to your blood; not forgetting the excitement of being hunted yerself when ould Glinnane, the keeper, smells his way to ye with his two big hounds for a nose.'

Bob's eulogy seemed to be addressed to a spot in the high sky from the angle of the gaze that looked from under the curled leaf of his hat. The cutty signalled an assent to his every utterance with bowing wreaths of smoke that laid to my nose the reek of twist tobacco.

'Any luck today, Bob?' I asked.

'Four coneys as fat as ever ye see, an' a wee bit pheasant that hadn't time to grow no bigger seein' she was only hatched this season. The family would have been minus another member only for Glinnane, bad cess to him, an' his thick-headed brutes of dogs. That ould divil can smell me a mile off, an' against the wind I'm thinkin'.'

'Still, you haven't done too badly,' I consoled.

'It could be worse, thanks be to God,' he agreed, 'but the divil a thanks atall to ould Glinnane.'

There and then I put the question that was trembling on the tip of my tongue for as long as I knew Bob the Poacher.

'But isn't it stealing, Bob? And stealing is a sin.'

I held on to my courage with both my hands when I popped the question, and hunched my skimpy shoulders under the blue knitted jersey against the edge of the answer I expected. But Bob took the question in his stride.

'Now if that question was put to me wance, I must have heard it a million times. What bates me is why it should addle the mind of a baby, for the answer is as plain as the nose in yer face. And that's plain enough, the Lord knows. To my way of thinking, a man can own the things without life, his hat, or his house, or his biteen of land: provided, of course, that he has the money to pay for them. His claim on the wild wans of the earth can only begin when he tames the wildness out of them an' puts them to his own use for gain, like a horse, or for pleasure like a dog or a cat on the fender. But a wild dog belongs to God; a wild cat no less; a wild horse is His till wan man matches his wits an' the strength of his arm with that horse, an' comes out on top in the struggle. In the same way, all the coneys, an' all the pheasants, an' all the trout an' salmon in river or loch belong to God: an' sure He wouldn't begrudge a few of 'em to a child of His that's in need of vittles for his feed. That's what He put 'em there atall for in the first place, the theologians tell us.'

'But if a rabbit is on a man's land don't it belong to him?' I argued.

Bob's brown face screwed up into a ball of pain. He squirted a top-heavy spit out of the corner of his mouth into space with dint of contempt for the poser.

'Atrocious reasoning I call it. Take Jim Shea for instance, an' Mikie Lynch his next neighbour. When a coney is on wan side of the ditch he's supposed to be Jim's, an' when he takes a dander over to the other he's supposed to be Mikie's. Did any man ever hear the like of it for reasoning? But by that same line of reasoning I calculate that when the same little coney is in my pocket he's mine, an' I'm fixed in my mind that the Almighty feels the same about it.'

To my mind his argument was sound as bell metal, and my conscience was clear on a small project that had festered for long at the back of my head.

'I'd like to spend a day with you, Bob,' I asked, and my whole heart hung on his answer. The Adam's apple rippled in the hairy folds of his throat to the richness of his chuckle. He half turned to give me a look up and down like a Sheridan eyeing the lines of a colt at a horse-fair. He chuckled again, and shot a hard palm to the mane of my hair.

'Very well so, my poacher's curate,' he said, and derision had died in the green of his eyes. 'Any time that suits ye I'll be right glad to learn ye the tricks of the trade. There's no spice like company for the two best things on top of the earth: a bit of the sport, an' a pint of good honest porter. Yer not ready yet for the wan, but ye'll do prime for the other.'

'Tomorrow after school,' I blurted out, and my heart sailing away on the wings of the wild duck.

'Tomorrow it is, an' no mistake,' he laughed.

Then suddenly he had one of his rare serious spells that gave his face all the benignity and kindliness of a Saint Francis.

'Is the old man idle all the time?' he asked with great quiet.

'He is,' I answered.

'Well,' he said, 'we'll see that there's no shortage of mate for the pot between the two of us.'

'I must be off, Bob,' I told him. 'See you after school.'

'Here on the bridge I'll be waiting,' he promised, 'and whisper, son. 'Tis my honest opinion that while there's enough food on top of the earth for every mother's son of us, any man that's bate with the hunger is entitled to his fill where he finds it. Good luck to ye!'

I left him there with the dog and his cutty, and his gimlet-green eyes away where the sun was dipping fast behind Tomies Mountain with a wan white glow in its wake.

As I slipped through the stile my gaze lighted on the bonny black bag in the sconce, and a rare bulge to its belly. The devil prodded me with the thought of Bob's advice about the hungry man and his right to his fill where he found it. And I was hungry: and the ones at home. I shot a look towards Bob: his back was still to the parapet. I darted to my hunkers and in no time at all my right hand was groping in the clammy cold of damp, dead fur. When I sped away home that evening, past the dreaming alders with the whisper of the river in my ears, one of Bob's fat coneys hung limp on the crotch of my arm. Next day he laughed when I met him, and told me I was doing all right for a start. Today he laughed louder than ever, and his laughter is no louder than mine.

For, again I have met him on the bridge with his dog and his cutty, the same good friend. And as I look at the alders, and the river and the swell of the hills to the sky, I am wondering ... wondering about the wisdom of my turn at the crossroads.

The Miracle

Only yesterday did it hit me that there must be many a time when a saint could do with a sense of humour. Saint Teresa certainly needed to have one from ten o'clock yesterday morning until nine last night with the way Leary carried on. Oh, never in my seventy years was I so ashamed for anyone. We were butties on and off the sawmills' job and since we retired we spend the days together, from late weekday Mass until the closing of the pubs.

Before Mass we pool whatever few shillings we have. After Mass we buy a paper and spend the time until dinner studying the horses between sups of a pint in Pat Mac's. What happens in the way of high living after dinner depends on the horses. A bad day with Willie Barret the bookie means a couple of cold pints and bed early. A good one can mean brandies or hot whiskies and notions of grandeur by the time Mac closes the door on our heels.

And Leary is certain that what happens to his horses depends entirely on Saint Teresa. Hardly has he said the last prayer with the priest after Mass when he is off to light a candle to her. An ex-Fusilier who stayed thin and wiry, he still walks like a soldier, and the way he stands before the statue of the little saint makes me nervous that he's going to click his heels and give her a soldier's salute at any moment.

'She's my little friend up there,' he says, touching his hat to the clouds.

'And she's a great judge of horses.'

'You have the faith that moves mountains,' I say.

'All I ask her to do is shift a horse,' he says.

'There must be times when she doesn't get your orders right,' I tell him. Oh, very sarcastic.

'There can be no such thing as all we want in this life,' he says, like a missioner. 'If there was we wouldn't strive hard enough for Heaven; but you must admit she gives me more winners than losers.'

He does win more than he loses. I'll grant him that. But all the same, the days come when we are stony broke. And yesterday was one of them.

'Have you anything?' he asked as we climbed the chapel steps.

'Not even a ha'penny.' I told him.

'Not even the penny for the candle?'

'Not even,' I said, poking in my pockets.

'I hate going to her without the wing for the flame,' he said.

'She'll understand,' I told him.

'I know that,' he said impatiently.

And it was then I came on an old penny in an ear of my waistcoat.

'Here,' I said.

'That's better,' he told me. 'Because today I'll have to ask her for a miracle. After all, 'tis one thing to ask for a tip about a horse, but 'tis another altogether to have to ask for the money to back it.'

'God help the living,' said I, dipping a finger in the stone font in the porch.

The morning looked nice in the chapel. The sun put the colours of the windows on the altar steps and found silver in Father Harty's chair. He is of our own age and we tell our few sins to him. I think of him, respectfully of course, as a sort of second butty. He says the Latin as if his lips like the taste of it. He makes you feel that if you get to Heaven there will be someone there that you know. So in spite of being broke I was at peace when he put on the biretta and pushed one old shoe after the other into the sacristy.

I had enough giddum for a smile to myself when I noticed that there wasn't the usual spring in Leary's step when he went to light the candle to Saint Teresa. Man, I'd go as far as to say that he was bashful. I heard our penny drop through the slit in the oak box beside the brass tree of candles.

I hid the smile in my hands so he wouldn't see it when he turned.

I wasn't a bit prepared for the parade-ground rap of his heels on the aisle. I looked up in surprise. If the organist was in the loft playing a martial air Leary wouldn't have been more cocky in his stride. He had a superior smile on his bearded little wedge of a face as I grabbed my hat and stuffed the beads into my pocket to follow him out.

'The miracle happened,' he said in the chapel yard, his black eyes blazing up at me as I eased my way down the steps.

'What are you talking about?' I asked.

'This,' he said, flourishing a span new ten-shilling note.

'Where did you get it?' I asked.

'Saint Teresa gave it to me. The miracle, I tell you,' he said.

'How, man?' said I, pinching myself to make sure I was awake.

'I asked her nicely to put a few shillings in my way for the horses,' he said. 'I bowed down in apology for having to ask such a thing. And there I was looking at this ten bob note in the slot of the money box.'

'And you took it?' I gasped, in horror.

'Now wouldn't it be a terrible snub to the little saint if I didn't?' he said, his voice climbing the heights of amazement at my lack of manners.

'Someone put it in the box as a mark of thanks for a special favour, and the growing pile of coins brought it to the top,' I said, stiff with annoyance.

'You're in second childhood,' he snapped back at me.

'Then the second child I am has more sense of right and wrong than you have at seventy,' I said.

He wheeled on his heel and made for the bridge across the road as if he was marching a man to the guardroom. We always smoke on the stone bridge between the lime trees and listen to the river for a while before we hit for Mac's. He was standing with his elbows on the parapet when I got there, the tip of his meggle of beard sticking out between his palms, and the way the smoke signals were going up you'd think his hat was on fire. We let the river talk away to itself for a spell.

'When did you ever see anyone put a note in a candle box?' he fired at me, of a sudden.

'Never,' said I. 'But that doesn't say it isn't done.'

'And coppers dropping into the box would weigh the note down surely, not lift it back to the top,' he argued.

'Coppers and notes do odd things at times,' I gave back.

''Tis a note never touched by mortal hand by the look of it,' he said, with wonder in his tone.

'Straight from Heaven,' said I.

'Well, a miracle anyhow,' he claimed.

'Who's in second childhood now?' I asked.

'Wait till you see how the nags will clip for me today,' he said. 'That will be the final proof.'

And I have to admit that his luck was amazing. He left me in the window corner in Mac's to put five shillings on a horse called Noah that could have come out of the Ark. It won at twenties. A pound on a clothes horse at the Curragh made him the richer by twenty pounds. A favourite at Doncaster must have stood aside to let Leary's outsider stagger on to win him a tenner. In no time we had brandies in posh glasses in the sliver of sun through the window.

Every time he came back from the bookies he looked more like an owner getting a bit bored with leading in so many winners. He stood drinks to the house for every face he hadn't seen since dinner and if he saw double now and again no one put him wise. He doled a fist of sixpences to homing schoolkids until he twigged that he was seeing the same redhead for the fourth time.

When he made the mistake of taking things for granted he dropped two tenners and a five-pound note on the nags, but he was more than thirty pounds to the good when the bookie closed shop.

'The losses were to remind me that there is no such thing as perfection this side of Heaven,' he said.

'I don't have to look farther than yourself today to be reminded of that,' I told him.

But an hour of slow brandies and tall talk later my worry about the welfare of this soul was a goner. By the time the singing stage set in I hadn't a care in the world. When Mac put the lights on to keep the dark at the door I was in the chuckles. And it was when I was sore from laughing that I came alive to the change in Leary. Between song and yarn going on around us he kept darting gimlet looks at my face, as if he was trying to recall where he saw it before.

'Drink that up and we'll be off,' he said, all of a sudden.

'Where?' I asked.

'I'll tell you in a minute,' he answered, walking to the counter.

He put a grubby ten-shilling note between two dribbles of froth and asked for coppers. Mac gave him the metal in two of the small green paper bags he had ready for the bank in the morning.

'Come on,' said Leary, and I followed him out.

'Where are we going?' said I.

'To the chapel,' he said.

Not a word could I get from him till we were in the chapel porch.

'I'm doing this for you,' he said.

'What?' said I.

'Putting the ten bob back in Saint Teresa's box,' he said.

'For me?' I gasped, sobered of a sudden by the shock.

'I believe the little saint put the note in my way,' he said. 'But you don't. What I did with the note since then was no sin for me, but it was for you.'

The stagger I had in the half-light of the porch had nothing of liquor in it. I was flabbergasted.

'To live high on what grows out of stolen money would be a mortal sin, and in your own mind that is what you did,' said Leary.

'I never thought in that way,' I said.

'Don't worry, because now I'm going to put you right. Come on,' he said.

It was so silent in the chapel that you could hear the beads in Ma Murphy's hands as she prayed in the cowl of her shawl near the door. Millar the postmaster was doing the stations with a look of resignation on his face that was out of place. The four of us had the high-pillared quietness to ourselves as Leary walked straight to the statue. And there he was for the next few minutes, dropping coppers into the box.

Putting things right with Heaven for me. Me, if you don't mind! I was fit to be tied. I could hardly wait till he came back to kneel beside me.

'If you're so sure about that note this morning, why didn't you put a note back, never mind your bags of scrap metal?' I whispered.

'I was thinking about what you said about the chance of a note coming back up on the coins,' he whispered back. 'If our note came back like that some caffler might think it was put there for him by a miracle. And he might take it.'

And the face he turned to the saint in the candlelight looked as if it was expecting a halo at any moment. But do you know, I'd have sworn there was a smile on the little face of the saint. A trick of light maybe, the sway of a flame. But I'd be easier in my mind if I could be sure she really did smile. As I said, she needed a sense of humour for Leary.

March Thrush

It sounds odd to say that people from all over the world came down our lane to listen to Moss Downey's caged thrush but they did. The lane is a relic of the old days in our town, where today you can meet Chinese and Japanese and groups of any skin colour you can think of in the streets when the tourists take over from June to September. The white strangers with the readies can be from England, Australia, New Zealand, colonized South Africa or any part of Europe: the Yanks are themselves with a harness of cameras and more readies than the rest put together.

On fine days all of them are away on mountain, lake and old road trips in country that God took special care in making and men built a town in to line their pockets with dollars and pounds and roubles and rupees, wearing a fixed smile that must make it a pain in the face to part with for sleep; like any tourist town in fact.

On days when the tourists give the trips a rest they traipse through the town itself in search of the quaint and the ancient and, of course, find the cobbled lanes where the old stock make ends meet and laugh when the wolf is made to yelp away from the door once again; once a day maybe.

The tourists stand in the archway entrances to rows of houses that are limewashed in lozenge colours; ready-made postcards framed in the arches for their cameras.

But at our lane they were lured by birdsong to the sixth in our single row of houses to see in an open window a caged thrush that sounded as if it thought it was in church, unless it was giving out notes that danced as if they were leading a fast fiddle into a new tune. That was Moss Downey's March thrush.

Moss was a cobbler with the face of a happy monk and a tonsure of baldness to go with it. He wore specs that rarely balanced properly across his nose and supported his stiff left leg with a stick. The fact that his thrush was born in March made it the remarkable singer it was, the experts said. Only song thrushes of the rarest kind dared to set up house in March they said, when tree and hedge and shrub had only buds to show at best and the only cover for a nest was in evergreens like holly and laurel.

And it was in the chapel-yard laurels on a late March Sunday that Moss found the nest of four young thrushes. He and his wife were crossing the gravelled yard to Mass when Moss spotted a bird flying with a worm in its beak. 'Go on in to Mass, girl,' he told Kitty in a hurry as he disappeared after the bird into the laurels.

'The worm wriggling in the bird's beak instead of being swallowed meant that there was a family to be fed in the nest,' he would say day after day in his shop. 'A nest of young March thrushes mind you. My heart was in my ears thumping with excitement as I stole inch by inch through the laurels. But I was quick to see that the cock and hen, yes the two of them, were flying a shuttle service with morsels of all sorts to one particular bush. I propped myself with the stick near that bush until the time came when the two were away together. Then I moved in on the nest. There were four young ones in it, fully feathered; all they were short of was tails. They would be leaving that nest any day, any hour, and there was no time to lose.

He would go on to tell how he decided to be fair to the parent-birds by leaving two of their young in the nest and taking the other two home with him for rearing in a cage. But when he lifted the nearest one out of the nest the others fled in a wild flurry of wings and feathers. The old birds went separate ways: the hen darting and clucking comfort to the frightened three, the cock following Moss to the chapel yard shrieking with rage. Mass was over and the emerging congregation were just in time to see Moss get clear of the laurels with his stick in one hand, the young thrush in the other and the old bird flying screaming circles round his ears.

'Of course Kitty was mortified, weren't you, girl?' He would call over the thin partition that separated the shop from the kitchen. And Kitty would snap back: 'Hadn't I every right to be? And it made you miss Mass of a Sunday as well.' That thrush was the last thing she wanted Moss to talk about, or anyone else to talk about for that matter.

Childless Kitty doted so much on Moss, who was all of fifteen years older than her, that few of the neighbours got much more than a nod from her. Anyway, if there was a trickle of feeling leftover she wouldn't give a drop to the thrush.

Ma, who was everybody's friend, came nearest to winning her trust and affection when they met at the pump to fill their gallons for the kitchen. ''Tis strange the way she turns on anyone who has a good word for that bird,' Ma used to say, 'as if we should blame it for sending its song down the lane to us. A cat in the house would be better she says. For the sake of the bird Moss won't let her keep a cat, she says, and the mice in the kitchen are laughing at her. Then she moves off with her gallons, pushing and dragging the old pair of Moss's boots she wears as slippers, scolding to herself about the bird.'

She carried on the same way when Moss had an audience on bird lore. The cage hung between him and the ash tree that rose above the chemist's garden wall across the way. When the sun shone and a breeze stirred the leaves the thrush sang loud and clear. It was at times like that that tourists came to the window to look as well as listen. Many of them wanted to buy the bird but Moss always smiled and shook the head that would have looked at home in the wine cellar of a monastery.

On one of those occasions I remember Kitty shouting over the partition: 'You're a fool, Moss Downey. It would be fitter for you to sell the bloody thing and let it pester the life out of someone else at the other end of the world.' But Moss went on to tell about the stranger who said a nightingale sounded like a thrush singing in its sleep and Moss had said that was the greatest compliment ever paid to a bird and the stranger said 'You mean the thrush?' and Moss replied, 'No, sir, the nightingale.' And Kitty chanted, 'Birds, birds, nothing but birds,' in derision.

Moss never answered back in anger. One time he told me with a grin: 'Always give a woman the second last word Michael. Keep the last for yourself and never use it unless you have to.' Ma, who was supposed to have insights about people, said if Kitty had a child she would have been more tolerant about the thrush.

Mind you, the thrush was the only thing they didn't see eye to eye about and I ought to know. As the only child of a widow our house felt empty when Ma was out at work in the kitchen of one of the local hotels. So when I wasn't playing football or handball or doing homework for school I was soaking in the chat and banter that Moss with his hammer presided over in the shop. When Moss got the heart attack I did the messages for Kitty and looked after the bird; in between I was company for Moss until Ma called for me on her way home.

Poor Moss had to be propped with pillows in the room over the shop. But there was an open window for the cage and the thrush still sang between him and the ash. Old butties called: they couldn't all come together like the shop days but each did his bit in trying to talk Moss back to being himself again. They didn't succeed; no one succeeded. Kitty woke one morning to find that Moss had died beside her in his sleep.

She was shaking in a stupor of fright and grief when she rushed in with the bad news to Ma and Ma took over on the spot. She sent me to the presbytery for young Father Slattery, put Kitty in the care of a next-door neighbour, sent the neighbour's youngster running to tell Kitty's aunt and Moss's brother and brought two of the older women with her to prepare the corpse for the wake.

In his last serenity Moss looked more like a monk than ever in the brown habit with the crucifix in hands more used to a hammer or a glass of grog. No one, least of all Ma, would hear of taking the thrush away from him, but Father Slattery, who was a songbird fancier himself and knew what to do, tied brown paper round the bars of the cage to darken it and keep the bird quiet. The thick mist that began to fall outside made the day itself anything but bright.

It was so quiet in the room you could hear rain seeping down the ash leaves and so still that the candle flames burned without flicker. Kitty looked younger in her black dress with good stockings and shoes. Her eyes showed more pain than tears; her mouth was twisted to one side and she whispered whatever it was she kept saying to herself.

Dusk was in the lane when she switched on the light to help the candles, and with the sudden burst of light the thrush began to sing on the instant. Whether or not it was the sudden light or something to do with the dawning sunset outside that confused the bird the sound had no place in a room that burning wax made to smell like a mortuary.

Everyone in it seemed stunned until Kitty screamed. 'The thing, the thing, the cursed thing,' she screamed, her body stiff and her fists high over her head. Before anyone could stir she ran to the cage, tore it off the hook and flung it through the window. Then she leaned out into the rain and shouted, 'Damn you, damn you to have the gall to sing over his corpse.' When Ma got her away from the window she began to weep her first real tears of the day.

By that time I was climbing the ash. The fretful sounds of the thrush in the half dark guided me to where the cage was jammed out of shape between two of the branches. The bird fluttered with fright against the bars as I eased the cage free and climbed down. Every leaf I touched sent raindrops soaking through my jersey and I felt rain like a mesh over my hair and face as I ran with the cage to Ma's kitchen.

When I switched on the light I found that the thrush looked as wet and perished as I was so I put the cage on a chair by the fire and poked the coals into giving flames as well as heat. Steam was rising from my jersey as I wiped the cage dry with a towel, pressed it back into shape and put crumbs soaked in milk into the feeding bowl.

It was a while before the bird began to straighten its feathers and comb the wings with its beak in bright heat. It was a while more before it began to eat but after the first few beakfuls it was looking at me sideways, as sleek and cheeky as ever.

And it was singing in the sun the following day as Moss in his coffin passed the laneway in a hearse. Everyone must have heard it as the funeral passed the archway. I said to Ma in the car we shared with two neighbours: 'I hope Kitty can't hear that.' Ma said: 'Oh, let her. She'll have to put up with it. You can't put a muzzle on a bird.' I felt that was a bit severe on Ma's part, but on a second thought I put it down to one of her insights.

Anyway, Ma was at Kitty's elbow at the graveside and helped her as she stumbled through the long grass between the mounds and crosses away from the grave. When we were clear of the graveyard Kitty put a hand on my shoulder and said: 'Your Ma told me you have the cage and what's in it, Michael. Well, keep it, I don't want it, I won't have it in my house.'

Still, in the days ahead she came more often to the pump with her gallons than she used to; she rinsed them more often than was needed and
most of the time her eyes were on the cage in our window. When she had
to close the window in bad weather she would cross the lane to chat with
Ma in the kitchen but there was hardly a minute when she wasn't looking
at the thrush. Her parting words were always about the bird and always
bitter: 'Will you look at it? When 'tisn't singing 'tis hopping and dropping
but always looking for notice. Will you look at the beady eye sizing you
up like a hawk on the prowl? Showing off, always showing off, old bloody
show-off!' That kind of thing.

So it was all the more strange that it was after one of those sessions that
Ma aired another of her insights. I was reading in the corner as usual
when she said: 'Michael, would it hurt you a lot to give the bird back to
Kitty?' I was speechless for a moment and Ma took advantage: 'Moss was
all she cared about ever,' she said. 'Not only is her life all but empty without him but her house is as well. Will you give her back the bird?'

I blustered to hide the hurt the very thought gave me. 'She hates the
sight of it,' I said, but Ma didn't seem to hear. 'Moss would like it if you
did, that's for sure,' she said. There was no answer to that: not as I saw it
anyway. But it took a while before I could get myself to say—'Will I take
it to her now?'

'No, not now,' she told me. 'That's not the way to do it. Leave it to me.
I'll pick the day and the time.' Then she added—'You're a good lad,
Michael,' as if the whole thing was my idea.

The day she picked had a hush of heat that let birdsong go a long way
and the thrush seemed to know that: the notes were never more mellow
in the hymn parts or more lively in the jig and reel whirrs of its performance. Kitty looked cool at the pump with her gallons. The black of
mourning suited her blonde good looks and the careless way she pinned
her hair behind her ears made her seem nearer twenty than the thirty-five
she really was. Besides, the way she pushed and dragged the old boots had
a lot of the kid playing games about it.

'Kitty looks smashing today,' I said from the window. 'Where is she?'
asked Ma and when I told her she added: 'Tell her I want a word with her.'

When Kitty came through the doorway I retreated into my corner
seat. Ma was sitting at the table near the window knitting a red jersey for

me. The soft wood top of the table was white from years of scrubbing. The sun shining through the cage cast a web of shadow over the needles darting daintily in Ma's big hands: a web that swayed when the thrush sprang from perch to perch between songs. 'Sit here, Kitty,' Ma said, pointing to the chair beside her. Kitty put the full gallons on the floor and sat on the edge of the chair, looking frail and uneasy beside Ma. 'What is it, Nora?' she asked.

'Kitty, I can't stand sight or sound of that bird any more,' Ma said. 'What!' said Kitty. Ma put the knitting aside and got to her feet. 'Listening to the same thing over and over day in and day out is driving me crazy,' she said. 'And when it isn't singing 'tis hopping and dropping filth in the cage.' Ma was playing her part so well that it was only then it dawned on me what she was up to. Her voice was harsh when she said: 'Kitty, if someone doesn't take that bird out of here I'll do what you did, Kitty—I'll throw it out the window, cage and all.'

'No. Oh no, Nora, no,' Kitty said, rising to face her.

'I mean it,' Ma insisted. 'Kitty, I want you to take it out of here, I want you to take it back. Are you listening? I want you to take it away with you.'

Kitty closed her eyes for a moment, then opened them to look, straight into Ma's face. 'Are you sure you know what you're saying, Nora?' she asked. Ma said: 'I was never more sure.'

With that Kitty turned towards me. 'How do you feel about it, Michael?' To gain time I closed the book I was pretending to read. 'For Ma's sake it will have to go out of here. To someone, anyone,' I said. I felt it was a good answer at short notice. I felt mean about fooling Kitty but it worked. She turned to Ma and said: 'I'll take the bird back, Nora.'

Straight away Ma was back to being her honest self again as if nothing had happened. She sat and took up her knitting and said in her usual cheerful way: 'God love you girl, that takes a weight off my mind.'

But Kitty remained standing. She hesitated hand to mouth before she stammered: 'Things were so sudden, so fast like, but could it be now, I mean, could it be now, the taking away?'

'That's what I meant, love,' Ma replied. 'Michael, take the cage down for Kitty. That cage is a bit awkward, so you'll take the gallons home for her as she takes the cage.'

To reach where the bird was I had to stand on a stool. Kitty held her arms out looking up at me, waiting for the cage. When I lowered it into her reach she closed her arms around it without a word, and the bird made neither sound nor stir as she held the cage against her body and made for the lane as fast as the old boots would let her.

She didn't get her tongue back until she was well clear of the door but then the words poured. From there on she was a new Kitty. I had all I could do to keep up with her and keep the gallons from spilling at the same time. She skipped over the cobbles as if the boots were shoes and she was really young again. She was talking away to the fluttering bird but it wasn't till she paused for breath that I could hear what she was saying.

'I'm taking you home,' she was saying, 'I'm taking you home. The neighbours are nice like Nora and Michael but there's a way that they'll always be strangers. I'm taking you home and Moss will be pleased and I'll be at peace because the place wasn't the same without the pair of ye. I'm taking you home where you can sing when you please and shut your gob when you please and let go with your droppings without asking anyone's pardon.'

She laughed young laughter like a girl's as she skipped ahead with the thrush in the cage. And as I followed on with the gallons over the cobbles I got back into good humour too. In fact, I found time to smile as I wondered who codded whom in Ma's latest insight.

Last One Home

From O'Connell Bridge to Deenagh Bridge in five hours, give or take five calls to bars along the way. Paddy whiskey doubles neat or with water at each call. Five hours, five Paddy stops: that was how Mac figured his car lift by a friend from Dublin to where he found himself on his very own on that bridge below the town where he was born and reared.

He had asked to be put off at the Deenagh rather that anywhere else in town because he wanted to gather his senses before he faced his mother at home. He didn't want her to find what she called the sign of drink on him. She didn't mind the smell, as long as he was what she called in charge of himself. The way his father died was the cause of that.

Loners just now, his mother and himself, she at home and he on the bridge, he told himself as he grinned wryly down at the Deenagh River. His wife Jennie was in Lourdes on a pilgrimage. They had no children and that more than likely was the reason for her pilgrimage.

He was sorry they hadn't a child, even a girl. But he'd have preferred a boy because he was the last child, the last male of his line. His father, a tinsmith who made and played tin whistles, died when he fell out of a car in the middle of a reel on his way home from a football All-Ireland in Croke Park. Too many Paddy stops likely.

That was when his mother took up dressmaking to rear and care for him: an only son an only child and last of his line. His mother didn't worry about the line as long as he was all right: mothers were that way. He didn't grin at the river on that thought: he smiled. A wry smile because he cared about the line. Then he listened to the river and remembered how he once said in a lecture that heredity was a murmur in the blood like a river talking to itself under a bridge. But the crooked smile was stopped in its tracks this time by an organ launching Gounod's 'Ave Maria' into the silence between him and the cathedral across the roadway and a lawned and gravelled yard.

Choir practice. The cathedral held its cross very high: it had to because the masons who built the spire in Famine days wanted it to go on climbing into a forever of pay days, so it was said. The 'Ave Maria' died suddenly in its tracks, as the organist no doubt called a singer to order for a wrong note or poor phrasing in the Latin.

Latin. *O Salutaris* … *Introibo ad Altare Dei* … and so say all of us … He had been an altar boy in that cathedral in days when Latin seemed to be synonymous with the state of grace. Mitre-bearer to the bishop, crozier-bearer, even train-bearer, the clean paws of the poor woman's son getting a grip on the tail of the bishop. His grin to the river this time was short lived when he realized that the organ was silenced. Then the mosaic of coloured light in the choir window flicked out to cue him into getting a move on.

The choir would be on their way out at any minute and he wanted to be a few steps ahead of the posse. He grabbed off the parapet a punch-drunk briefcase holding a book, a notebook, a shirt, pyjamas and a noggin of Paddy for the morning cure. Then he half-hurried along the river walk.

On his left was a high misshapen hedge that had gaps made down the generations by people like himself and the tin-whistle tinsmith. At some of the gaps he could hear more clearly the chatter of the river over stones; at others there was the ball-gown swish of an eddy or the deep silence of pools.

All gaps made by boys and men down the generations to fish for trout, wade with glass jars after fingerlings or swim in pools that were deep enough. And at any of the pool or eddy gaps if there was the splash of a trout you'd hear it.

No splashes this time, Mac told himself. But the cool breath from the river once again smelled of Woodbine from the hedge especially for him.

Right turn, he drilled himself. Into a road as old as time that was called new in spite of that; yes, the New Road that was made into a green tunnel by limes on either side that reached to touch branches overhead. And the only Woodbine he remembered here was a fag you got three smokes from by snipping the top off twice at hour-spaced intervals with a beak of nails from thumb and finger; that way the fag like the teacher's essay had a beginning a middle and an end: the end was always so sweet you sucked your finger with it.

And there on the right the dark stone monastery where he got the scholarship under the ashplant rule of Brother 'Jawsie' La Salle ('I'll make you use that brain of yours if I have to knock on your skull with the ash'), and there the alley in the yard where he could beat the best of the hand-ballers because he didn't have to grow more that his 5'4" and a bit to be a handballer. Come to think of it he never asked anyone how tall his father was.

Carry on, Mac, he told himself, yes. And there on the right the college he went to with his scholarship. And there the football pitch where he played corner forward on the college teams because he was too small to be put anywhere else and too good to be forgotten on the sideline. Four games, two medals, in inter-college finals before another scholarship took him to university in Cork.

Keep going, Mac, he told himself; and there on his right was Saint Mary's Terrace that had small houses for the best part of a mile of big families and no shortage of heirs for cabbage patches that in the long run might be better than chalk and a blackboard. Hah, that was a spake as long as the terrace. Breathtaking.

Watch it, Mercy Convent on the left he went to before the Brothers got hold of him. Sister Joseph—'Never take an intoxicating drink, Mac McCarthy'; Sister Peter—'Mischiefs wait for you to make them happen, Mac'; Sister Benignus—'I'll tell your mother'; Sister Camillus—'Some day someone will knock your little head off'; Sister Brendan—'Don't mind them, Mac, they don't understand.' Good old Sister Brendan, God rest your soul. God rest all their souls in fact but yours in particular.

So, with nuns to the left of him, Canons to the right of him, into the valley strode the last of the 600 ... left ... left ... you had a good job and you left ... left ... pick 'em up ... left ... left ... You're in the army now, you're not behind the plough, you'll never get rich, you son of a bitch, you're in the army now … left … left … And suddenly it came to him that he was marching upright in time and step with the thought in his head and he laughed. Outright.

Halt. At ease, he told himself … Easy now. At ease … if somebody passed and saw—and then he realized it would be one chance in a hundred that the somebody would know him, even recognize him. The unknown bloody soldier, how are you. It was nothing to laugh about but he allowed himself one last laugh out loud.

Then he called himself to attention again. On his left was the main road home but parallel and a bit beyond the wall facing him was a pathway out of a scoured-out sandpit that locals nicknamed the Burmah Road. He'd go that way home he decided, but first he'd have a drink. But where for the drink? There were so few places now to talk over a drink to yourself or to other people or indulge the luxury of listening to old clocks do ancient silences.

In seven out of ten of the haunts he knew would be bawds now with thrombosis thumps on the big fiddle and cat-gut screams from the small.

Wait now, The Place Hotel a few stops to the bottom of the hill on his right. Quick march. The Place kept half of the bar public and the other half semi-private for tourist residents. He took a quick look into the crowded public part and decided to play tourist in the big room at the back, where one of the few things that wasn't upholstered was a picture of O'Connell over the mantelpiece in what the knockers called his whoring heyday.

He pressed a button under the black marble mantelpiece and a shrill bell made itself heard in the bedlam the width of a partition away. A hatch opened near him and a man's voice said: 'Yes, sir, what can I do for you?' Mac said: 'A large Paddy with water,' and waited. The whiskey and a glass of water duly appeared on the hatch shelf and the disembodied voice said: 'That'll be a pound-fifty, sir, things are a bit dearer in the lounge.'

Mac raised the glass to O'Connell and chuckled at the certainty that if the now were there then the young Danno would wink back: greatness was always, well, nearly always full of certainties like that, letting little men like Mac feel occasionally like gods.

Mac sat under the picture at the table near the empty fireplace, just in

time to get the full broadside of 'Professor Mac is back' from the familiar
loud-hailer voice of Mick Lee, long, tanned, bone-hard boatman extraor-
dinary. Five strides brought Lee to Mac's elbow; his tweeds smelling of
cigarette-smoked salmon. The hum of whiskey on his breath would have
thrown flames if he lit it. 'You poked your nose in at the door outside and
I saw it. That bloody nose,' he told Mac.

'It often was bloody. I was too small. Remember?'

'You were able for the lot of them: in another way you're too big for
them now. Professor, doctor, that's what they call you in the newspapers.
What are we to call you at all?'

'Call me Mac or I'll lay you low as long as you are.'

'Lectures you give to societies and so forth.'

'But never to Alcoholics Anonymous because they might wind up lec-
turing me.'

'OK Mac, that's a nice way of reminding me I didn't get you a wel-
come-home drink,' Lee said, raking his fingers through the lick of black
hair that dipped across his forehead.

'Two large Paddys,' he called into the faceless hatch and the drinks
dropped into sight without bell or pronouncement. He lifted the drinks
onto the table as the three pounds he placed on the hatch shelf were fisted
away by a hand with a ring on it.

'Your mother is in great heart, Mac,' Lee said.

'Thanks for calling on her as often as you do,' said Mac.

'A great pleasure, a vintage lady, she's waiting up there for you now.
You're travelling light and alone, Mac?'

'Got a lift to the bridge below the town. Saved me the trouble of driving in the shadow of the inhaler. Jennie is in Lourdes on a pilgrimage.'

'Praying for you.'

'In the black-sheep section. You'd be there too, of course.'

'A bit of a ram, yes. And that brings me to my special question for you
this time. Mother Church is at it again: making it harder for fellahs like
me to stay in the fold, ram or no. And 'tis no disgrace for a ram to put too
many lambs in the sheep business.'

'What in God's name are you spouting about?' Mac cut in. Then he
said quietly: 'Sit down, Mick. You're not quite taller than me sitting down.'

Lee sat to stretch the upholstery on the biggest chair in the place. 'I'm talking about Mother Church's rigid rule against contraceptives. Contraceptives. Now there's a big word that we all got to know about.'

'You don't have to spell it out in letters,' Mac quipped.

'Letters, pills, what have you,' said Lee.

'It would appear that I don't need to have any of them, more's the pity,' said Mac and the wry smile twitched in the corner of his mouth again.

He got to his feet and moved around the carpeted room, bantam size, light on his feet but the face had a look of being hit too often; still, the eyes had glee when they weren't serious and they were only half-serious now.

'Why the hell can it concern you so much? You have six children ranging in ages from fourteen years to four. A few more won't make much difference, will it?' he said, watching the smoke from his cigarette do a rope trick through the still air to the ceiling.

'I only came into this along the way,' said Lee.

'Not half,' said Mac, still looking at the ceiling.

'I'm talking for young fellahs starting out in marriage with an average-paid job and enough feeling between them and their other halves to have too many children in too few years for their own good or the good of the kids,' said Lee.

'Go on,' said Mac, looking at his shoes.

'Two is a handy family,' Lee confided. 'Three at the most if the arrivals could be controlled and ended when enough is enough in the numbers game.'

'Bingo,' said Mac, prodding the air with a finger.

'But there is no foolproof control except the letter or the pill, so where do you go from there?' asked Lee.

'Away from you,' Mac told him, the glee glinting in his eye now. 'You always have only one way of looking at anything.'

'Like Mother Church, Mac.'

'The Arts is my game, MA, PhD, and nothing to do with my ass or feck-all I'd have you know. The Arts, yes.' Mac said, with a skip back to his drink at the table. 'Not theology. I'm no bishop. I'm barely a paid-up member of the laiety; a Mass a week, man, always of a Sunday. But suppose ...'

'Suppose what?' asked Lee, rising to stand over the small man.

Mac looked up at him in a way that indicated he'd be satisfied with a point's win.

'Look at the telephone on the wall in that corner, Mick,' he said, prodding with the finger again. 'Keep your eyes on that blower.' Lee surprisingly did as he was told.

'You have six children, Mick, three boys, three girls. If you had been permitted by your Church to use contraceptives in your marriage bed, three of those children would never have seen the light of day, and the light of any day is good when you're as young as they are.'

'Oh here, Mac, where the hell are you going?'

'Eyes on the phone, Mick, I told you, eyes on the phone. Now. Suppose I could walk to the phone like this, lift the earpiece like this and talk straight through the mouthpiece to God.'

'Don't be blasphemous,' Lee told him.

'Not intended,' Mac gave back. 'Suppose I got through to God and told him your view on contraceptives and how you think three is a handy family and God said—keep an eye on that phone, Mick—suppose God said—"Mac, tell Mick that by a miracle I'll take back to my care any three of his children he nominates."'

Mac paused for a moment. Then he said: 'You can take your eye off the phone now, Mick. I didn't get through. But suppose I had got through. Which three of your children would you give back to God?'

Lee gaped, then swung away to face the picture of O'Connell, his long arms outstretched on the mantelpiece as if the bantam had spun him with an uppercut. He lowered his chin to his chest and was silent as Mac waited with a glass in his hand. For one reason or another the hubub beyond the partition had settled to a murmur.

Then Mac said: 'No deal?'

Lee, without stirring, said: 'No deal.'

'Jesus, I asked for it.' Lee added like he was talking to himself. 'And I knew who I was asking.'

Then the big man swung round to face Mac and there was laughter with the voice that said: 'Mac, you're a bastard, but you're a nice bastard, you've done it again.' And the small man smiled. 'I'm glad,' he said. And he was laughing when he went on to say: 'One of the ones you'd give back might be a cardinal.' Then he put the phone back on the receiver.

'Do you know what I want to do now?' said Lee.

'Rush home and see them all.'

'Right again, Professor Mac. So it is a drink for the road, the Burmah Road.'

'My twist,' said Mac. 'But you say the ritual words to the hatch. I'd have to use bell, book and candle to get service.'

'Two large Paddys,' Lee told the hatch and the drinks appeared and Mac's money vanished in a sweep of hands. 'Magic,' said Mac.

'To the road,' Mac said. 'The Burmah Road,' said Lee, and their heads tossed back as they emptied the glasses.

Lee grabbed Mac's bag and made for the door. 'I have a pocket of money after the Gap of Dunloe trip today: easy money in duck-pond calm. If I don't get a handful to Jessie in a hurry she'll be late for the shops.'

'Do as of old.'

'How do you mean?'

'Blame me for delaying you.'

'And you'll blame me with your mother.'

'Quits?' said Mac.

'Quits,' said Lee, and both of them laughed their way out into the street. As usual their meeting made each of them feel younger.

'I'll leave a boat and rod at Ross for you on my way out in the morning,' Lee said.

'They'd have to jump into the boat for a start, I'm sure, but suicidal trout taste as well as the sane ones any day.'

'Mind the step, Mac.'

'Mind your eye, Mick.'

They crossed the street to the spent sandpit that was to be a park in urban plans for the future. The rough track called the Burmah Road that climbed out of it was made by the hundreds who used it as a short cut from town to the Villa houses on the flat hill like a steppe that overlooked the streets.

The hill was surprisingly high. The publicans had signalled night with neon signs that made the people down below look as if they had strayed into a carnival before the hurdy-gurdy music blared. But the sun on the mountains along the skyline had other ideas: going it was, yes, but by no means gone while the peaks looked like copper in the old-gold light.

The two men stood on the hill without a word; looking back. The hundreds of crows passing overhead had silence for the taking but they mocked it with caw-calls instead. Tattered flight after flight flew home to the rookery beside the Protestant church at the far end of town. Mac was now giving all his attention to the crows, from the swish of their wings overhead to the circular flight before they dropped into the church trees.

'All crows must be Protestants,' he said.

'Don't they look it,' said Lee.

'Now, now,' said Mac and Lee said: 'I take that back. Come on. All the crows are gone.'

But Mac didn't move. 'Come on I said,' Lee told him. It was true that all the crows were gone but Mac wouldn't stir. Lee stretched patience for the better half of a minute before he tried again.

'Oh come on, Mac,' he said.

'Wait,' Mac told him.

'For what?'

'He'll be here any minute.'

'Who will?'

'Ah, there he is,' said Mac.

'Who, who, who!' said Lee

Mac pointed to the sky. A lone crow was soloing home, cawing to himself. Mac watched him go by. Then he raised a valedictory finger.

'That was he,' he told Lee. 'That last one home. In all the years I've watched them there always was a last one home. Now we can go.'

The farther they went up the road after that the nearer they came to the loud, sometimes shrill voices of children at play ahead on the terraces. And they were almost done with the Burmah Road when three dark-haired children, two boys and a girl, raced towards them calling 'Daddy!' at the top of their voices.

The nearest boy hurled himself at Lee's chest where he was caught in full flight by Lee's big hands and transferred to the big man's shoulders. The other gripped his father's right hand and the girl swung from the left. 'What did you bring us, Daddy?' was the song now. The boy on his shoulders was tugging at Lee's hair, the girl was doing a kind of dance and the other boy was tugging at the nearest pocket.

'Wait till we get home will ye,' Lee told them. 'Manners please before someone gets hurt. What I have for ye is in my pockets and I can't empty them now. Silence I say but say hello to Professor Mac.'

'Yer Dad didn't give me time to buy anything for ye, little lady,' Mac told the girl as he put a pound into her hand. 'Buy an apple or something with your brothers.'

'Liar,' said Lee.

'Quits?' Mac queried, and Lee said, 'Quits,' with a grin as he moved away with his children.

Lee's voice in answer to his children's chatter drifted gradually away as Mac swung his bag down the back way home.